Lyn,

Heavenly LOVER

♡ Sharon Hamilt

BY NEW YORK TIMES AND USA/TODAY BESTSELLING AUTHOR

SHARON HAMILTON

DEDICATION

This is a special book to me. In 2008 our house burned down. A lifetime of possessions were lost, and oddly, some survived. Thankfully, no one was injured. The fire was as indiscriminate as fate is. What happened as a horrific event turned into a miracle.

While we were recovering and deciding what to do with the house, haggling with the insurance and our mortgage lender (being taken over by the Feds in another cruel twist of fate), a new vision began to emerge. It took several years to finish this project, but along the way, I was visited by what I can only say were Guardian Angels, who held my hand and helped me deal with all the decisions and life-changing things going on around me.

I began to have dreams of these angels. I wondered what their personalities were like. The image of Claire, the scrappy, highly successful and bright-spirited angel came to mind. Just like I was recovering from the depths of despair, I had Claire ministering to people who had found themselves devoid of the tools to go on. She brought my hero, Daniel, the strength to realize the beauty of his own life, just as she gave something to me. Something priceless.

I became a writer.

In thinking about Claire and her needs, I wondered if she could fall in love. What would that love look like? Is there such a thing as angelic love? Guardian Angel love? What would that feel like, and how would she be able to do this?

And so my story was born. So was the career of a new writer, from a place hidden by "stuff" I no longer needed, uncovered and purged by a fire in the middle of a February night.

I was lucky to meet a group of amazing writers through three RWA chapters I joined: San Francisco RWA, Silicon Valley RWA and Black Diamonds RWA (sadly this chapter has closed). I also joined Redwood Writers and California Writers Clubs. I joined a multi-genre critique group called the Tuesday Group (which now meets on Thursdays). I contested this manuscript and rewrote it more than 57 times. I finaled in contests and took dozens of classes, searched for an agent, a publisher and a following.

It all worked. I was given not always what I asked for, but what I needed most.

This is more than a story. It is the work of my heart, once damaged and full of pain, rehealed by stories of true love and a happily ever after.

Because that's where I really live.

Enjoy!

CHAPTER 1

This was all wrong. Wrong that there was a cemetery in Heaven. Wrong that angels could die.

Claire followed behind the older Mother Guardian. A crystalline path separated multicolored hedges of rocket snapdragons, red roses, and Sweet William, framing the gardens beyond as if to hold them at bay. Afternoon sunshine reflected off the greenhouse windowpanes, warming her bare skin. A syrupy aroma from crimson lilies assaulted her nostrils, making the air thick and breathing difficult.

So peaceful.

So deadly.

The scent of the end of things and of loss surrounded her.

She'd been summoned. But instead of asking her to come to the familiar third floor office in the Administration Building, Mother Guardian had chosen *this* place, forbidden to young Guardians. It was a place Claire had never been.

The angel cemetery.

The messenger had spewed out the order in a rush, fracturing Claire's afternoon reading of an erotic romance she kept tucked under the silk pillows of her lounge. "Come packed, and ready to go," she'd said. So, Claire's yellow transport bag was now slung over her right shoulder, hanging half empty like the flesh on an old horse.

But why was she to start her new mission at the place of unhappy endings?

Father works in mysterious ways. Mother Guardian's anxiety-laced thoughts filled Claire's mind.

Did they find my books? Claire couldn't help the errant thought from sweeping through her mind, but it was too late to take it back.

At the ancient, rusted gate, Mother turned to face her but did not smile. Her gnarled hand rested on the crooked handle above an empty keyhole. Her skin was wrinkled, like a flesh-colored prune. "You shouldn't read such things."

Claire knew it was true. Did Mother understand how hard she'd tried?

Not nearly hard enough, Claire.

So this was it. Punishment. The consequences she'd dreaded. They'd discovered her secret. Mother pushed the gate open, and Claire jumped as the rusty gate screamed in protest, like the helpless cries of an injured animal.

A strange and eerily peaceful world colored by green grasses and brilliant white stone markers opened in front of her. A chilling breeze blew back the hairs at the sides of her face. Unseen fingers pulled at her skirts, clawed at her bodice, whispering warnings. The wind writhed through the fabric of her white gown, disturbing the silver and gold hand-stitched symbols of her station. Her badges. Each represented a troubled human life saved from suicide. Each chronicled her perfect track record.

Tall, dark trees leaned into the cemetery plot, as if bowing out of respect for the elder Guardian, then swayed backwards, signaling that Claire wasn't worthy. Her senses were on full alert, as every leaf or blade of grass presented a threat.

As they made their way between the rows of graves, Mother's fingers patted the tops of the marble headstones, one by one. Claire was careful not to let any part of her gown or bag come in contact with the silent markers. Another blast of cold air traveled down her spine. The gown billowed out like a parachute, and then just as quickly, deflated, getting caught between her legs as she worked to keep up with the older angel.

Mother stopped, slapping her leathery palm against the top of one gravestone with a whack.

Time to face the music.

Her mentor's lips formed a grim line, indicating she knew of Claire's unease. "You *should* be scared, child." The old woman's half-lidded eyes scanned wearily over the undulating grasses behind Claire, a scene that would have been peaceful and serene if not for so much sadness hovering like a shroud over a meadow dotted by pure white stones.

"A very powerful dark angel did this," Mother whispered, then peered directly into Claire's eyes, burning a hole all the way to her soul. "He makes them believe they are falling into his arms, but instead they fall into the pits of the Underworld."

There were several dozen grave markers, all arranged in crisp rows, cooled by the swirling air and tickled by an occasional stray leaf or twig.

"One dark angel took all these sisters?" Claire asked.

"Like you, my dear, he has never lost a soul." Mother's eyes scanned Claire, as if she waited for a reaction. "There are others, of course," she motioned beyond the trees, "fallen, but not at *his* hand. This one has a particular taste for Guardians. He seeks them out on purpose, considers it his calling."

Claire searched the relief chiseled out of the smooth marble, hesitant to touch the design of a harp. Above the image, one name was etched in block letters: M-E-L-O-D-Y. Her fingers twitched with desire to connect with the spirit of the angel there, wanting to touch the flowing lines and sharp angles of the block letters. She tensed her hands at her sides. No dates were listed, nothing else written to describe the buried angel. Claire grieved for the loss of this being, someone who must have been loved as a human and who'd been cherished and trained as an angel to give some other human a second chance. A chance perhaps she never had. Such a harsh end to a gentle soul created to bring brightness and life to a dark and dying world.

Preyed upon, Claire heard Mother's mental warning.

Had Melody's trusting nature been used as a tool against her? The permanence of the angel's grave made Claire shudder.

"I wish I'd known her," she said.

"Would make no difference. I knew them all. Only one of us needs to bear this pain. I'm trained for it. You're not."

Claire had felt the same loss when other Guardians came home from unsuccessful missions. The crying and wringing of hands would go on for a few hours until the angel was carried to the wash, where the memory of their failed mission in the human world would be erased. They would emerge fresh, eager to study again, to garden, or to commune with their sisters. Heavenly smiles would be etched into faces as permanent as the symbol on the stone marker. Claire had assisted in several of these ritual cleansings over the years, and they were never easy. She'd resisted the urge to ask her angel sisters questions, to learn what had gone so horribly wrong.

"No. We can't have the memories here." Mother's terse comment tore through Claire.

Claire forced her mind in another direction. "You have a mission for me, then?"

"Yes." Mother handed Claire a sheet of white paper featuring the picture of an attractive young man with dark curly hair cascading over his forehead and down to his shoulders to end behind his ears. "This is your new charge, Daniel DePalma."

Claire traced her finger across the paper, down the slender nose and across full lips, barely aware she'd caught her breath.

"Those are not proper thoughts for a Guardian to have." Mother said.

Claire could see the older woman's right eye twitch, and her crooked smile with pursed lips seemed barely under control.

"He's been preyed on by this dark one," Mother added.

"Thought the dark one only liked Guardians."

Mother shrugged. "I think even a Dark angel gets lonely. Who knows? I don't study their habits, and neither should you."

Claire nodded. She flipped the paper back and forth, noting information was listed only on one side. "No file this time?"

"No. We think he decided tonight to take his life. You're going to have to hurry to get there in time. It may already be too late."

Claire tensed, irritated they'd wasted so much time. She turned, anxious to leave the cemetery and get started on her new mission.

"Just a minute." Mother's fingers dug into Claire's shoulder, spinning her around.

Something is still wrong. Claire rubbed her collarbone.

"Let me give this charge to another Guardian, Claire," Mother said. "I asked that it *not* be you. I was overruled." Mother's black eyes watched her intently, eyes that had begun to water.

Which meant Father had chosen Claire especially for this mission. But why?

Father works in mysterious ways.

"You can refuse it. In fact, I wish you would," Mother insisted.

"You think I'll fail? I've never failed."

"Careful of the pride, child. Every Guardian eventually comes across a human she cannot save."

Now Claire was determined to take the mission. "I won't refuse it. I can't refuse Father."

"I understand, but I was hoping you would anyway. You see, this is going to be your last mission. You're to be retired here, to become an instructor."

Claire's blood began to boil. She clutched the white paper, squared her shoulders and said through her teeth, "How could you do this to me, after all my faithful years of service to the Guardianship?"

"Shame on you, Claire! Teaching is an honorable profession. Think of the inspiration you will be to the younger ones—an instructor with a perfect record."

"I'm a much better Guardian *doing* the work, not *teaching* it," Claire spat, but she knew it was no use. She'd learned long ago not to try to change Mother's mind. It was as permanent as life eternal. Repositioning her yellow transport bag, she turned to leave.

"No appearing in his dreams, or in real time," Mother said to her back. "Don't talk to him, either, and no whispering. No notes! Don't give messages to someone else to tell him things." Mother's voice rose as Claire left, walking at first, then breaking into a full run. "And just so I can tell him I've covered it, don't use your dust for anything but helping him dream, Claire. No one must see your dust or feel its power. But most important, he is *never* to know you exist, *never* to feel your presence. Is that clear?"

A well-dented taxi, covered in spray-painted graffiti, idled as Claire emerged from the garden path. Sprays of diamond dust covered leaves and flowers at her side like a coating of sugar. She hopped into the rear bench seat and closed the door.

Thank God it's Doris.

The cabbie's eyes watched her in the rear view mirror as they descended through the clouds. Claire stared at the back of Doris's head, noting the short, unnaturally bright red hair that stuck out under a weathered cabbie hat worn too far back and at an angle.

Doris never said much on the way down. She had lots of questions and comments when she brought Claire back up. Claire sensed in her a kinship, a certain rebellious spirit. And she guessed the cabbie had been warned not to interfere with a Guardian and her mission.

Claire never knew another Guardian angel, except one, who had any memories of life as a human before the wash erased the memories. Just as she was certain she would never need to eat or sleep and wouldn't age, she knew she remembered things about being human—like the day she was murdered. She had carefully guarded this secret. It meant something was wrong with Father's wash mechanism.

Or something was wrong with *her*.

In a matter of seconds, she was running down Daniel's crushed granite drive-way in the dark to the two-story stone cottage tucked behind two massive homes. Claire smelled the loamy, wet earth coated with the heavy fog that covered most of the area as she looked up to see a tiny window in a small gable under the eave.

She willed herself through the wooden front door, remaining invisible. She hoped Daniel hadn't heard her transport bag drop at her feet. The room air was hot and stifling, filled with pale grey smoke that burned her eyes and scorched her throat, causing her to gag. She held her breath and checked her invisibility, her sensors scanning the room. No sign of the dark angel.

Seated in front of a lit fireplace was her new charge, muscled and bare-chested, holding a large carving knife in his right hand, working his way up from deepening the shallow cuts he'd made on his left forearm. A thin trickle of blood dripped onto his black slacks, the only clothes he wore. He was curs-ing in a foreign tongue, sweat streaming down the sides of his cheeks. His lips curled in a sneer as he held his breath, ready to cut.

Claire saw the alarm keypad to the right of the front door. She willed her-self there and pushed the red fire button, sending a shrieking noise throughout the living room. Daniel took too long to put his hands to his ears. *He must be drunk.* She saw the smashed neck of a wine bottle and pieces of green glass littering the floor at his feet. Remnants of a painting, torn and ripped apart from its frame, bubbled in the fireplace, sending a black streak of oily smoke up the wall.

Before Daniel could stand, Claire willed herself back to him. She rubbed her thumb against her first two fingers, producing dust, and applied the sparkling mixture to the raw flesh on his forearm. Golden threads began the work of restoring his skin. He didn't notice.

He danced around the glass, stumbling over to the flashing red alarm. Claire smelled the stench of terror and sweat mixed with the acid burning paint smoke coming from the fireplace. His chest was streaked with wide ribbons of red wine; his cheeks were flushed, and his full lips were stained deep burgundy.

The fury inside him was so intense Claire almost stepped back, but she held her ground as he punched a code into the pad that did nothing to stop the noise. He tried again, then ripped the keypad from the wall and left it dangling by two wires. The head-splitting sound abruptly stopped and he watched the pad sway back and forth, its red light refusing to submit. He turned his back on it.

She leaned against his massive shoulder muscles, feeling the heat of his body, reading the torment in his soul. She wrapped her arms around him. The salty smell of his body was an elixir. Claire tingled with energy.

"I am here, Daniel. Nothing can harm you now," she whispered. As if he could hear or feel her, he sighed in unison, a small moan from deep inside his throat, interrupting the few seconds of calm they shared together.

A faint siren got closer; she wondered what he would say to the rescue team that was surely on its way.

"Christ," he whispered. "I can't even do this right."

CHAPTER 2

What am I doing? What the hell's wrong with me? Daniel staggered over to the gas shutoff on the fireplace and turned the handle downward. He coughed, covering his mouth from the cloying, unforgiving smoke. He was as irritated as his throat felt. Irritated with himself, with his painting, with everything in his life. "*Filch da puta,*" he cursed, kicking the remnants of the painting he'd dismembered and thrown into the fire not more than twenty minutes ago. He used to gaze at the image that stood guard over the fireplace when *she* rode him there on the green velvet settee, on those long languid evenings when they'd drunk too much wine. All he could think about had been filling her little pussy over and over again near the devilish orange glow. It was the same settee she'd screwed the doctor on a week ago when he caught them in his living room.

My own fucking house!

He used to get hard looking at the painting when she was at work or out with her friends, so strong was his craving for her, like some kind of addiction he didn't even want to think about shedding. Except now he had to.

"Don't sell it," she'd said. "I want you to think of me, how we are made for each other." It was the first blue leopard he'd painted. Those big green eyes the size of fists used to stare back at him no matter where he was in the room. When he was creating the piece, he'd paint for a few minutes, think of her, and then get so hard he'd drive all over town to find her.

Never before had he felt this way—felt this insatiable lust for a woman. His cock had been in a constant state of arousal. They'd made love in closets, at the supermarket, at the nursery, and many times at the gallery, Craven Image, her favorite place. His mind had been in a constant fog, temporarily cured by a few precious moments when he'd sink himself deep into her pink folds. His attempts to satisfy himself without her body had been a dismal failure and only made his craving worse.

He could hardly have lunch with her in public he was so driven, the ever-present tent in his pants making it even difficult to cross his legs. The big blue leopard had kidnapped his desire for her deep in those green eyes, holding his lust like a vault at the bank, like his talent had been plucked from his body and held for ransom in the soul of this beast. It was the sum total of several months of work.

But now he'd destroyed it, like he'd destroyed his life. *I can't paint worth shit.* It wasn't a self-indulgent thought. It was the awful truth.

The faint siren was getting closer. He'd have to deal with them next.

He felt something warm against his back. Turning around, he glanced down, expecting to see some female companion, maybe Audray, but instead his gaze traveled to three more sets of yellow eyes on big cats in his jungle paintings hanging at the stairway. They were waiting.

"*Va se foder!*" he swore at them in Portuguese, but they didn't tell him to fuck himself in return. They sat there with no expression.

Maybe I'll burn them all. They're worthless pieces of garbage anyway. No one wants them.

He had been halfway ready to forgiving Audray's infidelity. She'd tearfully apologized and the makeup sex offered had been the best ever, though excruciatingly painful. The sex had been a bit rough, and not his usual tastes, but Audray had no limits, and showed him things he'd never considered. He'd tried to forgive her—told himself he did anyway—and had spent twenty-four hours screwing her so many times he'd lost count, but in the end, it was obvious she'd moved on, even though he hadn't. And his need of her and her body only increased the more he was without her.

He'd even convinced himself punishing her could help purge the self-loathing he felt for not being able to walk away.

Yeah, he could understand the guy getting caught up in the moment—Audray knew what she was doing, bringing the doc here under the guise of selling him a painting. The guy probably could feel the scent of lust and sex as soon as he walked in the room and before she took over. Like she'd done to Daniel months ago at the gallery party. No, he couldn't blame the poor son of a bitch for a little dalliance, even at Daniel's house. Just one taste of that sweet ass and he was hooked, hogtied, able to be led around by the nose. God knew, Daniel himself had been living that way for months now, almost a year. Daniel had always been a one-woman man, and had convinced himself he might be able to withstand the pain of her infidelity, as long as she came back to him. *Am I nuts? What was I thinking?* He didn't like the man he had become, the boundaries he had crossed, and had continued to cross every day he spent in her proximity.

But the last straw had been today when she told him the gallery was dropping his paintings. She was so sorry, she'd said. Then she'd told him it was difficult to be around him, since her feelings were compromised.

Compromised? Was that what it was, all that screwing? "Fuck you and your toilet seats," he'd shouted to the room. The gallery owner, Beau Bradley, had been the lead guitar for Spacetravelers, a rock and roll band from the '60s. Beau had gotten into autographing toilet seats and doing flashy canvases so wealthy owners could have a "Bradley" signature in their living room. The sales also helped with the cost of dialysis a couple of the boys in the band were under due to their past drug use. But was it art?

He leaned backward with his face to the ceiling. "When will this be over?" he groaned.

Now. It's over now. He didn't hear it. He *felt* it. There was a warm tingling sensation against his back again, like a woman's chest leaned up against him, like he'd been held in invisible arms, a cloak of safety surrounding him. His pulse quickened. It was unmistakably female.

"Who's here?" He whirled around, searching the room, the stairs and the balcony at the top.

The animals were silent. Even the bubbling painting stopped crackling in the fireplace. He raised his arms out to the sides and thought he saw a shimmer of dust slide down his forearms to his fingertips.

He rubbed his scalp, shaking off the crazy sensation, noting the steady beat of the heart he had tried to stop earlier this evening. He couldn't figure out if he was happy or sad to be alive.

He felt just as poor now as he had in his barefoot childhood years at that house near the beach, the one with no windows, the ocean as his shower. Difference was, back then he'd thought he was a talented artist and the world was his oyster. Now he wondered if he could ever stand to touch another canvas. The unsold inventory hung like tombstones at Beau's gallery. Of course they had to move him out. They were not in the charity business.

Leopard eyes were laughing at him. He didn't like their smirk. He'd rip that smug look off their faces, send them to a fiery grave just like their sibling. He was halfway to the stairs when he heard a tap at the front door. Turning, he saw a tall shadow in the frosted window, and felt a chill.

Might be a neighbor. *Well, screw it. Let them see the bonfires of my soul.*

Darting back to the entrance, he swung the door open so quickly he almost fell over. White fog with pointed tendrils snaked into the room. Daniel scented the exotic spices that always surrounded Josh and heard some kind of music. "God, Josh. Your timing is pretty pathetic."

"That's a hell of a way to greet your agent. I've come to check up on you. Got an inkling something wasn't right." Josh was dressed in black: leather knee-high boots, black jeans and turtleneck. Covering everything was a long black rain slicker, giving Josh the look of an oversized crow.

Daniel stepped to the man and gave him a stiff hug, which was not returned. "Thanks."

Josh remained at the doorway. "May I come in?"

"Might as well. Cops are on their way, though." Daniel shook his head and winced.

Josh marched into the center of the living room as Daniel closed the front door quietly and kept his eyes down.

"I see." Josh said after a quick survey, nodding. "We're having a temper tantrum, are we?"

"Fuck you," Daniel barked. He noticed laughter on Josh's pale face. His dark hair, pulled back in a ponytail, was shiny, and a lock of it had come loose, draped over Josh's left eye.

"Not what an agent wants to hear, my friend."

"Yeah? Well, I didn't send out invitations."

"Invitations? Invitations to what?"

"My demise."

"Ahhh. Now I see." Josh walked over to the fireplace and jabbed the still-smoldering painting with the toe of his boot. "Well, if you ask me, you got rather close. This time."

"This time? There's never been another time."

"True." Josh nodded in agreement, smiling.

Something about that smile disturbed Daniel. "You like my new piece?" Daniel gestured toward the paint smeared on the wall. When Josh didn't reply, he added, "I call it *Death of an Artist*." He picked up watercolor crayons scattered about the floor and smeared them against the wall, creating a burgundy paste. The cool, sticky substance made a mushy sound as he swiped his hands across the wall. "There. I call it finished," he said as he threw the remnants of the crayons at his feet. He wiped his hands on his black pants, already smudged with paint.

"Ah, yes. Death. That the friend you were seeking tonight?" Josh scanned the room as if searching for something. He sniffed the air, then coughed.

Daniel continued to wipe his hands and tried to focus on Josh's face but got dizzy. His stomach began to gallop.

"Don't you think this is a bit of an overreaction, my friend? Or, was it what you wanted?" Josh watched Daniel without expression.

Daniel focused on Josh's voice, which seemed to settle him. "What I want? How about a decent night's sleep? How about something to erase my memory? Everything I look at reminds me of *her*. How's this?" Daniel leaned over and snatched the knife at the floor. As he aimed it at his chest, he felt it slip out of his hand, as if invisible fingers wrenched it from his grip. Dumbfounded, he watched the trajectory of the knife as it flew through the air, clattering on the floor in the corner, and out of reach.

Josh crouched in a defensive stance and he searched the room, his eyes wide and fully alert.

"How'd you do that?" Daniel asked, in shock.

"You mean send the knife flying? You honestly think I did that?" Josh's dark lips lightened as they formed a thin line. "You're hammered. You couldn't hold onto your dick if your life depended on it."

Daniel leaned towards his agent, anger searing a hole in his gut, ready to argue against the accusation, but as nausea overtook him, he had a change of plan. He ran for the bathroom.

When he came back, stomach contents gone, he found Josh sniffing the wall. Both men turned as red lights strobed through the living room window and front door.

"Not a word about your intentions tonight, hear me?" Josh said.

"Sure."

"You take anything?"

"Just the Meritage, on an empty stomach."

"Ah yes, the Meritage. The wine you were saving for your wedding night."

It hurt more than Daniel expected, and again, his first reaction was anger. Then he heard pounding on the front door and took a deep breath to face the consequences of his behavior. Josh beat him to the door, opened it, and bowed to two uniformed policemen standing on the stoop in the evening fog.

"Good evening, officers."

"Officers Lopez and Sprague. We got an alarm call." The taller officer, Lopez, waved the smoke from his eyes and winced.

"Where's the fire? Is anyone hurt?" Sprague asked and stepped close to Daniel, giving him a sniff.

Josh cut in before Daniel could answer. "Problem with the fireplace. No one hurt. Ego bruised a bit is all."

"Yeah?" Lopez said as he looked from Josh to Daniel. He took out a pad and pen from his breast pocket. "Need some ID, fellas. Who owns the house?"

"I do." Daniel shoved a hand in his back pocket and pulled out his wallet. He displayed his driver's License. "I'm Daniel DePalma. This is—"

"Joshua Brandon. I'm his friend, and his agent," Josh said, opening his wallet up to examination.

"May we come in?" Lopez asked.

"Why not?" Daniel said and stepped aside to let them pass.

"What the hell happened to you, sir?" Officer Lopez asked, pointing with his notebook to Daniel's chest, stained with wine and smeared with paint.

Daniel bristled.

"We walking into a quarrel between you...two?" the officer said and gave a crooked smile, showing no teeth.

Daniel boiled at the implication. "What the fuck is *that* supposed to mean?" Josh grabbed his arms, restraining him from going after the officer, who had put his hand on his gun.

"Hold it, Daniel," Josh murmured. "Not wise. You're being an asshole."

Josh's strength surprised Daniel. He shook Josh loose and rubbed his arms where his friend's fingers had dug in.

The second officer, Sprague, Daniel thought, stepped in front of his partner. "Anyone else here?" he asked, before beginning to search the downstairs.

"No. He lives here alone. I just got here myself," Joshua answered.

As his partner wandered through the living room and to the open kitchen, Officer Lopez examined the alarm keypad that dangled by the two wires. He raised it delicately with his pen.

"I think the smoke tripped the alarm," Josh offered. "Then Daniel had an unfortunate accident with it, trying to get it to stop."

Dropping the keypad, which hit the wall with a light tap, the policeman pulled on latex gloves as he walked over to Daniel. He flashed a light in Daniel's eyes.

Daniel flinched. The bright light hurt. He was having difficulty standing up. Lopez twirled Daniel around and the room kept spinning. First checking Daniel's pockets, both front and back, Lopez then examined his back and hands. Lopez paid close attention to the small abrasions on Daniel's left forearm where he had nicked himself with the knife.

"When did you do this?" he asked Daniel.

"Roses. He pruned his roses Monday. Or was it Tuesday, Daniel?" Josh volunteered.

Daniel gawked at the almost healed gashes that had bled not more than fifteen minutes ago. "What the fu—"

Josh stepped on his foot. Hard.

"Okay, these look to be a couple of days old," said the officer.

"I'm fine." Daniel yanked his arms away and crossed them over his chest. He glared at Josh.

Officer Lopez was stern. "Look, don't bullshit me. You're far from fine. What have you taken?"

"Wine. One bottle of Ravenswood Meritage Estate Bottled 2005." Daniel sat down abruptly. The room continued to wobble. "It was as good as recommended."

Josh smiled and shook his head, looking at his feet.

"Look, Officers, I think I should tell you he has been dumped by his fiancé recently. And today, he found out his paintings are being dropped at the gallery, okay? It's been a blow both personally and professionally."

Yeah, and these dudes think we're a couple.

"If the fire department comes, you'll get a big fine for that too," Lopez said, moving to the fireplace.

Daniel shrugged. Didn't matter. He had no money to pay for it anyway.

"This is destruction of property."

"*My* property. *I own* this house," Daniel said.

"Yes, but it's against the law to willingly set it on fire."

"I didn't fucking cause—"

"Daniel," Josh said, "don't be more of a shit than you've already been. Apologize, or they'll take you to jail. And then you still will have to apologize, but it will cost you a few grand. I happen to know you don't have that kind of money to burn."

Sprague returned and nodded to his partner. "Okay, I guess we're done here," he said.

Daniel watched as Lopez kicked the twisted remains of the smoldering painting protruding from the fireplace. waved his hand in front of his face to rid himself of the cloud of soot and smoke.

"What's this?" he asked.

"Uh, that was a jungle scene with a leopard. It was an especially nice one," Josh said. Josh could spin anything.

"So what was wrong with it? Why'd he burn it all up like this?"

Josh took his time with the answer. "*She* liked it."

CHAPTER 3

Joshua spoke to the two policemen in hushed tones and they left, nodding their heads, laughing at something the three of them shared. He had promised he'd stay to watch over Daniel. Claire was sure Josh used some kind of power over them. She relaxed when the uniforms got in their patrol car and disappeared. Daniel was seated, leaning over his knees, head propped in his color-smeared left hand. He was focused on the floor and seemed oblivious to anything else around him.

She saw Josh continue scanning the room, as if looking for something he didn't see. His eyes shot a beacon of red light as he swept his gaze across the corner where Claire had been standing, invisible—or so she thought. The red light left a pricking sensation on her skin. She felt a sharp pain, jumped, and then saw Josh do a double take in her direction.

A chill ran up her spine. Claire dropped her eyes and willed herself to the opposite side of the room. This had to be the powerful, dark angel Mother had spoken of.

He can feel my pain. She knew he could probably feel her fear as well. It would be a mistake to reveal her presence. Tossing the knife had been an ill-conceived move, but she'd been out of options. If Daniel had drawn blood, she knew he would have earned an escorted trip to the hospital, and then most likely to jail afterwards. But if she'd healed Daniel, Josh would know for sure he was being watched over by a Guardian and not some other angel. She wasn't about to show off her special powers until she needed to.

Josh stopped scanning. He shrugged and rolled his head around to the back. His neck made a loud cracking noise. "I need a drink myself. I'm seeing things."

"What?"

"Never mind. Okay, Romeo, get your butt upstairs and take a shower while I fix you something."

"Josh, I'm fine. No need for this…"

"I'm going to insist. Besides, I promised to take care of you."

"I don't need a nursemaid."

"*Au contraire, mon ami*, you need a nurse *and* a maid. I've got a couple in mind and somehow I don't think the cops would object…"

"Stop it, Josh." But in spite of his drunkenness, his pants were tenting.

Josh noticed Daniel's groin and howled with laughter. "Oh, that's right. Your heart's breaking. My apologies, I forgot." He bowed deeply, raising his left arm above his head, little pinkie in the air, right palm over his heart.

Daniel glared at him. "You asshole. You don't take any of this seriously, do you?"

"No. I don't take much in life seriously."

"How can you say that? Don't you care about anything?"

"Oh, I care, I care deeply. Fact is, I care about things you have no fucking idea even exist. You're shitfaced. One minute you were ready to kill yourself, and the next you'd hump anything in a skirt, maybe one of those cops—"

Daniel lunged at Joshua, screaming Portuguese obscenities. With one small movement, the dark angel flipped Daniel end over end. Daniel's body collapsed on the floor where he lay dazed and confused. He struggled to get up. Josh finally gave him a hand, which he refused, with a curse and a glare, and righted himself.

"No more of this bullshit, Daniel. Behave."

Daniel scowled and turned away, rubbing his rear and moving his shoulder.

"You're just a victim of the human condition." Josh leaned on a high-backed overstuffed chair and said, "Now, get that stink off you and let's eat. We'll worry about getting a replacement for Audray tomorrow, or the next day. Fair enough?" He grinned, showing perfectly even white teeth.

Daniel hesitated a second, then lumbered to the stairway, mumbling something not in English. Claire willed herself up to the top landing, near the entrance to what she assumed was Daniel's master bedroom suite. As Daniel passed through her, she smelled the wine, the sweat, and trace elements of his lemon aftershave.

Telling herself she was concerned he wouldn't try to injure himself further, she followed him into the bathroom, leaned herself against the door for support, and watched as he slipped the tight black slacks with paint smudges down over his briefs. In one smooth move, he bent over and slipped off the gray briefs, exposing the tanned and muscled cheeks of his ass. She blushed at this intimate view of him from behind. The smooth, tanned flesh made her quiver.

He was healthier than the charges she usually got. Lean and well toned, this one didn't resemble the usual cadre of suicidals who had done years of damage to themselves, usually through drug and alcohol use. Simply put, Daniel was perfect in every way, from his broad smooth shoulders to the smallness of his rear and tightness of his thighs that were dusted with just a little dark hair. She watched the muscles move under his skin as he pulled aside the shower curtain and stepped in. When the water began to run she waited, giving him privacy.

Truth was, she usually liked to shower with her charges, but it was not the recommended way. She would give him a little more distance tonight; let him show her his dreams and the true source of his torment. Her instincts told her to be cautious. Something in her internal radar was bleeping off the charts.

She inched her way closer so she could smell the shower gel he used. She leaned against the wall, letting the lemony steam cover her invisible but sensitive angel flesh. She closed her eyes and listened to him reprimanding himself in Portuguese. It wasn't important to have a word-for-word translation; she understood perfectly what he was saying. The way the sounds rolled off his tongue and the deep resonance of his voice was soothing. She knew in that instant that she could save him. He didn't want to die. He wanted to live. He was fighting with himself, and right now that was a good thing.

She was still daydreaming when the water stopped and he reached for the towel located on the wall Claire was leaning against. His hands went through her shoulders to grip the blue terrycloth hanging there. She didn't move as he pulled the fluffy cotton to his face, burying it and then reaching behind him to towel dry his hair with one strong arm as he arched backwards and gave her a first class view of his chiseled abs, and more.

The place where he had touched her was warm. The full length of this slick, wet Adonis who smelled of fresh lemons was no more than four or five inches from the edges of her gown, but her body underneath began to glow and she was suddenly shy, and blushed. This had never happened to her before. When his hands again went through her body to replace the towel, and he exhaled a release, filling her nostrils with his mortal breath, she knew she had to get out of the room.

Willing herself into his bedroom, she rubbed her upper arms until the sensation of his palms was gone, and took a deep breath. Daniel dressed while she stepped out onto the upper landing and occupied herself watching Joshua tinker around in the kitchen below.

In a crisp white shirt that smelled freshly laundered, and a pair of blue jeans with sandals, Daniel brushed by her angel gown, not knowing he barely grazed her back. She followed the trail of his scent as he danced down the stairs, fingers of his long dark hair trailing behind him.

Close one. Other Guardians had told her if some kind of attraction occurred between the angel and the charge, her invisibility could be compromised. And if she appeared to him in the flesh at any time, it might mean a quick trip home to Heaven. She would have to be extra careful to make sure that didn't happen.

Josh washed the large carving knife and laid it on the counter top, then foraged in the refrigerator. He sighed. Almost closing the door, at the last minute he brought out a carton of eggs, some cheese, and an onion. He went back for the butter. He looked up at Daniel and gave a curt smile. "Better," he said.

"Yeah, nothing like a shower."

"All's right with the world, then?"

"Wouldn't go that far."

Josh sang some little ditty under his breath; it sounded to Claire like a pub chant. He whipped eggs furiously, creating a light froth. He unpeeled the golden onion and then halved the white meat with one quick slice, using the Henkel knife. Both parts of the onion sprung back and rolled slightly, freed forever from each other.

"Josh, you don't have to do that."

"Well, I'm here and I'm doing it. You…" he pointed the knife directly at Daniel, "can make the coffee."

Daniel flinched at the gesture. Claire went into protect mode, ready to spring. Josh followed Daniel's gaze and, noticing the knife, sighed.

"Thoughtless of me." He tapped his forehead with his knuckles, still clutching the knife. A small piece of onion fell into his black hair. Josh didn't notice. "I don't use my head sometimes. Sorry."

"My best friend is trying to kill me—with the knife he bought me for my birthday," Daniel mumbled, lips attempting a crooked smile. Claire loved that smile already.

"Shut up and get the coffee."

Daniel brought out a bag of coffee beans and poured them into the grinder. Both men jumped as it whirred to life.

Claire loved the smell of freshly ground coffee. It brought memories of previous missions, sitting at outdoor cafes, mingling anonymously in human form with the rest of the population. She liked looking ordinary, unremarkable.

The chopping and grinding completed, the two men waited for the eggs to cook and the coffee to brew. Josh painstakingly rinsed the knife, using his fingers to remove the onion parts and juices that remained there. Daniel watched him lay it carefully on a towel. After an awkward pause, Daniel began, "Bet you never thought I would use your knife to do myself in, did you?" His eyes were dark and hooded.

Josh shrugged. He looked up at Daniel slowly, and with a smile, said, "I guess I could feel sort of responsible, then? That what you're saying?"

"Not at all. You're not my keeper." Daniel frowned.

"Am I not my brother's keeper…?" Josh recited, with eyebrows raised.

Claire choked on hearing the Bible verse. *He's clever; I'll give him that.* She noted how Josh twisted things around, like buying Daniel the knife to kill himself. No doubt Josh had another kind of birthday in mind—a new black soul. She wondered if he was responsible for the broken relationship with Audray, too.

"Seriously, would you let me do it, if you caught me in the middle of it?"

Claire didn't like where this question led. As if sensing her concern, Daniel added, "Oh forget it. That was stupid."

"Depends on what you wanted." Josh looked down at his black boots. The smell of cooking eggs and butter caught his attention and he flipped the omelet over.

"So, you'd let me do it?"

Claire tensed. Why was Daniel still thinking about it?

"Is that what you wanted this time? Or did you want to be saved?" Josh asked as he dished up the eggs onto two small plates. He dropped the pan into the sink, adding water that sizzled when it hit the hot pan.

"No. I wanted to die. I have no money. I can't paint. I can't sleep without those fucking nightmares torturing me all night long."

"There're a lot of guys who would love those fucking nightmares, my friend."

Josh looked into the corner. Claire felt the pinpricks on her skin again and saw the faint red light emanating from the center of his eyes.

Daniel followed his gaze. "What is it?"

"I was just thinking how close you got. Mere seconds, from the sounds of it." He gave Daniel a wicked grin as he walked to the eating bar next to him and passed over the plates of food. "Divine intervention," Josh said. He stared at his plate and frowned, "Nah, no such thing, is there? You just didn't really want to do it, otherwise you would have. That's what they say, anyway."

Daniel started to say something, but seemed to think better of it.

"Time to get something in your stomach," Josh said as he set down a steaming mug in front of Daniel. They sat at the kitchen countertop, side by side, eating silently.

"You make good eggs," Daniel managed to get out around a mouthful.

"Ah, it's nothing. I didn't have much to choose from in your refrigerator. Going for the wine and cheese diet are we?" Josh retorted.

"I haven't been home—eating on the run, when I eat at all." He paused again before inserting another hot cheesy forkful of eggs, and swallowed. "Gotta sell the house."

"Why?" Josh's face was full of surprise.

"Money. The memories. Every time I go to bed I see the same dream—I see her in this house." He pointed to the green bench, standing unharmed amongst the carnage. "I'm broke. Beau's even left me messages to get my paintings out of his gallery in Healdsburg. That last big sale was what, eight months ago now? I think a change of scenery would help me…recover…if that's the word I'm looking for. Move to some place less expensive. It's been a tough year."

"Aghh! Things could be worse. Just wait." They both laughed. "Can't help you with the dreams, although I've tried to get you another space to exhibit. Things are tight everywhere."

"Yes, you have, and I appreciate it. But right now you've got to be asking yourself why you bother. Nothing seems to be working."

"Daniel, I see the potential in you. Trust me when I say I am a good judge of character. I've rather made a study of it." He got up and topped off Daniel's coffee. "One thing I do know is women are complicated and not really worth all the pain." Josh delivered this line with his nose screwed up tightly, as Daniel hunkered down on the stool and nodded his head, agreeing. "And sex is as good with one as with another. Best to fully play the field, my man, if you know what I mean? You're talking to an expert."

Daniel chuckled, looked at the remnants of his food, then sighed. "I thank you for your friendship, Josh," he said "You're the only one who cares whether I live or die."

"Hey, what are friends for?" Josh said.

"Well, I'm lucky you're on my side."

Josh smiled. He leaned back against the cabinets and rubbed his belly. "I'm still hungry—you got any bread? We need some carbs, man."

Daniel pointed to the refrigerator with his fork, "In the freezer. There's some wheat bread in there."

Josh opened the freezer door, pulled out four frozen pieces, and dropped them in the toaster. He was acting like he was watching Daniel eat, tapping his fingers on the countertop, legs crossed at the ankles, his black form casually leaning against the base cabinets. Josh's head was slightly tilted to the left side, eyes small slits looking into the far corner toward Claire again.

Daniel turned to follow Josh's gaze.

"What do you keep looking at over there?"

Josh shrugged, rolled his neck. "This whole evening has been rather interesting to me," he said. "I'm just taking it all in."

The toast popped up. They all jumped.

"You call that toasted?" Josh complained, holding up one of the pieces like a piece of stinky laundry. The bread drooped as he turned it horizontal.

"It was frozen. Put 'em in again."

At last the toast popped up a second time, smoking. Josh waved the grey cloud aside with his outstretched palm and arm. He carefully picked up the dark brown pieces with his fingertips.

"Ah, finally." He slathered butter over them.

"You've ruined them, man," Daniel said frowning at the charred remains.

"Better for you this way. Eat up, now." Josh threw two slices on Daniel's dish while he chomped down on his own. "So I gotta ask you, what happened with the alarm?" he asked, then licked his fingers.

"Fireplace smoke, I guess." Daniel made designs with the tip of his fork in the leftover eggs. "Halfway expected to find you standing there. Something must be wrong with it."

Josh coughed, stuffing down a laugh as he ambled across the kitchen to the front door. Holding up the dial pad with his index finger, he bent over like he was carefully pointing out a clue in a crime scene, and said the obvious, "There *definitely* is something wrong with it." He released his finger and let the pad flap as it hit the wall.

Daniel paused. "Happened just as I placed the knife at my arm. I was going to cut." He shook his head, and shivered. Claire could see he was trying to purge the image from his mind.

"I find the timing very interesting."

The two men were silent for a moment. Josh inspected the smoldering fireplace, the splash of colors on the wall. He sniffed the air, then the wall.

He is still looking for something.

"I guess my time was not up tonight," Daniel said softly as he turned around on his stool to face Josh. "Just lucky, I guess."

Josh gathered himself, inhaled deeply, and walked tall into the kitchen. He leaned over the countertop and placed one elbow next to Daniel's seated form and said, "No, man. Nobody's that lucky. I'd say you have a Guardian angel." He stood up. "She's probably standing right over there."

He pointed directly at Claire.

CHAPTER 4

C laire stood frozen in place, looking at the two men. One could sense her, the other could not. She was grateful neither could see her.

She willed calmness over her like a warm fuzzy bathrobe, making her breathing slow and deliberate. If she could keep her fear from surfacing, she might not be detectable to Josh. She knew Josh was trying to draw her out into human form so Daniel would see her.

"I don't see a thing."

"Well, Daniel, neither do I, but I feel her there." Josh pointed to Claire's corner.

"Apparently I'm not the only one who's had too much wine tonight." Daniel said.

Good. He doesn't believe him. Claire was relieved.

"No, you can laugh. Make fun of me all you want, but I believe in such things." Josh turned, facing Daniel head on. "I think there are spirits, even angels."

Daniel looked at his feet, shaking his head. "I'd have thought you'd go more towards the dark side, you know, demons of the flesh and all, considering your appetites…"

"Guilty." Josh smiled at Daniel then whispered, "You have no idea how I love the dark side. Who'd want a perfect world? Now, you and Audray were…"

"Fuck off, Josh." Daniel punched his friend's shoulder and frowned. "I'm beat. Gotta crash." His voice was hoarse and cracked.

The two friends shuffled to the door and hugged, slapping each other on the back. "Seriously, thanks, man," Daniel murmured. "I live to paint another day."

"Be careful, Daniel. Don't go letting fantasies in your head, making up stuff. Stick to reality, the here and now."

"But you saved me."

Josh winced. "Nah, I was in the neighborhood anyway. Glad I could help." As he walked through the open doorway he turned. "You going to be okay for now?"

Daniel nodded and closed the door. He turned off the lights but left the mess in the living room. He stared at the scene one last time, then shook his head as he climbed the stairs. Claire followed several steps behind, yellow bag over her shoulder. Daniel sighed heavily. He unbuttoned his top while climbing and was bare-chested by the time he approached the last step.

She was startled by a noise downstairs and turned around to see Josh emerging through the front door without opening it. Claire froze. Josh looked first in the corner where she'd been hiding, then around the room, landing his gaze at the bottom of the stairs, ensuring Daniel was out of sight. Josh bowed to the room, looking around afterwards. It was obvious he could not see her.

"Round One goes to the challenger." He delivered the statement with a smile and disappeared back through the door the way he had come. The thin trail of grey smoke left in his wake smelled faintly of cloves.

Her heart pounded. Everything else was eerily silent.

She focused on the temporary save, pushing away any lingering fear. *I told Mother he wouldn't die tonight.*

Anticipation coiled in her stomach and tingled down her spine. She was alone with him now. Time to start her job.

Daniel changed into navy silk pajama bottoms he wore low on his hips, but remained shirtless. He got into bed.

Claire loved the smell of a man's bedroom when he lived alone—soap, cologne—the personal stuff of a man's life. *This is just the best job in the whole universe.*

He lay on his back at first, right arm bent over his head. His long fingers were curled in the palm of his outstretched hand as if he were holding something delicate. A raised blue vein extended from mid forearm all the way to his

25

elbow, snaking across the muscles underneath. He closed his eyes and drifted off to light sleep.

Claire likened these first dream encounters to how an inexperienced young human bride would feel on her wedding night. It was private, this intimate look inside a man's thoughts to see the secrets of his soul. She never got over the miracle of being inside a dream, exploring the parts of his life. "Rest well, Daniel. I'm here now to help you," she whispered. "Show yourself to me."

Startled, she saw a smile on his lips. It soon faded.

He was a delicate balance of beauty and strength, she thought. The moonlight made the well-developed muscles of his shoulders and forearms look like marble. He took good care of his body. She lay down to watch him from the side in the quiet of the night.

No one would ever know about the chaos that occurred this evening, or how close he came to spending eternity in the underworld, his soul lost forever. It made her cold to think of the many files on Mother's desk. Daniel's file could have been one of them.

He must be saved. He touches me with magic.

The moon had a crazy effect on humans. It was good they were asleep during its reign. Perhaps it was for protection. Like most Guardians, she preferred the purity and warmth of the sun.

Why not level with these people, tell them Father didn't run things alone? He was the creator and organizer, but angels were the technicians.

Guardians fix things that are broken.

So the job before her was to inspire Daniel. Her specialty was landscapes screaming with color. She'd done some large purple buildings, turquoise sand and pink snow that looked liked cotton candy. What a delight that he was a painter.

She gently stroked the length of his injured arm, tracing the shallow cuts that crossed a deep blue vein down into the palm of his hand, which suddenly squeezed shut as if to capture her fingers.

Claire sat up at full attention, noticing Daniel stirring. She checked her invisibility. He became fully awake, staring at the ceiling. She cocked her head to the side and watched his sparkling eyes in the moonlight, waiting.

Daniel still felt sick to his stomach. How close he'd come to killing himself, to ending the pain. How stupid he'd been. Yeah, Audray had done a number on him, and his career had crashed, but had that been reason enough to give up on life? He mentally thanked the messed-up alarm system, Josh, and the cops who'd stopped him from self-destructing completely.

Yeah, his life was still messed up, but he'd been given a second chance to fix things. He could let that chance go and finish the job he'd started, or he could continue wallowing in self-pity. Or he could pull himself up by the bootstraps and figure out how to get himself out of this nasty mess. Easier said than done. But maybe the only choice. He thought about how far he'd fallen and how fast the ride had been.

He couldn't get the picture out of his head: Audray being pumped and pleasured on his green couch by some guy with a really hairy ass. After he'd caught them, he'd been left alone with the painting she loved to look at while being fucked silly. His painting. Her favorite.

He'd had to kill that painting.

As his eyes got heavy, he felt his life unravel before him. It all began the day he met her. He used to call it his lucky day. But now he saw there had always been an edge to her. Something otherworldly. Something dangerous. She was different than all the other women he'd ever loved. He was addicted to her presence. His cock was in a continual state of arousal, harder and fatter than it ever had been. That woman pulled him into doing things way outside his comfort zone. Not that he was afraid of life and its sensual side, but Audray demanded he push past his limits. She was always more than he could afford, emotionally, causing some element of pain along with the pleasure. He was powerless to do anything about it until it was too late. She had him in her claws with every ministration, every sensual pleasure she extracted from him.

Daniel allowed the sleep to overtake him and closed his eyes.

Claire hovered above his sleeping form and spread her arms out to the sides, lengthening her legs and arching her back. She could delve into Daniel's dream without this, could catch his REM waves by focusing on his resting brain, but she wanted the full on sensual experience of possessing his physical form first. She had learned this method in the past, with no ill effects.

The pull of his skin sucked at her breasts, thighs, and shoulders, as she laid her head at the top of his heaving bare chest, then turned to expose her cheek to the warm spicy underside of his jaw and down the right of his neck. She inhaled his moist man scent there, allowing her lips to wander up, cross his chin, and linger in the airspace between them. Feeling the pull, she allowed herself to be drawn into him. She breeched his body, warming herself inside his soul, which burned hot, flickering with red flames of torment.

Like brushing across a delicate flower with her fingertips she calmed the fires and immediately felt his body relax and remain open to her. She repeated the motion and was rewarded with a moan traveling up his neck and a stirring in his groin. The flame inside him flared golden, without sputtering.

Claire smiled. She was closer to him now than anyone had ever been in his life. If she wanted to cause him harm, he was vulnerable to anything she could do. She held his soul in the palm of her hand.

Daniel, you are mine now.

"Yes," he whispered as his flame turned bright yellow.

Claire gasped for air. She withdrew and scooted over to the edge of the bed, resting against the wall of the room.

He feels me. Was this a good thing or not?

She put a thought out to her Guardian friend, Angela. Going higher in the angelic chain of command would be acting smart, like she'd been trained. She hovered in the doorway of indecision, and recalled the admonition Mother Guardian gave her just before departing Heaven. She could not make herself known to her charge.

It had been clear every other time she took over a charge. But something was different about Daniel.

She decided against getting a second opinion and came back to his body.

What can it hurt? Just a little taste of what humans feel.

Once again she descended on him and, as she floated closer, she felt the heat of his body and the movement of the muscles and sinews underneath his flesh. She rubbed her first two fingers against her thumbs, sending a sparkling trail of dust down onto his closed eyes. The magnetic pull began. His breathing developed a catch and his abdomen flattened lower as his chest expanded, full of air. He bit his lower lip, a crease forming at the right side of his mouth. Those full lips curled in a smile and his hips undulated upward.

She wondered what would happen if she remained there awhile. Was this wise? The magnetic attraction pulled her nipples until they hurt.

Can this develop into something else?

The torch inside his soul began to spark, became erratic. She continued the breech until she was able to settle him down again.

He appeared in the white room. She remained invisible, stood just behind so she could whisper suggestions in his ear.

"Show me, Daniel," she coaxed. She stood one breath away from his back, leaning her head into his shoulders and wrapping her arms around his chest. "Show me where it hurts."

Daniel stood alone in the room, the light blinding him at first. Looking down, he saw there was no floor. He extended his arms to the sides, palms up, and felt warmth swirling out from his outstretched fingers all the way to his chest. A warm blanket of air covered his back. He was naked.

He thought he heard a sound. He quickly whipped around, but no one was there.

"Show me where it hurts," came a voice in his ear.

Tiny fingers of flames descended down his chest. His cock came to life. There was a female presence here, something he desperately wanted to touch, to taste and feel. He turned slowly but again, was alone in the white space. He walked forward, then stopped.

"Show me," the whisper caressed his ear.

The voice was definitely coming from this room. She was close, but where?

"Here I am. This is what I am," Daniel said to the white air. His cock lurched, eager with expectation. He chuckled as he looked down, hard and ready. He fisted himself, and his balls ached and began to pulse. It was going to get uncomfortable soon.

"Paint your life," the female voice whispered. Her voice sent an electric chill down his spine and images began to form in the distance.

He saw Audray for the first time at one of Beau's gallery parties. She was tall, like a model, but with curves. Her shoulder-length blond hair was tossed under in thick graceful curls, which accentuated her pale, sultry face and big green eyes. A few glistening strands caught in her thick lashes. She pulled those strands aside as she laughed at someone from across the room. Her red-tipped fingernails were painted to match the color of her full red lips.

At the first sight of Daniel, her green eyes widened. A crease toyed with her smile, just to the left of her mouth. It had distracted him.

Daniel stirred, almost waking up. This dream usually caused a cold sweat, accompanied by a hard-on he'd quickly have to take care of, or sleep was out of the question. And sometimes, on the bad nights, it came back. The engagement had been off nearly a month, and he still missed her body.

But tonight he felt stronger, as if some invisible armor protected his tender heart, along with the alcohol that deadened his senses. He released himself to the visions floating in the white space, and didn't fight it this time. Deep REM sleep engulfed him.

"Daniel, I'd like you to meet the very lovely Audray Steele," Josh said with coolness. Daniel's heart skipped a couple of beats when he came to stand so close to her that he could make out every eyelash. Her green orbs hit their target, and she pierced him with her lidded gaze. He felt like an insect on a pin. Still, his body warmed to her immediately, and he felt like he was coming alive for the first time.

Her greeting, hushed in an intimate whisper was, "Welcome." He felt the need to lean into her to catch the secret. She sighed, looking relaxed, aloof, like she was considering something, maybe hatching a plan in her mind that pleased her. He smelled an ancient musky fragrance rising from her dark cleavage. He was having difficulty keeping his eyes off the fully exposed mounds that rose as if in an attempt to escape her tight, fuzzy sweater.

She stimulated every part of his body. The sight and smell of her was intoxicating.

He was aware other eyes were on him as she sized him up openly, like a piece of meat at the market, but found he liked her scrutiny.

"I'll leave you two to get acquainted," Josh said, then left and blended into the crowd. In Daniel's periphery, he saw famous faces and aging rock stars. There were young college-age groupies and couples dressed in business suits. It was an eclectic gathering, all drinking wine, indulging in chocolate-covered strawberries, studying the bright art, and enjoying the music—and parting with their money in huge amounts. Checks were being written. Credit cards handed over. The room smelled of ego, money, and sexual prowess.

This didn't feel like any of the galleries Daniel had visited before. The evening didn't seem to be about the art at all. It was more about seduction and power.

He recognized Beau Bradley, owner of Craven Image art gallery. The former lead guitarist for the Spacetravelers was waving his arms, entertaining a group clustered in front of a huge bright canvas. The painting was about six feet square. It looked like someone splashed red and yellow liquid on it and then dragged something across it—most likely a woman's ass, based on what Josh told him about Beau's reputation.

But Daniel's concentration was honed in on Audray, who drew him into a succulent embrace and left her scent all over him like the marking of a predatory animal. The caution in his head only heightened his attraction.

She reached up to touch him just above his left pocket with her red fingertips. He leaned into the touch, involuntarily. Her fiery gaze tethered him; he felt as though his wrists were bound. She walked backward two steps, and then turned, walking straight ahead in a long graceful gait. Everything around him slowed as he watched her walk away. Her hips swung in easy rhythm from side to side with a bit of exaggeration. She turned her face in profile, making sure he was following. Of course he was. He couldn't help but to follow behind. She pulled him by an invisible cord.

Daniel was aware of the other partygoers in the room as he followed her, slicing right through the middle of the room. Faces blurred past him like he was on a merry-go-round. Nobody seemed alarmed. They just stared or nodded, eyes full of envy.

What am I doing?

Josh gave him a little bow and pulled his pale redheaded companion closer. She kissed his neck. He studied Daniel from a dark place, far away, and then turned back to engulf the girl fully with a deep penetrating kiss.

Daniel followed Audray outside the main gallery into a cool and unlit storeroom that was filled with wrapped paintings leaning against the sides of the walls. She continued walking without saying anything, her red fingertips a beacon as they grazed the tops of the covered rows of paintings. She turned the corner and started to climb a set of metal steps. The red spiked heels accentuated her smooth, creamy calves. The polished leather soles under the balls of her feet made delicate tapping sounds on the metal stairs as she climbed higher. She touched the railing with lightness, stroking the metal with her charm bracelet, hips and thighs swaying in unison to the thumping of his heart.

He stopped halfway up the stairs. She turned and looked at him for the first time since they'd entered the storeroom. He waited under the buzzing glow of the overhead light.

"Where are we going?" he asked. He tried to sound casual, but his voice wavered. His mouth dried up, and he found it difficult to swallow. He hung onto the metal handrail, his knuckles turning white.

She pulled her lips back in a huge smile, revealing perfect white teeth. "You don't trust me? How sweet."

A shiver slithered all the way down his spine. Somewhere inside his head there had been a warning to run, but it faded in the thrum of his desire.

"Would I hurt you?" she asked. "Do you really think I would? Come. Let's talk." She entered a small room at the top of the stairs. Daniel looked behind him to find the warehouse still deserted. The only witnesses to his actions were a row of silent canvases. They waited. Party sounds rippled through the storeroom in muffled tones, coupled with the buzzing of fluorescent lights. She reappeared at the top of the steps, bent down, and held out her hand in a plea. "Come, please, Daniel. Step into my office."

He proceeded up the steps until he came to the final rung, then hesitated. She stood firmly at the top without flinching a muscle. Her gaze pulled him forward and he took the last step to close the gap between them. He was aware that if she pushed him he could fall backward to the concrete below. The danger whetted his sexual appetite. *Be careful, Daniel,* a small voice inside him cautioned.

But he couldn't help himself. He drew close, close enough to feel the mound of her breasts against his chest and the electric tingle made by the connection of her thighs as they rubbed his with an almost imperceptible back and forth motion. Her breath against his neck was warm and uneven. She traced his lips with her forefinger. His ears buzzed. He was going to put his arms around her, but at the last minute she moved out of his reach. He swallowed hard and felt his groin swell.

They entered a small office through a glass door, which she closed behind them. When he caught her waist and pulled her to him, claiming her lips fully, she reached for something. Daniel felt her melt into him and she gave a little moan. His ears buzzed again. She pulled away. His fleeting thought was that this was reckless, but he didn't care. He was a man dangerously in need of what she could easily provide, if she was inclined.

"I have a better idea. Come here." She led him by the hand to one of two red leather high-backed chairs in front of a carved wooden desk. She pushed his chest and he collapsed into a seated position supported by the chair. He had been holding his breath. He exhaled now. With a mixture of dread and excitement, he waited. The tent in his pants was clearly visible, and yes, she noticed, and smiled.

She hitched herself up on the edge of the ornate desk and crossed her long legs, a movement that revealed her pale upper thigh. She leaned back to reach a file, the curve of her right breast visible. Her movements were catlike. He felt his common sense evaporate. His pants were getting uncomfortable. His imagination ran wild with erotic visions.

"I have a whole file on you, Daniel." She looked over the top of the manila folder. "And I have to say, I like what I see, on all fronts." She flashed him a smile, parting her lips deliciously for him. "Beau has asked me to look out for a new painter just like you. Someone to add to the gallery. He attracts people who love art, have lots of money, and, in Beau's words, *'part with it easily.'* Are you up for it?"

Of course he was up for it. He was rock hard. Under normal circumstances he might have considered his behavior a little too careless. But Audray held in her hands the keys to the two things he wanted most right now: to be recognized as a talented artist and to find a woman to share his passion with. Almost out of money, he needed the break, and it was worth the risk.

"I'm glad you like my work." He thought he sounded too eager. "So, what kind of a file is that?" He pointed to the folder she held in her hands.

"Talent. It's a talent file." She said it like a librarian would speak to a second grader. "Certain people I choose, or they get recommended to me—as in this case—Josh…"

"Josh recommended me?" Daniel had only hoped to be able to score some smaller gallery space, but Beau Bradley's? This was a huge coup. He was thankful he'd chosen his agent wisely.

"Of course."

She was almost too beautiful to paint. Some sights were that way. He imagined her naked, sitting in front of him, looking up at him in his bed, needing him to stoke her fires. He knew he definitely was up for it.

"We'll want to see your work, your originals, of course."

Was this an interview or did she just want sex? Did it matter?

She sat on the desk, tapping the surface with a fingernail, as if impatient. She was studying him. But the pleasure reflected in her face seemed to come not from studying him, but from the fact that she could choose.

He needed to give her an answer without appearing desperate. It had been a long time since his last sexual encounter, and the dry spell was turning his thoughts, as well as his resolve, to mush.

"Of course. When would you like to see them?" He wasn't sure which need was greater: bedding her or having his paintings perused. *What is wrong with me?*

"Well, right now wouldn't be too convenient." She pouted and slid off the desk. She stood above his seated frame, cocked her head to the side and regarded him for a second before she slid down an imaginary pole and deposited her rump in his lap, her long legs dangling over the arm of his chair, crossed at the ankles.

Startled, at first he didn't know what to do with his hands. She rested her head on his shoulder, and after tracing a line down his throbbing vein with her tongue, she whispered, "How about we look at your paintings tomorrow morning when we wake up at your place?"

CHAPTER 5

No woman had ever talked to Daniel that way, and the more she forced herself on him, the more Daniel wanted her. She tugged at his shirt. The muscles in his lower belly tensed. His hand smoothed over the surface of her skirt where her thighs were taut and firmly developed. He traced the groove down the small of her back. The pressure of her breasts against him took his breath away, filling him with need. She steadied his head between her palms as her lips gently pulled and suckled his, her sweet tongue finding its way, fanning the flames of his desire. With his growing erection, it became painful with her on his lap.

Before he knew it, his pants were unbuckled and unzipped. She stood, hiked up her skirt, and turned around. Bending over, she showed him her soft behind that looked like a peach, bisected by a strap of red lace. With one finger she pulled the fabric to the side, revealing her sex. She sat down on his shaft, groaning as she looked over her shoulder at him. He was deep inside her wetness. His willing cock lunged, seeking the depths of her folds, seeking oblivion.

The leather of the red chair groaned. He could smell the musky hide of the beast it had belonged to. He slid his hands under the front of her sweater and up to her breasts, the heat of her skin warming his palms. He buried his face in the cloud of her scent at the small of her back, and then raised the sweater to taste her flesh. His hands glided down to her thighs, pressing them further against him as he raised his hips to penetrate deeper. He was overcome too soon and spilled his seed inside, feeling there hadn't been nearly enough time. He leaned his head against her back and exhaled as he stroked between her thighs. A part of him wanted to apologize.

She raised herself up and off him. Smiling, she stroked his member and purred, "It's going to be a wonderful night, Daniel."

He was certain of it as well.

He trailed behind her down the stairs as she did her runway walk in front of the canvas audience. They returned to the party and separated, but he never lost track of where she was. Every time he saw her he felt the bulge in his pants. He felt invisible fingers massage the back of his neck, and he'd turn around to find her green eyes burning, looking at him like he was naked. He found idle conversation useful in the interludes between stolen glances at her ass, her breasts, or the way her red lips kissed him in the air from across the room. He imagined doing all kinds of things to her when he got her alone. How could he be so conscious of how very wrong this was but still be powerless to do anything about it?

Toward the end of the party, Josh stood beside him as they watched Audray hug a skinny old rocker with long grey hair pulled back in a ponytail. The guy tried to grab her bottom and she politely took hold of his hand and presented it back to him as they both laughed.

"Isn't she exquisite?" Josh shook his head from side to side.

"Have you...?" Daniel asked.

"God no. She's as pure as the driven snow. A virgin for the plucking." Josh's eyes danced, mocking him.

Daniel chuckled at the obvious untruth, and nodded, staring at his feet.

"How do you feel, man?"

Daniel wasn't sure how he felt. Of course he felt good; he'd just had sex with a goddess. But he also felt like he'd dabbled in his first taste of sexual heroin. His appetite was only partly sated. He needed more. "Unbelievable."

"Yes. Nice, isn't it? I like going over the edge like that."

"But you..."

"She's all yours." Josh leaned into him and whispered, "You're a very lucky man, my friend. I haven't tasted, but have it on good authority you are in good hands."

"Yes, she has nice hands."

"Easy to let yourself go," Josh said.

"Hard to believe she's unattached."

"I didn't say *that*."

"Who?" Daniel noticed a growing wave of jealousy. Ownership rights.

"The one to watch is Beau. He lusts for her between his girlfriends."

"And you?" Daniel asked.

"You mean would it be okay to screw the ex-girlfriend of your agent? Would it have made any difference at all?"

"I'm sorry, Josh. Of course. I didn't think…"

"Oh please, don't waste your breath. She isn't my type. Never has been. You're free to roam. I prefer the red-haired angel types." He scanned the room. "Like that one over there." He pointed to a sweet-looking pink-skinned red-head in a dark corner, alone. At Josh's gaze, she looked up and beamed.

"Readheads or angels?"

"Both," Josh said, and winked.

Claire watched another dream interrupt the party scene. It came over him in a wave, and then yanked him away. He was in a field of grape vines on a bright, sunny summer day. Audray led him down between the rows, her red lips singing a little song that went with a dance she did.

Lady in Red.

Audray twirled, flashing Daniel a white smile as she beckoned him farther down the dusty rows bordered with the lush green foliage. She held a corked wine bottle in her right hand, the left clamped over Daniel's first two fingers as she led him deeper into the fields. He stopped to spread out the blanket.

"No, Daniel, let's go farther," she said as she pulled on his hand.

He knelt on the blanket. "No. Now." He was urgent.

She approached with a pout, standing over him with her legs apart, then started laughing as his hands slid up her thighs to grasp her panties.

Claire was flushed, her eyes pinned to what he was doing to Audray, at the sight of him pleasuring her with his tongue. Claire could feel the texture…

The blond vixen looked out above the vines like a queen at court. She stopped him.

"I'm hungry," she said.

"So am I. So am I." Daniel tried to pull her down but she easily got loose.

"We eat. Then we play some more. Come, I will feed you."

Claire felt his arousal through the dream. She was embarrassed for him, and apprehensive.

They ate a picnic of cheeses, olives, and red grapes. Claire felt his complete enchantment with the way Audray talked, the way her body moved on the picnic blanket in the sun. Her skin was translucent, blushing red from effects of the wine. Her hair sparkled golden. She laughed a lot. They both did.

They made love in the field under the blue cloudless sky. Claire had seen couples having sex before in dreams, but not with this abandon. Daniel was possessed. The angel wondered how it would feel to have her body worshiped in such a way by a man, *this* man. He took Audray hard, but was attentive and careful at the same time. He watched the signals she gave, intent on giving her as much pleasure as he took. Claire was enraptured with the way his body played hers. She could not take her eyes off them.

He threw Audray's clothes over the vines to the next row and soaked in the view as she ran down the dirt path stark naked to retrieve them. He lay on his belly, watching her looking for an opening big enough to crawl through to the other side. He was laughing again.

Afterward, he noticed they had an audience of farm workers who whistled as Audray turned and waved to them, unconcerned she showed them every part of her body.

Claire could feel the question growing in Daniel's dreamstate. *Does she love me more than she loves herself?*

"Good Daniel. There are things I can use here," she whispered in the dark, in the moonlight. Perhaps now he would sleep. But soon he began to stir. She hovered above him. "I can bring you peace. I can heal you. Show me. Show it all to me." Her gentle words were met with a smile, and then a frown as another dream snagged him.

She held her breath as she saw Audray wildly unzipping Daniel's jeans in a men's restroom. As his pants dropped to the floor, Audray reached into his underwear and pulled out his cock. Claire was alarmed at the way Audray coldly exposed him to the cool bathroom air, jerking and pulling on him before she softened and put her lips on his firm length and knelt down. Daniel's head leaned back, his back arched. He was enjoying the initial feel of her sucking, in spite of himself. And then objected, but way too late.

"Audray, I can wait—"

"Maybe you can, but I can't."

Daniel was reaching to check the door, but she stood up and pulled his hand away.

"I took care of it," she said as she hiked up her skirt.

He thrust into her from behind as she leaned over the sink. He was caught up in the excitement of screwing her in a bathroom, which only seemed to intensify his need for her. He heard the tinkling of wineglasses and civilized titters of laughter from the tasting room on the other side of the door as he pumped her.

Claire should have taken her eyes off them. She could have switched his dream off, or directed him elsewhere, but she couldn't take her eyes off the face of Daniel's reflection in the mirror, a man who felt the pleasure being inside this woman. Claire read in his soul how he thought this was what he needed, and knew how very wrong he was.

But was this why she couldn't stop looking at the muscles of his butt as he drilled inside this woman with abandon? Did she not find something a little thrilling there, hearing the slap of skin against skin, the groaning of their combined lust? What would she do if he looked at her right now? Leave? Or beg to watch some more?

The moment was lost as a dapper man in a linen suit barged in, stunned by what he witnessed. The partial view of Audray's soft flesh paralyzed him; but like Claire, he didn't turn away, as would have been appropriate. Audray looked up and smiled at the stranger through the mirror over the sink, then drove a sultry look right into Daniel's heart. Claire felt Daniel's pain as well as the pleasure of his cock thrusting deep inside Audray, with a stranger as witness to his lack of control.

The man's eyes widened. "Excuse me, I…" At last he released himself from the trance of Audray's hold and closed the door without a sound.

"We seem to be attracting an audience everywhere we go." Audray's voice was deep and husky.

Daniel started to withdraw, but she reached around and pulled him into her again.

"I'm not done."

When Audray was finally satisfied, Daniel was just spent. She dragged him through the full room of tourists by his belt buckle after he'd hurriedly dressed. The healthy chatter at the wine center had stopped abruptly as soon as Audray strutted across the room, Daniel in tow. Claire knew Audray liked it that way. The woman looked into everyone's eyes with a triumphant smile, lording her sexual prize over any woman brave enough to return her gaze.

Claire couldn't find one willing to do so.

Daniel's dream screen faded to black so suddenly Claire had to catch her breath. His sleep was dark and deep. Now she understood the hold Audray had over this man. He was infected with their intense sexual relationship, and she could see why he had stopped painting. He had become obsessed with screwing his muse instead of having that muse inspire him. Audray never would be able to inspire any of the men she devoured. Her energy used them, drained them for her own satisfaction. His paints were relegated to the back of his mind somewhere, like the memory of a broken childhood toy. It made Claire sad.

It was disturbing hearing about Josh and his preference for angels. *He must take special delight in turning them into his willing companions.* No wonder Mother said he was powerful. She wondered if he made his own brand of dust, requiring the recipient to do his bidding. There had to be some physical tool in his arsenal she had never been told about at the school.

Claire was going to let Daniel sleep since his body was in need of it and she needed time to plan. But she was anxious to hear more about the story of this man's journey into darkness. While she knew Josh was a dark angel, she would have to meet Audray in the flesh to determine if she was human or another of the dark angels.

Moonlight from Daniel's single bedroom window filled the space, just like moonlight filled her own room in Heaven. Soothed by the milky white glow, she settled down to think. Some of her best planning time was spent while her charges were in a deep sleep outside of dreamstate.

Several minutes passed and then suddenly Daniel jerked and caught his breath as if drowning. Claire thought he would awaken. But he fell back deeper into the pillow and his eyes began to move back and forth under his eyelids, indicating he was beginning to dream again. She wasn't about to pass up this opportunity. She dove in.

"You're just like several other painters we've had. You're a no-name, not like Beau. Why do you think we are always looking for new talent?"

Daniel watched Audray lace her fingers through the golden yellow hair he used to lose himself in. "But people love my paintings. You told me so yourself hundreds of times." He could see she was unmoved by his plea, and she turned her back to him. He persisted. "You used to believe in my work.

"Used to, Daniel. Used to, as in past tense."

That hurt. Something began to crumble inside him. "Look, I forgave you for fucking the guy. You made a mistake. Perhaps wanted to be caught. And I got angry, really angry. Look, I think we can work past this, in time. Let's forgive each other, and move on. But the gallery..." *I have nowhere else to go.*

"For your information, it was not a mistake."

Daniel's insides boiled.

She lowered her eyes. He saw the kill shot coming. "Sure, you have talent. But no one is willing to fork out a penny for your great masterpieces. They look like crap that belongs in a child's bedroom, not on the wall of a bank building."

"And you think a toilet seat is more suitable?" Anger was rising in his veins.

"They sell, Daniel. They're commercial."

"So it takes a while to get my name out there. I wasn't doing drugs, screwing teenyboppers, and taking off my clothes on stage to get famous. I was studying art. Learning my craft."

"Craft? You call this craft? It's shit and you know it. You guys start out great—the next Picasso—then just fizzle. Happens all the time. Just deal with it, and maybe stick to children's books." Audray was deadly in this mood.

And he was starting to believe her.

He felt alone and thoroughly worthless.

Claire's heart ached at the pain in Daniel's soul. She felt Audray's bitter heart and saw bloody claws in Daniel's chest. She'd never seen a man so torn apart by another woman before.

Daniel's eyes moved again as another dream consumed him.

He stood outside his dining room window in the dark of night, face pressed against the glass, reflecting the orange glow of the fireplace. Claire saw he recognized the blonde, naked on the bench.

"Hairy asshole." Daniel mumbled. Large hands dripping in black hair kneaded her white flesh. "Get your hands off her—" He said some things in Portuguese. Claire felt the pain in his chest, saw the sweat build up on his upper lip. Daniel's fingers clutched and crushed leaves from a bush under the window ledge.

"She arches to his touch. She wants him…" The man's mammoth hands dimpled the delicate white skin with fat probing fingers. Her red lips kissed him, everywhere. Claire swallowed as she saw Audray suckle the strange man's member between her red lips.

In his sleep, Daniel groaned, and she focused her attention on his sleeping form instead of his dream world. In spite of the dream, Daniel was getting an erection in bed. His arm rubbed his groin above the covers. Claire's cheeks turned bright red. She brought her attention back to his dream world.

The scene changed. The thick Henkel carving knife was balanced between his fingers. It gleamed in an unearthly patina as he turned it in silence. The blade was capable of effortlessly slicing through flesh. "I won't have to press hard at all…"

Claire's stomach turned as she watched him imagine the cut, dreaming about something that thankfully never occurred. The blood was warm. It spilled over his legs. She was certain every time she looked at that green bench that she would remember both scenes: love and death. *The curse of being human.*

"No more nightmares. Peace at last," he murmured. She knew this was folly, but he was trying to kill off his own passion.

Claire could feel Daniel's pain as he relived those hollow, sex-filled days. But she also picked up how much he missed the excitement and unpredictability of this woman. Audray was a complete distraction, consuming his thoughts. His desire for Audray came from a place of need, a true addiction. Claire blushed frequently at his thoughts, she did not view his appetite as being healthy. She could not remember a charge being so tormented.

Claire leaned over and laid her hand over his forehead and eyes, not quite touching. Warmth radiated up to her fingertips. She rubbed her thumb back and forth over her first two fingers, producing sparkles of dust, which fell to his face and on his closed eyes. He succumbed to a dreamless, deep sleep.

She smiled at the sight of his uncovered chest. She held her hand above it, feeling the warmth, and moved closer, looking at the delicate black hairs leading down below his waist. His pajama bottoms had slid low, revealing a flat stomach with two delicious veins extending below. Her hands warmed and her fingers tingled. This was a new sensation, this tiny charge of electricity passing from his massive upper torso and traveling up her arms. He smiled, as though responding to her gaze, which caught her breath up short. The smile faded.

Claire laid her head on the pillow next to him to wait for other signs of a dream, but doubted it would be tonight. Next time, she would try to give him some color, something other than the vision of his own blood or the blonde he could no longer have.

It would be morning in a couple of hours. She stretched her arms and legs, just inches from his sleeping frame. His breath in her face was delicious. She was glad she never slept. This meant she had at least two, maybe three, hours of this Heaven on earth before Daniel's normal routine took over.

Claire searched her feelings. Her desire to heal him remained strong and true. She knew she could do it, even with all the dark dreams. It was his passion she wasn't sure about. Although it was uncharted waters, and perhaps a bit dangerous, her confidence lifted her.

Her search for adventure lifted her higher still.

When sunlight first began pouring into the window over Daniel's bed, Claire watched Daniel pull the sheet over his head to protect his eyes. At last, she felt him surface and become fully conscious.

Claire held her breath as he sauntered to the bathroom and dropped his silk pajama bottoms. His smooth bottom was slightly whiter than his muscular thighs. His back rippled with definition she had never seen before on a man. An urge to run her hand over those smooth cheeks and press herself into his bronzed shoulders left her no choice but to get up and follow her eyes. She stood barely an inch behind him to see if she could feel the warmth of his flesh, and found she could. The nipples of her breasts twisted in little knots under her white gown.

He stepped into the shower, lathering up with that spicy citrus soap he'd used last night. It tweaked her nose, making her sneeze. She leaned against the bathroom wall, doing her deep breathing exercises, but found it difficult to resist the temptation of removing her gown and joining him. She had never experienced such a sensual attraction to a human charge. She was sure she would be breaking so many rules this time around.

Anything of value carries with it great risk. Father had told her that. There was always danger when she was learning new things about humans.

And it was exactly why she loved being Guardian above all else. Perhaps above the *calling* as Mother described it. It felt more like a pulling, an attraction. An irresistible urge to what?

To be part of something else. To blend…

Daniel swung the shower curtain back so fast her heart jumped. He stood before her, dripping wet. She felt hot angel blood flush to her face. She immediately exited to the bedroom to calm down, listening to the muffled sounds of the fluffy towel do its work. She would have liked to—

Stop it. She needed to exercise control, but slipped back into the bathroom, sure he was about to perform the ritual of shaving.

He looked into the mirrored cabinet and foamed up his face with fluffy white cream. Claire held her breath in anticipation of what was to follow. She was sometimes guilty of hiding her charge's electric shavers. The sounds of the razor slowly sweeping over the fresh, menthol-laden surface of his cheeks and chin made her toes curl. She could have swooned. *If he were mine, I would do this for him every morning, and again at night, if he would let me.*

Steam came up from the hot water tap. His muscled forearm rippled as he rinsed off the razor once he finished. He tapped it three times against the porcelain edge of the sink.

He stared into the mirror. What did he see? Could he know she was standing behind him, that a droplet of the Mediterranean lime aftershave he used landed on her gown as he patted his cheeks? The moist air was as fragrant as any of the flower gardens in Heaven. The vision of his towel-clad body every bit as beautiful as the roses she picked. After drying his hands, he went to the bedroom. She buried her face in his towel and filled her lungs with his scent.

If he were mine, I would wrap myself in this towel and wear it all day.

What am I saying? Her friends would laugh at her if they knew this. *But wouldn't it be nice?*

He dressed, then she followed him down to the kitchen where he poured himself some cold cereal and made coffee. Claire sat across the table, chin in hand, and elbow resting on the wooden surface. He bore no resemblance to the man she first met last night, like the journey she'd been on in his dreams had never taken place. She was pleased her healing hand had washed his soul.

He was rushing, checking his watch and hurrying out the door. He never looked once at the remnants of the destruction in the living room. Claire decided she would use the day to explore, mingle with humans in human form. She would go to the café she saw in the picture, or maybe to the gallery to see his paintings.

The instant Daniel left, Claire pulled herself out of her invisibility and walked in human form down the hallway leading from his bedroom, which was still filled with Daniel's scent. She tore herself away, ascending the stairs to the attic, her yellow transport bag in tow. She could have willed herself up there, but loved hearing that delicious creak of the door as she pressed it open. She climbed the narrow stairwell like a human woman seeking a new adventure. It reminded her of secret rooms she had read about in castles in Europe.

The attic was tall at the roof's ridge, but both sides sloped to a dormer and window. The little window she had seen from the street last night had an old wooden chair beside it, as if someone used to sit and watch who came and went. The place was dusty, but on the windowsill there was a fine layer of sparkling dust, like some gentle hand had pressed the glass, waiting for a glimpse of someone coming home.

Or, maybe that was just the story she told herself. Like one of her novels.

She touched the dust. It was from a long time ago. Had another angel sat there? Had she waited for her charge to return from his adventures in the human world? Did she succeed? Did she love her job as much as Claire did?

She set her bag next to the worn and scarred dresser in the middle of the room and tugged off her gown. She pulled on a t-shirt, then a hooded sweatshirt, and slipped into blue jeans.

Much better. She almost felt human.

Almost.

CHAPTER 6

Claire sat under an awning of the outdoor café, watching people hurrying down the sidewalk that shone from the morning rain. Wetness in the air melded with the smell of fresh hot coffee and griddlecakes. Even the smell of wet pavement was pleasant. *I will miss this when I return.* It never rained in Heaven; it misted.

She tapped her nails against the green and white-checkered plastic cloth that covered the little table as she searched the crowd for a familiar face from one of her previous missions. It could happen. But no, not today.

She felt alone in spite of the people surrounding her. She dipped her tongue into the soft whipped cream piled atop the steaming chocolate drink warming her hands. It was considered dangerous for angels to taste things, as that could lead to eating, which could eliminate an angel's powers of invisibility. Yielding to temptation made angels visible. It wasn't forbidden, just not advised. Eating was an aphrodisiac—at least, the way many humans ate was. The hunger inside them had nothing to do with their stomachs. This was a dangerous experience for an angel and could lead to a fall from grace.

But the scent of warm chocolate was one of her all-time favorites. Ignoring the danger and repeated warnings, she savored the way the sweetness caressed her tongue.

"That is just one of the sexiest things on the planet." Josh had slipped in so quickly she hadn't seen him.

Startled, Claire jolted, spilling a little of the warm mixture. She felt trapped in her human form, but remained seated and set the messy mug down. A small dollop of the whipped cream stuck to the tip of her nose. She reached up to dust it off but Josh stopped her.

"Ah, love. You've messed your face. I can help." He rubbed it off with his forefinger, then put the tip of his finger in his mouth. His eyes danced with an unearthly fire. "Very sweet, very sweet indeed."

Claire's heart pounded so hard surely Josh could hear it. Bound by the rules, she couldn't just disappear without people noticing: she was caught. Josh tilted his head to the side, squinting, as if he enjoyed watching her squirm. She had no choice but to talk to him.

"So now that we've met, what lovely name do I call you, or do I get to pick one?" His velvety smooth voice washed over her face and made her ears tingle.

Claire focused on her mug of chocolate, remaining mute.

"You know that when we turn a Guardian, we get to choose their name? Surely they taught you that in school?" The words rolled easily off his tongue.

Claire was confused and Josh saw it. She knew he had something to do with that, that his breath carried with it something that made her feel things…

She became distracted with his mouth…

Keep calm.

So this was something else they hadn't taught her. Fear began to rise, pressing cool fingers all the way up her spine one vertebrae at a time.

Deep breathing. Keep on your feet.

"No?" he persisted. "I can see they didn't. But maybe they don't know."

"And I'm not turned," she spat out.

"Ah, lovely. She speaks. The angel talks to me." Josh consumed her with a warm smile that sent a thin erotic cover over her whole body.

"I said, I am not turned," Claire insisted, despite the tingle down her spine. The mental erotic caress was not unpleasant, but the circumstances were.

"Not yet, my lovely. Not yet." Josh's voice purred. "You're much prettier than I thought. Most of you are too vanilla. I'm partial to redheads, but you probably already know that, if you've snooped in Daniel's dreams at all." He leaned into the table, whispering, "How'd you like Audray? Did they have you panting in the middle of the night, hmmm?"

"I've seen it before."

"Of course you have," Josh said. He straightened up and chuckled. "You guys never get in the game. Human life is just a spectator sport—something you can go home and gossip about with your friends."

"I don't share your cynical view of human life. Didn't they teach that to you in the Underworld School For Bad Boys?"

Josh's eyes widened. Three deep forehead creases appeared. He tilted in a subtle bow. "Very good, little one. I like the fire and spirit in you. So then, tell me your name."

"Claire."

"Nice. I like it. I think you can keep it, for now."

"How did you find me?" Claire curtly asked, ignoring his implication.

"Hard to miss the big yellow taxi with the only redheaded cabbie I know."

This annoyed her. She felt vulnerable being so easily spotted by this dark angel. "What do you want?" Claire knew it was impossible to mask her fear. She didn't think he could read her mind, but knew he felt her fear.

"You." He smiled. His eyes became translucent and she could see traces of red light coming through again. Claire looked down to avoid his eyes, unsure of his powers. Josh reached across the little table and raised her chin with his thumb and forefinger, causing a warmth that blotched the skin at her chest. "Now, now. I'm not here to hurt you. There'll not be a scene. I'm curious about you." He smiled and released her.

Claire wasn't used to the mixture of emotions. Her pulse quickened. No doubt he observed this. Her frustration was tinged with a bit of anger that she worked to stuff down. She could see how Josh had manipulated Daniel so skillfully. Appearing as friend when he actually was the enemy.

Feeling unprotected being alone with him, she was grateful for the surrounding crowd. After considering all her choices, she thought it best to let him deliver his communication, anticipating it would be some kind of threat. Then he might leave her alone.

"May I?" Josh pointed to the hot chocolate. "I mean, I know you girls don't drink or eat." His knowledge of angels both impressed and frightened her. Her insides were scrambled.

"Help yourself." She barely got the words out. But at least her voice didn't waver.

He leaned back in his chair, inhaling through his teeth in a kind of reverse whistle. "Don't *ever* tell me that, Love, if you know what's good for you." He smiled, and shaking his head, he leaned forward for the warm mug of chocolate. He sucked in the whipped cream off the top loudly, leaving a white moustache on his dark and handsome face.

Claire wanted to look away, but something held her gaze as she watched him remove the whipped cream from his upper lip with his tongue. He dabbed his mouth with a napkin and waved his eyebrows up and down, playing with her.

"I saw you thinking about tasting it. You're not supposed to, but you want to drink and taste, don't you?" He looked with that tilt of the head again that would seem so innocent on someone not so devious.

I should have known better, been more careful. Why couldn't I sense him before?

"Do you think He would mind if you just had one little taste?" He pointed to the heavens and shrugged. "I don't think so." He held out the mug. It was still steaming, and the rich chocolate fragrance filled her head.

Claire steeled herself. She would need to overcome her emotions. Time to show him what she was made of. She'd resist, even if he liked it. Sounding more determined than she felt, she said, "I have no interest in what you think. I don't care anything about you. I want you to leave me alone."

"Ah, yes. Well there is that, too," he said as he raised his eyebrows and smirked at the subtle rebuke. Holding the mug to his lips, he paused. "I admit. I am an acquired taste." His face jerked back after taking a sip. "Ow, too hot, even for me." He blew over the top of the drink with enough force to push back the hairs at the sides of her face.

The effect of his breath on Claire's face startled her. Her eyelids became heavy and she released her composure, relaxing into the fear. She became dizzy and aglow with sensuality, as though drugged. For a brief second, looking into the dark eyes across from her, she could feel a pull towards him. She wondered in a flash what it would feel like to kiss those smiling lips and feel their power on her body.

It wore off just as fast as it came on. Josh toasted her with the mug.

"That was a beautiful thing to watch," he said as he winked. He didn't mask his arousal.

Claire was losing the battle and needed escape to safety. She was not used to being outmatched, so she leaned forward on one elbow, chin perched on her upturned hand. Under the table she rubbed her thumb against her first two fingers, filling her other palm with dust. She motioned with forefinger for him to bring his face closer to hers.

Eagerly, he leaned into her, elbows matching and almost touching hers, chin resting on his fingers. Josh's face was only a foot away from hers. He spread that affable Cheshire cat smile. He smelled of cinnamon and cardamom, and she heard deep organ music.

She inhaled deeply, and in one long movement, brought her other hand up to her chin, then slowly opened her palm full of dust and blew it in his face. His eyes widened initially as he appeared temporarily immobilized. Fear brushed across his face for one brief second. At last, he recovered with a sigh. Then he sat up straight.

"You're very good," he said at last.

"You're very bad." She gave a tight smile in return. She was hoping her shaking didn't show. No sense to stay to do battle all day. So she stood. "I'm leaving."

"Yes, you are." He rose slowly to his feet, appearing enchanted. "It has been a pleasure, Claire." He made a hint of a bow in her direction.

"I'm not going to play this game with you. We aren't friends and we have nothing in common."

"Is that a challenge I hear?"

"This is *not* happening," she replied, putting on her jacket.

"Oh, but it already has begun, my dear."

"Well, perhaps in your mind. It's something else entirely to me." She turned to leave. He grasped her forearm over the jacket sleeve firmly, showing his need to touch her, pulling her toward his chest as he inhaled her scent.

"Tell me what it is for you," he murmured.

She saw a flash of something in his eyes—need? Emptiness? Something had shifted. She didn't know what, but she'd seen something Josh wanted to remain hidden.

Claire held her breath to ward off the effects of his power at this close distance, and then blurted out, "You'll never know." She yanked her arm from his grip. Knowing he expected his seductiveness to work on her, she added, "I can say this: I saw a lot of wet, slimy frogs and snakes. I saw mushrooms and rotting leaves. I was chilled to the bone. You *do* have *that* effect on me."

It was a complete lie, of course. Her heart was racing. Her eyes felt like they were going to burst into the tears she stubbornly would not give him the satisfaction of seeing. She wanted to run, but turned and walked out into the street.

Claire didn't look back at him as she walked away, feeling the warm sun on her face. This was the best she could muster today. She needed help. Now she understood how dangerous Josh was and how he'd gotten his hooks into Daniel. Claire was worried, for both of them. Josh made it clear he'd shifted his sights to her. She needed someone else's advice, immediately.

If I'm not careful, Josh will have a twofer.

CHAPTER 7

Daniel burst through the front door as his phone rang. He dropped his portfolio bag and ran across the broken glass left over from his last night's indulgences.

"Shit." He gripped the cordless phone, then heard something squawk as it fell from his fingers. He could hear "Hello? Hello? What the fuck?" from the handset.

He bent over, grabbed the phone off the floor, then brought it to his ear. "This is Daniel."

"What just happened? You okay, man?" Beau Bradley's speech was slurred. Daniel assumed the slur came from Beau's steady diet of Quaaludes and Southern Comfort.

"Sorry, Beau. Dropped the phone."

"Okay. Woulda hurt, if I could still hear." Beau chuckled, bringing on a rheumy wheeze. He coughed, clearing his throat. "You haven't answered my phone calls. Okay, I get it. You don't want to talk to me about your shit—sorry—your paintings."

"I'll be down next day or two. Gotta borrow a truck."

"That's why I'm calling."

Daniel heard a door close as Beau whispered into the phone, his voice muffled as if he were buried in a cave.

"Two IRS agents are here and they are asking questions about your stuff, you know, like when was the last time one sold, if any were waiting for pickup, that sort of thing."

"IRS? I don't get it. I've not gotten any notices, and my taxes are current."

"They're talking like you had some big windfall, some large sale you didn't report and they're looking to take 'em."

"The paintings?"

"No, my toilet seats. Of course I'm talking about the fucking paintings!" Beau coughed into the phone. "Be glad it was me here today. Audray would have told them to take 'em all."

Sweat rolled down Daniel's back, soaking his shirt. He threw off his jacket, swearing under his breath, then undid the top button and pulled his shirttails out of his slacks. The last several months, he'd been plagued with banking overdrafts, declines on his credit cards, and now this.

What's going on?

"But fuck me, Daniel, trouble with the I Fucking R S is not something I need right now. Catch my drift?" Beau said.

Daniel understood Beau's aversion to any form of law enforcement. "Yes, I understand."

"And, I'm fucking bursting at the seams here. She's got this new photographer she wants to display, and I got no fuckin room."

"Photographer?"

"He's a doctor, really. Not much of a photographer, just my opinion. But I like having nude pictures of Audray adorn my walls, if you know what I mean."

Daniel did. He could imagine she liked it too.

"I haven't got a clue, Beau. They taking the paintings now?" Over the cell phone, Daniel heard a creaking door and then the sound of it closing.

"Can't tell yet, but they're writing down shit in little notebooks, you know, like cops."

"I'll come down there and talk to them. Don't worry. It must be some kind of mistake. They've got me mixed up with someone else."

"You know, Daniel, I'm not so sure you should come unless you bring an attorney. These guys look like major bruisers. They don't smile. They grumble."

"I have nothing to hide."

"Are you sure, cause…"

"Yes, I'm sure. I'll give Josh a call, maybe he can come on down with me. I need his Hummer anyway."

Beau sighed. "I gotta ask, why do you pay Josh anything? The guy is worthless."

"He found you, didn't he?"

"He found Audray. Josh doesn't fuck men."

That made Daniel smile. "He's a good friend, and he cares about the artists he represents."

"Then how come they all wind up dead? No, Daniel, the only one he cares about is himself." Beau mumbled curses. "I coulda told you not to get involved with her, though. What *were* you thinking?"

"I wasn't."

"Your lower brain sort of thing. Been there myself a time or two," Beau continued.

How many times?

The crash Daniel heard sounded like something in the gallery had shattered to the floor. Beau swore. "These guys are gorillas. That cost me about five Gs."

Daniel's finances were precarious, and his pride was buried under debt. He had enough to replace the paint he'd squandered last night, but not much else. That would mean not making his house payment this month, which would mean month number three. A foreclosure notice would be coming any day then. He had equity too. He'd be flushing that down the toilet if he didn't come up with some cash in a hurry.

He heard a banging sound on Beau's end of the phone, along with a muffled yet booming voice that said, "Sir, you want to step out of the closet, please?"

"Shit! Daniel, gotta go now," Beau whispered.

"Tell them I'll be right down," Daniel said.

"Your funeral." Beau hung up.

Beau's statement worried Daniel. Did Josh like to represent suicidal artists for some particular reason? Tortured souls?

This morning he'd met with an old friend from art school in the San Fran—the author of a couple of popular children's books—and was supposed to start some sketches for him. Thank God he hadn't forgotten to get up. There wasn't any money in it up front, but a possible book tour and percentage of sales if it did go to print. It was a chance at some kind of future. He was finally starting to get it together. What had he been thinking last night, wanting to end it all? Today, he was seeing possibilities.

But first he had to take care of the IRS. *What am I missing?* He shook his head and dialed Josh's phone.

"How are you feeling today, my friend?" Josh asked.

"Seems like I just get done with one crisis and another pops up. Beau called me and two IRS agents are at the gallery, acting like they're going to take my paintings. Is there something you're not telling me?"

"You think I caused this?" Anger laced Josh's words.

"No. But I've received no notices, my bank account is all screwed up, and now this. They think I sold a ton of stuff and didn't report it, or so they told Beau."

"Makes no sense."

"I need to take the paintings back. Can I borrow your Hummer?"

"Yeah, I'm downtown now. Meet you there or pick you up?"

"Meet me there."

Daniel hung up. The pit of his stomach felt like it had a hole in it.

On Daniel's way to the gallery, Beau's comments dislodged something that bothered him about his agent and Josh's fondness for dark and dangerous things. Everyone Josh introduced him to had some sort of huge flaw. Even he had one now: he needed money. And he needed to stop getting hard at every turn. When he was fourteen, he'd found the potential amazing. Now, however, a perpetual hard dick got in the way. He remembered a time when his cock acted like that of a normal man—hard when required. But ever since Audray, he'd been a walking Viagra commercial.

Shit, I'd rather have acne.

He needed to find a way to get release. He was going to get carpal tunnel from biffing himself so much. Time for some serious dating.

He was also flawed in that no one even looked at his paintings anymore. But even concerns about his lack of talent took a back seat to his financial precariousness. Once Audray had signed him on at the gallery and his work had garnered the attention of the art crowd, he'd set aside his other commercial work, which paid very little, but had in the past gotten him by. The big splashy canvases displayed at Craven Image, initially selling for thousands of dollars, were his real meal ticket. At the gallery parties—almost orgies, really—the rich and famous had loved his work and had stroked his ego. He'd raked in the dough then, hand over fist.

But then all of a sudden, the attention had dried up. Just like his affair with Audray. It was like one minute he was a member of this exclusive club and the next he was being barred at the door by a really big bouncer.

He knew sleeping with the gallery manager had been a mistake, but he hadn't been able to help himself. Audray had come along just at the right time, right when his career was beginning to take off. And, as fast as he made the money, she made sure he spent it—on her. He could see the slight nod of acknowledgment by other men as he walked with her on his arm.

He thought further about those stares now—were they looks of admiration as he'd always assumed? Or were those men wondering why he didn't see the danger there?

He shook himself.

Stop it.

He arrived at the little gallery on the Square in Healdsburg and found a slip of a parking spot just big enough for his old two-seater Mercedes he'd bought with the proceeds of his first big sale. What a day that had been. Before the interest in his art had crashed.

Josh's black Hummer was conspicuously taking up two spaces people would soon kill for, come noon. The gallery doors were open. A sandwich sign out front advertised his paintings for half price. He cursed a string in Portuguese.

Josh was already in dialogue with two men in dark grey suits. Beau had been right, both were beefy, not the typical IRS pencil-pusher types Daniel expected. He figured they were the ones that scared everyone into paying up. Looked to him more like Russian mobsters. But this didn't matter. He had no money and he was certain he owed nothing.

"Ah, gentlemen, this is Daniel DePalma, the artist," Josh said, touching the elbow of the beefstick closest to him as he rolled his eyes. Daniel looked to the two, making sure they didn't pick up on the disrespect. He stuck out his hand.

"I believe we have some sort of misunderstanding," he said as he pumped the fist of the first man, then followed with the second. The bones of his hand were crushed by the vice-like grip each had placed on him with their handshakes. He made sure his face didn't show the pain.

So much for a civil outcome.

"This is Agent Fisk, I'm Agent Rossetti. We've been asked to take an inventory of the paintings." Rosetti's puffy cheeks were pock-marked, and his beady hazel eyes darted from side to side.

"Inventory?

"Mr. DePalma," Agent Fisk said, pulling out a folded paper from his vest pocket. "Were you aware of the fact that you owe the IRS over one hundred thousand dollars?" He placed the folded sheaf on Daniel's palm.

Anger flooded his chest. Hot blood flowed through his veins, down his arms and to his fingers. The document almost burned him. He unfolded the paper and examined the notice for an IRS levy. "I've never seen this letter before."

He crumpled the paper like it was a sandwich wrapping and held the notice above his head. "This is bullshit. I haven't *made* that much money this year. How could I owe this in *tax!*" He glared at the two agents. "You fucking assholes. What kind of a game are you playing?"

Josh stepped between Daniel and the agents, but part of Daniel's anger was aimed at his friend as well. "Daniel, look," Josh said. "I think we can settle this. You need to calm down, man."

"Calm down?" Daniel reached around Josh to punch Agent Rossetti, but only landed a glancing blow on man's shoulder, which hardly moved. Rossetti grinned.

"Do that again, and we get to take you in." His little teeth were stained yellow and crooked. He wasn't used to grinning, for good reason.

The two agents were hungry for more, Daniel saw.

"Whoa, there!" Beau shrieked in panic. "If you're going to get into fists and all, take it outside, man. I got glass and breakables in here." He opened the door and gestured for them to leave. The two agents stood their ground, not even considering him.

Josh kept Daniel and the glowering men separated and turned to them. Although Josh was their height, they outweighed him by at least double. "Gents. There has to be a mistake. I'm this artist's agent. I can vouch for the fact that he hasn't sold a painting in over six months. The owner, here, wants him to remove all this, making room for something that will sell. Believe me," Josh said with conviction, "If he sold something, I would know about it."

"Yeah, where did you get your information?" Beau said with unusual bravado, taking one step closer, adding his sneer to the mix.

Daniel watched the four men jockey for position and banter among themselves. All because of him. He glared at Agent Fisk, whose red, bloated face made him look like he had a Helium hose secured to his ass.

Behind the IRS agent, the long, unsmiling stares of the big cats peered through jungle foliage and remained passive witnesses. Daniel scanned all of them, one by one. Their eyes followed him as he backed up and out of the cluster of controversy, as if to ask, "What will become of us?" Orphaned children in a divorce proceeding. Did they know their beautiful sibling had met a fiery grave?

Daniel sat on a park bench in the town square and felt as poor as the guy dumpster diving in the pretty little square. How could his life have fallen so far apart? Josh had worked his magic on the agents, who, for now, agreed to leave the paintings in place. Josh promised them sales receipts for the past twelve months and convinced them it was in everyone's best interests to get the paintings sold, even if it was at half price.

Half price. Is that what my life is worth now? I'm a sale item.

He couldn't shrug off the loneliness, the pain of his uncertain future. He was hoping this was all a bad dream he'd wake up and find didn't really happen. What a strange time, a series of unfortunate events all coming together in a great cluster fuck of a convergence.

Perfect storm.

It *had* to get better. It *just* had to. Couldn't be worse.

He got out his sketchbook and began penciling some images of children walking past. He looked up to see a young woman with short scruffy blond hair standing outside the gallery, interested in the sandwich sign. She went in.

Daniel's pulse shot up. Was she interested in his painting, or the sale? Dressed in blue jeans and an oversized man's white V-neck tee shirt, she didn't look like the typical tourist, but rather a local. Maybe he had a fan.

He put away his pencils and tablet and crossed the street, then shadowed the doorway, hesitating to go in. Through the glass door he could see Beau pointing to one of his paintings. The woman tilted her chin, then nodded her head.

Someone is actually looking at my paintings. He could see she was studying them, and was drawn to watch. He knew it wasn't a good idea, but he couldn't help himself.

Daniel took a deep breath, and then put his hand on the doorknob, and entered.

He walked up behind her as Beau scowled a reproach. She turned around, her large blue eyes flashing panic. She temporarily lost her balance, falling against his chest. He held her up, his arm wrapped around her waist, touching the small of her back with his fingertips. Beau's sales pitch went on in the background. Daniel's whole world poured into her eyes for just a second, bringing him some peace. The merciful cessation of pain for that all too brief moment. She looked down immediately, and the ache in his head returned.

He thought perhaps she was looking at his crotch, and almost chuckled at her forwardness, but then saw her lashes sweep up and a bright rosy blush come to her cheeks. The short blond wisps of hair about her face formed a halo effect. Her pink lips were entirely kissable. Not knowing what had gotten into him, he leaned toward her and then stopped as he saw her alarm. He released his grip on her waist immediately.

"I'm so sorry. Didn't mean to startle you. Just trying to keep you from falling," he said, and then mentally cursed himself.

This all you can say to this nubile young woman?

He couldn't figure out her age.

Without saying a word, she brushed by him and went out the door. Pieces of glitter swirled in the sunlight as she stepped onto the breezy sidewalk. The hairs on his forearm where she had barely touched him stood to attention. And, oh yeah, his bed buddy was pointing like a bird dog.

"Well, that's just fucking great. Blow your own sale," Beau said as they both watched the glass door close, tinkling the bell above it.

But Daniel was drawn outside, the string of curses behind him fading as he pursued the girl. She scampered through the crowd and dipped into a shop. She glanced over her shoulder just long enough to make eye contact, and again, Daniel picked up her fear.

Have I seen her before? Trying to recall the luscious ladies Josh had introduced him to over the past few weeks, he couldn't place her, and somehow didn't think she would be someone he would know.

He followed her into the blown glass shop she'd entered. The lighting was minimal, but high intensity blasts twinkled down on the translucent marbled glass in mixed colors and shapes, leaving the rest of the room in shadow. She was standing behind a display of glistening paperweights with embedded designs that looked like long tendrils of jellyfish. Through the case he saw her outline, and the way her chest rose and fell. She was nervous. She was as delicate a being as the pieces of glass. And she enchanted him.

He walked to the case, and through the glass said, "I mean you no harm." He couldn't see her full face.

She surveyed the sides of the room, ducking as if to get a clear view of the front door. He saw her pink lips and the blush at her cheek. Otherwise, her skin was flawlessly light and seemed to glow from within.

"Please. I just want to talk." He dropped his shoulders and raised his palms. "I'm the painter. I think you liked my paintings back there."

"They're nice." She looked down.

"Can I show them to you? Would you let me?" He started to come around the corner of the case, but she tensed.

"Don't! No. I'm not…I have to be somewhere else." She tried to slide by him. He grabbed one of her hands and felt warmth and a tingle that ran up from his fingertips to his elbow. He delayed her, unwilling to let her go, but did not pull her to him, letting the distance remain. Her soft flesh aroused him in spite of himself.

There was something about her scent.

Sunshine. You smell like sunshine.

Heartened she hadn't struggled to get away, he thought perhaps she might feel the same attraction. He cocked his head to the side and looked down to catch her eyes, rubbing the back of her hand with his thumb. "I'm Daniel," he said, placing his other palm to his chest.

Her eyes lingered there.

Yes. You watch me.

Slowly her lashes rose as she enveloped him in the blue water of her gaze, which seemed to take in his whole face, ending at his lips. The connection between them flared as she opened that mouth he desperately wanted to kiss.

"I really have to go, Daniel. But it's nice to meet you."

She was looking at him like she would never see him again. When she turned and firmly retracted her hand from his, leaving him standing there in the glitter, his heart sank.

He dashed to the door she had just exited and called out as she picked up speed in the crowd of tourists. "One minute, please. Just one minute," he shouted above the sounds of the crowd.

She stopped, turning towards him, but she looked at her feet. The flaxen hairs at the top of her crown glowed gold, almost like they were on fire.

"What is your name?" He held his breath until she answered. It seemed like forever.

"Claire," she said, giving him a quick look that told him not to follow.

"Nice to meet you too, Claire," he murmured.

And then she was gone.

Claire rounded the corner, gasping for breath. She wouldn't trust a look behind her, just in case Daniel hadn't gotten her intent. She was running away, yet her body was screaming to run back the other direction. She was filled with a strange glimmer and wondered if she would actually glow come sundown. With Daniel's borrowed tee shirt stuck to her sweaty chest, she felt parts of her body awaken for the first time, the scent of this man's body mixed with her angelic one.

And she loved it.

CHAPTER 8

From the back seat of the transport, Claire could see Doris was having a bad day. The cabbie's hair glowed an intense red and stuck out from under her cabbie hat with obstinate disregard for the rules of coiffure. It matched the way Doris fidgeted and mangled paper messages in the front seat.

"Summons to Heaven for a meeting with the transport director," Doris said, tossing the ball of paper to the floor.

Something about the cabbie angel made Claire feel she could trust her with anything, including her secrets. Her unusual friend could be counted on to tell it exactly like it was.

"You have any idea what the meeting is about?" Claire frowned with concern. She hated to see the angel so tense.

"Yep, I know exactly what it's about. I had myself some fun last night."

Claire wondered what kind of fun Doris meant. "Sorry to hear it," was all she could think to say.

"Since you're not gonna ask, I let the air out of a kid's tires last night." Doris's voice was laced with an obvious sense of pride.

That was fun? "I don't understand."

"He cut me off. Got the little misfit's license and ran a check. Went over to his parent's house and deflated all four tires. Nobody was hurt. But I'll get the warning anyway."

Claire laughed. Doris looked at Claire in the rear view mirror and grinned.

"And here you thought I'd gotten myself a boyfriend, right?"

Claire shrugged. Doris did spend a lot of time in the human world.

"Nah, tried that once, Claire. We only kissed. I adored the guy but he didn't feel the
same. Story of my life. My real life."

"Wait a minute, this happened when you were human?"

Doris nodded her head. Streaks of sunlight flashed across her face.

Someone else who remembers their human life. Are we the only two?

"What happened to the guy?" Claire asked.

"He's right here in my heart." Doris patted her chest. "He died on the job not long afterwards."

"Maybe you'll see him some day. You think he could go Guardian?"

"Beats me. Don't know how they do it. He'd be a good one, though. Saved a bunch of lives that day, including mine."

"You should ask Father."

"I keep my distance. I'm usually on his list. And not the good one. I find it difficult to behave as it is. Don't you go telling him, okay?"

Claire smiled, touched by this little revelation from the spunky cabbie. It was the only bit of softness she'd shared with Doris in all the years they'd run back and forth between Heaven and the human world. She really didn't know anything about Doris.

"Guess I'm not the kissing kind. No, I leave all the lovin' to all youse guys, the Guardians. Your charges are safe from me at least." She leaned back and laughed.

Doris dropped Claire off to meet up with another Guardian doing duty nearby, Angela. Last year, Angela had lost one of her human charges to a dark angel. Claire had been on assignment at the time, but heard the stories when she returned to Heaven. The experience had caused quite a stir in the Guardianship. Failures were hard to take. Tears flowed like water for weeks. In the end, Angela was able to return to work, without having to go through the wash.

Today, Claire found Angela reading by a picture window at the large bookstore.

"Hey, Claire, what a surprise. Didn't know you were down here." Angie's blond hair was longer than Claire's. She wore it back in a ponytail; a few golden strands had pulled free and framed her sweet face and fair complexion. Claire thought Angie looked exactly how humans pictured angels to look, except for the clothes. She sported a red pair of Converse high-tops.

Another angel with a shoe fetish.

"Just got here last night. Who you got?" Claire asked.

Angie smiled, blushing a little. "A sex therapist."

Claire's eyes widened. "No way."

"Go figure." Angie rocked back and forth, then curled her lip. "You wouldn't believe what this guy does in his therapy sessions." She leaned closer. "I've learned a lot."

"Like what?" Claire's cheeks were hot.

"He sometimes watches couples, you know, doing it. I mean, they come into his office and he coaches them. Can you believe it?"

Claire could only shake her head.

"Promise me you won't tell Mother."

"She'll pick up on it as soon as you're back. She doesn't miss a thing, especially if it's something you enjoyed doing."

Angela laughed.

"So why would a sex therapist want to kill himself?"

"He has performance issues. Even though he's a therapist, helping men with their problems, he can't get it up himself."

"Wow."

"Ladies expect him to be Casanova in bed, but he can't perform. He's self medicated with Viagra and tried everything else, but it doesn't help. I'm a little perplexed, but I'll get a fix on him, I always do."

Claire nodded. Angie had been the only other angel with a perfect record, until last year. She looked down at her hands folded neatly in her lap and became very still. She wasn't sure seeking Angie's help was such a good idea now.

"So what's eating at you?" Angie finally asked. They were not close friends, but Angie was quick to read a situation.

Claire winced a bit as she began, "I have a gorgeous Brazilian artist. A painter."

"Nice! And…"

"He's being tortured by a dark angel. I mean, this guy is his agent and they've become best friends. Daniel—the artist—has no idea how dangerous his friend really is. I need to get him away from the dark angel. I can't tell if

Daniel's ex-girlfriend is one too, but the relationship breakup is apparently what sent him over the edge."

Angie nodded her head, then glanced outside, watching cars maneuver on the wet street.

"What's his name?"

"You mean Daniel?"

"No, silly, the dark angel."

Claire frowned. "Josh. Joshua. Why?"

"Yeah, that's what I thought." Angie's gaze reflected some inner pain as she aimlessly looked nowhere in particular. "I've heard of him. The darks always take Bible names. They can't help themselves. Disarming, aren't they?"

"I *thought* maybe you'd seen one before."

"Unfortunately, yes." Angie leaned in and grabbed Claire's hands. "Be careful. Be very, very careful."

"What do I do?"

"Don't let him see you. Stay out of his way. Try to curb your fear when you are around him."

"Too late. He just spoke to me at Café Contada."

Angie sat up and whistled. "In the flesh?"

"He came without warning, sat across the table, and drank my hot chocolate. Close as you and I are right now." Claire summed up how Josh had sensed her at Daniel's and perhaps followed her to the café the next morning.

Angie thought a moment, then asked, "How's the charge holding up?"

"Fine for now. I think the immediate danger is over. I'm monitoring him. So, what do I do about Josh?"

"Dark angels usually go away once they see the charge isn't responding. There are easier marks, millions of others they could go after. They're usually, well, lazy."

"What if he doesn't want an easy mark? What if he likes the challenge?"

"Hmmm. Haven't run across that. Just try to keep your distance from him. Keep your emotions in check too; that's how they find you. And keep a close eye on Daniel. These dark angels are real bad boys, and I'm not talking about bad as in exciting." Angie raised her eyebrows for emphasis. Then she tilted her head and hesitated before asking, "Is there anything about this Daniel that's different than your other charges?"

"No." Claire lied. She thought about his body, his muscular arms in the moonlight, the way he made love in his dreams, the fullness of his lips and what they would feel like on her pink angel skin.

"The Dark has to want something else. It isn't Daniel any longer. Once they can't get the suicide, they usually give up and move on."

The comment struck Claire across the face. Her fear rose. She could feel the cool breeze on her face in the cemetery as she looked down on a lost angel soul that day.

So that's how it's done.

"You finding this one kinda, um, nice or something?" Angela squinted, as if unsure how Claire would take it.

"He's pretty nice, yes."

"Nice, or hot?"

"Hot." Claire hadn't wanted to answer but figured Angie sensed the truth anyway. "I ran into him today in Healdsburg."

"You've *touched* him?"

"More like he touched me."

"Uh oh. Houston, we have a problem." Angie spoke into her sleeve like transmitting something from space. It would have been funny, if not for the circumstances.

"Why do you say that?" Claire asked.

"Get out, Claire. Get out now. Go home." Angie's lips formed a thin line, without a smile.

"I can handle it. Just give me some pointers."

"There are no pointers to give. He's done with Daniel; he wants *you*."

Claire didn't like the confirmation of her own feelings about this shift in Josh's trajectory. "I sort of thought so. I'm not worried he will turn me, though, Angie. Call me foolish, but I think I can outlast him."

"You have one tiny problem, Claire."

"And that is?"

"You care about Daniel. That, my friend, is what the dark angel is counting on. When you don't care about Daniel any more, Josh will no longer be a threat. Until then, hold onto your dust. It's going to be a bumpy ride."

CHAPTER 8

Claire sat on the corner of Daniel's bed, propped against the wall. Quiet sounds of his slumber made her wonder what it felt like to sleep. Something she'd have to ask Father.

She often got a private audience with Father, initially because of her perfect record, but the more time she spent with him the more she considered him her real father. Something about their relationship was special to both of them.

Claire wondered if he picked up on some of her concern now. *Of course he does. He knows everything.* Perhaps she should ask to speak to him. Josh was making her nervous. And Angie's words echoed constantly. "Get out now. Go home." She had never quit before, and wasn't about to now.

But as she settled down to her second night, watching him fall asleep, she drove out the niggling thoughts in the back of her head. Time to go to work.

Claire watched Daniel's dream, finding herself projected onto sand. She recognized it as his home in Brazil. He was a boy of six or seven, running on a wide beach. Squinting from the blinding white sand and reflection of sunlight dripping on the waves in the ocean, he ran free and shirtless in a dirty pair of cut-off jeans secured with a worn piece of rope. The soft foam of the warm ocean licked at his small feet and skinny brown legs. He dug his feet into the wet sand and smiled as he ran toward the waves. He dove in just before a small swell could crash on him.

He floated face up, looking at the blue sky with white clouds changing shapes before his eyes. The water made melodic sounds as it tickled the sides of his face, ears and neck. Above him, in the sky, shapes appeared in the clouds, familiar faces, animals and pictures of houses and birds. Lots of birds.

Claire smiled to herself. She had done the very same thing hundreds of times in her open-ceilinged dorm room in Heaven. The clouds there were identical to those in the human world.

In the ocean, Daniel's body weightlessly rocked back and forth on the bed of water. A wave drove over him and filled his eyes and nose with salt water. He stood up, coughing. He waded through the waist high foamy water onto the shore. A gentle wave washed over a pair of footprints in the wet sand. Today the ocean had left two gifts for him: a brightly colored piece of glass and a partial shell, a curled piece from a pink and orange home of some sea creature. He held the glass up to the sun and felt its energy as it bathed his eyes in color. He squinted.

His sandy fingers explored the pieces, turning them over and over, looking at the dance of pink and white, light and shadow. A work of art, complete in its own texture and pattern—not something broken.

He put the glass and shell into his pocket and folded over the button flap, safely securing the glass and shell in this secret place. Claire could tell by his ragtag appearance that Daniel was probably unused to holding onto anything of value, but he seemed to treat these items as if they were even more rare than money. She could imagine that when he got home, he would put them somewhere special—maybe in a special box of treasures he kept under his pillow at night.

Next, Daniel was older, seated at a campsite in the early evening, the glow of sunlight giving way to a sprinkling of stars in a turquoise and violet sky. He picked up a piece of charcoal and started to draw on a discarded piece of brown bag. A small group of preteen girls sat in the sand, carefree and laughing as they showed off their smooth tanned bodies. He liked looking at them, especially his favorite. His fingers sketched outlines of her face.

They hailed him over. These were friends from school, slightly older girls who typically made fun of him. They teased him constantly about his good looks. They told him how he would break many hearts when he was older.

The girl giggled at her likeness on the brown canvas, holding the sketches upside down, laughing as she maneuvered it to the right and to the left. He leaned back on his elbows, watching her. She laughed all the time, her bright white teeth a sharp contrast to her bronzed skin. The small hoop earrings on her delicate lobes twinkled gold, playing a bit of sultry hide and seek in her long dark hair. He basked in her warm smile.

The look she had given him one day at school when she turned around and found him staring at her made him wish he were ten years older. She let him stare, without embarrassment, when her friends weren't around. The stolen gazes became a secret they shared. He thought maybe he could be in love.

Daniel saw other images of a back alley in a poor village without paved streets, all the children running barefoot down the sandy path. He sketched a likeness of a dirty Coke bottle in the sandy soil outside his back door. He discovered he could make the translucent sketches with blue green pencil and chalk resemble a photograph.

He drew by candlelight in his shared room with two other brothers, looking out the glassless window at the dusty streets to a golden orange and pink sunset. The faint outline of a dark, ominous jungle died into the horizon, filled with the sounds of creatures that squawked and screeched all night long as he lay in his bed.

Next, he was a young man, walking the streets of San Francisco, sketching brightly colored houses, little boats with blue water. He drew in classrooms and coffee houses, smoothing the chalk with his third and fourth fingers, a curl of his dark hair falling across his wrinkled brow as he concentrated.

Claire considered all the images he showed her in his dreams. What touched her most was the little box of "treasures," those pieces of colored glass and shells washed up on the beach. He probably considered these trinkets as having come from some faceless benefactor. Claire had met that benefactor, knew him enough to call him Father. These were obviously young Daniel's most precious possessions. In a world filled with wonderful things, she was struck that he chose to cherish pieces of broken shell and glass—miracles of the human world, worn by time and polished by the ocean.

She wanted to wander the streets again as a human, get a feel for the town and Daniel's world. But tonight she sat at the corner of his bed, propped against the wall, watching his chest rise and fall in peaceful repose. Nothing could touch him now that she was on guard.

CHAPTER 9

Claire settled herself over Daniel's sleeping form, loving the pull his body commanded over hers. She could easily fall into the fantasy of his kiss, up close and oh, so personal. Elongating her neck, she angled her head as if his lips had opened and beckoned her. The urge to whisper in his ear pulled at her soul. She was desperate know him, to feel every muscle, every electric current between their bodies. She allowed her thighs and lower torso to bond with him first, then lowered her spine down so her breasts lay against his chest. With outstretched arms, her fingertips extended all the way to his wrists. Almost joined, their arms prayed, flesh to flesh, mating together from wrist to shoulder. Her forearms felt the steady pulse of his life force as she submerged her chest, and at last allowed her head to sink in the warm cavity under his jawline. Before losing herself in his dream, she filled her lungs with his sleeping scent and enjoyed the resulting vibration in her core.

Was there a little melancholy, because this wasn't real? She had never before felt this way. She knew her soul glowed amber and wished he could reach out and touch it, aware that a portion of him already did. It was one of the most wonderful things she'd ever felt.

The trick tonight was to direct his dreams, not just watch. She would have to be careful not to become visible to him in her exuberance.

You must make sure that he never knows you exist, Mother had said.

Get out. Go home now, Claire, Angie had warned her.

Oh, but it already has begun, Josh had said.

You were handpicked by Father himself.

She entered the white room and stood behind him as he saw doors open to a freshly washed street. A purple school bus pulled up, opening its doors with a burst of pink steam that engulfed him.

There was no driver, but he got in anyway, the doors closing behind him. He came to a table with a translucent white surface that lit up when he touched it. An easel with white tablet was propped there. His chalk crayons and pencils were laid out in the same order as at home in his studio.

His fingers laced over the crayons, and he felt the vibration unique to each color. They were alive, breathing under his touch. He heard whispers, each color telling him intimate, private stories.

The colors have emotion.

The bus relocated to a sandy road at the edge of a dark jungle. A window next to him became a doorway Daniel walked through. Someone on a red motor scooter buzzed by him with a turquoise dog in a wicker basket, leaving a trail of white dust in its wake.

Curious.

He followed down a path littered with shiny dark leaves as long as his body. The earth beneath his feet felt spongy. Brightly colored birds flew between the curling vines and room-sized blooming flowers, wafting in and out of the scented mist. He turned around quickly, and saw a lighted table and easel behind him, waiting.

Never had a table follow me.

He went on. Hearing water, he came upon a green steaming pool. Looking around and finding no one, he shed his clothes and dove in. The surface of his skin tingled, opening to the feel of the liquid as warm as a bath. He felt someone's eyes on him, but searched the jungle and saw no one. Underwater fish moved in schools of bright yellows, turquoise, and red. He floated on his back, listening to the sounds of the water tickle his ears. He looked up at the clouds changing shapes, showing him faces of people he knew. Stars twinkled in the daylight sky.

There was that feeling again. A female. He searched the bank for a face.

Could I be in someone else's dream?

Claire sighed. She could watch him for hours. The way he moved his body through the pool of water was an art form all its own. While colors and shapes inspired Daniel, Claire was inspired by the look of his wet male body floating in the steamy pool. She could easily create another dream, inserting herself in it, but that was a dangerous thought.

Albeit a very nice one.

A path appeared, drenched in a beam of sunlight at the other side of the pool. Daniel thought he saw the faint outline of something in white. As he got out to explore further, he saw a terrycloth blue robe hanging on a branch. He pulled it on, and the material was soft on his skin, hugging his body, warming him when he draped it around him. The path was covered with crystals of sand so fine they were like finely ground diamonds, sticking to his toes and ankles, making his feet sparkle like sunlight on water.

He came to a clearing, a large meadow filled with acres of flowers—snapdragons, foxglove, lavender, and sunflowers—lined with rows of fully blooming rose bushes in deep shades of red and pink. Walking through the meadow, his fingers danced on the tops of the garden bounty. He quickly turned around. Someone's eyes were on him again. But again, partly in the sun and partly shaded, the lighted table and easel waited patiently. "Odd," he murmured.

Claire almost pinched herself she was so annoyed. If she wasn't careful, she would give him too much and he would wake up confused and disoriented. Belief was important. Disbelief was unproductive. She didn't want him thinking he was losing his mind.

A flock of green parrots flew overhead and chattered noisily in the trees at the sides of the clearing, dropping fruit and making the large flat leaves and vines shed their drips of water, bobbing in the sunlight. Their screeching made the sunlight dim as the jungle became dark and covered in shadow. He sensed something evil lurking, watching him, at the other side of the pool. He felt dark eyes on his back as he ran through the jungle path until he got to another sunny clearing. All of a sudden, he was filled with unspeakable joy and peace, as if being held by some invisible golden arms.

I must remember this.

He quickly turned. He still felt eyes on him. *Her* eyes. *My muse is playing hard to get.* It brought a smile to his face. He saw the table in the distance, next to a little cottage covered in moss and green vines.

Muse of my paintings, are you there, where I can see you?

He walked under the open doorway, ducking to avoid hitting his head. A massive chair made of tangled branches called to him. He sat. Sprigs of moss and ferns adorned the back and arms of the massive chair, tickling his fingers.

He closed his eyes and leaned back, listening to the chatter, inhaling the steamy scent from the flowers in the meadow.

Where are you?

He exhaled, opened his eyes and, just as he thought, the lighted table sat before him, the chalk calling to his fingers.

In Daniel's bedroom, Claire heard a loud scooter pass by his window. She quickly put her hands over his ears so the putting sound wouldn't affect his dream. The horizon was starting to turn pink as the real world came back to life.

In the distance, Daniel saw a golden dome with spires of brightly colored flags flapping in the breeze. There were gardens, and golden paths…figures in white almost floating along the paths. *Is this the land of muses? Does my muse live here?*

The scene began to break up, the edges turning black, blotches forming in the middle. His last thoughts as he sailed off to sleep were filled with a longing for this place of the golden spires.

Or is this Heaven?

Oops. Claire had caused her homesickness to creep into Daniel's dream. She'd showed him the playhouse and teaching garden. *Note to self: stay present with Daniel. Only show him things he would see in the human world.* Exaggeration was acceptable. Revealing parts of Heaven, not.

She sat in the corner of the room as the light through the window showed a softening sky, and watched her charge. He grew a smile. His bare chest rose and fell with his deep breathing. Then he rolled over to his side, exposing his muscled shoulder. She traced the line from his tanned bicep, down to his elbow, his forearm with the dusting of black hair extending to his wrist. The backs of his hands showed the veins of someone who used them often. His long fingers splayed on the sheet next to his body, delicately holding onto the night air.

She could wait or she could go, as he probably wouldn't dream any longer tonight. She decided to just wait and watch him. She had a feeling this could become one of her favorite things.

At last, the first glow of sunlight started coming through the window. She stirred, realizing she'd been daydreaming what she would do if she took him there.

It would be Heaven.

Can't wait to see what he paints today. She knew it was going to be magic.

Several days and nights passed, and Claire settled into a routine. Daniel would dream every night, then he would get up, shed his pajama bottoms, and jump into the shower. Each morning, Claire resisted the temptation to jump in with him, imagining what his tanned body would look like all lathered up. His morning showering and shaving routine became her reward for a long night of dream work. She blushed to herself. There were no words to describe just how curious she felt.

Daniel would emerge from the bathroom, his familiar scent surrounding him, and would get to work and paint every morning. Gone were his urgency and concern. He had not dreamed about Audray now for almost a week. Claire took credit for this permanent change in his mood.

Through his dreams, she fed him things she liked to do when she wasn't with him, or things she'd done on previous trips to the Real world, like going to some of the flower shows, craft fairs, and the planetarium. She even threw in a couple of tours to a Laundromat to smell the fresh scent of clean clothes, and the perfume counter at Macy's.

A couple of times she felt he was looking for someone. *Is he looking for me?*

Claire had no need of sleep, so there were large stretches of the daytime when Daniel was going about his daily life that she replenished herself. Even an angel couldn't go forever without these necessary recharges. And humans didn't sleep usually as much as they were awake, so it was never a problem for an angel to find the time.

She let Daniel initiate the dreams now. Often this could be a tug-of-war with her charges, but not Daniel. He seemed especially susceptible to her suggestions, as if he walked beside her, holding her hand. He'd start out on his own in some scene, but then she would creatively take it further, exaggerating and embellishing the dream. Usually it was something he thought about during the day, sometimes very briefly. She would take him there sometimes in a roundabout route, but she always started with his idea. The goal was to show him the beauty of the world in which he lived. She revealed to him small wonders that he could find around him.

Occasionally, Claire heard him murmur, "Thank you," as he dreamed. She was sure it was an expression more appropriately meant for Father.

This isn't work. This is communion at the altar of life. She worshiped human life, especially those gifted souls who could understand the magic and majesty of the creative process.

I am a life sculptor. She was good at helping them to take that most important step into the light away from the darkness, but by their own free will. She could show them anything from her imagination, but she couldn't make them take that step.

Yet, every single one of her charges made that step. She knew Daniel would be no different.

The local junior college's planetarium was one of her favorite places to go, the show like a movie of Heaven, or at least the only part humans saw from below. She was touched by how humans were always searching the heavens, trying to make sense of it all.

The twinkly lights in the sky were like angels looking down on her—her friends up above awaiting her return and her stories. She imagined that as a real child she must have laid out on warm summer nights and stared at the stars and the beauty of the sparkling sky, listening for some kind of sound, waiting for something to happen in her life, as if her calling was up there among the stars.

"Twinkle, twinkle little star,

How I wonder what you are,

Up above the world so high,

Like a diamond in the sky,"

She remembered this little childhood song humans sang to their children. *Did my mother sing this to me at night?*

To Claire, the galaxies were unfinished projects, other worlds with stars like earth's own sun, where life was being created, mixing light, combining it, like a painter. As far as she knew, there was no limit to creativity. She didn't need to know everything about the universe; her little part of it was enough. And since she would live forever, there was no rush to learn all its secrets any faster.

She regularly took Daniel to the planetarium in his dream state. She left out an audience so she could have him all alone and fully to herself. Though dangerous, she preferred to remain in human form, leaning forward to smell the scent of his clean hair.

And she wanted Daniel to have a sense of someone looking down upon him and his life, someone who cared and protected him.

So, on this particular night, he dreamed about the trees overhanging the flower garden he abandoned in his back yard. This was the perfect segue to taking him to Lake Ozette and the mighty forest that awaited them. She chose the bright green time of late April.

CHAPTER 10

She could see Daniel's curiosity as he stood at the trailhead next to the ranger station. He began the journey down the forested trail. Within a few yards, except for the wooden planks, no evidence of man existed before him. There was no sound but the wet dripping of the mist off the huge canopy of trees, to ferns and shiny leaves below, resting at last on the brown, loamy soil. One big drop of water fell on his face as if it took a century to fall from the bow of a very tall tree poking at the underbelly of Heaven itself.

He called forth his easel and chalky paints and sat working over the pages in the forest at the edge of a large, golden-lit meadow. The mist and droplets of water created the moisture needed for his pencils and watercolor chalk. He blended them with the pads of his long fingers. In his dream state, he seemed to work easily and happily alone, drinking in the glory of the forest, producing an impression that captured a glimpse of this great story.

A magic love affair lay somewhere between the pads of his fingers and the smooth white paper. He pressed into the paper the chalky substance, smoothing just here, shading just there, like a lover deciding which portion of his sweetheart's body he would grace with the warmth of his lips.

There she is again. He looked up, slowly glancing around.
Careful.

Claire could hear his thoughts. She must have made her presence known somehow. But it was so hard to distance herself from Daniel as he painted. She could watch forever, she thought. Perhaps sweeter to her was the fact that

Daniel, unlike her, did not have forever. This made his life more urgent and precious. Her heart pounded in her chest, and she reminded herself to breathe.

Daniel worked intently on a jungle scene, this morning incorporating bright tropical flowers and dark towering jungle greenery. He drew little scratches in pencil with two or three colors, and then added chalk to bring out more intense pigment. He added a dab or two of water from his rinse glass. He coaxed the color over the page with the pads of his third and fourth fingers.

Claire felt the intimate act of painting like fingers on her own skin. Sometimes he put his lips up to the paper and blew, drying it just so and just enough so more layers of color could be added. He then removed half the intensity of the color with a soft stroke of his finger or tiny wet sponge on a stick. It was a give and take of color and form, a sensuous meal of both light and dark.

Sometimes when Claire studied him painting, it was difficult for her to breathe, like right now. She felt the little fluttering in her heart like tiny harps with strings made of fuzzy yarn that resonated and deferred to him in some ancient harmony. It wasn't really music; it was a vibration of her soul. In his presence, she could completely lose herself.

She liked to put her face close to his to watch every little change in his eye movements, and to absorb the smell of his hair and the trace of lime cologne he put behind his ears. She loved the feel and smell of his breath as it bounced off the page. She would close her eyes and inhale the warm sweet scent of him. On this day he smelled a little like limes and warm, fresh earth.

Daniel stood back now, examining his work. After another adjustment and another step back to double check, he seemed pleased with the end result. He smiled faintly as he moved his head from one angle to the other.

He was prolific in his new commission for the children's book. This was perhaps the tenth or so painting he'd completed in as many days. She felt a rush of warmth flow through her body—pleasure in Daniel's success.

Daniel whipped his head up and looked around, as if he could sense her—see her. She tamped down the human emotions inside of her. He was her charge, and she was to do a job—heal his soul. That was all.

She wondered how Daniel would paint her story, if he knew she existed. How would he paint her face, her countenance? What colors would he use to show her emotions, and the depth of the love she had for her work in the human world? Would he be able to draw all the exquisite things she remembered from Heaven: the golden pink valleys and mountains of clouds; the sky that could go from pale blue to a deep midnight, almost black; the way everything sparkled with diamond dust? Would he be able to draw how happy it made her to sit and watch him sleep, or how wonderful it smelled when he was shampooing his hair? She wondered if all of that could be captured on paper.

She was an angel helping real humans live in the real world through the fantasy of their dreams. Claire understood that fantasy could create reality, but could the opposite happen? Could Daniel's experiences change her? *Am I becoming changed?*

She thought about the Brownings. Elizabeth Barrett and Robert Browning had fallen in love—not by the physicality of their being, but first with each other's words, poems, and letters; then their fantasy love became real. Could two people fall in love through art, color? *Would Father deny me just a taste of this?*

Perhaps a real and lasting love like Elizabeth Barrett and Robert Browning had shared could be made a part of Heaven and that love could live forever.

Daniel washed up his paints and laid the brushes out to dry on the table. His final act was to wash his hands. Claire noticed his third and fourth fingers now always had a stain, half purple, half brown, even after washing. Anyone who knew him as well as she did would be able to tell how inspired he'd been lately by this one telltale sign.

He made dinner and sipped a glass of red wine, with soft guitar music playing in the background. If she were human, these would be the times she would enjoy the most. He was very still and usually quiet at night. She especially liked one effect of the red wine he drank: it made his cheeks blush a bit and gave a wonderful redness to his full lips. *What would his lips feel like on my skin?*

Claire liked to sit next to him in the overstuffed chair, watching the lights flicker from the fireplace on his smooth masculine face. She would trace the little laugh lines, the wispy part of his hair at his temples, where it was unruly. She knew he would be very striking at any age.

The flickering firelight brought Daniel's paintings to life, as if created to be watched near a flame. The pink and yellow leopards and multi-colored birds almost danced in and out of the profusion of green strokes that had been made by his fingers and brushes to create the jungle foliage of the painting. Their wide eyes stared as if startled at being discovered and followed Claire around the room as she moved. *Do they think I am stealing him away?*

She'd never steal him away. Where would she take him? Something tugged on her heartstrings. Her time here was finite. There would come a day when she would need to leave this charge to the beauty of his human world. And she would go home to the vanilla world of Heaven.

Wouldn't it be wonderful if somehow this could last forever? For the first time in her angel life, Claire sensed that in being an angel, she was missing something.

I don't want to go home!

Her disobedient thought shocked her. What would that look like? Feel like? What if she could eat and sleep? What if she could…

No. Stop. You can't do this. She needed to gain control over her rebellious side before those in Heaven heard her thoughts.

Daniel had gone upstairs. Claire went back to his easel. She shifted out of disappear into human form, touching the chalks, the watercolor crayons and acrylic paints. She picked up a blue crayon and wrote across the surface of a fresh white sheet of watercolor paper, C-L-A-I-R-E.

She used residue water in Daniel's paint tray to brush over the letters the watercolor crayon had made, which bled and blended into the white paper. But her name was still visible underneath. Her finger still wet, she made a thumbprint in the upper right corner of the paper, and then carefully tore it out of the tablet. She blew on it like Daniel did with his work.

In her hands, she held evidence that she existed in the human world. She had changed the physical human world with something uniquely her own creation.

"You are never to let them know you ever exist," Mother had said. That was the hardest part, for she knew she did exist. She was proud of her work. Why shouldn't she show Daniel, let him know he was being watched over? What could it hurt, really?

In the universe Father had created, with all the variety and free will afforded angels and humans, surely there was room for one little angel to show a tiny part of herself, and how much she loved her job, particularly how much she enjoyed the company of one human above all others.

Claire wanted to save the paper with her name on it, so she waited until she thought Daniel was fully asleep to ascend the attic stairs at the end of the second story hallway. Although she could will herself up there, the paper would not be able to follow her, being of the human world. The small door creaked as she opened it.

Claire carefully tiptoed up the narrow stairwell to her little attic space, her private sanctuary. The few clothes she brought from Heaven were neatly folded in the dresser. She had hung the crystal from her dorm room over the single window, which sparkled rainbows over the bare studs and walls in the daytime. But at night, one flat side of the crystal caught a glint of the moonlight, illuminating the space. Claire laid the white paper on the empty trundle bed frame, spreading over her written name with the tips of her fingers. The paper felt completely dry.

Just then, she heard a creaking of the stairs. Someone was coming up.

CHAPTER 11

Daniel peered around the side of the doorframe, but it was pitch black. Expecting an intruder, he gripped a baseball bat in between his hands, steeling himself for a quick swing. He tiptoed into the room and scanned it, eyes glancing over the four corners illuminated by moonlight.

No one was there. He looked behind the dresser with the cracked mirror. Nothing. But yet he sensed something watching him.

"Who's here? Show yourself." The wind outside shook the rafters and whistled. The hairs at the back of his neck stood at attention. After a few more silent moments, he released his hold on the bat, dangling it with his right hand and started to leave the room, but a sheet of his drawing paper resting on the wire bed frame caught his attention. He quickly turned around, to see if it was some kind of trick to distract him, but seeing no one there, went back to the paper. He bent over and brushed his fingers over the top, sensing slight dampness only his fingers would be able to feel. He traced the letters he saw there in blue.

"Claire," he whispered. "Who is Claire?"

He picked up the paper, brought it to his nose and sniffed. A slight floral scent remained.

My muse. She paints.

He set the paper back down, scratching the back of his head with one hand. Some movement caught his eye and he immediately looked to the window, noticing the crystal blinking on and off, caught in the rays of the moon.

He approached the window, and with his forefinger, touched the crystal hanging there, watching it twinkle and dance.

Was this here before?

He scanned the top of the dresser, seeing a small sample perfume bottle. He picked up the bottle, smelled the delicate floral scent remaining and sprayed it into the air. Tiny glistening particles softly fell like magic rain.

What is this?

He wiped his hands on his pajama bottoms, then stuck the spray bottle in his pocket. With another careful glance around, he called out, "Show yourself." He waited.

This is ridiculous. But he glanced around the room one more time, then he silently left the attic, closed the door behind him, and locked it with a resounding "click." He made his way slowly down the stairwell, touching the sides of the wall with the fingertips of his left hand. The bottom two steps groaned under his weight. He closed the lower door and locked the latch as well.

Back in his room, Daniel stared up at the ceiling in his bedroom with a smile on his face.

It was completely insane to believe that a muse lived in his attic. But it was a pleasant vision. And one he decided to entertain.

Though the baseball bat was leaned against the bed by his head, he doubted he'd need it tonight. He liked the idea he had captured his muse and locked her in his attic.

Sleep well, my little one. Show yourself to me and I will let you out.

Daniel shopped at the organic grocery store on Friday afternoon, sorting through the extensive wine section. He held the green plastic basket casually in his left hand, brushing it near his thigh against the black knee-length raincoat with the slit up the back. His right hand moved across the labels in the red section. He had no idea what he came to the store to buy.

"This is what you're looking for?" Josh handed him a dark shiny bottle of Ravenswood Meritage without smiling. They looked at each other carefully. Daniel saw a slight challenge in Josh's dark face.

Daniel held the bottle by the neck and slid it back on the shelf. *Not going there again. Ever.*

"Thanks, but I think I'll try a different brand. I'm not fond of the memories." Daniel selected a Sin Zin, showing the label to Josh, who beamed.

"Nice, very nice choice," Josh said.

Both men continued shuffling down the wine and beer aisle.

"So, where did you crawl off to?" Josh cocked his head, watching.

"I've been working," Daniel responded flatly.

"Yes, I can see. Too much, I fear."

Wondering why his agent and friend wasn't happier, Daniel asked, "You're not pleased, then?"

"All work and no play…well, you know how it goes," Josh answered.

Daniel shrugged and stepped away from the wine section towards the meat counter, across the wide aisle. Josh followed. Daniel looked over the cuts of lamb, pork, and beef, arranged in pink rows silently lined with little borders of green plastic imitation grass, then requested a large New York steak.

"Go for the rib eye," Josh leaned in and whispered in his ear.

Daniel felt a calmness travel down his spine. He'd missed his friend. "If you want to come over, I can get another one."

"Tonight?"

"Sure. Or tomorrow, whatever works."

"You still don't have much of a social life, my friend," Josh said as he leaned over and put his arm around Daniel's shoulders.

The camaraderie made him happy. "I'm in love with my painting right now, Josh. That's probably hard for you to believe. I almost can't believe it myself."

Josh dropped his arm and stared at the ground, rocking back and forth on his heels. "I'd say you've made a rather remarkable recovery, Daniel. You went from despair to inspiration all in the space of what, little over a week?"

The butcher was waiting with the New York on a piece of white-waxed tissue held in the palm of his hand, tapping his fingers against the counter with his other hand. He looked pointedly at the line of customers behind Daniel and Josh. "You want another one or not?" He said loud enough for three waiting women shoppers to hear.

"Ah, sir, if you would, we'll have those two rib eyes," Josh spoke up, pointing to two large steaks toward the front of the tray. The butcher sighed, slapping two pieces of the marbled meat unceremoniously onto the scale, then wrapped them in pink butcher paper. He handed the package to Josh with grim determination, not asking if he could help them with something else, and wiped his gloved hands on his bloody apron. They'd been dismissed.

The two men walked down the dairy isle.

"Tonight." Josh said after a long silence.

"What?" Daniel didn't understand.

"I'll come over tonight. We'll have our steaks—then I want to take you out for a little R and R."

Daniel nodded in agreement. Perhaps it was time for a break.

"You are wound up tighter than a drum, my friend," Josh whispered in his ear. "Being celibate *and* alone is downright unhealthy."

Daniel stared at him. It hadn't occurred to him he had been celibate for what, a month now? He was surprised his needs hadn't surfaced like they had been. How could Josh know this?

Several women walked past them, suddenly primping their hair and straightening their posture. A skinny blond girl in her late twenties with enormous breasts leaned into the glass case, almost cutting the two men off midstride. As she opened the door, bringing out a half gallon of non-fat milk, she revealed a huge cleavage and breasts that almost leapt from her stretchy white v-neck top. She didn't look at the men, but she smiled knowingly. Daniel smiled at Josh, who tilted his head to the side and watched the girl's ass wiggle alluringly down the aisle. She wasn't Daniel's type, and then he realized he was comparing her to Audray.

There was no comparison.

Am I losing my manhood?

"You need female companionship, bad," Josh said, tearing his eyes off the blonde to look at Daniel.

"I have a meeting in the morning. Can't make it too late of a night," Daniel answered, creating an excuse why he hadn't gone for the blonde. "But I probably do need a break. I'm stoked for you to see what I've been doing."

Daniel was slightly disappointed when he heard Josh's flat response behind him: "I can hardly wait."

Josh and Daniel were finishing up their dinners, sitting at the dining table next to the open kitchen. Daniel made an occasion of their re-connection by setting a formal table, complete with candlelight and good wine. When he wanted to be, he was a very good cook. He and Josh usually dined on a fare that was heavy on lean, slightly rare meat, light on rice, heaviest on greens. Over dinner, they'd shared a bottle of red wine, and it was now at the bottom.

"So you haven't said you if like my new stuff," Daniel said, offering Josh the last of the bottle.

Josh grinned. "Sin Zin, of course, my friend." He held out his goblet. He inhaled the scent, then sloshed the wine in his mouth and closed his eyes as he swallowed. "Heaven."

They both laughed. "God, I've missed you, my friend. Forgotten how much fun it was to eat and drink," Daniel said.

"And screw. Don't forget the screwing part. Part of your Latin heritage, Daniel, and very important to your physical well being," Josh said, pointing his fork at Daniel's chest.

Daniel frowned. He didn't need to be reminded.

Josh grinned and played with a piece of steak with his knife, not looking up at Daniel. "You amaze me. Where do you find this recent inspiration?" He pinned him with a serious stare.

"I think it's the bounce," Daniel answered, not even sure why.

"Bounce?"

"I was at the bottom, I mean, really at the bottom. I hit, but I recovered. When you're at the bottom you have nowhere else to go. The only way is up." Daniel shrugged. "As for inspiration, I don't know, Josh—it's coming from somewhere. Somewhere out there." He wanted to remain a little guarded.

Josh sat up straighter and scanned the room before he answered. "Daniel, *you* see this talent of yours as something given to you from somewhere *else*. Don't you understand the talent is coming *from* you? Can't you accept the fact that you can do anything you set your mind to do—it's just a matter of confidence?"

"Well then, why do I feel inspired some days and not others?"

"That's just the human condition—just life. Look to yourself for the source of that power to create. It's all here, man," he said as he tapped his own chest with his clenched fist. "Have faith in yourself. Believe it. There is nothing else to believe in."

"Maybe I have a muse."

"A muse? What the bloody hell are you talking about?" Josh's face got red. He started to stand, then seemed to change his mind and remained at the table, but threw his knife and fork on his plate in disgust.

"You know, a fairy, a spirit—someone or something watching over me. I've sensed it in dreams lately."

Josh scanned the room again. "That's pretty crazy, my friend. I'd be careful saying things like that."

"What could be the harm? If I choose to believe it?"

"Be careful believing in things that will cause you pain, Daniel. Be very, very careful." Josh's brow was furled, eyes squinted. Then his face relaxed and he checked his watch. "We should go. I took the liberty of making some plans on your behalf. A new place on Fourth Street just opened up. I've not been there yet. Some friends will be stopping by."

Josh stood up, and as Daniel pushed his chair away from the table, he noticed how under the dim light of the dining room, Josh's skin seemed almost translucent. A faint blue vein extended over his jaw line and disappeared into the tissues of his cheek. His features were not the classic good looks of a great lover of women, but he commanded a handsome presence, perhaps less from his features and more from a place of power.

Daniel started to speak but noticed the center of Josh's dark eyes flash a sharp red light for just a fraction of a second. Josh kept scanning the space, as if searching for something.

"What do you keep looking for?"

Josh held up his keys. "Keys to the kingdom. Let's go rule the night, and get some serious ass."

A tingling sensation ran all over the surface of Claire's body, like a threshold had been breached, almost as if the tiny flash from Josh's eyes had been a probe of some kind. Had Josh recognized her? She felt a chill of fear run up her spine.

Two seconds later the door opened again. Daniel hit the "set" button on his repaired alarm system, which began a soft repeat rhythm. Claire stared at the closed door and waited. Her angel intuition told her this act wasn't over yet.

There was movement at the doorway again. Josh appeared at the window, and then he entered the room *through* the door without opening it, just as

Claire had earlier. He stood as if addressing the space in general. He inhaled deeply as if needing to smell her fear.

She held her breath and tried to think of nothing but pure white light.

Before he exited, he turned, gave a low bow, and vanished through the door just as he had come.

It was past midnight and Claire was reading at the attic window when she saw the headlights come up the driveway and heard the sound of a car door opening. She peered out. A young redheaded girl was kissing Daniel. Her hands slid to the front of his pants, making him jump. Laughing, he extracted her arms and pushed her gently back into the rear seat of Josh's car, closing the door. Another redhead was in the front, arms outstretched. He leaned in and gave her a kiss as well. She nearly pulled him into the car through the open window, dragging Daniel's shirt up almost over his shoulders. He worked hard to get disconnected from the woman's arms, just like he had the first one. Both women were pleading with him to stay.

Josh stood next to the driver's seat, car door open, and addressed Daniel from across the top of the car. Music played in the background. Daniel tucked in his shirt, and said something back. Everyone laughed just before Daniel turned to go up the driveway. Josh called out to him, loud enough for Claire to be able to hear.

"Daniel! Think! Think, man!" When Josh didn't get an answer, he continued, "Your loss is my gain."

Daniel waved over his head in acknowledgement, but did not turn around as he made his way to the front door.

There was a second where Josh looked up to the attic window and gave a little nod. There was no red flash of light and no prickling sensation on Claire's skin, but she held her breath just the same.

Josh backed his car down the driveway and away from the house. Headlights disappeared around the bushes and down the street.

Claire willed herself through to the top of the stairs and watched as Daniel sauntered up. He staggered a bit, but he was dancing, humming a Latin tune and moving his hips, turning a fantasy partner. The sight of him took her breath away. The sound of his gentle singing set up a buzzing in her ears.

Off came his shirt. A wave of strong cigar and whiskey smell overtook her. He laid his pants over a chair and then removed everything else. He warmed the shower as he danced naked in the room. Claire watched his reflection in the floor length mirror. Steam entered the bedroom from the readied shower, fogging up her view.

Under the warm water's splash, he continued singing. Claire poked her invisible head through the shower curtain and watched him soap himself then let the water sluice the white bubbles down his skin. She loved the smell of the spicy gel he used tonight, a hint of cinnamon and orange. He shampooed his hair. She followed ripples of water over the natural tan of his smooth muscular body as his hands scrubbed at his scalp.

Daniel toweling off intensified the smells for Claire. Mixed with the fading scent of the cigars, soap, and shampoo was the smell of his clean skin, and something else she was beginning to recognize as well as feel and almost smell: the passion of his soul. The emergence of this scent was usually a good sign; it meant the charge's recovery was well underway. Claire was pleased.

A lingering doubt crept in when she realized he hadn't painted today. Perhaps a little change of pace was all it was, since the passion was returning to his soul. That couldn't be bad.

But of the most concern to her was Josh's reoccurrence in Daniel's life. She was going to need to do more research on this. She remembered the white stones Mother had shown her and hoped that once she separated Josh from Daniel permanently, she would never think of those cold stones again.

CHAPTER 12

When Daniel went off to a meeting with a client, Claire put in a voucher for money so she could wear something other than what she'd brought in her duffel. At night, when she was at work, she wore her beautiful eyelet lace gown, which resembled a man's nightshirt. Claire assumed this was Father's design; he seemed to prefer his Guardians be dressed in clothes that did not show off their curves when they were working in case they became visible in their exuberance. But what they wore on their off days was up to them. She hadn't had time to properly pack. Except for her favorite pair of jeans, her wardrobe was simply lacking.

Doris drove her to Macy's and tossed a purse of money over the cab seat. When she looked at the amount, Claire had no idea how much it would buy.

"He wants receipts, you know."

"I know."

"And, Doll, nothing flashy."

"Oh, I know." She grinned. She'd done this before.

"Usually you go for the sporting goods stuff, Claire. Macy's today?" She gave her a wink. "And don't even try submitting a receipt from Victoria's Secret."

They both laughed. What a picture that would have been, Mother Guardian looking over the receipts and seeing one from a lingerie shop.

Claire needed shoes so she could ditch the black slippers. She had an affinity for light colors, but being late fall, there weren't any. Everything was black, maroon or shades of brown. On the back wall of the shoe department, a display of Crocs caught her eye and she was immediately attracted to the bright colors. She picked out a yellow pair in Mary Jane style, and placed them on her feet.

Perfect.

With her slippers in one hand, she found some plastic charms in various shapes and sizes. Someone had placed these inside the holes of the display Crocs. They called them "jewels."

Too good to be true.

She picked out several: pink daisies, yellow and gold stars, a couple of red hearts, and a couple of gem-like stones in purple and green.

A separate holder had jewels with logos she didn't understand, including a red bird with a topknot, a shark, and a bull's head. She liked the one that was a letter "A" with a halo over it.

Get that one for Angela. She found one with a stylized "C" for Claire and went to the checkout.

The charms cost more than the Crocs, which surprised her.

Oh well. She had to have them.

She told the saleslady she would wear her yellow Crocs out.

"Go Cubbies," the lady said as she handed Claire the bag. Curious. What could she possibly mean?

She gave the lady a smile, but had not a clue.

Claire was aware of the makeup and fragrance counter to her left. Although she needed neither of makeup nor fragrance, the brightly lit display cases, track lighting, and music attracted her. She touched the silver and gold trimmed gift sets wrapped in cellophane, loving the sensation and sound as they crinkled under her fingers. She overloaded on scents as she walked around the aisles, sampling the fragrances on her human "skin." Soon, however, her nose started to itch.

One of her favorite things to do in the human world was to spray the scent in the room and then walk through it, something an older guardian taught her. That's what they did in Heaven with their dust, but there it was a multisensory experience. Dust brought forth emotions. Perfume was a faint imitation.

Just for fun, Claire occasionally liked to wear a little makeup, something she wasn't allowed in Heaven. It did commit her to staying in human form, because the makeup couldn't disappear like the rest of her body. A made up face walking down a mall without a body attached to it scared humans. It had only happened to her once before and she was loath to repeat it. A woman had fainted, then woken and made the sign of the cross, which Claire had found ironic.

Risky or not, one of her most favorite things was to have her make-up done at Macy's. The counter girl bounced in like a brightly colored flag on the end of a ship. Her jet-black hair spiked out in tufts at the back and sides of her head behind her ears. She was short, Claire's height. She was probably in her twenties, with a flawless, pale face with large brown eyes done brightly in shades of green and fuchsia. These were not colors Claire would have thought to wear together on her eyes.

"Can I try something on you?" the girl asked in a perky manner.

Claire agreed, and placed herself on a white and chrome stool. Peering into a mirror, she noticed her short blond hair had spun out of control but glistened under the overhead lights. She wasn't used to seeing herself. Her blue eyes were lighter than she remembered. A young man wearing lots of eye makeup with streaked blond and black hair asked her if she wanted some sparkling water.

"Perfect," she said. Though she didn't usually drink anything, she liked the way the bubbles felt on her tongue.

The makeup artist started the process of showing her the cleansing products. She pouted a bit when her cotton square revealed not a speck of dirt on Claire's face.

"Your skin is exceptional." Counter girl scrunched up her face as if deep in thought. "You must have just showered. There's not a trace of anything on here." She held up the brilliant white pad, flicking it back and forth with a small wrist action. Claire nodded, since there was no way she could explain the truth.

She enjoyed the sensuous experience: the gentle facial massage, the warm water rinse, the application with the pads of the artist's fingers as she applied moisturizer. The girl possessed a cheerful disposition and bantered on about what she was doing and why. It was background noise, like the music in the store. Claire loved the whole experience. She wondered why there never was a place in Heaven where angels could enjoy this kind of happy pampering.

Maybe someday Father will let me open a spa in Heaven. She almost giggled at the thought.

The girl wore a very flowery scent Claire liked as well. She thought the tattoo on the girl's forearm of a small frog was out of place on her delicate white skin.

"Can you make me look sexy?" Claire surprised herself when these words came out of her mouth. She blushed a bit, but that was what she wanted.

Countergirl gave a devilish giggle. "Right on. Hot date tonight?"

"You have no idea."

Countergirl sighed. "Okay, Let's knock his socks off and make you a real sex siren."

I'm thinking about him taking off more than his socks. She wished she could show Daniel that side of her. Perhaps she would chance it and appear to him just once this way. She wanted to see the reaction in his eyes as he beheld her painted face. What other parts of his body would respond?

Now was time for the dramatic eye paint. Claire watched with a handheld mirror as the girl applied each layer of color, starting with a pale green, going darker in the crease of her eyes. She added the fuchsia to the ends and a bit in the crease, blending the color. Claire had to admit, with the dark eyeliner, blackened lashes and bright eye shadow she looked completely different—completely desirable, she hoped.

The woman Claire saw in the hand-held mirror at the end of the session did not resemble the girl who'd walked in. She was shocked at the change. Her face was as bright as one of Daniel's canvases. Her eyes were mysterious and dark, and she practiced flashing them. But her lips were luscious and pink, the lip-gloss plumping them up. She could wear them like this every day, she thought.

"Oh, honey, you are sexy. And your skin is fabulous!" Fabulous was a word they hardly ever used in Heaven, but Claire loved the way humans said it. Several of the other helpers came over and admired the canvas that was Claire's face.

Countergirl gave her more of the light pink lip color, glazed over with gloss that tasted like cherries. Claire had to have it.

"Now just one more thing." Claire was trying to imagine what could possibly be missing as she looked at her transformation in the mirror.

The girl brought out a small silver can and shook it. "Close your eyes." There was a hissing sound that lasted only a second. "Ok, now open them."

On Claire's forearm were tiny sparkling particles that caught the bright lights of the counter. In the mirror, she saw this sparkle had fallen all over her hair, her forehead, nose, and shoulders. Countergirl held up the little metal can, her big smile showing large white teeth.

"What is it?" Claire asked, halfway expecting her to say "Dust."

"Seasons Sparkles. They make it every holiday. 'A Spray To Add Sparkle To Your Day!'" It was a perky advertisement, and it worked. Claire had to have it as well.

She was finishing the sale when she noticed a woman so beautiful she looked dangerous enter the area two counters over. It took a moment for Claire to realize why she knew her. Audray! Her long blond curls fell and bounced in mid-air as she leaned into the counter to examine something. She sprayed perfume on her wrists and smelled it with eyes closed. She seemed to enjoy mesmerizing the sales clerk, who was a young man. She held up her wrist to him.

"What do you think?" She flashed him a smile.

"Uh, nice. Very nice. Good on you," he responded with a blush and quickly looked down.

Audray looked back at him as if to say, "Of course it's nice." Even Claire had a hard time pulling her eyes off her beautiful face and slender body.

Audray purchased the bottle and then wandered off. Claire watched her stroll the counters, salespeople feigning friendship with broad smiles as she passed, especially the men. Claire suddenly felt a bit challenged. Something boiled inside her stomach. The taste in her mouth was slightly sour. Did this woman know the effect she was having on everyone around her? *Of course she knows.* Does she think about Daniel at all? Claire decided she did not. She hated this woman, a very unpleasant emotion for an angel, and not one she often felt.

The pink bottle Audray sprayed on her wrists called to Claire. She applied one spray and rubbed the other wrist on top. She liked the fragrance, an infusion of sweet flowers including jasmine, and a little orange spice. The bottle read Pink Passion.

A poor substitute.

She took the offered sample and added it to her bag, then went in search of Audray, who had entered the Men's department.

Audrey stood with the hairy man from Daniel's dream. She held up a blue and white striped long-sleeved shirt. He gazed at it from behind her, chin on her shoulder. His hands found their way under her shirt. One was on her breast, the other headed down under the front of her skirt. A couple nearby gawked in disbelief, then moved away, whispering. Audray watched them leave with a sultry smile, like she relished making waves. She stepped back, pressing into the man's crotch and threw her head back in a laugh. The man's mouth was on her neck. She turned her head to do a quick scan of the area, when her green eyes rested briefly on Claire. Her eyes narrowed, as if to say Claire was not worthy of her attention.

Claire stood her ground and stared back without a smile. She truly despised this woman and tried to say so with her eyes.

Audray raised her chin, and then abruptly turned to face the man, whispering in his ear. They walked arm in arm to the dressing room area, grabbing a fistful of shirts right before they disappeared around the corner. Audray released a hard steely stare that was predatory and vicious.

Claire shivered. She was not afraid of them, but repulsed. By the look on the dressing room monitor's face, even she knew they were going to have sex. Probably happened all the time. If Claire had respect for the couple, and she didn't, she would leave them to it. She showed a sweater to the monitor as she took the room next door to the couple.

As soon as the door closed, she went into disappear mode. She heard sighing followed by the soft shifting of material and the metallic clinking of a belt buckle. Claire stood on the vinyl-covered bench and peered over the top of the partition.

It actually excited her to see him with his pants down around his ankles, his engorged cock seeking to enter Audray from behind. They had not bothered to remove her skirt, which was bunched up tightly around her waist. Her blouse was unbuttoned. Her hands were stretched out in front of her, pressing onto the glass of the mirror where she was watching herself. The man pushed aside her white lace thong underwear. She bent her knees and extended her ass toward him as he entered her from behind.

"Oh, baby, yes," she said. "Oh, give it to me, give me that fat cock. Ram it hard."

The man grunted, his hairy legs jerking to the actions of his groin. He reached forward, grabbed one breast, and squeezed. He yanked her body roughly to him, impaling her deeper, a large hairy hand buried in her lower belly. Her long locks bounced in time to his thrusting as she raised her face to the ceiling.

Claire was hoping to dampen the couple's pleasure just as Audray looked up and their eyes met. Of course, their eyes couldn't really meet, because there were just dark pockets where Claire's eyes would be, carefully outlined in black by Countergirl, shaded in beautiful hues of green and pink. What Audray saw was only the makeup. No neck or body attached to it, either.

Audray shrieked.

Claire's made up face, with the wide Cheshire cat grin, lowered back down to her side of the wall. She shifted back to human form before she left the dressing room as whispers, protestations, and the sound of arms and knees knocking into the tiny booth came flying behind her. With her keen angel senses, she heard the door to the cubicle swing open, but Claire was already around the corner and well out of sight.

Claire couldn't remember when she had felt so completely satisfied.

She walked past the salesmen in the cologne section and batted her eyes seductively. The younger one of the two blushed and looked down. Good. The makeup was working. *There's more than one siren in this store.*

Doris was waiting for her outside Macy's, but looked at her in confusion when she waved her down. "I wish I had a camera! They just won't believe this at the transport station," Doris said. "I didn't recognize you!"

"Don't tell them, Doris. I didn't buy anything for my face but lipstick… and some sparkle," Claire was timid about this. She handed Doris the receipts.

"Sparkle? They sell dust there at Macy's?"

"Well, it's not the same. I mean, it's just for looks; it doesn't give you anything else.

"I should hope not. Can it be healthy then?"

"Oh, I think it's harmless. It comes in a little can with a spray button on it."

Doris shook her head from side to side. "You are one hot lookin' babe. You look more like those girls of Carmen's."

She meant the guardians that worked with the streetwalkers in the human World. Many of these young human girls were addicted to drugs. These tough angels were responsible for saving a few of them, but not many. Their risky lifestyle, considered a form of suicide, was what brought them up to Triage's attention. Most of the time it was too late by the time the call went out.

Since Claire respected the difficult work these angels did, she didn't take offense at the comment.

She looked at the vision of herself in the large glass window just outside Daniel's dining room, saw the price tag on the new jacket she was wearing, and pulled it off.

CHAPTER 13

"I've got a lead on a new gallery for your work." Josh told Daniel as he sipped on his beer. "It's in Marin, but I think the location is perfect. Old, restored building they are just finishing up."

"Good, I'll need the space soon." Daniel dove into his spinach salad as the waitress brought over some whole grained bread in a wicker basket. After she left, he leaned into the table and whispered to Josh, "And, I need the money. Big time."

"I hear you. How about I spot you some cash until your next sale?" Josh pulled out his wallet, fat with money. He started to peel off hundred dollar bills.

Daniel held up his hand. "No, man. I don't do that."

"Don't be stupid, Daniel. Just consider I bought one of your paintings—how about the one in the fire?"

"Josh, that's charity and you know it."

"I know a talented painter when I see one." Josh stood up, "I need a trip to the loo. Be right back. Here," he said, handing Daniel a wad of bills, "study those for me while I'm gone."

Daniel looked around the room to make sure no one had noticed, covered the bills with his palm. The wad of money was tempting, calling to him through his flesh, but there was no way he would accept Josh's generosity. It didn't feel right to him. He moved the substantial cash under Josh's napkin so he didn't have to look at it.

Just as Josh was returning from the men's room, Audray and her new boyfriend entered the restaurant. She was syrupy sweet as she made a point to bend down to kiss Daniel on both cheeks, revealing her cleavage. She smelled of fresh sex. Her boyfriend looked pissed.

"Ah, sweetie, how've you been?" she said to him, feigning concern.

Neal cleared his throat. Daniel thought perhaps he was looking for an introduction. Audray ignored him, of course. Being someone she cared about was a dangerous thing, he reminded himself.

Daniel stood, although she didn't deserve the respect he showed her. "Audray." Turning to Neal, he continued, saying, "My name is Daniel DePalma. We've met before. You were screwing her on my loveseat—the green one, by the fireplace—where she and I used to do it all the time." He turned to Audray. "Remember that, *sweetie*?" He addressed Neal again. "She always did like that place."

A definite chill had descended upon the restaurant. Josh grinned, but Daniel could see the smile was forced. "Neal, Daniel here was Aud—"

"I know who the hell he was, God damn it." Neal tugged on Audray's arm. Her eyes widened as he led her to another part of the restaurant, but she managed to secretly blow Daniel a kiss. Josh and Daniel sat back down. With eyebrows raised and a sigh on his lips, Josh picked up the money and stuffed it back in his pants.

Daniel watched Audray's ass as it swayed from side to side, almost hitting the little tables in her wake. *The woman is diabolical. And damn hard to forget.*

When he looked up, Josh was studying him.

"I have a cure for that, you know."

"Time is doing a pretty good job."

Josh nodded his head slowly. "Yes, I can see that. It's doing a really remarkable job."

"Fuck it." Daniel stood up and threw his napkin on the table. He motioned for the check.

Josh got up. "Daniel, don't do this, man. Look, I've got some ideas. Let's get out of here and go grab some coffee across the street."

The waitress came back with a sheepish smile on her face. "Mr. DePalma, I'm sorry." She was a little too loud. "Your credit card's been declined. I'm so sorry."

Daniel's hands made fists at his sides as he looked around the room at a few patrons who had noticed the interchange.

"Not a problem, this was supposed to be my check, anyhow." Josh handed her a one hundred dollar bill.

The two men strode down the rain-swept sidewalk, headed for Starbucks. "Just one more thing I get to deal with," Daniel grumbled. "There should be plenty of money in my account. Lately, though, it's like the bank's computer just doesn't like me. I have never seen so many holds and rejected checks—all of them mistakes. It's damned embarrassing."

"You don't have to justify anything to me, Daniel. I believe you. I just think you should take some of my money, as an investment in your future."

"No, then I would owe you."

"Suppose I make it a purchase, a gift." Josh stopped. "There is no crime in taking money from a friend who freely gives it."

"Except that you will own me."

Josh let out a chuckle, almost a cackle. His eyes began to water. "I'm going to remember that line for eternity." He shook his head and continued walking.

Daniel insisted on paying for the two cappuccinos, with cash. They stood at the coffee bar and looked out through large picture windows onto the traffic outside.

"I get to feeling pretty good about myself, and then this crap happens," Daniel said.

Josh nodded. "You're getting your professional life back on track, but you still need some serious female attention. You need to lock yourself in a room with three or four lovelies and just have at it, my friend. Get good and drunk and good and screwed."

"Not my style." Daniel couldn't help but bring a smile to the corners of his lips. "Although it's sometimes a pleasant thought."

"Consider it done! My gift from me to you. You won't take my money? There are a couple of lovely ladies that owe me big time, and they will blow your mind. I'll set it up for this weekend, then. I won't take no for an answer. It'll be my investment in your well being."

After stuffing her Macy's shopping bag into her transport duffel, Claire elevated to the second floor hallway, and then opened the doorway leading to the attic above Daniel's bedroom.

She could fully stand about two feet on each side of the ridge board. Late afternoon sun gilded tiny particles of dust kicked up by her yellow Crocs as she crossed the room to look out one of the two dormered windows. They faced each other on opposite sides of the wide but shallow space.

It seemed the perfect place to be. It was warm, still, and filled with sunlight. She removed her jacket, laid it across the back of the chair, and sat down. She inhaled the scent of old dust and wood. It felt cozy in spite of her nearness to the windowpane.

The house is waiting for him too.

There were no interior walls in the attic. Wooden studs merely stood as a testament to someone's idea that this upper space could be a room—a glorious room. She could visualize it painted a light color, or perhaps partially covered with wallpaper in a flowery pattern.

Joyful.

In the middle of the room stood a dark brown scratched dresser with an attached cracked mirror. She regarded her reflection in the damaged glass, cut in two. She turned herself invisible, and then visible again, reliving the scary scene of a floating face in the dressing booth. She smiled and shook her head.

I'll hear from Mother on that one for sure. But it was worth it.

It always amazed her how Father had made angels able to appear and disappear at will. Just one of many tools in her arsenal, she thought. She would need all of them this time around.

One thing would have to be remedied before Daniel got home; she would have to lose the makeup.

A bare mattress sat atop the mesh platform of an old trundle bed frame. Claire went over to it, clutching her red shopping bag. She carefully pulled out her purchases. Two white boxes remained at the bottom. She opened them up to find little pink vials of perfume. She hoped the girl wouldn't get in trouble for giving those to her for free. She sprayed the room and walked through the cloud of spray. She hoped she smelled better than Audray did.

Daniel will be home soon.

Time for a shower.

Claire removed her clothes and stepped into in his shower. She loved the feel of the warm water and the soap against her human skin. After finishing her shower, she faced Daniel's mirror, drying off. Turning back to disappear, she took a quick check to make sure she left no trace of the makeup. A little water shadow remained, but no other evidence that she had been there.

Before she could dress, she felt something cold, like the forefinger of a cold spirit trace down her spine. She shook herself loose of the feeling.

The towel she used was Daniel's. It contained the scent she had grown to love. Before replacing it on the rack, she buried her face deep inside the warm cotton, inhaling. Her body tingled with excitement, every cell. She opened Daniel's medicine cabinet and took out his lime cologne and inhaled it with eyes closed.

The best. She sighed. She'd guarded humans who smelled good only some of the time, but he smelled good to her all the time.

Which do I love more, smelling him or looking at him?

Claire returned to the attic to await his arrival, then slipped on her gown. She picked up the perfume, sprayed it in the room and walked through the wonderful jasmine scent again.

After retrieving her Sonnets from the duffel she curled up in the chair by the window and felt the last bits of golden sunlight slowly die off as she read E.B. Browning:

"How do I love Thee? Let me count the ways."

This poem always made her shiver. It was curious to read about love, a human emotion she had not experienced. She felt joy and sadness, and she could say she loved Father, but it was a kind of devotional love for him, not like what was described in these poems.

Like an angel, Robert had come to Elizabeth's bedside and coaxed her to health. Claire loved that story. They had fallen in love with each other's words, and then they met and fell in love in the physical sense. Claire tried to imagine that kind of love. It seemed to be in short supply in the human world. In Heaven it wasn't necessary.

Or is this what I'm missing? She had never felt she missed anything before.

If the Brownings had become angels in the Guardianship, they wouldn't know each other, she thought, as all their human memories would have been washed clean. Perhaps they lived together in a different world—one of the other ones she knew existed.

Maybe there's a Land of Great Loves...

She would have to ask Father about this. All she knew was the Guardianship. What are those other worlds? Most angels had never seen them, except her friend Carmen. The Ladies of the Night had tremendous access all over Heaven, especially Carmen, who was the oldest angel she knew.

Rumors about other worlds and other goings on in Heaven sometimes caused big "clarification meetings," because the imaginative angels on her squad were susceptible to exaggeration or embellishment. It sometimes brought on trouble. Mother Guardian was always on the lookout for trouble, or for things that would distress her girls. Some of the male angels in the guardianship had traveled between worlds, but they'd been sworn to secrecy, keeping the girls naive. Mother liked things to be peaceful, simple. Claire knew the angels were only told what they needed to know, and no more. But sometimes she wished they knew more.

A few hours passed before Daniel arrived home, later than usual. His mood was somber.

Something is bothering him.

Claire was a bit alarmed. Last night he had been out with Josh and had met the redhead and her friend. She doubted he would pine for her, remembering how anxious he was to be rid of her wandering hands.

He sat by his fireplace in the big chair, his stocking feet up on a hassock. He proceeded to drink almost the whole bottle of wine without the use of a glass again, like the night of his suicide attempt. This was not a good sign. He rubbed his eyes with his fingers, like the fireplace had caused his eyes to water. Claire looked at his pencils and chalk. Untouched today. Untouched yesterday as well. This also was not a good sign.

The near empty wine bottle sat on the floor beside the chair and ottoman. He leafed through one of his books and sighed, then looked into the fireplace as if searching for answers. He fell asleep with the open book propped on his chest.

Claire came around and admired her poor, beautiful charge. Once he fitfully entered dream state, she dove in.

She could tell immediately where it was going again.

What has triggered this encounter with Audray? Here it comes. I hate this dream!

Daniel walked up to his front door, and, seeing his key wasn't necessary, was about to open it when he heard sounds inside. He walked around to his dining window and saw Audray on the couch in front of his fireplace with the hairy man. The man looked even more ape-like than before.

Each time the man got hairier, and fatter. Daniel was embellishing his own dream, although Claire had planned to do the same if she had the chance.

She knew what would be coming next. Deciding to use some humor to help break up the ache in his heart, she gave the gentleman an even wider butt than he already had, and added more body hair. Claire didn't like this man either.

But Daniel didn't seem to notice the embellishment. His eyes were glued elsewhere, tears streaming down his face.

Not acceptable!

This dream undid days of contentment. She knew it would keep coming back over and over again. Claire had to stop the downward cycle. She smiled as she came up with a devilish solution.

Humor. Use humor.

Claire forced the fire to flame out of the firebox several feet. It lightly touched the man's bottom as he was pumping into Audray. The man squealed in pain as he rubbed his sore behind, cursing. Claire could see it was starting to turn bright red and hoped Daniel saw the welts forming.

Audray threw her head back and laughed. Claire wasn't surprised. That would be the end of the lovemaking.

Was that a thin smile on Daniel's face?

Claire was relieved. A little comic relief was often good for a broken heart. But her relief was short-lived, as Audray rose and stood, with her perfectly formed body on view, fluffing her hair, stretching like a cat in the glow of the fireplace. Though there was lots of movement from the agitated man, Daniel's stare could not be swayed from glow of her flesh, and Claire felt his craving and heartache return.

This calls for drastic measures. This dream will end permanently tonight. I'm sick of it.

Claire put a wrinkle in the rug, so when the goddess walked across the room, she tripped and fell, landing on her rear.

Audray wasn't one of those women who fell well. For one thing, she had artificial breasts and they stayed pretty much in the same location – out front and center, pointed to the ceiling like a plastic doll. They were too rigid and did not look real. Claire looked at Daniel's face again, hoping to see some relief.

Instead, he looked like he wanted to rush in to her aid.

Disgusted, Claire couldn't help imagining his thoughts. She needed something to get this scene ended once and for all.

Then another idea came to her. Audray and Neal had been having some sort of snack by the fire. With not much little effort, Clare repositioned a red napkin strategically, and, as Audray arose gracefully and turned around, there was a very obvious and hard to miss red napkin stuck in her butt crack. Hoping Daniel would find this as hilarious as she did, Claire looked to his face and was rewarded with a huge smile.

Then he turned and looked behind him. Did he know she did it?

I have the best job in the whole universe. She danced a jig and fluttered with enthusiasm, almost levitating.

Daniel awoke with a big smile on his face. Unpeeling himself from the living room chair, he began a slow ascent upstairs to his bedroom. He shook his head from side to side, chuckling. He rubbed his fingers through his shiny black hair as he yawned. Then, to Claire's great pleasure, he stepped into the shower.

Claire could do nothing else but join him this time, though she had already showered. She was completely invisible and undetectable, but she did not remove her gown, out of respect for Daniel's nakedness. The gown, made in Heaven, would not get wet.

Concentrate on his face, shoulders and chest.

She inhaled the spicy steam, the shampoo, soap and warm water. Her eyes did drift down to view his full naked body, first from behind, and then as he turned to rinse the shampoo from his hair…She held her breath.

Heaven help me.

She watched his hands touching and smoothing off the soapy goodness, touching himself in the places that she wanted to touch.

Wonderful. She couldn't help looking. Her body heated.

He stepped out, buffed his fully packed torso and legs. He did one last rub to his hair and face. Then he sniffed the towel—the very one Claire had dried herself with earlier. He did it again, before placing it back on the towel bar.

Uh oh.

Daniel lumbered slowly to his bed, and sat, chin in his hand, one elbow perched on his bulging thigh. Moonlight made him look like a marble statue.

Adonis. Statue of David. I have touched this beautiful statue before.

He looked out the window at the stars, then lay back on the bed fully exposed to her in his nakedness. She tried not to look.

You've seen a naked man before. Oh! God help me.

Claire's eyes seemed to have their own volition as they ran over him, ending far below his face and chest.

Touch him. No! Stop it. Stop it.

She was almost relieved when he covered himself up with the sheeted comforter, head propped on the light blue pillow she would share when he was in dream state. His arm rested under his head, exposing the muscles and ribs of his torso just above the hemline of the coverlet.

He went quickly to dream state again. Claire had only just wrapped her arms around him and inhaled his clean, wet hair when she saw he was standing in a rose garden lined with star jasmine plants. He was picking the delicate vines, smelling them deeply, with eyes closed.

Claire realized it came from the perfume scent on her wrists.

Note to self: no perfume before bedtime. Especially *her* perfume. A little too careless, and risky.

It could affect the outcome of his dreams and put focus on her. She had to stay invisible to him forever.

And then there was that part of her somewhere that wanted him to see her. Would she have another close encounter again? Would he touch her and smile? Would she disappear this time?

"Unsafe thoughts, Claire." She could almost hear Mother's voice.

She gave Daniel and extra dose of dust so he would sleep soundly without dreaming. She needed time to sort everything out. She needed to plan tomorrow.

She had to find out more about this Audray. No sense putting it off any further, Claire thought. Perhaps she had underestimated Josh and his connection to the vixen. She hoped she hadn't waited too long.

CHAPTER 14

Claire was drawn back to the Farmer's Market. Daniel was off looking at gallery space out of town. She would go in human form, so all her senses would be heightened, but she would stay in angel uniform just in case.

Doris dropped her off by the fairgrounds. Claire had heightened senses in the human state, immediately smelling freshly ground coffee and a nut roaster. Today was grey, but the overcast was to burn off by eleven. Small patches of blue sky already broke through, laced with occasional ribbons of sunlight on the wet pavement. She passed several people with gloved hands holding steaming Styrofoam cups. She walked past a long table with bright orange tangelos, yellow-orange Meyer lemons, limes, and oversized Chinese grapefruits. The pungent citrus made her mouth water. She took a slice of the orange fruit, savoring the sweet, cold segment with her eyes closed.

What would it be like to feel hungry? Claire greatly enjoyed just smelling and tasting. Being in the human world was unlike Heaven. It was richer, fuller with more choice and variety. She enjoyed the emotional responses she got from her heightened senses. The human world was almost like a kind of dust to Claire—its powerful effects often left her daydreaming.

She remembered the first time she walked past a Laundromat; the fresh laundry soap and clean clothes smell burst out onto the sidewalk. The warm space was lined with humming machines spinning colorfully. She'd been so mesmerized by it that she'd closed her eyes to enjoy it fully. When she opened them she was surprised to find several of the patrons staring at her. Did they not appreciate the warm smell of soap bubbles? She guessed not.

Claire heard music from a stringed instrument. Anything with strings, like guitars, lutes or cellos were of special attraction to her, and she wandered in the direction of the music. On the way, a bright flower stand called to her. She bent down to smell a bouquet of long-stemmed deep pink roses displayed in a white bucket. She closed her eyes. These floppy, almost overripe roses were her favorite. Next to them stood several other containers of mums, stock, and roses in varieties from purple to yellow, red to orange. Kneeling there before the altar of color she felt her heart swell with the goodness of it.

Claire walked toward the music again. The harp-like instruments were played with nimble fingers. The sound sent ripples of joy down her spine with each pluck of the strings. Claire wondered if she could bring one of those harps home to Heaven when she was done. She thought it looked small enough to fit in the transport bag, when the time came.

She scanned the marketplace, feasting on the colors, smells and sounds of this happy place. Tears came to her eyes as she realized how much she loved being in the human world.

A cheese vendor handed her a sample of a creamy white soft spread on a cracker. She tasted the cream, loving the tangy saltiness of it, and the way it made her taste buds stand to full attention. An Indian woman sold wild berry preserves. She spread the globule of glistening red jam on the small, white plastic sampling paddle, then placed it on her tongue. She closed her eyes to savor the sweet and sour combination that filled her head.

"I have cherry," the woman told her. That was Claire's favorite sweet taste. The old woman's cherry preserves were definitely going back to Heaven with her. There would be no other way Claire could describe the flavor of this compote to the new guardian recruits.

She heard a tinkling sound that instantly attracted her. A vendor had made wind chimes of flattened silverware. He displayed them on an overhanging metal rack, which Claire ducked under. She stood in the middle of several of these chimes in various sizes, some made with large flattened serving spoons, others with combinations of forks, spoons and small knives, occasionally twisted or folded into an unusual shape, all glistening in the early morning sunlight. With her eyes closed, again she let her fingers drift up to the chards of silver, hearing a Heavenly chord of perhaps twenty tones only an angel could distinguish. Again, she felt her heart soar. This was a good day.

"They're beautiful, aren't they?" The voice seemed to come from within the waterfall of the chimes music. It washed over her like a smooth elixir. She was lost in it, so natural, so safe…

Daniel's voice. The realization jarred her to the present. Her stomach knotted with excitement. She turned sideways to avoid looking in his eyes.

"Yes, they are lovely." Claire smiled and looked down at her feet. *He talked to me. I'm talking to him right now.* "Excuse me."

She began to walk away, but Daniel called out to her. "We've seen each other before. We've met, I think. I saw you here, maybe last week?" Daniel said to her back.

Her cheeks started to flush. *He's following me.* Even from several feet ahead of him she could smell his cologne and shampoo. Turning her head slightly, but still looking down she replied, "I think you have me confused with someone else. It happens all the time." Claire's heart raced, and she started walking again, increasing her speed to lengthen the distance. His voice pulled at her heart, spoke to it. Her heart wanted her to stop.

Her mind knew it was dangerous and that she had to get away.

Between two stalls a large vegetable truck loomed in front of an alleyway. She quickly slipped in the empty space and looked around carefully. *No one here to see me.* In the privacy between this truck and another stall, she shifted into disappear.

Claire made a hasty exit around the other side of the truck, until she stood right next to Daniel as he stood, watching the alley. He walked forward, and finding the alley vacant, he turned fully around, scanning the area. Since there was no sight of her, he repositioned the flowers he had bought and the green handle bag containing something lumpy, and walked off down the aisle. His head moved from side to side as she watched him walk. He was searching still.

He wants to find me. He looks for me.

She watched his casual gait, the way his jeans covered the tops of his athletic shoes, the black hair on his forearm that held the bouquet of roses to his chest, and how the other arm swung back and forth clutching the green bag full of the market's bounty.

She trailed farther behind Daniel, catching glimpses of his back or the sides of his face between the crowds. He stopped, examined and tasted samples, and looked over other stalls before finally moving off toward his car. Before he unlocked his door, he turned and surveyed the market one last time, his eyes looking right through her without detecting her presence. He finally drove away, leaving Claire standing in the wet parking lot, invisible, breathing hard. Something in her chest was throbbing with a dull ache.

Deep in her heart, she felt excitement that Daniel had actually gone looking for her. In all the years of being a Guardian, no one had ever done that. Though it was not a safe thought, she secretly hoped it would happen again. For the first time she wondered what would happen if she gave in to the attraction she was feeling for Daniel.

If God made all things in the universe, how could it be wrong?

"Macy's again? Boy, aren't we the little spendaholic? You know they have meetings about that." Doris pulled up in front of the store. "Receipts, remember the receipts," she said to Claire's back.

Claire didn't pay any attention. She was on a mission to speak with Angela again.

She met her at the mall and they spent the remainder of the morning and afternoon together, taking turns getting their makeup done at Macy's, wandering through the perfume counters, sitting to watch the shoppers in the mall over hot chocolate.

"You'd best be careful, Claire," Angela said seriously. "Sounds like you are getting a bit too influenced."

"So, what do you do, when the influence...flows?" Claire wasn't sure how to put it.

"Flows?"

"It just seems like it flows. I don't know how else to describe it."

"You're falling in love."

Claire felt like Angela had slapped her. She wasn't sure whether she was more upset about not knowing the obvious signs or that Angela thought she wasn't able to complete her mission. "That's silly, Angie. It's impossible."

"Are you having trouble staying away from him when he is in the room? Does your skin seem to leap out to touch him?" Angie looked amused. "Could you pick his scent out from a crowd of people? Can you hear his voice from a block away? When he speaks to you do your ears buzz?" The older angel looked at Claire with concern in her eyes. "You don't have to tell me—I can see it in your face."

Claire looked down. Her emotions were confusing her, forcing tears into her eyes. She looked at her friend, now feeling the pain and the peril of her predicament.

"What do I do?"

"Ah, the age-old question. I have spoken to Father about it before—not about you, of course."

"Are our conversations here private?" Claire whispered, her eyes wide.

"What do you think?"

"No."

"Tell me, have you ever seen anything Father does not know about?" Angela asked.

Claire shook her head slowly. But she wasn't sure about her secret memories of her human life. "Why is this happening? It never happened before." Claire needed answers.

"I have a theory about this. I think sometimes we get paired with someone we would have been paired with in the human world. Then it is more difficult, you see. It's harder to keep your distance. I think he knows your struggle."

"Daniel?" Claire asked.

"No. Father of course!" Angie shook her head. "If Daniel ever finds out about you, there will be real trouble. You can't show your human form to him in a dream. Don't go there."

"What kind of trouble?" Claire asked.

"He could lose his soul and be lost to us forever. He's not to know anything about having a Guardian. He has to think they are his own dreams, not ones you embellish." Angela took a deep breath. "It happened to me. That is how I know."

"What happened?"

"We fell in love. I couldn't help appearing to him, not in the flesh of course, but in his dreams. We were inseparable. He wanted to dream all the time. I was in danger of, well, you know, appearing to him in the flesh, and thought about having sex with him. I went home to ask for some advice, get some help, like you're doing now. When I returned, he thought I'd abandoned him. I even warned him all about the dark side, and he still went there. Some dark angel grabbed him. It was my fault. I have to live with that, forever!" She looked up at Claire. Her eyes were wet too. Claire took her hand softly in both of hers.

"I am so sorry, Angie. I didn't know. This was James, your charge last year, right?"

Angie winced. "You know there is a theory on that too. I can't say his name, or I will summon him."

"Again, I'm sorry, Angie."

"You want to know the worst part about it?" Angie's eyes showed all the internal conflict of her words. "I look for him everywhere."

Both angels paused, watching humans pass them by—families—whole families, with children. "Have you ever thought about being a mother?" Angela asked.

"Not really."

"Well, I did. I thought about all of it. Marriage, children—even breast-feeding. Isn't it funny? Something I'll never have, but I would never have minded getting up at one or two in the morning to feed a child. Some humans complain about their kids, even resent them. That is something I just can't understand. They don't know what a miracle life is, do they?" She sighed again. "No, I was confused, very confused, but I was one of the happiest angels you have ever seen." She smiled to the mug of hot chocolate.

"What did Father say when you asked for his advice? Was he mad?"

"Not really. But he said to find another way without breaking the rule. Find the strength in my heart to make it work, somehow. Never give my whole heart away. Keep that part of me an angel forever. And then come back home. I thought I could fix it somehow."

"What else could you have done?" Claire was curious.

"I've asked that question millions of times. I honestly can't say."

"Father still lets you come down here, knowing about your failure?"

"Guardians fail all the time. Look at Carmen and those girls that work with the streetwalkers. They lose more than half of their charges. It was only once for me. I think he has enough faith in me that I can still do my job. I was never the risk taker you are. This guy just came on me right out of left field. I went home to get help, before we did anything irreversible. You understand."

Claire did.

"I have no idea what they would have done with me if I let this relationship bloom. I was going to have the full on experience, and I returned still not sure what I would do. One thing for sure, I'd have been ruined as a Guardian."

Claire asked, "You know about the cemetery?"

"What cemetery?"

"The one behind the greenhouse. Mother ever take you there?"

"Nope."

"Mother showed me just before I came down here." Claire told her about the scene.

"Holy cow. You remember any of the names?" Angela asked.

"One was Melody."

"Melody! I knew a Melody. Bright red hair, gorgeous. I thought she got transferred. That was years ago."

"Transferred to where?"

"Beats me. You think she's buried there?"

"Looks like it. No date on the stone, just the etching of a harp."

"Yeah, she played the harp beautifully. It was almost mesmerizing. She made everyone cry when she played, the music was so beautiful. Especially the Mothers. There was something very sad about her."

"Like she had a broken heart, you mean?" Claire probed.

"She tried to talk to me, and we just never got together. Then she was transferred. You think she's actually buried, I mean, in the ground there?"

"Why else would there be stones?"

Both angels thought in silence. Claire was a little nervous Mother had confided in her now. She looked back at her friend. "Angela, what will you do if you see him again?" Claire asked.

"If I see him again, one of two things will have happened." She looked at Claire with no expression, "Either he has come back to battle with us as a dark angel..." she looked off to the side, not wanting to meet Claire's gaze, "or I have gone dark."

"No! Surely there are more choices than that," Claire pleaded.

Angela shrugged. "Maybe I will know what to do when the situation arrives. Maybe I just need to trust in our training...One thing I know for sure, Claire. Don't appear to him in his dreams. Please don't do what I did."

CHAPTER 15

After sunset, Claire looked into Daniel's living room through the large picture window. He was drawing, fully engaged.

Good.

She willed entry just inside his front door, staying invisible. She resisted the temptation to watch him paint.

Not wise. I need to be in control.

Don't do what I did. Angela's words stuck with Claire. She couldn't put Daniel's life in jeopardy. But the truth was glaring: she was falling in love with him.

He had already completed three other pictures that were drying by the fireplace. The white papers curled slightly from the heat. He stood as he worked, the table adjusted to counter height. His head moved from side to side so he could look at the shapes and colors at different angles. First right, then left, then at a distance. He leaned forward and was working on a delicate part, his face not more than a couple of inches from the paper. His fourth finger on his right hand was working in a beautiful color of dusty rose. Claire resisted the temptation to place her head next to the paper so she could feel his breath on her face.

The roses were in a clear vase on the dining table. She thought them an odd color for a man to buy, but she recalled how these had been the most fragrant—almost spicy. She looked over at the fireplace, now lit and without a trace of that awful scene. He had put a new area rug over the stains on the light brown carpet. The walls were re-patched and painted, courtesy of the crew he'd hired last week. This actually was a very pleasant room, she thought.

He had put on a Gregorian chant. Another strange choice. Apparently satisfied with the results of his painting, he picked up his glass of wine and went over to the overstuffed chair and collapsed in it, holding his wine by his fingertips around the top of the glass.

He appeared deep in thought, as if searching out answers in the flames that lived there. The cream color of his flannel shirt seemed to soak the warmth. Yellow light from the fireplace reflected from the deep pools of his dark brown eyes. The soft shirt raised and lowered with his breathing. The wine stained his lips. She watched as he sipped the red liquid, swirled it, and then swallowed sensually.

The movement of his throat all the way down to where the black hair from his chest appeared just above the unbuttoned top of his shirt enchanted her. Fingers on his hand tapped the upholstery along with the music of the chant. His shirttails were out, and his long lean body ended in black stocking-clad feet crossed at the ankles.

Claire wanted to see what was left on the easel. She eased forward to get a good look, and her cheeks turned flaming red when she stared down at an incredible likeness of her own face staring back at her from the paper. Her whole body shook. He had remembered every detail, along with the intricate embroidery pattern on her gown. She looked at the painting again. Her short golden hair framed her pale face and blue eyes like there was a light shining just behind her.

Claire saw an emotional connection there. The painting made her eyes well up. Her angel heart was beating so loud she was sure he must be able to hear it. He had seen her before. Could he feel her presence now? She thought not.

Her eyes darted over to the paintings now completely dry in front of the fire. One was a side view of her bending down to smell the pink roses at the market. It showed the delicate detail of the hairline at the edge of her face, the smaller unruly hairs that resided there. He had framed the way she touched things with the shape of her hand. This was a picture from today, she realized. The roses on the dining room table were the ones she had touched and smelled at the market.

The painting to the right of this one was also a scene from the Farmer's Market. It was a frontal view of her inhaling the pungent scent of a large pink grapefruit. Her eyes were closed.

He was watching me long before he saw me at the wind chimes!

The last one was a dark picture. She squinted to see what it was, and after some seconds realized it was a drawing of the inside of the planetarium. He was sitting in one of the cushioned seats, and behind him, was a golden image of Claire leaning forward, close to the back of his head. She hadn't been paying attention, as she'd been so wrapped up in the smell of his hair. How had he seen her?

What is going on?

She thought about her conversation with Angela this afternoon again. She'd been bold enough to ask Angie, "So, what is it like, loving a human? I mean, having him love you back?"

Angela had sighed and closed her eyes. She'd taken a minute before she responded.

"Better than anything I have ever experienced in Heaven."

CHAPTER 16

Daniel walked through the front door, dropping keys in the brown wicker basket on the stand, interrupting Claire, who'd been reading *Warrior of the Highlands*. She loved him in the azure blue shirt he wore today. It contrasted with the tanned skin of his face and neck. His long, strong neck disappeared into the top of his shirt as he turned his head.

His portfolio case strap slipped down his arm as he leaned the thin black bag against the stand. He sighed. He had not shaved yet, so his stubble was thick and blue-black. Claire thought maybe she'd get lucky tonight. Other than watching him paint, watching him shave was her most favorite thing.

Now so familiar with his patterns, Claire knew that after showering he'd either get ready for bed, or go out. That meant no more reading, for now. She could leave the book next to the table with the book clip light attached, as both these things had arrived with her from Heaven; they would stay invisible.

Daniel unbuttoned the blue cotton shirt as he mounted the stairs to his bedroom. Claire then heard his belt buckle signal its release. She pretended this strip tease was meant for her eyes, so she sat back in the overstuffed chair and enjoyed the view. But when she spotted him completely naked at the top of the stairs, headed for the bedroom with his clothes over one arm, she bolted up the steps three at a time to stand behind him.

She had seen naked men before many times. But not like Daniel. Her skin felt pulled in his direction.

The tips of his black hair lightly kissed his smooth broad shoulders. She watched the muscles in his lower back move in rhythm as he leaned down to put the clothes in the wooden hamper. Almost a foot behind him, she could not miss the warm male scent of him. She closed her eyes and let his aroma overtake her.

He heated up the shower water, waiting a few seconds before stepping into the tub and pulling back the curtain. It didn't take long for Claire to smell the shower gel he bought at the farmer's market. *Lavender and grapefruit, hmmm.*

She felt drawn to the curtain, though she knew it was unwise. She removed her white angel gown with the seed pearls and gold embroidery, placing it carefully, invisibly, over his towel on the bar. After inhaling once more the soapy scent, she willed herself through the curtain and stood behind his beautiful body.

He was just too perfect. Too beautiful. She ached to touch him, but was not ready to break this rule, which would separate them forever. She couldn't bear the thought of not being in his presence, limited as it was.

Claire noticed her nipples grew hard and knotted into little nubs. There was a glowing that started at her belly button and extended down to a place between her legs she did not know existed before. But from her books, she knew this was a full-on arousal. Another first. Another gift.

Her arousal made her curious. So she put her hands up to the backs of his shoulders, keeping a very small distance from his flesh. She could feel the warmth of his skin below her fingertips, but did not touch. Carefully she laid a cheek against the airspace at his upper back. She let his warmth come into her body as she melted in its deliciousness.

But then something amazing happened.

He started, and then slowly turned around to face her, looking through the steam as if trying to focus on something.

He senses me.

Caution would have told her to withdraw immediately, but she was too curious about this human experience. She stepped back slightly as she noticed his full erection.

How can this be? He couldn't even see her! She knew his active imagination had conjured up a picture he obviously liked very much.

She raised her palms to his chest and felt the warmth again. His dark brown nipples contracted when her fingers laced the air above them. His brown eyes with the long silky lashes were wide, searching the steam.

He's looking for me.

He parted his lips and licked them, leaving them open for her. She couldn't stop herself from rising to touch the air space close to his face, then down to brush her lips over his luscious mouth. She wished his lips could kiss her right now. Her heart was pounding. She couldn't take any more. She dropped her hands to her sides.

He slowly closed his eyes and his hands came up to where her face was. He stopped just short, and pressed his thumbs against the air next to her lips, his fingers under where her jaw would be. She parted her lips for fingers that could not touch her.

He feels my heat. He knows I am here.

He began to bend to her mouth. Lips on lips that would not really touch. She held her breath.

There was an instant where she thought her body was going to override her invisibility control. This scared her. She immediately willed herself out of the shower and stood watching the curtain, breathing heavily.

Close. Too close.

Daniel whipped aside the curtain and searched the steamy little room as if looking for evidence of her, and then turned off the shower.

When he grabbed his towel, Claire hoped some part of his clean scent would remain on her white gown, which had rested there. This would leave something for later while she was alone. He placed the towel around his thin waistline as her gown sank to the floor, invisible to his eyes. Claire quickly pulled it over her head and stood at Daniel's side. He looked into the mirror as he combed his hair.

He pulled out his lime cologne and dabbed his cheeks. Did she see a little crooked smile on those lips? Was there a twinkle to the side of his eye? What was this new behavior? Claire almost went into orbit.

He's playing with me. He knows I'm here.

Uh oh.

She realized what she had done. This would be hard to explain. All this was new territory for her. But it was such an attractive fantasy, Claire couldn't help but follow him into the bedroom as he pulled back the covers of his bed, dropped his towel and stretched his long lanky frame into the bedding.

His torso with the dusting of black hair at his upper chest was propped against the headboard and blue pillows. He had a smile on his face, but his eyes were serious, half lidded.

What does this mean?

And then he said the words she never thought she would hear in all her years as a Guardian. He stretched his massive arms out at his sides and whispered, "Come to me, Angel."

CHAPTER 17

In all of Claire's years as a Guardian, none of her charges had asked for her to appear. None of them had known she existed, even though she had some close calls. But then, she hadn't showered with any of them either, like she had with Daniel. She'd never been attracted to the look of their skin, their scent; she hadn't found the sound of their voice intoxicating. She didn't long to sit by the hour and watch what they did. She used her dream interventions to get the job done efficiently. With Daniel, she wanted to have a relationship. And this was new, and very dangerous.

She'd appeared in her charge's dreams, sure, but not so they knew it. If she appeared in Daniel's dream tonight, he would know her. Things would ever after be altered.

And Claire knew she was going to do it. There wasn't a question in her mind. She knew appearing to him was wrong, but would anyway.

What would the consequences be?

She shuddered. The doorway was opened, and she was going to walk right through. She hoped that somehow Father would find a way to understand. Maybe he would see this as a different kind of love, one worthy of a pardon.

Part of her wanted to hold his soul in her small hands, protecting him forever. Wanted to lay her head on his chest and have him know she heard his heart beating there. Wanted his arms to wrap around her waist and hold her tight, as if she was human.

But Claire would never be real. He could see her in a dream, but not touch her skin. They could touch only if she appeared in human form outside the dream, but this could get her tossed from the Guardianship forever.

She felt energy emanating from her expanded heart, beating wild and free. The look of him, and the knowledge he wanted to be with her brought sweet sensations all over her body. It stimulated places she had not known existed.

Rubbing her index and third fingers with the thumbs on both hands, Claire created dust that sparkled as it fell to his chest. He angled his head and his eyes widened when he saw the dust falling around him. As the sparkles fell, she blew her dust into his eyes. They closed. It was the first time ever her charge had seen the dust coming.

It feels so natural to do this.

Daniel's chest rhythmically rose and fell while he accepted and inhaled fully the scent of her breath, laced with her dust.

It used to take several minutes before he would enter the dream state, but of late, his motivation had been keen to get there right away. Tonight was no exception. Claire wondered where he would choose to begin this encounter, in light of the sexual overtones of the shower.

Let him show me first. She could always adjust, if necessary. Claire felt excited and impatient, waiting for something to show itself on his screen, like waiting for the film to begin in a dark movie theater. Waiting, like a young girl searching for the sight of her lover in a crowd. This was going to be something special. This dream was going to go where others had not before. *For both of us.*

Claire wasn't surprised to find the dream begin on his bed, but instead of his bedroom, he had positioned it in front of the fireplace in his living room. She blushed at the thought he expected a night of passion, and it tickled her. Yet, as wonderful as the thought was, she knew it would have to be the first thing she adjusted in the dream, as this could interfere with her job. It was also very dangerous.

In dream state, Daniel opened his eyes and beheld Claire sitting on the bed next to him. He immediately reached out to touch her face, but his hands went right through her image. Disappointment spread across his eyes. His brow furrowed.

"We won't be able to touch each other." Claire's voice was soft, watching him explore her. He looked thirsty. "But we can talk," she added.

"It's you." His face showed surprise.

Does he remember me from the farmer's market? Claire lowered her eyes. *Perhaps I am blushing.* She did not want to reveal too much of the confusion going on inside her. Her heart pounded in her ears at the sight of him examining her all over.

"I've seen you before. Or I've seen glimpses of you. You wear white, just like now, don't you?"

"Yes, Daniel."

"What do I call you?"

"Claire."

"Claire," he murmured.

How wonderful that sounds. She would remember this forever.

Recognition hit his face, "Like on the paper that night. You wrote your name on the paper."

"Yes." Claire blushed and looked down.

"You were there in the room. You put up the crystal." He scrunched up his eyes. The creases at the sides of his mouth formed and disappeared as he spoke.

"Yes. I stay up in the attic sometimes when you're not home."

"Why can I feel some things here? The fire. The bed. I feel the air around me, my skin." He rubbed his own fingertips together. "But I can't touch you?" He reached forward again to take her hand, but moved right through it like it was a hologram.

"We're in the dream state. I don't fully control it. I can help you see things. Some images you direct, some I do. You probably feel like we're here, but we are not real right now." She sighed. "I mean I'm never real, but right now neither are you. This is a dream."

Claire watched him grapple with the idea. She could see he was having difficulty understanding any of it.

His chest was bare, since he had shown up in his dream just as he went to sleep, completely naked, legs covered by his bedcovers. Though she had seen him so many times, she admired anew the smooth tanned skin and muscles underneath, the sinews and smaller muscles at the base of his neck, and the way his full lips had moved when he'd spoken. She gazed at the shallow furrows between his eyes beneath his wide forehead. He seemed to look right into her angel soul, like he knew every part of her.

Was he seeing in her a masterpiece? Was he inspired? Did her face bring to him the joy his brought to her? Was it possible there was a place in Heaven or Earth where this relationship without touch could be allowed to flourish? Maybe that could be enough…

She showed him the image of what his real body was doing, sleeping soundly, stars in the distance shining through the window above the bed. The hologram played a few feet in front of his seated frame. In it, his arms were outstretched just as he had left them when he'd said, "Come to me, Angel."

But his eyes were closed and he was obviously asleep.

"This is what's real," she said as she looked from the image back to his face.

How many times had she traced the line from the top of his forehead along the curly hairs at the sides of his face, down in front of his ears with the twin creases there, down the long neck to the beginning of his substantial chest?

He turned to face her, just a few inches away. She was not afraid to show the devotion she felt inside. For the first time in her angel life, she wanted a human to recognize her feelings. She wanted him to see her for who she was.

"I have questions," he started, then paused.

How like him, wanting to know how things worked, what the medium was. "Go ahead," she whispered, feeling timid.

"Why are you here? Who sent you?"

"You know who sent me. I am your Guardian angel, Daniel." She saw he was still puzzled, so she added, "I was sent to save your life. You remember, the night you…" She cleared her throat, then started again. "I was the one who pushed the fire alarm. That night I intervened on your behalf. But tonight, I am part of your imagination, your dream."

"No. Impossible. You are real to me."

"But not real. Not real…" she repeated.

"Am I dead?"

She laughed. "Noooo. What a silly question!"

"Will you be with me forever?"

"No."

"How long?"

She paused before speaking. Best to tell him the truth. "Until my work is done."

"When will that be?"

"I don't know that. It depends on you."

"What can I do to keep you here?"

"Nothing. I'm not real, remember?" A tightness grew in her chest. She sucked in air.

"Why?"

"Father's rules. Do you make the sunrise, the wind, the fragrance of roses?"

"You brought those back to me, those colors, those smells."

"Not really, I helped you find them. They were always there. You had just forgotten. They didn't change. You did. Your inner vision changed."

"Why?"

She bit her lip, not wanting to remember that black night. "To save you."

"Save me from what?"

"Death, by your own hand."

"But we all die. You can save me from death?"

"No, not entirely." She shook her head. "You will die too, but not for a long time, I hope."

"Have you died?"

"Yes."

"So you lived? You were real at one time?"

She nodded.

"But you are not alive now?"

"No, not in the same physical sense as your body."

"Why? How did you become an angel?"

"I was chosen by Father for this job of Guardian."

"But you died."

"Yes, some ten of your years ago, and then I was chosen to be a Guardian. And don't ask me how that happens, because I have no idea. I interfered with your temporary decision to end your life, but I cannot save you from death."

"Who decides this?"

"Father."

"God."

"We call him Father."

"Are there other angels?"

Claire's smile was wide. "Thousands of them. They are all around you, you just didn't know it."

"So you take care of other people too."

"No. I am your angel. Your Guardian angel."

"Why can't I touch you?"

"In your dream state you can see me. Touching only occurs in your human state. I can appear in human form, but that is forbidden."

"Why?"

"It's just the rule." She looked into his eyes, and with a bit of hesitation added, "I'm not supposed to appear to you in any form, even dream state. But I'm breaking the rules a bit for you. I wanted to clear up your confusion. I knew you could sense me."

Claire saw Daniel deep in thought. She knew, under normal human circumstances, he would hold her hand, would put his arm around her. He'd whisper words in her ear, and she would feel his breath on her face. She knew exactly how she would feel as a result. But this was a dream, and these things were not possible.

I have to keep telling myself this.

"Can I command you to do things?" Daniel asked.

"Like what?" She held her breath, felt a little electric current run down the back of her neck.

"Stay."

"Not possible," she said with a slight smile to her lips. She liked where this was going, although it was dangerous ground.

"Make love to me," he said looking at her again with those brown eyes that reached deep into her soul.

"I already love you." This was true. She added, "An angel's love is special, different than any other's. And it never goes away. We live forever. We love forever."

"Can you love me like a human woman, like the human woman you were?"

Claire had to be careful here. Her feelings for Daniel were already more complicated than she'd ever experienced before.

"I'm not allowed to physically love you. I can only love you like an angel does, in spirit. Is that not enough?" She tilted her head slightly, feeling full of lightness and grace.

"So if you live forever, why can't you stay as my angel forever?"

"I stay until my work is finished. Father makes that ultimate decision. You are a person of the Real World and I am a person of Heaven. Perhaps someday you will join us there too."

"Why is it a rule not to touch?"

"So humans will have faith. When you don't know, it requires more faith. You live here. You can't live with me. I can't live with you." She was surprised by the wave of grief that washed over her when she said this.

"What if I chose to be in dream state twenty-four seven?"

"Then I won't have saved you, Daniel. That's escaping reality. You will need to make better choices than that to truly live."

"So, I can't touch you. Ever."

"That's right."

"But I can choose to see things in my dreams."

"Yes, within reason."

"Show me what we would look like making love."

This caught her completely off guard. She looked down at her folded hands, embarrassed. She knew in the Real World she would have let him advance on her, kiss her. The constraints she was under made her job very difficult.

"But our relationship isn't physical. It never will be." She searched for a reaction from his face and got it. *Is there a little pain in his eyes? Just a little?*

"But what about the shower? I felt your presence. I felt…something there. We felt each other, I know we did."

"I didn't say it was impossible, just against the rules," Claire admitted. "I was surprised about the shower too. I'll have to do a little research on this."

Daniel opened his arms out to his sides, the strong biceps flexing under his smooth skin. "Research all you want." He made that crooked grin again. She wanted to touch the little laugh lines at the corners of his eyes. She wanted the strong arms to enclose and encapsulate her small body. But this would not be for today. She sighed.

In the Real World, Claire would never have been able to resist him; he would have had his way with her long ago. She knew with certainty there could be no physicality in the dream state. But she loved lingering in the place where they both experienced that desire. *I want to feel this a little while longer.*

"Can I ask you a question?" she asked.

He nodded.

"What did you think I was when you saw me in your dreams?"

He smiled. Now he looked down at his hands folded in front of him. With boldness she did not expect he replied, "You were and are the girl of my dreams. My muse."

The excitement that coursed through her body took her by surprise. She had trouble breathing. However, the truth of their situation quickly set in. Once again she became aware of the infinite space between them. They were only inches apart, but in reality, worlds apart. Each longed for something the other could not give.

She wanted him to take her in his arms and crush her mouth with a delicious kiss. It was a pleasant vision, but it also broke her heart. The silent communication of their eyes fed her soul, but gave her pain.

Who will push the fire alarm in my internal living room now? Am I not considering suicide of my immortal soul?

Claire broke it off to ask another question. "When did you first see me?"

"It was at the planetarium. I was looking at the heavens, the twinkling lights, and, well, I just seemed to lift out of my body. Soon I was above my head looking down and I saw you sitting behind me." At Claire's nod, he added, "You saw the picture?"

"Of course."

"Just like that. You didn't notice me looking. At least, I didn't think you did." He hesitated to ask the next question. "Does this mean I have special powers too? Maybe we are a match, then?" He looked up at her as if searching for good news.

"No, you fell asleep and you saw me in your dream. Sorry, Daniel. No special powers."

Claire made a mental "note to self." That night she had been distracted thinking about running her fingers through his hair. She must have projected herself there. It was a dangerous accident, due to her lapse in concentration. But she was secretly delighted with the outcome.

"What about the other times?" she asked.

"I saw someone in white in a couple of my dreams. I thought you were perhaps a fairy, a muse. I looked for you. I tried and tried. Couldn't make it work. So I decided to go for it outside of a dream."

"The Farmer's Market?" she said.

"Yes, I recognized it in my dreams. I went to re-create the colors I remembered, and I saw you there. I saw you later, at the wind chimes place, remember? It was you, wasn't it?"

"Yes. I was trying to avoid looking at you. I'm not supposed to in human form."

"I touched you that day. I touched your arm," he said, reaching to touch her there again, but his fingers went into the image of her.

"Yes. I felt it too." *Careful, careful.* "But I'm not going to let that happen again. We can't do that, Daniel. Sorry. It would be the worst kind of transgression for me. Possibly for you as well."

He frowned and searched her face. Claire found it intoxicating to be studied in such detail by a human male. He continued to study her and said, "I thought that if I was dreaming these places, I should go see them in real life. Then when I kept seeing you, and you didn't want to talk to me, well, I kept hidden. I watched you. That's how I got the inspiration for the paintings."

He leaned back, a puzzled look on his face. "I understood the planetarium, the flower market, the Farmer's Market, the beach, the bookstores. But why take me to the Laundromat in my dreams?"

"Um, the smell of clean laundry, fabric softener sheets, soaps?" Claire answered and winced. He laughed, and she shrugged.

"The perfume counter at Macy's? I thought I was having a gay fantasy for a while. I mean, I love perfume, but on a woman's body."

She was tantalized by his soft Brazilian accent when he said "woman's body." He was smiling at her when she looked up again. *Healthy male. Confident. Used to getting what he wants. Ah, and patient too. Oh no, can't go there.*

"So you felt led?" *Have to say something.* Claire was seeing herself spreading massage oil over his body. She was irritated with herself at the images. *This is not helping. Think!*

"Oh yes, definitely. I was a willing participant but I didn't see these things as coming from my memories. That's why they affected me so. I loved, almost"—he had a twinkle in his dark eyes as he smiled—"almost all those places, or grew to love them."

Do they make lavender massage oil? Stop it!

129

"You found them inspiring?" Claire raised her eyebrows and tried to look serious, studious.

Daniel, inspire me. Take me away from this prison I call my angel life.

She sucked in a quick breath. *What am I saying?*

"Very. Look at how many paintings I've done in the last month. I've never been so prolific."

If I was human, we would have sex several times a day...Stop it. Stop it. Stop it.

"That's the way it's supposed to be. That's your gift," she blurted out.

You bet it is. Why couldn't I have met him when I was human?

He nodded.

"Daniel, I want to ask you about Audray," she began, needing to change the subject. He lowered his eyes. "You are still in pain there, I think."

Think? Claire, are you nuts?

"That will never go away." It was almost a whisper coming from him.

"You don't know everything about never," Claire corrected him.

"You don't know everything about pain," he answered.

True enough.

"So." He started to smile a bit as he asked this question, "How do you... save...me?" His brown eyes flirted shamelessly.

Those eyes. The crease at the corner of his mouth. Not fair, not fair at all. Claire was blushing, again. The fourth time at least.

"In a way, all I do is stay around until you save yourself."

Daniel immediately frowned. Not the answer he was looking for, apparently. He sat silent for a moment, then his expression lightened. "And so who saves you?" he asked with an innocent look, pressing with those eyes.

A very good question.

"I have the very best job in the whole world," she said. *What kind of a non-answer was that?*

He nodded in quiet agreement, and then furrowed his brow. He raised his eyes up to meet Claire's face. He whispered, "I wish you were here for me and not because it was your job. I wish it was the very thing you wanted to do most in all the world."

They looked at each other, neither moving. Daniel's dark eyes pinned Claire.

"But I'm not really a part of this world. Thank you, though. It was a wonderful thing to say."

Yes, wonderful. It was also wonderful also how it made Claire's heart do flip flops, made it sing. *So this is joy. So this is…*

He came to a kneeling position in front of her. "I still want to see us making love. I want to feel what that feels like."

It would have sounded good with any accent. *So do I. You have no idea how much I do.* "You have your fantasy world where all that happens. I only lead you in your dreams. I am not to be part of your real world."

He closed his eyes, opening them a few seconds later. "Did you see that?"

"No, Daniel. I don't see your thoughts." *But how I wish I could.* In Claire's fantasy she reached down and kissed his luscious lips and…

Then she remembered her job, her station. This was getting out of hand. Outside the dream, she rubbed her fingers together with her thumbs and added dust to his eyes.

This put him in a deep sleep with a blank screen. Claire sat the rest of the evening and watched his wonderful body. She drew herself up, encircling his waist and resting her head on his heart, listening, waiting, pretending there was a morning coming in a few hours where he would awaken to find her there in the flesh.

But tonight, no harm would come to her human as he peacefully slept in the cradle of her loving arms. She hoped tomorrow she would have better control over her emotions.

And then again, she hoped she didn't

CHAPTER 18

Things had changed. Daniel was painting, which was good, but he talked to her while he was doing it. He talked to her while he was cooking. He asked questions that got no answers. But he still kept trying. It was driving her crazy.

"Claire, I have an idea for a scene." He fought to scowl. "Guess what it is?" He looked around the room. "Just give me some sign you are watching me. I know you are."

About the fifth time he said it she picked up one of his chalks and threw it.

"My, we are angry today. Testy. I'm going to have to dream up some punishment for you tonight."

If only.

One day he brought down an armload of clothes from his hamper upstairs. "I have something for you." He held up a towel and one of his tee shirts. He put a load in the washing machine and turned it on. "Do you smell that? Isn't that wonderful, Claire?"

She was beginning to rethink her conversations with him in the dream state. He knew far too much about her. *Am I really so predictable?*

Claire decided she needed a break. *Too much temptation to appear to him in physical form.* His questions needed to go unanswered.

Claire would explain tonight what the rules were. Until then, she was on edge. She wanted to kill some time.

She went to investigate some of Daniel's haunts and decided to start with the gallery, willing Doris to appear for transport.

"God, I love it here," the cabbie said, leaning her head back. Her hat almost slid off. "I was so happy when I got your call. This place is just gorgeous. You got your wineries, the beautiful little country roads. This is a good gig for you this time."

"Sonoma County is lovely, isn't it?"

But I'd love anywhere he lived. He could live in the middle of an industrial dump and it would feel like Heaven…Listen to me. I've got it bad. Angela was right.

"So, where to, my dear?"

"That gallery, Craven Image. You know it?"

"Oh, yeah. The one that has all the rock stars' stuff in it?"

"Yes, that's it."

"You know what they have? I heard they have a toilet seat signed by the whole Spacetraveler band. Can you believe it? Framed and everything."

Claire laughed.

"Good idea to have it under glass, just in case, you know what I mean."

"I'm getting grossed out, Doris."

"Yeah, too much information. Well, here we are. Not open yet. You wanna go somewheres else?"

"No, I'm fine. I'll wait."

The bistro next door, aptly called Ravenous Ravioli, was open, and did a breakfast out on the patio, so Claire ordered a hot chocolate and waited. She loved to watch humans walking by.

At a quarter to ten, Audray made her way down the street, carrying a black portfolio bag. She was wearing a tight purple straight skirt and a cream colored silk blouse with a self-tie at its low neckline.

Claire could smell her cloying jasmine scent from the distance. She watched as delicate fingers managed a fistful of jangling keys, and then heard the door creak open. A rapid beeping alarm was abruptly terminated. A few minutes later, Audray returned to the front, bringing out a sandwich sign announcing a sale. The sign had a color picture of one of Daniel's paintings, now half price.

Claire's stomach churned. *I hate this woman.* She gripped the hot chocolate so powerfully she feared she might shatter the mug. The thought of anything Daniel had created being discarded or sold off at a discount made her blood boil. She abandoned her chocolate and decided to investigate.

Entering the gallery, she heard, "Welcome to Craven Image. Is this your first time to our gallery?" Audray's green eyes were bright but deadly. Even though her voice was lilting, Claire felt scrutinized like a piece of dirt. No doubt Audray had a keen scent for money. The woman frowned, leaning back to give a half-lidded look at the angel as if she was missing her glasses. Her red lips pouted and then turned into a snarl.

"Yes. My first time here." Claire was relieved to see Audray didn't recognize her face from Macy's. But then, she had been rather busy with the hairy guy, and Claire looked completely different without makeup. The angel felt a little wicked recalling that scene in the dressing booth, though it was one of her best performances.

Claire walked along the tiled floor, looking at several large canvases. There were six of Daniel's, done in hues of green and turquoise, jungle scenes at the edges of a beautiful white beach. Animal faces popped out from the dark green foliage. Their large eyes stared at Claire.

"I like these very much," Claire said. She hoped her voice didn't waver.

"Oh yes, the DePalmas. I've just put them on sale last week," Audray said. She had a small frown on her face as she studied the paintings.

"How come? I think they're lovely."

"We have to make room for new things. We've had them awhile."

Claire walked around looking at the violent splashes of color done by other artists. There were three large black and white photographs of Audray completely nude.

Audray followed closely behind, scanning the photographs like she was reading a newspaper.

"This one is by Beau Bradbury, lead guitarist of the Spacetravelers. See, he's signed it here."

"Ten thousand dollars! My gosh, why would anyone want to spend that much on such an awful painting?" Claire focused on her attitude, wanting to display superiority. She loved how it felt, especially in front of Audrey, who was a master of the mood.

"You can probably have it for eight."

Claire nodded and headed back to Daniel's paintings

Audray followed, then leaned into Claire and said, "These don't sell well. Not compared to the famous musicians. That's really who we cater to. We need the space. But Daniel is…" she sighed as she traced a pink spotted leopard's ear on one canvas, "…he's a good painter. The owner just wants to move on."

Like you have. Revenge, is this revenge I feel for the first time in my angel life? Mother would chastise her for these thoughts.

"So, tell me how much for all of them?" Claire suddenly didn't want anyone else to own them, or to know they were on sale. She wondered what Father would say about the expense chit.

"I'll have to call the artist, first."

"No, that won't be necessary. What would your gallery owner sell them for? I don't want the painter to have to decide. You know how it is with artists. They work so hard and then give everything away. Just doesn't seem fair. I have means."

Audray's smile was almost angelic, Claire thought. *Unless you knew what was going on inside her. Glad to be rid of him so soon?*

"Well, I have authorization to sell them for fifty percent, but maybe we could go, say forty-five percent? I might be able to do more if I call him. I know how to reach him."

You know how to dump him, you mean?

"No. Not necessary." Claire feigned going into deep thought. "Oh, why not? Let's do it. I'll take them all." The penniless angel tried to sound like she spent money frivolously and that this investment in the paintings wouldn't put a dent in her trust fund.

Audray took all six of the canvases down, stacking them carefully behind the counter between large sheets of bubble wrap. Claire had almost expected her to stack them on top of each other unprotected, but Audray was a better businesswoman than that. But she wasn't going to wrap them up until the sale was complete.

The calculation was done. "Ok, that will be thirteen thousand, eight hundred dollars. Let's just call it thirteen thousand even."

Claire was stunned. She was in a panic, but covered it up, summoning strength to return Audray's piercing stare. *How in the world will I get my hands on that kind of money?* How could she ask Doris for this? But her pride loomed. No way she would turn back now.

"Give me your bank routing number. I will have my manager wire you the funds this afternoon. Then I can pick them up later today. Does that work for you?"

"Absolutely. Uh, I should get a deposit."

Perfect.

"Miss, or is it Mrs.?" Claire made a point to bat her blue eyes, showing no concern.

"It's Miss. Audray Steele."

"Miss Steele, if I am going to spend this amount of money, it's important we trust each other. If you don't trust me, I will take my business elsewhere. Let's face it, there are a lot of gallery owners in Sonoma County who would love to make a thirteen thousand dollar sale today or any day, wouldn't you agree?"

The look on Audray's face was priceless. Or, maybe, Claire giggled, worth thirteen thousand dollars.

Claire collapsed on the bench seat as she got into Doris's transport.

"What's eating you, doll?"

"Uh, I just did something I probably shouldn't."

"Oh, just because we're angels doesn't mean we're perfect." Doris turned around in her seat, facing Claire. "Spill it."

"I just bought all of Daniel's paintings—on sale."

"What's wrong with that?"

"I don't have any money. At least not that kind of money."

"How much do you need?" Doris pulled out her wallet.

"Thirteen thousand dollars." Claire winced.

Doris tossed her man's billfold onto the passenger seat. "Oh, boy. No way Father's going to authorize that. What the blazes were you thinking?"

Claire shrugged, looking down.

"I'm glad I came, not one of the other drivers. I can fix this, no problem."

"How can you fix it?" She was worried this might make it worse.

"You don't want to know. You gotta promise not to tell anyone I can do this, though. And I might turn you down another time."

"Doris, you're not doing something illegal, like stealing or anything? I won't do that."

"Nope. No one is hurt. No stealing. But I'm not telling, either."

"Fair enough. Can you have the money wired to this account?" She handed the cabbie the slip of paper Audray had given her with the bank routing number on it.

"Yep, I'll do it this afternoon, unless you have other plans."

"No other plans. Thanks so much. Guess I got a little carried away. I appreciate what you're doing for me. Drop me a few blocks from his house. I want to walk a bit."

"Sure."

They drove past a couple of wineries. Claire thought she would like to try a tasting some time. *Better try it soon. No telling how much longer I'll be allowed here.* She decided she needed to make a list of all the things she wanted to do before she went back to Heaven. The paintings would go well in her bright dorm room with the single window…

"Uh, Doris, there is one other thing." Doris slammed her foot on the brakes.

"What now?" She frowned.

"Can you pick up the paintings for me later and take them home?"

"Jeez. I can see the gossip flying when I take those puppies up to your room. Claire, you owe me a big one."

Yep, that she did. Although what coming up with thirteen thousand dollars meant in the angel world, she had no clue.

That afternoon, Audray watched as a cabbie picked up the neatly bubble wrapped and well-taped canvases. Audray had expected a messenger service of the white-gloved variety. She thought it odd, watching the female cabbie drive away, that two of the paintings extended through the sunroof of the little cab. She didn't think she had ever seen a yellow cab with a sunroof, and could have sworn there wasn't one when they started loading the first two paintings.

And she certainly had never seen any of the art she sold sticking out of the ceiling of a car, flapping down the street. In fact, she'd never sold six in one day. She wondered where they would be hung. She hoped, for Daniel's sake, it was some place important.

CHAPTER 19

Tonight's dream started in the mall. Daniel watched Claire's eyes sparkle as she realized where they were going. She turned the Victoria Secret store into a candy shop with clear tubes filled with brightly colored candy sold in bulk.

Two can play this game, Angel.

Armed with the new knowledge he could control many things about his dream state, he walked over to a shelf filled with boxed sets of jelly beans, stacked about ten high. Under all of them was one black and pink box he carefully pulled out. He opened the lid while watching his angel blush, her eyes wide and her mouth open in shock.

Tucked neatly inside the box was a very light pink silk teddy with white gossamer ruffles glistening under the lights. He'd seen it in a magazine ad earlier in the day. Dropping the box, he let the teddy hang between his fingertips. It would only barely cover her belly button if she had put it on. Examining the box now laying at his feet, her eyes went wide when she noticed there were no panties. She blushed in earnest then and wouldn't look at him. When she did, he thought she would melt. His eyes refused to let her go.

"Will you wear this for me?" he asked, surprised at how rough his voice sounded. His pants had tented as he saw her struggle with an answer.

Yes, my little angel. Feel how I desire you. He knew she was grappling with the new experience. She was unprepared.

She looked around, as if needing help.

He ducked his head down to try to meet her eyes, still holding up the skimpy plaything.

"You can do this, Claire. I command it. As my Guardian. I want to see your body in this—this device of fantasy."

"Absolutely not."

"Why?"

"First of all, it's against the rules. And I am your Guardian, but I am not your sex slave."

"Ah, but you know what a sex slave is?" Daniel couldn't help but chuckle as her eyes darted around the room. Then she abruptly turned around with her back to him.

He leaned into her, his lips just above the pink flesh of her tender neck. He searched the spun gold of her hair, the tiny hairs along the velvet of her earlobes. She smelled like fresh rain on a bed of roses. He could see she had closed her eyes.

"I want to see you." His voice was husky. She arched her back and inhaled sharply at the sound of his voice. He stepped closer, feeling the quivering heat of her body against his chest and thighs. His groin ached.

"I want to see you naked, my love."

"You see me now," she answered back, carefully.

Her flushed cheek seared the miniscule airspace between them, and flamed his own.

"I want to see you in my arms. I want to feel your face when I kiss you in… places."

She couldn't look at him yet.

Turn, turn to me, Angel.

He placed his hands on her shoulders through the gown, and she allowed him to turn her around to face him. Daniel gazed at her full pink lips and wanted to explore further. He brought his hands to cup under her jaw line, without being able to touch her, and moved his lips just to the point at which the sensation of the warmth between them ended, before the nothingness.

She seemed to lean into him as he scented her heat. He felt she would let him draw her to him, letting him impose his will with her.

I want to touch you. Kiss you.

He inhaled deeply and closed his eyes, locked in the microscopically small space between them. The physical touch of skin on skin was the only sensation he was denied.

The swirling closeness of her enveloped him in shapes and color. His lips parted, hot with lust for the touch of her pale skin. He noticed the small changes in temperature as he inhaled her and then released her back to herself a changed being.

Daniel's eyes locked fully on Claire's face as he pressed her to a pillow somewhere where their mutual pleasure was possible. She was unashamed to be examined by this man. She felt like a kite, tied to his tether, and wherever he would go, she would have no choice but to follow.

Following him would be so natural, so human.

But she was not human. Sadness consumed her. She dropped her eyes and felt tears well up. For the entire world right now, she would have given almost anything to be real, to be a real woman, flesh and blood, belonging to Daniel.

His hands and arms motioned for closeness again and she felt the warmth of his body pressing against hers through their clothes. She laid her head on his chest and felt, as well as heard, his heart beating there, the miracle of the aliveness of him and the wonder of this perfect man. She wished he could hear it. She could feel it, but he could not.

They now walked through the mall side by side, his arm around her waist. The normal mall lights turned into the ceilings from the planetarium with all the millions of stars twinkling, lightly illuminating their path. A gentle music of harps and guitar teased her ears. She realized with a start of joy that he was giving her something he thought she would love. His intuition was creating a world for her, like a lover improvising, exploring, and heightening the senses for her enjoyment.

She willingly walked through his dream, feeling his body next to hers, moving in rhythm, and sometimes burning with the touch of his arm around her waist, sometimes with the brush of a thigh that spread its full length of muscle against hers. She was a fully willing participant, as though he was her angel and he was directing her dream.

They were standing in a store, arms entwined, looking down at a display of long sleeved evening gloves. With a little crooked smile, he unwound his arm from her waist and bent over, picking up a long black glove. He intimately opened the end of the stretchy material with his long, delicate fingers, looking into her eyes as his fingers encircled the opening and stretched it to gape open.

Her fingers seemed to have no choice but seek the folds of the fabric as she slid her hand up into the dark opening, filling the silvery black glove fully to the tips. She felt him pulling the material along her arm up all the way to her elbow.

The black object came to life and curled in the air as her fingers felt the pleasure of being so confined to his instrument of play. Encapsulated in the slinky material, now her fingers would be able to touch his skin and he would be able to feel her caress. He traced a line with his forefinger from where the glove ended at her elbow, all the way up her arm towards her fingers, slowly until his hand warmly found that it fit fingers to fingers between the little protrusions. He closed in on her gently.

Then he opened her hand, cupping it like one would hold water. He brought it up to his lips and pressed them into the palm of the glove and kissed it, drank from her spirit there.

She almost collapsed. Her breathing was ragged and heavy. She grew wet.

He brought her gloved hand up to his face and placed it tenderly against his cheek, looking at her, his eyes consuming her. Her fingertips traced the lines of his face, the little wrinkles at the corner of his eyes, across his hairline, and over his warm lips, feeling his breath through the black fabric as she felt his face for the first time. With his hand on her gloved forearm, he moved his fingers up and then slowly down, back and forth in a caress.

She dove the black glove deep into the shiny long hair she had wanted to touch since the first day she had seen Daniel. He delicately kissed her palm again, and, through the glove, nibbled all the way down her forearm to the crease at the inside of her elbow.

He tugged at the end of the glove, bringing his finger underneath it, not able to feel her skin, but exploring there as intimately as if he had slid his hand underneath her shirt to her breast. He wanted more of her to touch. She was thrilled.

How many times had Claire dreamed about what it would feel like to run her real fingers through his hair, have the touch of his warm hand on her arm, on her face? She had spent hours thinking about these things while lying next to him, protecting him as he slept at night.

She opened her fingers and extended them again through his hair, squeezing it in her gloved fist.

He closed his eyes and said, "You have no idea how wonderful that feels."

All of a sudden, his eyes started to frown slowly. The view was changing, breaking up. The dream was bordered in a black edge, which moved to the center, becoming larger and larger, and then everything was black. His screen had gone blank.

Daniel jolted awake from the dream. He had been holding a pillow to his bare chest, and as he opened his eyes, he tossed the pillow with frustration across the room. Annoyed that he'd woken up, ending the sensual dream, he stood up, moving away from the bed. Away from the source of his pleasure and pain. There was no hiding his full erection, stubbornly signaling what had caused him to awaken from the dream.

He began cursing this particular body part in Portuguese for having deserted him in a great time of need, and hoped Claire didn't understand what he was saying. He could not see her, of course, but had no doubt that she saw his readiness.

"Now, you can't tell me that isn't real," he said pointing to his groin in disgust. "Time for a cold shower. Care to join me?"

He shed his silk bottoms and stepped into a very lukewarm shower. He poked his head out into the bathroom, not sure where to look for her. "Sorry, you had your chance." He abruptly pulled the curtain back and continued with the shower.

He finished it off with a totally cold splash, whooping as the cold hit his body. He dried off, placing the towel around his waist. The cold shower had taken care of some of his erection, but not all.

He walked back into the bedroom and faced the window. Daniel stared out the window at the horizon, which had already started to bleed pink. Removing the towel from his waist, he used it to rub his hands through his wet hair, shaking his head from side to side.

"Is this as frustrating to you as it is to me?" he asked to the silent room.

He threw the towel on top of the hamper then sat on the bed, and, as he pushed his legs under the covers, muttered, "Not fair, not fair at all. You get to see me naked and I don't get to see you, except in a dream."

He punched one of his pillows and planted his head there. He wanted to sleep for eternity. He did not dream this time.

Claire thought of what had just occurred. Her chest was still heaving from the nearness of him and the feeling of his warmth upon her face, his hands up and down her arm through the fabric of the black glove.

Perhaps a remnant of her human side was excited and glad at the intimacy now growing between them. She was developing a very deep and fearless love for this human, regardless of the risks that placed on both their souls. It was spinning out of control.

A physical relationship endangered her status as an angel. It was bad enough to be seen, that in itself was a huge violation, but to be physically present to him in the human world, that would classify as a "Fallen" offense.

The stark reality was that she was an angel and would always be an angel, forever. And he was a human male, who needed to live in the Real World with a real woman, someone he could commit to, grow old with, and die with.

That was something she would never be able to provide him, even if somehow she were granted permission to stay his Guardian forever, or at least for his lifetime. There was no precedent for that. No matter how much she wished it, no matter how real the dreams felt, in the real scheme of things, this was only a dream. That was all it could ever be.

I am not accomplishing my goal. She knew in her heart that this was wrong and would have to stop. And she knew she would have to confess her failure to Father. Overwhelmed with her choices, she wondered who else she could turn to.

Claire felt utterly alone and lonely for the first time in her angel life. She now understood what it would feel like to lose someone, to be separated from them forever.

Grieving was not something any of the angels had training in. She understood it to be the flip side of the love she felt for Daniel, which made her love feel even more precious. For hers was a love she would have to give up, in order to save him.

143

But that would be another day. Perhaps she could have a few days of bliss before she had to make that decision. She was at the edge, but not quite ready to really cross the line. She wondered if she would have the strength to stop before that happened.

She made a decision she hoped she would not regret.

CHAPTER 20

Audray slipped the check in the envelope and sealed it with her tongue. Her forefinger brushed across the outside where she had written his name on it: Daniel DePalma. There had been a time when she halfway thought he could be the one. But she was the serial dating kind, and Daniel was the kind to find a woman to love him forever. But that wouldn't stop her from getting him back into bed. The man had been amazing in the sack.

Her pulse quickened as she drove up to Daniel's front door to deliver his six thousand dollar check. She could have mailed it. But something in her wanted to see his face when she presented him with more money than he had seen in a long time. Would he be willing to give her just a little taste of his luscious body in the form of thank you sex? He was and forever would be the standard by which she would judge all men. And she wanted him. Not forever, of course, but just a taste. Just for today.

She had chosen red, his favorite color. The dress was made of a stretch fabric, very low cut in the front, exposing the "enhancement" Neal had so lovingly provided her. He'd wanted to enlarge her just one size, but Audrey went for two. No sense going through all the pain and hassle if she would be just a little bigger. She needed to be memorable. And she certainly did like the way they felt now. That wasn't a bad thing, after all, to be in love with one's own body.

She sucked in air and instantly got wet at the sight of Daniel at the front door, with his blue shirt unbuttoned half way, revealing the rippled chest and flat abs of his beautiful body. He always distracted her with how he liked to wear his pants, low and loose.

She could see she did not have the same effect on him.

"Audray. What are you doing here?" He was frowning and didn't invite her in.

"Have you lost your manners? I bring gifts." She flashed him her most flirtatious look, and grazed her breasts across his chest as she slipped beside him into his living room. The male scent of him was a welcome and familiar elixir.

He rubbed his hands through the shiny black hair that her fingers itched to touch, and closed the door.

"Well, this is a surprise. How is your boyfriend?"

His Brazilian accent was even sweeter now. She remembered coaching him on the things she wanted him to whisper in her ear, things that turned her on unlike ever before, or since.

"My boyfriend is fine." She looked him up and down, her gaze finally settling on his crotch. She did not see his usual response there. "But I have to say, I've missed you." She walked to him, pressed herself against his body, drew her arms up around his neck and plunged her fingers into his hair at the back of his head as she pulled his mouth to hers. Her need of his lips was probably obvious. Something new for Audray.

But he did not kiss her back and separated them immediately.

Oh well. She sighed.

"I think you should leave. If you have come here—"

"No, Daniel. But the sight of you takes my breath away." It was a true statement, after all. "As much as I wish we could enjoy other things"—she raked over his lanky body again, taking in every square inch—"I've brought you something I think you'll love."

"Oh?" He seemed serious. No smile on his lips, or in his eyes. Audray could see she was dead to him now.

"Money!"

Instead of exhibiting excitement, Daniel let out a short laugh. "Money?"

"I sold your paintings. All of them."

"When?"

"Yesterday." She opened her purse and brought out the envelope. She walked towards him as slowly as she could, hoping to see some semblance of sensuality in his dark eyes, and whispered, "Six thousand dollars, Daniel." She held the envelope out, her red fingernails blazing under the foyer light. His gaze dropped to his name on the outside. He reached for it.

Audray immediately retracted the envelope and put it behind her back with a flirtatious smile. His eyes narrowed. Damn. He seemed to be immune to her charms. "Come and get it. Wrestle me for it, Daniel," she said through half lidded eyes.

He didn't move. He looked at his feet, put his hands on his hips, his long fingers accentuating the flatness of his lower belly and the two veins that led to his crotch below.

"I'm not going to play these games."

She imitated his accent. "Dees games. Dees games." She frowned. Still no reaction from him. She held the check up and waved it over her head. "Can't I get just one little kiss for this? A kiss for a check? One kiss for six thousand dollars? That seems like a pretty fair trade. More than fair."

He carefully stepped closer to her. Grabbing the envelope from her fingers with a little pull, he kissed her on the cheek.

CHAPTER 21

Doris struggled up the circular stairwell at the Guardianship dorm. She was attempting to get two of the largest paintings up to Claire's room without injuring them. She wondered how long it would take before she would be detected.

She didn't get far.

Ava stood at the top of the stairs. Doris was a little relieved it was one of Claire's friends. She'd made a habit of being scarce and barely knew anyone.

"What are you doing, Doris?"

"New form of exercise all the rage down below. Haul bubble wrap canvases up and down stairs." She stopped as she lost her grip on one of them, but Ava ran to catch it in time before it went sailing over the handrail.

"Where'd you get these?"

"Claire." Doris didn't really need to say more. They walked down the hallway, each holding one large canvas, bigger than they were. "Hope you got a key, or I'm breaking in."

"There isn't one." Ava opened the door.

"Jeez," Doris exclaimed as she looked at the disarray that was Claire's private sanctuary. It had been ransacked. They hadn't even tried to cover it up. "Little shits. Oops, sorry, girlfriend." Doris halfway expected an electric jolt from some unseen finger.

"I completely agree. For all she does for us you would think they would treat her with more respect."

"Claire would never do this, even in retaliation. That's what makes her so good. They're just young and out of control. Selfish. Not enough supervision." Doris sounded more reasonable than she was feeling. But she was in Heaven, after all.

They leaned the paintings on an interior wall, away from the sunlight streaming through the one window.

"I think I'd better get the others from the transport before we get spotted. Can you help me?"

"How many more?"

"Four."

"Wow. She must be inspired."

"I wouldn't exactly put it that way. I was thinking of another word, but I'm supposed to keep my mouth shut."

They hurried down the stairs. There was a small crowd around the transport.

"Alright, alright, nothing to see. Go on now. Don't you guys have a class or something? Someone to save? A plant to plant?" Doris said as she shoed away the six or seven angels who were looking inside the windows of the transport. They stayed in one group, whispering as they retreated.

"Guess it's not a secret now," Doris sighed. She opened up the rear door and carefully took out the other four canvases. The two angels each took two, and started up the path to the dorm. "Next I'll get the summons."

"What will you tell Mother?"

"Beats me, kid. I'll think of something."

"Does this mean Claire is coming home soon?"

"Nah." Doris stopped to catch her breath. She wasn't used to this kind of work. "That angel is going to stay down there as long as she can."

They continued up the front steps of the dorm building.

"Can you tell me who made them?"

"Her new charge, Daniel. Boy, is he a stunner. I'd ride him around in my cab all day, if you know what I mean."

Doris saw Ava smile and consider her comment. She was pretty sure Claire's books were quite an education for the young angel. Doris preferred books about bad boys on bikes. She kept them in the trunk of her locked transport, and in the safety deposit box she managed to sneak past her auditors in

149

New York City. She figured Ava had no firsthand experience—that she knew of.

"Is she okay?"

"She's not complaining. And that's a little new for her. Last few times she was, I don't know, just not happy with the job."

"Is she going to keep her record?"

"From what I understand—now this is just rumor, mind you—as long as Claire is around, this Daniel guy ain't going anywhere. But I think they're on a collision course." She adjusted the grip on her two packages before mounting the stairwell.

"Collision course? Like an accident?"

"Honey, there's no accident about love."

Happy for you, Claire. About time that girl had someone who could love her back as intensely as she loved others. Doris still worried about her, though.

They set the other four against the wall, checking the coverings.

"Should we open them up?" Ava asked.

"God, no! Oops, sorry. I don't spend much time here; I'm out of practice. Ava, I honestly don't know what is underneath these wrappings. What if it was a bunch of nudes?"

Love to see it, though. Wouldn't that be a scene? "Kid, what if they were nudie pictures of Claire herself?"

"I see your point." Ava glanced at the condition of Claire's room and said, "I'll tidy up a bit, and then I'll sneak a peek under the bubble wrap."

"Don't say I didn't warn you," Doris returned with a wink, and left, closing the door behind her.

Ava straightened the silk embroidered pillows on Claire's daybed, and repositioned some of Claire's romance novels back onto the bookshelf. A couple of the books had spines so well worn, the pages fell out. She smiled as she remembered the tour she and Claire had taken that first day they met, on Ava's first day in Heaven. What a magical day that had been.

It had felt like she woke up from a deep sleep as someone kissed the top of her head gently and whispered, "Welcome to Heaven, child." She had passed through a warm lighted mist that left the faint scent of lavender and citrus on her skin. She realized she was dressed in a white gown, sitting on a wooden bench seat in a small boat behind a row of other girls similarly dressed. In the distance a cherub choir was singing.

These little ones are angels too.

At the front of the boat was a long neck of a swan carved in wood extending up into the mist so high she almost couldn't see the top of the bird's head. There was a small thump as the boat reached its destination and, as if on cue, all the girls stood. Beyond the dock was a golden landscape punctuated by green gardens of brightly colored flowers waving in the gentle breeze.

Straight ahead soared a translucent building several stories in height. It appeared to be carved from one solid piece of glass with a roofline so tall it extended up into the clouds and disappeared.

Ava felt a hand lock into hers and turned to gaze on the new angel she was paired with. Her short, blond hair spun out of control in the sunlight, and her pale blue eyes reached deep into Ava's soul. Her new escort had flawless white skin, looking like it was carved from alabaster.

"I'm Claire. Welcome to Heaven," the angel said.

They only had a week together before Claire was sent away on her emergency mission with the painter. But they were inseparable during that time and knew somewhere in their erased memories they must have known each other. She missed Claire deeply.

They both loved the playhouse performances. It was packed on Friday and Saturday nights. Old fashioned candle stage lights and torches were used for lighting, illuminating the room in a flickering, constantly changing form, like the wings of butterflies. And of course, fire was never a problem.

One couldn't ask for a better audience, as angels were a most enthusiastic crowd. Regardless of the quality of the performance, the angel crowds always gave standing ovations. On occasion, there would be a lot of fluttering. The audience would elevate happily and throw off their dust. Sparkle would be everywhere.

When it got especially exuberant, it was not only a heady mess of scent, but emotions as well. Occasionally there would be little ones younger than five in the audience. They had to be watched carefully. Ava had seen them run out of the Playhouse screaming. It was a lot for them to take in.

Father had an ornate box in the first balcony to stage right. He would sit in his box with several of the Guardian Mother Instructors, his ladies as he called them. Ava had seen his face light up and knew the playhouse had a special place in his heart. He never missed a performance of Peter Pan. Never.

Peter Pan was everyone's favorite, performed with an all new cast each month. They had lots of time to prepare. The play had been adapted, and the Tinkerbell role was extremely coveted, but since it was given each month with a different cast, anyone who wanted the role would have the opportunity.

They came to the part where Peter asks the house to clap loudly for Tinkerbelle. The clapping was supposed to help her survive the poison she ingested to save Peter's life. It was the house's favorite part.

The last time she and Claire attended, there was more than the usual flutter and sparkle spray and clapping. Seated in the first three rows was a large contingent of the cherub choir, recently expanded. It was their first performance and they were perhaps a bit on edge, fluttery already. Their rosy cheeks bloomed under the house candlelight, and their sweet scent, warm smiles, and rapt attention added all kinds of emotion to the stage for the actors, as well as the rest of the audience. In fact, the angel who played Wendy became so overcome, she started crying spontaneously on stage and forgot her lines.

These types of performances were, in fact, what the audience loved best. Her scene drew a standing ovation. Tinkerbell was saved, as she was every month, the house rescuing her from certain death by their exuberant clapping. All ended in a happily ever after. Peter vowed never to grow up, and, as an angel here in Heaven, he never would.

Next, the cherub choir made their way noisily to the stage from the first three rows, with their director hovering about, attempting an orderly rank and file. In the end, it was useless.

What the choir left behind in the three rows they'd vacated was an assortment of stepped on jelly beans, spilled sodas in colored plastic cups, popcorn, caramel corn, and M&Ms—all favorite snack foods. That was when she learned the little ones loved the rewards of candy and soda, and they were allowed these indulgences without limit. Heaven had rules for its older angels, but the cherubs were literally spoiled at every opportunity.

But the candy and soda made it harder for this choir to stand with freshly starched white choir smocks. Most of them were smudged with colorful smears or spilled drink. Most things in Heaven were perfect, but Father allowed these little imperfections. In Heaven, no two performances were exactly alike.

Violence was never tolerated, and when a little tugging match ensued, four cherubs fell off the stands. Someone was led off the stage by his ear. The rest of the choir got quite distracted by the events and stopped singing, though the pianist hadn't noticed and for about ten bars exuberantly played a solo. The song had to be started over.

They got a standing ovation, of course.

Ava closed the door to Claire's straightened room, and wondered if she'd have to do this again. But, she wouldn't mind. She liked being in her space, basking in the warm light this legendary Guardian spent so much time in.

Come home to us, Claire. Be safe. Come home.

CHAPTER 22

It was a difficult decision, but Claire knew she needed to seek Father's advice. She summoned Doris with the message, and had an answer back within an hour. Father would to see her right away, this afternoon. She hoped it would be a quick conversation so she could be back to Daniel by dinnertime. She hated to leave Daniel, but he'd be painting all day and into the evening anyway. He wouldn't miss her if she left for a few hours.

Daniel focused on work. He needed to finish more paintings, and, because of the windfall sale from the day before, he was out of inventory unless he sold his personal favorites. Now that he had a little cash in the bank, he met with the bank manager, who was clueless when it came to all the problems he'd been having.

"There's a gremlin in our computer system, I'm sorry to say. And he's focused on you. I will personally purge it for you."

Daniel hoped this was true. Perhaps his worries were starting to get behind him. He wouldn't have to let loose of his favorite paintings to make ends meet. Not just yet. But he would if he had to. The manager offered to hang one up in the lobby. Daniel only thought it fitting to give him one he did of Claire smelling the dusty pink roses at the Farmer's Market, which was not for sale.

The manager looked at the title, "'Guardian Angel.' Nice. We all could use one."

"I'm hoping she'll watch over my accounts here." Daniel was serious.

He had some things to do to get ready for his dream tonight. He wanted to push the envelope a bit with Claire. Used to getting his way with women, he had never pursued an angel before. And when he thought about it, the women had done most of the pursuing, anyway.

But first he had to get some preliminary sketches done. He waved to the bank manager and turned for home.

He was bent over his easel when the girls arrived. One had lifted her shirt and had pressed her bare chest into the glass of his living room window and the other stood with her hands on her hips. Daniel was filled with more alarm than attraction. He seriously preferred to paint. He had completely forgot about Josh's "gift."

Knowing they probably would not leave unless he talked to them, he muttered to himself and crossed the room to the front door. He heard bantering and giggles on the other side of the glass window frame.

He didn't know what to say, but before him stood two absolutely drop-dead gorgeous girls—girls he'd usually consider his type. One was a blonde with shoulder-length hair, accessorized with some of the largest tits he had seen. They looked like they were raging to break out any second. The girl had a tiny waist, but nice hips. Daniel liked curvy girls, liked meat on them, and this one fit his tastes to a "T." Boy, did Josh know him.

The other girl was a brunette with long hair worn straight at the sides of her face, framed by bangs. This girl had an almost white complexion, highlighted by her luscious red lips. This one, Daniel noted, appeared to be the leader. Her black eyes pinned him before he had a chance to say anything, almost casting a spell on him. For a second, he couldn't move.

As if releasing the hold she had on Daniel, the dark-haired girl walked past him into the living room, surveying the surroundings. She turned, dropping her long jacket to reveal a see-through pink dress and the absence of underwear.

"Nice, very nice. We can have some fun here," she cheerily remarked.

"Oh, lookie, Maya, a fireplace!" The blonde ran up to it and raised the back of her skirt to warm her bottom. Daniel didn't have to look. He knew she probably did not wear underwear as well.

"Ladies..." he wondered if that was the appropriate term. "Ladies, as lovely as you are..." He was sincere, they aroused his healthy maleness as he wasn't a saint and he wasn't dead, after all. "I'm afraid I have to ask you to leave." He gave them a mock frown.

The girl in the pink dress with the statuesque alabaster body came directly towards him. Before he knew what was happening, she had him in a lock-lipped suction kiss that left him breathless. And he was getting aroused, no denying it. Her hand to his groin was dangerous, but welcome. It had been awhile since that part of his anatomy had been touched by a female, and it responded like a thirsty animal in the dessert.

"Oh, you are a nice one." She sighed into him, and he felt suddenly dizzy. His ears began to buzz as he searched her lips and down her long neck to the place between her breasts. This one would be hard to get away from, he thought. And he only halfway wanted to.

But he found the strength inside. "Look, there's been some kind of mistake. My friend got the wrong impression. I'm really not interested, but thank you anyway. Maybe some other time." He thought he sounded respectful. Something about this encounter reminded him of the way he began his involvement with Audray. It didn't make him feel very secure. But something was tugging on his insides, urging him to partake in something that would interfere with his painting, and came up against his strong feelings for the angel. There was a tug of war going on and he wasn't sure he was winning.

"There's no mistake." The brunette slithered closer to Daniel as he walked away from her, backward. "We just want to distract you for a little while." She stalked him. "We're hungry, aren't you?"

Daniel knew they weren't talking food. And yes, he was hungry too, but for a different sort of companionship.

"No. The answer is no. I'm working tonight and I'm expecting company."

"We don't mind. We share if you do." The blond was cutest when she pouted, Daniel noticed.

Both girls descended upon Daniel, but he cut them off before they touched him again. "Enough! I want you out of here or I'll call the police."

He didn't figure it would scare them, but the strength and resolve in his voice he hoped would get them to stop. He was right. Both girls exited the front doorway, the brunette tracing down his cheek and over his lips with a forefinger.

"You will call me if you change your mind. If you want some private time, you know, just you and me, I'm not opposed to that." She handed Daniel a business card he refused to take. He pushed her fingers back toward her.

"I'm not interested. Not interested in any of this. You have the wrong guy."

They slinked their way back to their BMW. The blonde one made the sarcastic comment, "Way I hear it, you got the wrong girl, Daniel."

He thought about this for awhile as he watched them drive away, waving kisses. He had not mentioned Claire to Josh, although he'd been about to. He thought he would wait a little longer. Even though Josh was his best friend, telling anyone he wanted an angel sounded insane. But how the hell did these two know about Claire if Daniel never said anything about her to anyone?

He decided maybe they were seen together, but couldn't figure out how that could happen either.

Daniel went back to his sketching. He wanted to get the bones down on paper, and then he needed to run his errands. Claire had said she would be home later than usual.

Father stood tall, dressed in his usual brilliant white shirt and slacks, and looked through the rosette stained glass window overlooking the center. Although he never aged, his white hair seemed whiter today, framing a handsome face with clear blue eyes the color of aquamarine. His office sat atop a green flower-lined knoll, and he had the best view of the Guardianship.

"I am well aware of the dangers in the attraction to the world of Humans," he said. "After all, I made it," he continued softly, with a little catch in his throat.

On occasion, Claire had seen emerald and red spires of other worlds in Heaven, but never asked about them. Maybe soon she would. Maybe she would need this knowledge.

She could only see the side of him and his hands folded behind his back. The colors of the glass in the sunlight reflected complicated patterns across his face like the canvas of a colorful painting.

Like one of Daniel's.

He turned and looked down at her as she sat before him. She noted how his face was full of pain, his eyes moist with centuries of tears shed. These were things she never noticed before. Although never aging, now he seemed especially weary and sad. His demeanor reflected what her heart felt like inside.

"So then, Father," she began. She folded and unfolded her hands in her lap, as if their icy coldness could warm as she talked. "If you made all these emotions, these possibilities of feelings between my angel life and the life of this… human…" She could hardly get the word out of her mouth. "…Daniel…" Her eyes filled with tears, her throat constricted, and she could say no more. She drew her palms up to hide behind them for a moment. The warm tears flowed through them and dropped silently in her lap.

Claire uncovered her face and watched Father turn back to the stained glass window and close his eyes, as if he was struggling with something. She could tell this was not the talk he had imagined.

"What makes this more difficult, Claire, is I have built free will into your DNA. You have to understand, I mean, it must come as no surprise that I feel a special closeness to you." He paused again, looking at something in the glass, then following a line up and across the archway. "It is always difficult for a Father—and I am your father in every way but the human way—to do something that is going to hurt his child. But, sometimes we must make decisions in the short term for the health of all involved in the long term."

Claire sat very still, looking down at her hands again in her lap. She wished now that she had not come back.

"I didn't consider until today that giving you this free will would land us here, in this position. I knew you would have to make choices. I didn't understand it would be this painful for you. I probably should have known, but I honestly did not think of it."

"I'm sorry, Father." Claire was sincere. She sat still, staring at his back.

"I have to stop the pain from spreading before it gets out of control," he said, his jaw clenched.

Claire remained silent.

"You bring so much life-force to Heaven. You bring so much love." His voice broke a little. "Your bright countenance…do you know I miss you when you go on your guardianships?" He turned and looked at her while he said this, his eyebrows upturned.

Claire looked down. She could not return his gaze, did not want to see the pain evident there. Her eyes began to tear up again. Father turned back to the window.

"You walk along a cliff and you look below, aware of the large gash in the earth, and you are afraid. You imagine how it would feel to fall into it, how much it would hurt. You can't help it, what we call human nature. You revel in its beauty, the power of the danger lurking there, all the time understanding fully that if you jump, you will perish along with memories of everything you love."

So that was going to be the answer, Claire thought. "But Father, what if everything you valued was lying at the bottom, dead, unable to rise, unable to call out? What if you cannot rescue the only thing in the universe you care about? What then? What keeps me from jumping then?"

Father rushed from the window with a speed that almost frightened her. The full force of his being and his intense turquoise eyes steeled her, as he held her head in his two powerful hands. He drew his face within inches of hers and breathed into her that which had been done some ancient time ago with the making of the first man.

"Life!" he boomed. It vibrated every muscle, bone and tissue of Claire's body. "You have life and the will to live, always!" She felt suddenly small now, like a child, comprehending the awful truth just spoken. Preserve life was the prime directive. It always has been and always would be.

She closed her eyes, tears starting to flow freely in ribbons, dripping down her gown, staining his hands. She lightly nodded. Father wrapped his huge arms around her, drawing her up off the chair and into his chest. He had never done this to her before. He rocked her from side to side without saying a word. She shuddered in his embrace, knowing he could feel the pain, the fear, and the sadness that rocked her body. She felt the wet part of his shirtsleeve where her tears had found their resting place.

They remained in that embrace until Claire's eyes could no longer bring forth tears. Only in Father's arms was Claire partially sure she could go on. She needed his strength, the knowledge that she was loved in the larger sense. At last, she resigned herself to the fact that this calling, her life's purpose, was worth more than the love of this human, as difficult to admit as it was. But she wondered how she would be able to explain this to Daniel. And could she, really?

And who is going to explain it to my heart?

Father unlocked their embrace and held her at arm's length, and with his soft, deep voice, spoke to her. "You will go back tonight and tell him. You must find a way, Claire. And then you will come back home to us. You have one week." He drew her to him again and sighed holding her in his gentle arms.

"What if I can't do it?" she whispered to his chest.

"Then don't go back. Stay here now. Someone else can finish the job."

Claire closed her eyes and drew in her breath suddenly. As difficult as it would be, she couldn't just abandon Daniel without saying goodbye.

"Alright then. I'm ready," was all she could manage to say.

Daniel drove home in a festive mood. He ran from the car with a big bouquet of pink roses. He put some in the kitchen in a large glass vase. Others he put on the nightstand next to his bed so Claire would be able to smell them all night while he was in the deep dreamless sleep. He changed the sheets on his bed.

He was a little surprised she did not join him in the shower. He whittled away time, using lots of shampoo and lathering his body twice. Still no trace of her. He wondered if maybe she had returned when the two girls were there. Perhaps she was not coming, after all. Maybe she deemed him unworthy.

He rubbed his body dry, listening, trying to feel her presence. He opened the medicine cabinet and put the lime drops on the palms of his hands and patted his face. He strained to feel anything of her, and then quickly put a fingertip of lime at his belly button. Perhaps they could figure something out there.

He loved the idea and creativity this love affair was driving him to. Who would have thought the look of a long black evening glove could drive him so wild? He wanted to try other props. Why hadn't he thought to bring home a black silk scarf? He would kiss her through the material. Although he couldn't see her, he could pleasure her in ways her angel heart wouldn't be able to resist. Of this he was certain. He would rub a long pink rose the length of her body. Something to do tomorrow night. He had a lot of things to do tomorrow to get ready.

In the back of his mind, he wondered if the intensity of the dream would awaken him again.

Or, if she didn't look directly in his eyes, would she allow him to see her? That was the hardest vision to get out of his head. Just what did her naked body look like? What would be the texture and the exact whiteness of her skin? Where was it softer? Where did she want him to touch her? To kiss her? How would it taste? Would she be able to taste him? He wondered if she could touch him without blushing. If she did, maybe it would look like how it did in his dreams. He tried to imagine how he would feel when she talked to him in bed. What would her breath feel like on his face? What would that mouth taste like?

His biggest question of all was: would he be as important to her as she was to him? Only one thing was certain, he was going to try it all, to work to become the perfection for her that she was to him.

But where is she?

He put on a white flannel shirt and a pair of loose khakis, slid on his sandals and ran downstairs. *Perhaps she went shopping.* Maybe she resisted her natural angel goodness and went to a lingerie store, or maybe she was going to surprise him with an evening only she could come up with.

Yes, that was it. She was out planning something special. His heart raced with anticipation. Something wonderful was going to happen tonight.

He sat by the fire and waited. From time to time he would look around, try to catch some non-natural thing, a clear indication that she was here. But when nothing happened after an hour of waiting, he grew concerned. He knew she liked to surprise him, but this was a little too long.

He poured himself a glass of wine. He was certain she would come. He finished it standing there, poured another glass and returned to the fire. *Have I missed an important signal? A clue?* Had he miscalculated her desire to be with him? Or, had something happened to her? Could there have been some kind of accident?

Or could Claire have been summoned home?

This new thought left a hollow coldness at the pit of his stomach. Now that he had found her, how could he lose her?

The wine on an empty stomach made him sleepy. He closed his eyes.

There she was! She was sitting in her pretty eyelet dress on a soft quilt in the green rainforest she often took him to. She smiled as she let him come to her. Claire could be so exuberant, so full of life, so full of love, and he could see in her eyes she was happy to see him, yet she didn't run to jump into his arms as he'd expected. He ran to her and buried his head in her lap. Her sweet scent filled his nose. She wore a white shawl and placed it under her right hand as she rubbed his hair and bent to kiss him through it.

"You smell nice, Daniel. You washed your hair for me."

He wrapped his arm around her waist and kissed the bodice of the eyelet "uniform." He twirled the pearl buttons with his tongue. He tried to touch her under the flap at the button, but there was nothing there to touch. He could smell her, but could not feel her skin.

"We have to talk, Daniel." Her smile was one of the sweetest he had ever seen.

"Could we just do this a little more first? I have thought about nothing else all day." Could she hear the urgency in his voice? God how he needed to be in her presence.

She was shaking a little, and it stunned him, so he sat up. He could see she was softly crying.

"What is this, love?" With tenderness, he brought his hand up to wipe away the tears, but then held back, tilting his head to the side. *What had gone wrong?*

Claire lowered her eyes to look at her hands wringing in her lap. After a long silence, she began her painful message, practiced over and over to the mirror. Here, in front of him, in one of her favorite places in the whole world, the word would be much more difficult to speak.

"Daniel, I have to go home soon. Forever." She barely could steal a glance at him.

The shock and horror in his face was more than she could bear, and her heart wished she could reach out and take it all back. He shook his head from side to side.

"No."

"I have no choice; or, rather, the choice was made for me by Father. I spoke to him today." Daniel was still shaking his head. With hesitation, she added, "Daniel, I agree with Father. This has to be done before things go too far."

"No."

"It has to be. It is the way it's supposed to be."

Daniel stood up, hands balled into fists, the neck muscles extended, tense. "Why not just leave me a note on my refrigerator. 'Sorry, Hon, gotta go. It was fun.' Something like that. You so quick to get rid of me?"

"No, no it's not like that."

"Everything I love goes away. Everything I care about leaves me."

"I'm not leaving."

"Yes, you are. You just said it."

"I'm not leaving yet. Soon. I have one week, and then I must return."

"But why? Because I saw you in person?"

"Partly. I'm afraid the longer I stay the more difficult it will be to leave. And eventually I have to leave. You know this. It was going to come to this eventually."

Claire understood now what it felt like to stare down into that chasm and seek the lifeless form laying there at the bottom.

"Are you in trouble?"

"Not really. I have violated many important rules, but that isn't anything new. The big problem is that I was supposed to bring you back to your life, and instead, I've lured you to a dream state. That's where you want to live now. That isn't what I was supposed to do. Instead of saving you, I have condemned you."

"What body part," he said as he tugged at his shirt, his pants, his hair, "what part of me is complaining?"

"You can't have me. I've made you want something you never can have."

"Can't have?" He turned to her, animated again. "Can't have? I've had you. I've had you in my heart, my dreams. I've had you just today in about ten different positions." He leaned over and took the shawl from her shoulders. "In my world, this was black and see-through. The things I imagined doing to you tonight…"

Claire closed her eyes and smiled. Yes, she had to admit, she had some pretty vivid daydreams too.

"Can you see it, Claire? Can you see how I've had you, how I want you still?"

She nodded.

He dropped to his knees. "Dear Angel, love of my life, my soul, make this decision go away. Bring your magic here tonight and change my destiny."

How she wanted to bring her hands to his face and touch him there. "I have powers and strength, but this I cannot do," she said with sadness. "You have to go on in your world, and I in mine. That's the way it's supposed to be." She looked to his eyes to see if he believed her.

Daniel's shoulders dropped and he deposited the shawl back in her lap with resignation. Her heart was breaking for the disappointment he must have felt.

"Please, Daniel, see this as an act of love and not one of abandonment. I swear to you, if I could change it, I would make it so."

"You can't make me stop loving you." He pointed to Heaven. "He can't make me stop loving you."

"Nor do I want you to. My love for you will go on forever and ever, Daniel. Long after you are gone—" She broke it off as she was beginning to cry.

"You come to me, and you give me reason to live, and then you..." He looked at her with tears in his eyes.

"See, that's the mistake I made. I made the mistake. I supplanted your life with myself. I was supposed to give you your life back, and instead I claimed it."

He nodded.

"It's important that you go on living; if not for yourself, do it for me. Know that I love you more than anything. Know that I want you to fall in love and live your life—raise a family—I've seen all these things in my mind. These are good things. Life is worth taking. We can't spend our forever wishing it was different."

She stood, and Daniel followed her lead. "I have a little surprise for you. Not what you expected, but something I can do." Claire put the shawl over her face. "Kiss me, Daniel."

Daniel drew Claire by the waist to his body. He could feel the cheeks of her buttocks as his hands moved down lower. She was leaning into him, as if needing balance. He felt her shoulders and then, using the shawl, drew his hands under her chin and spread them at the sides of her face to bring her to him. Through the shawl he kissed her lips. They had parted for him. They were hungry for him. Even through the thickness of the fabric he could feel the electricity enveloping him and encasing his soul. He knew her spirit was no longer her own. It lay within the confines of his body, and he would not let it go ever again. Somehow he had to keep it forever.

CHAPTER 23

Claire loved it when she didn't need transport. Dream states allowed her to take her charges anywhere, and at any time of year. She directed Daniel so that they were riding in his little convertible on an early summer day. It was a pleasant break, and she hoped it would bring relief to his soul, and perhaps to hers as well.

A lot of her work came in the winter months when the weather was often wet and cold. Therefore, Claire usually conducted her dream states in the warmer months, depending on the human, because summer had more light and longer days. She found it easier to lighten their spirits in the sun, with the angelic light of God's grace having as much an effect on humans as it did the angel population.

Daniel had allowed her full access to his dream state, giving up all autonomy. Claire was driving all the images. She was hoping he would participate, but as of now, he seemed a somewhat willing passenger, a little morose, but willing to be in her presence. But she had a plan to change all that.

She had on a floppy white straw hat with large yellow bow sewn into it that she tied underneath her chin. There were bright felt flowers attached with buttons for centers all along the brim line on her left. Daniel at first looked at it and shook his head with a chuckle. He focused back on the road, but left the smile in place.

Claire turned to him, sensing a reaction of some kind and, behind large dark glasses asked, "What?"

"Do you put flowers on everything?"

"Just about. When it's appropriate."

"You think that's appropriate?" he queried.

"People who love flowers are special." She loved how his shiny black hair blew in the wind.

"You are that," he nodded with a small laugh. "Where are we going?"

"Just up the way a bit. We're close now. Turn at the next flashing yellow light."

They had driven through lush green hills covered with vineyards, olive trees, and bordered by hedge roses. In this dreamstate, the fruited vines had not changed color yet. She preferred the look of them to the bare brown stakes and dark "claws" that came out of the ground when the vines were pruned back. They had passed wine tasting rooms and country stores that sold everything from metal chicken wire sculpture to milk paint. If he got hungry, Claire could take him to a couple of great Italian bistros. Or they could go wine tasting. This being a weekday, there wouldn't be the tourists flocking to the cool rooms, hanging on every word from their tour guide.

Claire remembered Daniel's dreams about Audray and the vineyard. A little electric thrill trickled down her spine like a spider's web. She wondered if he had taken Audray to any of the bucolic bed and breakfasts they saw, the parking lots filled with BMWs and Mercedes. It seemed like it would be fun. *If I were human.*

She supposed that if there was such a place on earth, this could be Heaven.

They came to a four-corner caution crossing, slowed down, and turned right. They traveled out of the town to a more rural area where the hills were brown and unplanted. The houses started to stretch apart. There were more fence posts and golden straw-colored rolling hills and mailboxes. A green and white sign with a picture of an airplane on it stood by a big bay tree.

"Turn there."

The road was lined with eucalyptus trees for a few yards, and then the pavement ended and it turned to gravel, snaking around the hills with very few trees. They were going into what looked like a large warm, golden valley.

There was a temporary trailer behind a small gravel parking lot with a few small cars. Daniel parked where Claire pointed, next to a dusty Jeep with its top down.

"You can wait here while I make the arrangements."

"Claire, this is a dream—" he started to protest.

"Believe me, I know," she said slipping off her dark glasses and folding them at her collar line.

"Wait." He pointed to her flowered hat and nodded. "They might take you more seriously—"

"It won't make a bit of difference. You'll see." With that she marched up the ramp to the glass sliding glass door of the temporary building, giving him a feigned scared expression. Then she walked through the glass door without opening it first.

In a few minutes, she came out with a fistful of paperwork. "We're going skydiving, Daniel. See, I forged your signature. And you weigh 190, right?" She showed him the paperwork. "I'm making this as real as I can."

Daniel's face was filled with dread.

Claire didn't pay any attention to this. "This is perfectly safe. I am testing your faith. Listen very carefully because I don't want this to be a bad dream, okay?"

She took him over to a platform area and motioned to him to lie down on his stomach next to her.

"Spread your arms and legs and arch up a bit." She demonstrated it. He followed along.

"Now make sure you are making a big 'W' with your arms, like this." She showed him how to place her arms at her sides, bending the elbows. She could see Daniel was working hard not to look too terrified.

"One other important thing. Keep your mouth closed when we are falling. It will be way better for me."

"Falling?" he gasped.

"Excuse me, Daniel. Flying." Claire laughed.

A small plane appeared in the dirt runway. It was missing a side door. The equipment appeared magically on his back; Claire examined and pulled tight the straps going between his legs and over his shoulders. They stepped into the plane, sat down on a cold bench, and strapped in, they sat side by side. Instantly they were airborne.

The plane was so noisy it was nearly impossible to hear herself speak. She doubted Daniel could either. His hand was squeezed into a fist around the strap that hung from the ceiling. His other hand clutched the edge of the metal bench so tight his knuckles were white. Through the opened door, they watched the ground get smaller and smaller, and more distant. The farms and cars and roads became so small they looked like houses in a Monopoly game.

"You trust me?" she yelled over the drone of the engine and the wind coming from the open doorway. She had removed her hat. She could feel the short golden wisps of hair flying out in every direction. She smiled at the sight of him, completely helpless in her hands.

"Do I have a choice?"

She shook her head from side to side. "That's the purpose of this. It's a leap of faith." She matched the smile he was trying to make. He gave up and just shook his head as well. She handed him a helmet and donned one herself.

The plane circled around in a large spiral. The ground below was a hazy brown with a few splotches of color here and there, but individual buildings were now hard to see. In the distance was a row of purple mountains. A light went on in the cabin and Claire motioned with a thumbs up. She unbuckled both of them and they shuffled, hunched over, towards the door. Claire walked behind Daniel and snapped a couple of buckles in place, connecting them. She adjusted his straps again, reaching between his legs and around his shoulders. As one crablike unit, they moved right to the edge of the doorway, the wind blasting their faces. He looked down, seemed to fall back a little. She stood behind his body and pressed against him to keep him upright.

"Remember to arch, remember the W, and remember to keep your mouth closed," she said. He nodded.

"When do we jump—" He had started to say, but then they were falling from the doorway into the cool air.

The ground was so far away Daniel had more of a sensation of floating on a large upward burst of air than of falling. He felt like his head was sticking out of the top of a convertible going 100 MPH. The air was cold. The rush of the wind deafened him. The dark blue sky hovered above, and as they fell through a wispy cloud, he could see the horizon very slowly changing, coming to greet him. He corrected his arch, made sure his arms were out to his sides, and closed his mouth. For what seemed like minutes they fell, then Claire said loudly in his ear, "Hold on."

Daniel was thinking, "To *what*?" when the jerk of the parachute came. All of a sudden it got very quiet. The fall was gentle now. The bright yellow sail flowered and fanned out into the air.

"You okay?" she asked.

"This is amazing," he answered. He felt suspended in thin air, without the sensation of falling at all.

"That's San Francisco over those purple hills." She pointed, and then said, "See the ocean?"

Daniel's heart soared. He had never experienced anything like this in his life. He felt the air warm ever so slightly the farther they fell. Claire leaned, and they made some sweeping turns and dips, circling up and dropping down, like on a roller coaster without tracks. He felt her small warm body above him, strapped so tight she couldn't get away. He liked the feeling.

"I love this," was all he could say. At last he began to see little houses and some ribbons of roads. He saw the trailer and the airstrip that looked about an inch long.

"You wanted to know how it felt to fly. Well, this is the closest thing I can think of."

"It's—it's amazing." His heart was overwhelmed. He could feel tears collecting in the sides of his eyes, and then disappearing in the sunlight as they fell farther.

He had the sensation of the ground coming up to greet him in little degrees, and the air continued to warm as this happened. He began to smell the earth, the dust in the air. The vineyards in the distance looked like rows of green tight-looped commercial carpet. They floated and drifted lazily for nearly a half hour.

At last, there was the sensation of real falling as Earth came up to greet them.

"Put your feet out front but don't lock your knees. Let me touch first, then you can stand."

His feet shot out in front of him. The ground came up quickly and touched the soles of his shoes so that he merely walked forward as Claire pushed him. She unhooked them.

They faced each other and removed their helmets, letting them crash at their feet. His heart was filled to bursting. The look of Claire's smiling face thrilled him. She was the most beautiful woman he had ever laid eyes on. He trusted her with his life. He wanted to spend the rest of his life feeling this good, this happy. He'd been taken on a journey he never wanted to end.

Claire looked at Daniel's skin, which was blotchy red-pink. His hair stuck out all over the place. He looked utterly ridiculous. She couldn't help but smile. His eyes fixed on her lips. She knew he wanted to kiss her. It would have been a perfect kiss. She knew it as sure as the fact that there wouldn't be anything there if he tried.

He tousled his scalp with his hands, releasing some of the straw that had gotten entwined there. He let out a couple of shouts. Claire laughed at him. She danced a little jig, her flowered clogs kicking up dust.

"Isn't that the *best*?" she giggled. "I love it more each time."

He extended his arms wide and she jumped into them, wrapped her legs around his waist and they fell to the ground. Claire was on top, straddling him. He rubbed the back of her waist over her top, then lower, his hands caressing her bottom cheeks in tender, fluid motions. Claire felt the place between her legs lurch and ache for him. She instinctively rose up and pressed her mound to him just enough so his eyes grew wide. She surprised herself as well.

She was getting used to feeling the excitement when she was around him, especially when her body was pressed against his. She didn't want it to end. They looked into each other's eyes.

"Thank you," he said.

"My pleasure."

"Claire—"

"Sh, Daniel. It makes me feel wonderful that you enjoy this. Life is made to be enjoyed."

"With you." He rocked her hips so that under her clothes she ground against his hardness.

"No, you know that's not possible." She eluded his attempt at kissing her. He was only going to feel air. She released herself and started stripping off the equipment. She was doing it efficiently, trying to concentrate on the routine, but inside her heart was racing. It had flushed her face.

"How does all this work?"

"These are not clothes I brought with me. They are clothes of your world I brought into your dream. That's why you can feel them. Your body doesn't know the difference between a dream and the real thing, and I took some license with the dream. You are feeling the clothes and the straps, not me. You cannot touch or feel me, really, but you can feel the clothes in the dream."

"But this felt real."

"It was a dream. Dreams feel real, especially the dreams I'm directing for you now. You will remember the dreams I help you with, always, unlike your own, which will be fragments of thoughts and scenes. And don't ask me because I do not know why or how." She smiled. "That's what's so great about it. You get to experience it, but it never really happened."

Daniel spent the rest of the dream driving alongside the ocean, the wind and sun on their faces and in their hair. At one point they stopped and walked along a white stretch of deserted beach. Daniel brought her a hot chocolate, which Claire held between her hands as she inhaled the scent, and they watched the sunset, sitting next to each other on the beach. The sunset was especially orange and the wind particularly warm and soft. The mist from the ocean washed his spirits clean. As they watched the sun set in the horizon, Daniel wondered how much of this was his doing and how much was hers.

And then he figured it didn't really matter. He enjoyed it, not needing to know.

"This has been a perfect day," he said, finally. He lay back in the sand and closed his eyes. Claire wrapped herself around him and snuggled against his chest. He could feel her shoulder through the fleece top, and after tracing the line of her collar down to where the zipper part was, he pushed his two fingers inside to the warmth, but there was no skin to feel. He resigned himself to that fact, sighed.

Someday. There has to be a way. What kind of a God would bring me this angel and then not let me touch her, taste her?

CHAPTER 24

Claire was alone on a Friday night, Daniel off to a dinner appointment. Best place to stave off loneliness was to go to a planetarium show.

It was a sparsely populated group this evening.

She sighed and leaned back into the velvet rocker chair as the lights dimmed and the symphony music came on. The announcer began the program. He had a voice she could listen to forever, deep and soothing, like Father's.

Looking up at the twinkling stars, she was struck with a sense of homesickness. She was living between two worlds and not fully a part of either one. The stars reminded her of views from Heaven, which she missed. She longed for her sisters at home.

She wondered if, some day, Daniel would look up at the heavens and sense her—perhaps see a star and think of her twinkling down on him. Something wet dripped from her chin onto her collarbone and she realized then she was crying.

She felt warm hands cover her wet eyes and she tensed, ready to disappear, but settled down as she heard the familiar velvet words, warmed by his soft Brazilian accent.

"With so many angels looking down on you, how could you be sad? Don't cry, Claire." And then, as she was about to change form, Daniel delivered his urgent whisper, "Don't go, Claire. Stay."

The vibration of his voice swept down her spine, spreading out down the backs of her arms and thighs, awakening places she felt for the first time in her angel life. *I ache for him.*

She fell into the fantasy of belonging in this human world. This was the man she loved, calling her to his side. *This feels real, but it can't be.*

Her body desired more. She heard his heart beating too, heard the sound of his breath as he inhaled, and the creak of the theater chair behind her as it rubbed the leather of his jacket when he moved. His long, veined fingers were moist with her tears and his heat, as they bid her closed eyes to wait, his hands resting gently against her cheeks. Two thumbs circled the arches of her ears, causing her to shiver with expectation.

She released herself to the care of these fingers, these hands that smelled of lime. His long lashes fluttered on her skin as they brushed against her temple. His warm breath and a sensual kiss to the back of her neck raised the soft hairs there. *I am entranced by this man.*

The sound of his tongue as it lightly tapped the back of his teeth, to form the melody of his words, melted her.

"Don't open your eyes, Claire. Please don't open your eyes."

Yes, yes I shall obey. She nodded. Her only allegiance was to the soft voice that commanded her complete obedience. When he removed his hands from her eyes, she didn't move.

"Yes, keep them closed." That velvet voice again warmed her ear. She heard him move to sit beside her. Her body hummed in anticipation of where he would touch her next.

And then Daniel's warm lips were, at last, on hers. Lime scent filled her nostrils with the sweetness and urgency of his soul. Claire could smell traces of his shampoo and soap. It was excitingly new and familiar at the same time.

His hungry lips pressed deeper into hers as she acquiesced to his heat. She was on fire. This was how she imagined a kiss would feel, smell, and taste—only more intense. Her tongue touched his as she parted her mouth, granting him access. He made a little sound deep in his throat.

Were my lips coaxed to drink this elixir, or am I willingly inhaling it? Is there a place where I end and he begins?

He withdrew again with another gentle command. "Claire, see me. Open your eyes and see me."

When she opened her eyes, she first saw the twinkly lights moving slowly over the dome of the planetarium "night" sky. Then she saw his face, not more than a breath away.

"I see the face of my beloved," he whispered, kissing her in the soft spot under her jaw and back up to her lips.

Yes, that is the word. Beloved. Now she knew what the sonnets meant. *Beloved lover mine.*

His eyes searched every part of her face. His lips lapped and eliminated all the evidence of her tears. A pairing of color, scent, music and emotion shimmered around them. *He has a dust effect over me.*

"If your Father makes you leave at dawn, then we have the whole night together," he murmured.

Not enough time. Oh, not nearly enough time.

His thumb and fingers came up to brush her cheek, and then dropped to elevate her chin and fully expose her mouth to him again. His long kiss and probing tongue left need on her lips.

"But when I go, it will be forever." Her husky voice cracked. She could barely speak.

"Then this is all we have." His eyes underscored a faint smile. She saw what the evening could hold for them both. She blushed.

"It won't be enough," she insisted. Her eyes filled up with tears.

"Then let's take all we can while it is ours." He extracted another long kiss from her willing lips. "I won't be able to leave you tomorrow. Fair warning, okay? If one of us has to do it to save our souls, it won't be me."

She nodded at his confession, wondering if she would have the strength to do it either.

They stood in unison, then quietly walked the long aisle up to the top of the bowl of the planetarium, arms and hands locked together, swinging slightly. She leaned against him, not wanting to be parted from the warmth of his body or the feel of his muscles.

Outside, the real stars were triple in number. The moon was almost full. There was plenty of light on the path to his car. He wrapped his arms around her and bent to kiss her throat at the top of her collarbone. His lips nibbled the length of her neck up to her chin and then claimed her lips again.

She responded by pulling him to her. She needed to be as physically close as possible to him now. The lushness of their bodies together made her dizzy. He slid his hand under her shirt, looking into her eyes. She wanted him to look at her in the moonlight, all of her. She wanted to be touched, kissed, and claimed by this human. She wished for the first time in her life that he owned her, in every sense of the word.

"You touch me where no person has touched me before." She delivered this as the simple fact it was.

When they arrived at his house, she felt as though the wooden structure welcomed and celebrated her. At the front door, he released his arm that had hung around her waist to find his keys and disarm the keypad. She was jealous of the attention the keys received; she wanted those fingers on her body, playing and painting the feelings on her skin like he did with his watercolor crayons on paper.

I am your canvas, Daniel. Use me to tell the story of us.

Her thoughts were full of anticipation as they ascended the stairway to his bedroom. She had no sensation of walking. He released her hand to open the bedroom doors and she free-floated into him. She would have fallen had not his large hands found her rib cage.

She pushed her breasts against the granite muscles of his chest. The place between her thighs sent out a small current of electricity, demanding attention. She pressed it against him. Her arms came up and crossed behind his neck. She inhaled him and allowed herself to be taken away again by another long kiss.

His hands drifted down to her bottom where he cupped and pushed her into his groin.

I love his need. She exhaled as their lips parted. She explored the region at the top of his buttoned flannel shirt and kissed him there. Claire heard as well as felt a sigh emanate from his chest. Daniel turned her so that her back was to the bed.

"Wait right here a moment. Close your eyes." He kissed them closed.

Claire could hear movement but had no idea what was going on until he commanded her to open her eyes. He had lit several white pillar candles. The fluttering of the golden flames sounded like wings of a bird in flight. There was music–the music of harps. Her eyes filled with tears as she became overcome with bliss.

"It's an altar," Claire whispered. Her tears flowed freely down her cheeks.

"A celebration of our love," Daniel answered. He held her close again. "Do you trust me?"

She looked down, then up at him with a small smile and shook her head from side to side. "I want to be ruined by your love," she said through her tears.

"Tonight you will feel what it is like to be worshiped," he said.

She leaned into him again and wound her arms behind his neck, pulling his head down to press his lips against hers. Just before contact, she whispered, "Take me and never let me go, Daniel."

He sat her on the edge of the bed and kneeled at her lap, removing first yellow clog and then the other The jeweled charms sparkled in the moonlight. His warm fingertips explored the length of her calves, one at a time, inside, kissing a trail up under her gown.

She looked at the curly dark hair, the top of his head in her lap, feeling his breath on her thighs, savoring his need mixed with hers. She removed her gown, tossing it to the side. He cupped her breasts in both his hands, tickling her pink nipples with his warm tongue, sucking on them. The gentle pressure caused her nipples to tighten into knots. Her breathing was uneven, rising with every touch to her body.

Claire felt she was being treated like a rare and delicate flower.

Daniel removed his shirt in one smooth movement. She looked up at his chiseled torso, which gleamed, all the muscles in his chest and upper arms moving in waves. She held her breath at the beauty that was his tanned body, offered to her.

He pulled her to standing position. They kissed again, her bare skin pressed into his hard body, as he unbuckled his pants and slid them down his thighs. She watched him step out of them. His red silk boxers lay in a heap on top. He stepped closer, pressing his body fully against hers. His muscled thighs and erection pressed against her.

"Now do you trust me?" he said as he cupped her face in his large hands.

"Yes, Daniel," she whispered through her lips. "But you must show me what to do." She didn't want to disappoint him. He was a man of many past loves. "Can you show me?"

"The only thing you need to do is to love me forever."

"And that I will."

Taking her hand, he led her to the pillows near the headboard. He lay back and pulled her on top of him. She was still, her ear on his heart, listening, feeling every part of him as she covered him with her body. His fingers feathered over her back, down to her buttocks and then up again. He moved underneath, pressing one knee between her legs and rolling her to one side, massaging her belly, one finger tracing a path lower. He kissed her there, and then went farther down. Her fingers lazily laced through his hair as he continued to move. He stopped just inside the top of her thigh; she could feel his hot breath on her tiny opening. His thumb pressed on the button there and Claire jumped with pleasure. She looked down to see his eyes watching her intently.

Her awakening continued. Daniel was a careful lover. He didn't rush any part of the exploration so she could feel all of what he did. He noticed what she liked, what made her smile. His fingers slid inside her wet peach, pushing aside the flesh of her lips. She experienced a little shot of pain as he separated her folds with delicate fingers she had seen caress his art. He played her body like an instrument.

As his tongue replaced his fingers and stroked the insides of her opening, Claire thought she was going to explode. She arched to his kiss, pushing her sex hard against his ravenous mouth. Her lips gasped for air as she pulled his body up to cover hers, his lips engulfing and claiming her. Confined to the hardness of his chest, her breasts arched up against him, her lower belly pressed to his maleness.

The sensations of their skin on skin was as beautiful as anything she had experienced before, and better than she had imagined. It was so natural, him on top of her, warming her with his need, ministering to her desire and strumming her heartstrings.

She smoothed her hands down his back to his rounded cheeks and squeezed them. The firmness of his flesh under her fingers, the smoothness of his lower back and the bulges of muscles at the sides of his thighs were thrilling. Somewhere in the back of her mind, she knew she would not be able to live without the feel of him on top of her. It was natural for her to press him to her, to spread her legs and grind her sex against his warm cock.

"Make me real, Daniel," she whispered. "Make me a real woman." Her ache for his entry was unlike any hunger she had ever experienced.

Daniel looked in her eyes as he found her entrance. "Are you completely sure?" he whispered, the space between his eyes showing a tiny frown line.

Am I sure? Could I possibly stop it even if I wasn't?

"Yes, please, Daniel. Oh, please make me real."

He entered her carefully, just the tip at first. As her hands pushed his buttocks down and she inhaled, he forced the full shaft into her, forever altering her. He moaned. Claire felt a sharp pain and guessed what that was. She gave herself to him, wanting him to use her as his vessel. Their lips locked deep, tongues exploring and seeking.

I am becoming real. It's happening to me right now. I am yours. I am your woman. Over and over again the delicious thoughts sang to her soul. *Will you love me all night, Daniel? Will you love me always like I love you?*

His need grew as he penetrated deeper and deeper. Claire adjusted herself to accept him more fully with each thrust. She loved the arch in the small of his back and how it flattened each time he entered her deeper. She loved feeling the strong muscles working to bring them both the pleasure she'd thought would be forever denied her.

She'd read about love, the kind of love she now felt. The taste of his sweat pushed aside the little worrisome thoughts that attempted audience. His eyes seemed to water just a bit as she looked up at him. She felt her soul on fire as she gave herself so willingly over and over again.

The electricity brought on by contact of flesh upon flesh traveled all over her body. Her nipples were tight and hard. Her palms seared. Claire's forehead became moist as well as the space above her breasts. He kissed her there.

"You are my angel," he whispered.

I am claimed. I belong to him. I am as close to human as I can get...

Claire's muscles clamped down on Daniel's member, causing him to moan again, and in a flood of pleasure she felt like she was going to burst. Her body surprised her with the sensation of her erupting climax, satisfying something missing and now found. She let the experience take hold of her and carry her away outside her physical body. Every part of her that touched him made her want more. Her skin tingled with pleasure.

There was a brief moment where he was overcome, and began to shudder, which Claire felt inside her, filling her. She could feel the strength of his life force.

She was suddenly sad she had no womb to accept him, to grow his child. *I would bear you a child if I could. I would. I would.*

They lay together, breathing hard, touching, kissing, and lapping the sweat from each other's bodies. He whispered words in Portuguese, exploring and telling love poems. She tasted the saltiness of their lovemaking, the way his body excited hers where they touched. Claire loved the way the sparse hair on his chest tickled her breasts. The candles mimicked whispers like hundreds of angels who had come to watch this holy union. She felt a part of that secret society made up of all the angels who had gone before, who had experienced real physical human love.

He was spent, breathing hard into the side of her face, and even so he was kissing her softly on the cheek, in her ear and hairline. She wrapped her arms around him like she had done so many times before, but this time it was real. How wonderful to experience how he felt on her skin. Claire watched him breathing, restoring, and healing his body. Her legs remained entwined in his. She soothed down the bits of black hair at the sides of his eyes that had been ruffled out in the pillow, and kissed them into place. She traced the lines at the sides of his mouth. His lips took hold of her two fingers and sucked them.

She smiled at the love play. These were golden moments stolen from a timekeeper distracted with something else. For however long it lasted, she reveled in all of it.

"I have to sleep a little bit. Will you wake me up in an hour or so?" he asked.

"Yes, my love." She continued to trace all his little lines. Her fingers moved across his full deep red lips and rubbed against the roughness of his beard. The sensation to her fingertips was thrilling.

"If you keep that up you will kill me."

Claire frowned at him.

"Just kidding," he said softly, "But I promise to be a better lover if you let me sleep for a few minutes."

"I promise to leave you alone." She said with a sigh. She watched him, peaceful. His eyes were closed, but they did not move from side to side like in the dream state. When she tried to enter his mind, there wasn't anything there.

"I can tell you are watching me," he said.

"Yes."

"You are distracting me from sleeping."

"I don't want you to sleep, Daniel."

"Yes, I can tell."

Claire leaned over and kissed him long on the lips, pressing her breasts against his chest. He groaned and rolled over to his back. Claire raised herself, straddling him. She undulated back and forth, caressing him, looking for a hint that there was a friend between his legs. She leaned over him, and he was now looking intently at her breasts as she plied her sex against his groin, seeking its gentled manhood.

"This I didn't expect," Daniel said.

"You forgot I don't need to sleep." She kissed his chest, alternating between nipples. She let her breasts brush against him again. He squeezed her butt with both hands.

"I didn't count on the difference in our appetites," he said with a smile.

"Ahhh." She slid down lower. Her tongue explored his belly button. She covered his belly with tiny kisses. "Is this what a woman does when she wants more of her man?"

"Yes...sometimes. You know, I won't always be able to do this. I hope you won't be disappointed." He was trying to look to see what she was doing. Then her lips found him. He gasped, and she chuckled. Her tongue curled around the end of his shaft and she sucked on him gently, watching his eyes. The lust in his face matched the little quiver his body produced, which made her laugh. He was growing larger now.

"Do I act disappointed?" she asked him back as she licked her lips.

"No."

"You don't seem disappointed either." She licked the length of his enlarged penis, which was fully aroused. It responded to her tongue and the pressure her lips applied.

"You are sure you didn't have any classes in...this?" Daniel asked through clenched teeth. "You are a natural lover."

"What do you think we read at night, hmmm?"

"Well, I don't know. I thought maybe the Bible, a book of prayers, or..." Daniel was having a difficult time speaking.

"Yes, but we read love stories too. I have always wondered what this felt like, what this tasted like." She moved his head across her lips.

I see he wants me again. Look at him need me.

"You read romance novels? In Heaven?" He raised himself up on his elbows.

The long length of his flat stomach and muscled torso shone in the moonlight. Claire stopped for a moment to look at him on the bed. *I have dreamed this. I thought of this the first time I saw you in the shower. I belong to you now.* "I was made for you. I cannot help it if I need…more of you." She said this through her lips and teeth as they were pleasuring him.

This caused a reaction in Daniel, who sat up, took hold of Claire by the shoulders, and led her into the soft folds of the bed, positioning her beneath him. He looked into her eyes like he was asking permission. She smiled, the anticipation building as he spread her legs apart carefully.

I am yours for however long you want me. I cannot resist you. There is no turning back. We have now but we may not have much more. Love me now while we can.

"I want to stay in this bed with you forever," Claire spoke to his ear.

"And I will love you forever, Claire." They looked at each other. The candles infused lavender and vanilla throughout the room, and cast dark and light shapes onto the walls and ceilings around them.

This is the ancient ritual. This is how it feels to need someone so badly you cannot…

He touched her there. *Oh, that spot.* His finger massaged the little nub until it hardened. He was waiting for her, she realized, waiting for her to show him what her body felt like inside.

Oh please. I need you. Her body exploded into bursts of pleasure as he entered her again, slowly, working his way past her already engorged and swollen lips. Even the pain was a pleasure to her, as he rode her gently, claiming her, calling her body forward to do his bidding. His strokes continued until the pain turned to pleasure. The spasms in her body preceded his.

Exhausted, he collapsed into the pillow at her side. She felt a little twinge of regret that he could not make love all night long. She was not sure how many they would be able to share.

"Sleep, my love," she said while she caressed the soft hair at the nape of his neck. "Sleep and see us here. Then I can have you all over again, in your dreams. I want every part of you again." Claire had no more finished those words than she heard him snore. *I will wake him when it is time. Are the books real? How many times can he make love tonight?*

Pressed into the mattress with the weight of his sleeping frame on her body, Claire wondered what the days ahead would bring. She had knowingly violated a direct order from Father. Would He take away her remaining few days of pleasure as a consequence? For sure there would be a consequence. She saw a faint image of the garden with the white stones.

But the love in her soul was worth the price, every bit of it.

CHAPTER 25

With new light bleeding pink into the bedroom, Claire let Daniel sleep. It was Saturday morning. She imagined what she would do if she was human—go have breakfast at a restaurant somewhere or play footsie over a cappuccino. If they were in a hotel they could order room service and eat naked or wear those motel robes, leaving them open down the front. They could tease each other; stay there all day long; take a bubble bath together.

His head lay on her chest. She had spent the last five hours or so watching him sleep. Several times he half awoke as if to make sure she was still there, giving her a kiss somewhere unexpected before falling off to sleep again. She raised the sheet up to look at the length of his tanned body on hers. He covered one hip and thigh completely, holding her in place. If she tried to leave, he would awaken and pull her back down.

I like how possessive he is.

The pink roses by the bed had infused the room with their floral and spicy fragrance. This man with his strong male smell, the hair she loved to run her fingers through, the full lips that melted everything inside her whenever they claimed her—this man had picked these out for her and had placed them so she would have a reminder of what was in his heart. Now she was basking in the glow of what they had done, what they meant to each other.

Daniel's fingers stroked her shoulder as he inhaled and awoke. He raised his head, leaning his chin against her, midway between her breasts.

"Mmmm, you smell nice. Wonderful to wake up in the arms of an angel. Almost magic."

Claire smiled and traced around his eyebrows and down his nose with a forefinger. "It is magic, being here with you."

"How do you feel?"

"Wonderful."

"No regrets?"

She had to think about it. "No, not really. Oddly enough." She had pushed her concerns out the window the instant she saw his face.

"What will happen now?" he asked.

Claire looked up at the ceiling. She closed her eyes and smiled. Daniel chuckled as he began to kiss her nipples, sucking on them and turning them into knots.

"Mind reader."

"I told you I had special powers. And you didn't believe me," he whispered.

"I want those special powers again, right now."

"You're lucky I'm in a mood to please. I haven't even had my coffee and you have me wide awake." His penis lurched against her upper leg. He pressed his hardness slowly up. She groaned and pushed back against him with her thigh. She opened her legs to him as he maneuvered to the warm place between. He burrowed through her swollen lips, straddling her, then slid his arms under her back and pulled her onto him with his hands under her shoulders.

He was inside, and deep. As her muscles accepted his shaft to the hilt, the sensation instantly sent her pulsating. She ground her pelvis against him and pulled his buttocks. The strong smooth muscles of his lower back worked as he slowly and carefully stroked her passion. She could see him watching her pleasure ripen. She tried to keep her eyes open to drink in more of the intensity of his eyes, but found she couldn't.

The gentle motion of their bodies rocked them and they entwined limbs. They urgently played each other out in a rhythmic fashion against the blue sheets. His physical form was delicious to her touch, but even more so as she felt the muscles under his bronze skin, muscles taut and spent, then soft and tender. Her appetite had no limit. His deep breathing cooled her, and she was swept away by the force of his exertions. When she moaned in pleasure he covered her mouth with his as if to capture every sound, every breath coming from her body, as if to savor all of her pleasure completely.

His warm wet lips and tongue coaxed her, pulled her, and stripped from her any thoughts that there would ever be a separation between them. He kissed her neck, squeezed her breasts. His undulations increased and she felt the waves of pleasure coming over her, muscle contractions inside her coming again. He arched and plunged in deeper and slowly spent himself inside as she jerked in unison. She covered his face with kisses, smoothing her palms down his back while softly calling out his name, her body jolting in her climax.

"I love you, Daniel."

"I love you, Claire. Always."

It was a day of passion. Stolen passion. Was He being merciful or was He being cruel? To Claire it was the beginning of her life, a life she never thought she could have.

Is this what it feels like to be alive, to be a real woman?

They sat at a little shoreline restaurant fishermen frequented. The coffee was terrible, Daniel told Claire, but the chowder was to die for. She winced, and corrected him on the use of that term. It was probably time to clue Daniel in on Josh, so that he could be prepared next time he was tempted by the dark angel. Now that she was real to him in human form, she hoped she could deliver a message he'd believe.

"I need to tell you something about Josh."

Daniel looked up from tasting the steaming bowl of white chowder. "Josh?"

"Yes." She leaned across the red and white oilcloth to be closer to his face. She dipped a forefinger into the hot soup and inserted it in her mouth for a taste. Daniel's half-lidded eyes immediately went to her lips, sending a tingle down her neck.

"Were you Josh's Guardian too?" He furrowed his brow.

"No. He is like me, an angel. But he's a dark angel. A very powerful one."

Daniel leaned back in his chair and it squeaked. He chuckled, looking out the window to the array of boats in various forms of disrepair. Very few of the boats were seaworthy. Occasionally someone would show up, but not much work was being done.

"I just can't accept this. I mean, he's been my agent and my best friend for over a year, Claire." Daniel shook his head. "This makes no sense."

"You trust me, Daniel?"

"Absolutely." He reached for her hand and kissed it.

"For your own sake, you must believe me in this." Because Daniel shook his head again, Claire added, "He is only your friend to claim your soul. He is the one who tried to get you to kill yourself."

"No, it was Aud—"

"Who introduced you to her? Josh?"

He nodded his head.

"Don't you see? Why do you think he just swooped down that night? How did he know you were trying to kill yourself? You didn't call him."

Daniel dropped her hand, then folded his on the table in front of him. "So explain this to me. Explain how you know about this."

"He told me. He came to me the next day, put down the challenge. He thought he could scare me off." Claire left off the part about Josh saying he was going after her.

"But Josh has always been looking out for me. He helped me with the introduction to the galleries. He made calls for me, helped promote my work."

"How else to get in your good graces? You want to paint, to show the world your talent, to be recognized for it, right? Every artist does. He got to you in your softest, most vulnerable place." She lowered her voice to add, "And he introduced you to Audray. Was that looking out for you? Really?"

Daniel had to laugh at that one. "No, definitely no."

They sat in silence for a bit. Claire hoped he was convinced she was telling him the truth about Josh.

"So, how does all this work? Is Audray a dark angel too?"

"Well, the rule is that humans have to kill themselves to be turned. They have to agree to give up on their human life. They are denied access to Heaven permanently. And I don't know if all of them become dark, but darks are known for their skill in 'negotiating' death with people, making deals. And just for the record, Father never does."

"And what about angels?"

"To turn me, he would have to sleep with me, just once."

Daniel frowned.

"You can't think that would ever happen, Daniel. You know me."

"Yes I do. I do indeed."

Claire blushed.

"So, Josh is no danger to me unless I start wanting to cut myself again, right?"

"No, he's more dangerous than that. I mean, he could also take you if he got you to go on a drunken rampage, drive your car off a cliff, get you to overdose on something to drown your sorrows. Those would all count. There are lots of ways to do it."

"Or he could hold me hostage."

"Hostage?" Claire asked.

"He could give me what I wanted most in the world. You."

"No. No, Daniel. He can't deliver me." She leaned in again. "Look, you are never to trust a thing he says to you. He will say anything to get you over to his side. Anything, understand?"

"I understand. What about Audray?"

"I'm not sure. I need to do a little research on her. Darks have black eyes, and, as far as I know, hers are still, what…"

"Green," Daniel whispered.

"But I would say that if she isn't one already, she's headed there. Her vanity, her desire for conquest, desire for power and youth—all these things make her dangerous as well. I wouldn't be surprised if she turns soon. She would make a very stunning assistant. If she was a dark angel, she would be easier for Josh to control and impossible to break."

Daniel's body tensed.

She shivered. "Stay away from him, Daniel. Stay away from them both."

CHAPTER 26

Claire stood in the back of the children's section of the library and watched Daniel read the story about a family of jungle animals to a rapt audience of young grade-schoolers. Daniel had received the news two days before that a children's book he illustrated was shipping out and the author needed help with the book tour. He'd been given a list of arranged readings in libraries and bookstores in the area.

Now, at his first scheduled read, he'd already captivated his audience. The most expressive part of him, his hands, moved across the smooth surface of the pages, sometimes waving in the air around his head, and his eyes would widen and generate giggles or "ahs" from his enchanted young audience. He brings magic to everything he touches, Claire thought.

Even me, an angel.

Daniel's black hair kept falling into his eyes, framing the warm face of the handsome man she could watch for centuries. He had the children cheering at the parts where the hunters were scared out of the forest and the animals threw a big celebration.

"And so, Prissy Penguin shouted, 'ice cream! Let's all have ice cream to celebrate!'" Daniel looked at the audience.

"Who likes chocolate ice cream?" Immediately little waving hands went up. Daniel's eyes danced as he gave them a broad smile, "Me too. Chocolate is my very favorite. I like it with sprinkles or M&Ms."

Several others immediately agreed.

"How about whipped cream? Who likes that?" Daniel asked. The kids cheered as he laughed and looked at Claire, who caught a naughty twinkle in his eyes. She waved her eyebrows up and down, as if in agreement.

"Is he yours?" One of the mothers leaned in, asking Claire. She thought a moment before answering.

"No, but I am his, for sure."

Nodding and flashing a smile, the woman moved away quietly.

The mayhem Daniel was causing reminded Claire of the Playhouse performances of Peter Pan, where the audience of young cherubs was asked to clap loudly so Tinkerbelle would be saved. For, like any true angel, the love of the people she cared about would save her and bring energy back to her life.

Everyone laughed when he came to the part where the penguins' ice cream making venture failed miserably and they covered themselves with the sweet mixture instead. The whole jungle got to enjoy milkshakes they drank from cups made of exotic flower bowls. Claire wondered whether it was the author or Daniel who came up with the idea that penguins lived in the rain forest and that bright pink hippos could dance.

Bringing out an easel and his pastel crayons, he demonstrated how to draw. Several lucky participants got to leave the bookstore with hand-signed original sketches that she figured would be worth something some day, even if wrinkled or folded and stuffed into backpacks.

Afterward, Daniel signed books for his little audience and some of their appreciative mothers. Claire noted how many of them took a special interest in the dark good looks of this young passionate artist.

Who wouldn't? He's handsome, he loves children. He has talent. He makes me feel wonderful all over.

Claire could hardly contain herself when his signings were done, she was so desperate to be alone with him. They stayed in a Victorian bed and breakfast the first night, where Claire tried to keep him up until sunrise. They wandered around shops in the quaint town the next day, Daniel yawning. She smiled at the thought that her appetite for him was wearing him out.

They sat in the square and watched people. Claire was fascinated especially with the children. She bent on her haunches to speak to a blond-haired toddler who had come over. The youngster's mother and father were watching at a short distance. The toddler had a green balloon tied to her wrist, and her fingers and mouth were smeared with some shiny candy substance. Claire's palms went to her warm pink cheeks. Touching the face of this cherub, who was a miracle in every respect, she wished this little girl a long life and the chance to have children of her own.

"You have heard of cherubs in Heaven, Daniel?" Claire said as she watched the family of three walk away.

"They were children here? Oh, how sad."

"No, they have a very special life in Heaven. If only their parents knew." She smiled and waved to the toddler who kept turning around to look at her with big blue eyes, the green balloon bobbing in the carefree afternoon sun. "They get to eat all the candy they want, and they never get sick, and they never grow into teenagers!"

Daniel smiled, and nodded. "Of course. Life is perfect there, right?"

"Almost." Claire sighed and leaned her head into Daniel. He brought his arm around, gripping her shoulder and kissed the top of her head. She thought about the little ones who were in Heaven, called to serve in the guardianship, and vowed, if she made it back to Heaven, to be kinder to them. And for the first time she understood the loss these little bright beings caused their earthly parents, and was glad the cherubs would never know it. At last Claire knew the meaning of the word loss.

Although it was an idyllic three days during the book tour, it was also bittersweet for Claire. After all, she was living a life that was impossible to have. And the thought occurred to her on more than one occasion that perhaps she was taking him away from a life he should be living.

"Daniel, have you ever thought about what kind of a woman you would take as a life partner, marry?"

"That's not something you ask a man. For being so smart, that is a pretty dumb question."

"But surely you've envisioned the perfect woman?"

"Oh, well, let's see. Blond, short hair, blue eyes. Insatiable in bed. Oh, and I think she should know how to fly, perhaps even disappear."

Claire chuckled. "But did it ever occur to you that I am taking the place of a human woman who could give you children?"

"I don't think about that. I have you, don't I?" he told her.

"But I can't give you a life. I can't be a true partner to you. We live in two worlds."

"But not today. I have you today, Claire."

Looking at his warm brown eyes, Claire could see a life with this man. She could almost believe that just the force of their love for each other might somehow bridge the gap. Like some miracle could happen—like the Brownings and their undying love for each other—against all odds.

Stores with elaborate Christmas displays, complete with angels, shepherds and twinkling stars, created a festive mood. At one point Daniel turned around and couldn't find Claire anywhere. He went outside in the rain to look up and down the sidewalk. As he glanced up at the window display, he saw Claire, posing with the angels, hands pressed together, looking up at the heavens.

She saw his smile out of the corner of her eyes, as he seemed to take pleasure in the odd looks he got from passersby. A couple stopped to examine what he was looking at through the glass window. "My own personal angel, there," he told them before they walked off, shaking their heads.

Daniel took Claire wine tasting in the Dry Creek Valley. She loved watching him sniffing, swirling and tasting wine. She swizzled the wine as well, but much preferred to watch him do it instead. She loved the warm taste of his lips afterwards. She watched as he swallowed the liquid mixture, and was drawn to kiss his neck, and the top of his shirt where the dusting of black hair hid just above the first button. She loved watching everything Daniel did.

Being at a winery with him recalled his dream of the escapades with Audray. She wondered if he desired her with any of the same degree of intensity. Almost as if he read her mind, he pulled her into a dark corner and urgently pressed her against the musty smell of the massive oak aging barrels.

"It smells so old, so ancient," she whispered. Her voice echoed like in some of the cathedrals she had been in.

"And you smell fresh. You always smell fresh to me."

He put his finger up to his lips to ask her to be very quiet. His hands moved over her top, and then under it. She could not get enough of the feel of him on her flesh. She gasped, following his lead, bringing her hands up and under his shirt and pulling it up so she could press herself against the warmth of his packed chest.

She felt her body heat rise, and the space between her thighs called out in need. She undid his jeans and released his erection to the pleasure of her hand. He had her pants off in mere seconds and, after slipping off her yellow clogs, wrapped her legs around his waist and raised her sex onto his stiff rod. They had to be quick, and their urgency brought her to climax in ripples.

It was never enough. Even as he gasped and grabbed her buttocks, when he whispered her name in a groan, when he shot his seed inside her, it wasn't enough.

She never wanted to be separated from him after they made love, though she enjoyed their time afterwards. He always whispered to her in Portuguese, the words soft, sensual, and mysterious, making her body tingle as he charmed her in every way possible.

They rejoined the tour. A few heads turned. Claire was sure the tour director had seen them sneak off and knew it wasn't the first time such a thing had occurred. She remained as entwined as she could be with Daniel, walking behind him sometimes, with her face against his back, fronts of her thighs against the backs of his, arms wrapped around his waist.

"I can feel you inside me still," she whispered to his ear. "Do we have a fireplace in our room?"

"I will keep you warm, Angel."

"But I want to see you naked by the fire," she softly pleaded.

He grinned. "Then I'll look for a fireplace at the next stop."

And they had to go to three different inns before they found one with a bridal suite that had a double Jacuzzi tub and a huge four-poster bed by a roaring fireplace. They had to sleep with the doors open, but they were able to see the stars in the night sky under the golden glow of the crackling heat. She wrapped herself up in his arms as she daydreamed of a life that was only possible in her mind. The heat of Daniel's body covered hers as he slept peacefully, holding her with one arm around her waist, as if he needed just to make sure she wasn't going to leave.

She wouldn't be able to leave, not of her own accord. And every time the thought appeared, reminding her these days would end, she successfully pushed them aside, choosing to live and bask in the glow of the love they shared this minute, this day, these glorious nights. This love affair had become something she grabbed while it was hers for the taking.

CHAPTER 27

Daniel and Claire pulled into Daniel's driveway to find Josh's Jeep parked in front.

"Remember what I told you, Daniel?"

"Don't worry."

"You think he's inside the house?" Claire asked as she picked up one of their bags from the trunk.

Daniel pointed to the attic window. Josh's face was framed there; he waved.

Tension strained Claire's chest, anger at the invasion of her space. "He's up to something," she said with a knot at the pit of her stomach.

"Knowing Josh, he can't wait to tell us." Daniel scowled. He dragged the bags up the steps, then unlocked the front door and disarmed the alarm.

Josh appeared at the top of the steps. "Bravo," he said as he clapped with exaggerated arm movements. "The lovers return."

"How does this concern you, Josh?" Daniel gritted out.

"No doubt she has told you a few stories about me." Josh paused, looking up to the ceiling, as if looking for inspiration from the Heavens, then looked back at Daniel and Claire, a nasty grin on his face. "In fact, I don't think she knows the half of it. You have a naïve one there, Daniel."

Claire stood behind Daniel, who stayed on the ground floor. Josh slipped over the balcony and effortlessly floated down to the ground floor in front of them.

"She can't do that unless she disappears," he said in a conspiratorial tone to Daniel. "I much prefer my powers as a dark." He walked around Daniel to face Claire, who grabbed Daniel's arm for support.

"You look lovely, my dear, as usual." Josh bowed slowly, and then just as slowly rose to his full height. "I've just spent a few minutes in your quarters, my lovely. Does Father know about all those spicy books, hmmm?" He smiled, his dark eyes flashing with an energy spark. Claire knew he loved watching her squirm.

"Leave, Josh. There's nothing for you here." Daniel did not smile and his voice had an edge of confrontation to it.

"Sorry to be a nag, kiddies, but He won't let you have this little idyllic lifestyle for long. In fact, I suspect the order is on its way down here now. I'd be willing to bet she is about to be cast over anyway." He smiled and stepped closer to Daniel. "And then she becomes mine. Forever."

Daniel was going to fly after Josh, but the dark angel was quicker and shot himself through the door and in an instant was in his car, driving away. Daniel was left standing in the living room, chest heaving. Claire could sense he was having difficulty controlling his anger.

"Bastard," he said. Claire grabbed his arm and pulled him back. He turned to her. "Is this the way it works?"

"I don't really know the way it works, Daniel. All I can say is we both know we're violating the rules here. I've never met another angel who has done what we have."

He wrapped his arms around her, kissing the top of her head. "We'll find a way. Somehow we'll find a way."

CHAPTER 28

"You warm the dead, my dear." Josh told Audray. She appeared to take it as a compliment. Her oversized satchel sat on the bench next to her. The bistro was buzzing with a Friday night crowd. She sighed and worked her fingers through her golden hair, fluffing it.

"What's up?" Her green eyes sparkled. Josh preferred thinking this was a result of his effect on her.

A waiter asked what they wanted to drink.

"Absinthe," she said.

Josh straightened, his eyes grew wide. "You continue to surprise me, my lovely." He glanced at the waiter. "Mine as well."

Audray was grinning, mouth full of perfect white teeth. "We watched Dracula last night. Absinthe just looked like something I'd like to try."

"I love it when you cleave to the dark side."

"Yes. I know." Her forefinger rimmed the top of the candle flute. "You want to tell me why I'm here?"

"Why not think I just wanted the pleasure of your company?" He smiled and cocked his head.

"Because I'm not a redhead and I'm not that stupid."

Sitting back with a palm over his heart, he replied, "So delicious. So deadly."

Audray looked pleased with herself. "You have someone new you want me to meet?"

"Are you tired of the surgeon?"

Audray leaned forward, bringing her face closer. He did the same. "I've explored every inch of his body, and kissed most of it. Next time introduce me to someone who's had laser hair removal, okay?" She batted her eyes.

They both laughed.

Josh sighed, wiping away tears. "Ah, love. I do wish you were my type. Ever thought about us? Together?"

"Are you asking for an honest answer?"

"Not really."

"Didn't think so."

The waiter delivered their absinthe. Josh balanced the ornate spoons on top of the shallow glasses filled with the green liquor. He placed one sugar cube on each spoon, and then poured water over the top, dissolving the sugar into the liquid. The ancient ritual was important to him. He removed the spoons and handed her the concoction.

"To new things, and a dark future," Josh toasted as they touched glass to glass.

Audray sipped the green liquid, squeezing her eyes and mouth tight. "Ew."

"Acquired taste." Josh added, "Haven't had it in years. It's rather nice, better the second time. Have another go at it but finish it this time."

Audray tossed it back and shook her head. She gasped, her voice raspy, "One more thing I'll cross off my list."

"List?"

"Things to do before I die." She could hardly get the words out.

Josh tapped his fingers and mused. He was feeling joy, an odd emotion for him. The lively background conversations of the place felt like the happy chirping of little birds. "What do you know about me?" He watched her carefully.

"Know about you or suspect about you?"

"Either one. Take your pick."

"I know that I don't want to know."

"Meaning?"

"Things have a way of working out in a certain manner around you." She squinted as she said this.

"In a good way or..."

"In a good way for me. Not so much for other people. People like—"

"Daniel." Josh was nodding his head. "You feel a little bad about that one?"

"I'd have felt horrible if he really killed himself. Glad you stopped him."

Josh continued nodding. He was glad she had no idea the Guardian was involved. "Why?"

"You don't understand how it would be bad for him to die? Over me?" Audray gave a smirk. "Holy cow, Josh, you can't be that cold. Don't you care a thing for him?"

"Well, I thought with your appetites you were perhaps a bit too much for him. It wasn't going to work out anyway. You didn't cause it, you know."

"Yes, I did. I am solely responsible for his suicide attempt."

Josh grabbed her hand in both of his and kissed her fingers. "I need to explain something to you, Love. I don't want you to leave right now, Okay? Just stay with me a bit. Can you do this, Audray?" His breath coated her face and he saw her eyes became half lidded.

"Sure."

Josh wondered if the absinthe also had some supernatural effect on her. Her eyes turned deeper green, and dark.

"I've never met a woman who had such natural proclivities towards the part of the universe I inhabit. I know this sounds a bit crazy, but I feel like you are my sister, my ally. Audray, would it surprise you if I told you I'm not human?"

She was silent. He thought he saw her take in a quick sharp breath. Her eyes widened. Josh saw a combination of fear and pure excitement. She swallowed.

"So this goes back to the question of what I know...or suspect about you?"

Josh was completely still. He let her take it all in. *She'll get there. Just give her a little time.*

"So what you're saying is, you're something else other than human? What exactly would that be?" She swallowed again and looked up at him.

Josh could see she was trying to be brave. It thrilled him. "Guess." He was still holding her hand, stroking the backs of her fingers. She retracted her hand.

"I killed my imagination years ago, Josh. I'm a very literal person. Suppose you tell me."

"Yes. I know about that." When Audray gave him a quick look of surprise, he continued, "Oh yes, I know all about Bakersfield. I do my homework. I have sources you wouldn't believe."

Josh knew that Audray had a past she had successfully covered up, and was fairly sure he was the only person on the planet, save her mother and one other, that knew she had been raped at sixteen by one of her mother's boyfriends. The day after the incident Audray had hitchhiked to LA with a trucker and closed the door on that chapter of her life forever. Josh knew as well that she had a burning desire to get even with the man who had meted out this violence: Burt.

Revenge in a woman this talented is indeed a beautiful thing.

He could see she was getting nervous. "Just listen to me a bit more, Audray, and then I'm going to make you a proposition this one time and this one time only. You don't even have to tell me your decision tonight. You can take a day or two."

The waiter stopped by. Josh ordered two more absinthes.

"Do I have the option to say no? I mean, really no?"

"Absolutely. But I won't ask you again."

"But it will cost me either way, right?"

"You're safe with me. I'll not let any harm come to you. If you say no, nothing changes, really." He hesitated, then added, "Scout's honor." He held up his palm.

"Oh, that's just wrong. You should be ashamed of yourself."

Josh smiled and shook his head.

"You have a wonderful future with your surgeon. Well, I have another kind of surgery in mind, one of a more permanent nature. What if I were to offer you the chance to be young and look like you do now for the rest of your life? No surgeries, no boring workouts. Young forever. Making love forever in that gorgeous body of yours?"

"How could you do that?"

"Let's not talk about *how* it is done. Let's talk about *if* we can do it. If I could offer you that, would you take it?"

"What would it cost?"

"The cost is minimal, but free in terms of dollars and cents. We'll discuss it. Would this be something you would want to do? Be young forever? Twenty-five years old and gorgeous forever? Unlimited sex. No sickness. No sagging. No surgeries to make you look like a freak at sixty. No breast cancer, cholesterol problems, hypertension, stroke…no diapers when you're eighty-five. Any of this attractive to you, hmm?"

The waiter delivered their second round of absinthe. Again, Josh slowly poured water over the sugar cubes. Audray slipped in a second cube before he finished pouring. He gestured to her to drink up. Audray reached for her glass, downing it in one gulp. She didn't flinch this time.

Josh could see Audray was thinking about all of it, mulling over the pictures he painted. Her eyes fluttered to the sides and slightly upward, occasionally revealing a tiny line or two at the bridge of her nose. He was getting aroused watching her struggle to make sense of it. He breathed long, slow and deep, giving her a little help. He could smell her fear. He felt victory close at hand.

"God, you're beautiful." He meant it.

"Knowing you, there's a catch."

"Yes. One teeny tiny one." He held up his thumb and forefinger showing just how small.

"And that would be?"

"You have to kill yourself."

There, I've said it. He watched her. The fact that she didn't jump or throw up heartened him. He took it as a good sign—evidence of a good presentation. He expected she would have more questions, but was surprised with her next statement.

"I hate pain. It would have to be without pain."

"Of course. This can be arranged."

"Okay."

"Okay I'll think about it, or okay I'll do it?" Josh couldn't believe his luck, if he could have such a thing.

"I'll think about it. You said I could have a day or two."

"Quite right. You have up to two days, unless you are sure right now. Could you see yourself being young and living young forever?"

"Of course I could. I'm not a fool."

It thrilled him she was getting excited about the possibilities. He watched her flashing green eyes light up with an almost devilish fire he hoped would continue once her eyes turned dark. She was in a heightened state of alertness, checking out everything and everyone around her, smiling at walls, backs of diners and glasses of water. He could watch her beautiful face for hours, he decided. "Audray, you are a natural."

"Yeah, a natural. At being a dead person who will live forever. Do I have to drink blood or something?"

"If you like. It can be arranged."

"No thanks. What questions should I be asking? What kind of a being will I become? Same as you? I noticed you never told me exactly what that was. Will I howl at the moon, turn green every third Thursday? There has to be something I will be surprised at, or wished I knew."

"You'll wish you had done it before. And no, you will not turn green or howl at the moon."

"That's it? You promise?"

"Contrary to what you might think, I am telling you one hundred percent the truth. I never lie. You'll become a dark angel, just like me. You will go through a transformation, and shortly come back here to the human world, to work and play here. Forever."

"Dark angel. Not a vampire, not a ghost."

"Exactly."

"Besides killing myself, what else do I have to do?"

"Nothing you wouldn't love to do, my dear."

"That's a non-answer, Josh. Do I have to do you?"

"You act like that would be a horrible thing."

"If I can drink absinthe and bed Neal without itching, I could probably do it. But I would prefer not to."

"Done. Not a requirement. Do you want it in writing?"

"In blood." She smiled. Her excitement touched him. Josh loved the lively banter back and forth between them. She was better at it than he was.

"I do have a surprise for you. I was going to wait until the deed was done. Give it to you as a present."

"I want my surprise now."

"Of course. I should have expected." Josh smiled as he motioned for her hand again, which she gave. He pressed her palm with a long sensual kiss, his hot breath on her white flesh. He savored the fragile humanness of her. He tasted the salt of her skin and the delicate jasmine scent of her hand cream.

"I give you a toy, to do with whatever you like."

"A toy?"

"I give you Burt."

CHAPTER 29

All the way home Audray thought about Josh's proposal. Not that she hadn't considered proposals from past acquaintances, but none of them had the kind of permanence this one did. Even marriage was a temporary thing for Audray, who was not convinced it was normal to stay with the same person for the rest of her life.

But this wasn't about love, or even sex. It was about living forever. Being beautiful forever. There was a part of her that wanted to say yes right away. But a decision as grave as this deserved more consideration, so she took the time to reflect on her options.

There was no denying life was hard as a human. Audray had seen her share of the seedier parts of it. She was aware of the transitory nature of beauty and youth. It concerned her if she would be able to wield power and influence when she was no longer a coveted possession. And the thought of someone loving her for "who she was" brought tears of laughter.

What a cruel joke by some supreme being, whoever he was. It was certainly the type of joke only a man would create.

Who are they kidding? Josh had casually told her about the new love in Daniel's life. One who inspired him. She knew full well no one could inspire Daniel the way she could. Her crowning glory was to drain every drop of passion from a man, leaving him spent but wanting more with his last dying breath. And then she moved on. Whoever this new woman in Daniel's was would be a poor substitute. Besides, who could live on an artist's meager earnings? Live on love? That was another good one.

Wouldn't it be fun to screw Daniel in a vineyard when he was fifty and she was still twenty-five? Just thinking about it made her moist between her legs.

And what would happen if she turned? Would she still get the moistness, the horniness she lived for like vitamins? Would the touch of a man's tongue on her sex still send her through the roof? Would she still come? Josh better have a good answer to all these things. If she was going to go to the dark side, it damned well be warmer than a cold grave, or ice-cold fingers snaking up her spine.

Neal was a generous man. But he had a generous backside, and some day would look like just a frumpy older man with a pot belly. How she hated pot bellies.

She thought of Daniel's chiseled chest. She feasted on the memory of his smooth ass and his long lean looks. The way his beautiful skin felt against her bare breasts still made her wet. She had to admit, there were some things she missed about him. And he had been the best lover she had ever experienced.

Unlike Neal, who had been going through the phase of fucking anyone in skirts—anyone who said yes. Compared to Neal's other choices, Audray had been a goddess. So she made him pay for it. Lavish gifts. Trips. They had romantic weekends, cruises. She even got to send the girlfriends packing, relishing in their pain. *Did he notice I have to get drunk to screw him?*

And then there was the surgery. During their first morning after sex, he had cupped her breasts and told her she was perfect. *Perfect, but…*

"I could enhance you," he'd said. He methodically told her what he could do to her breasts. "You'll enjoy your body so much more," he'd insisted. *Did he really think I bought that line? Who is he kidding?* He fixed every woman he slept with more than twice. His office manager had complained to Audray that they had been doing too many gratis boob jobs for his girlfriends.

For most plastic surgeons there would be the issue of his medical license at stake. But Neal would not be denied his sexual liaisons, which were a form of payment for enhancing the women. If they signed the consent form, which had a morals clause inserted in very fine print—something his attorney had recommended—he was covered, or covered the best way possible. Going without sex outside of his long, boring marriage to a loveless woman was not really an option. Not to Neal. She gave him credit for that.

So, for now, Neal was a keeper. But it wasn't permanent. Even for him. Audray knew this as sure as she knew she was female.

The prospect of living forever in a perfect state was appealing. She had to admit, with no desire to have children or settle down, life would undoubtedly be on the upswing from here on out. Fantastic at twenty-five, ravishing at thirty-five, terrific at forty-five, stunning at fifty-five. From there a woman's allure was only referred to as her "inner beauty." This was not at all to Audray's liking. In fact, she had thought about taking her own life the first time she had a relationship disappointment. She had the sense her flawed past would catch up to her some day, anyway.

No, immortality was looking pretty good.

Audray waited at the coffee shop she and Daniel used to walk to. She halfway wanted to see his face one more time, in light of the decision she was about to make. Just to see if the look of him would change her mind. Even if she held her breath and lazily scanned the hardness and the passion of his beautiful body, she doubted she'd change her mind. There were other men like him everywhere. And, if she were going to live forever, she would have all the time to explore them.

And that was her greatest concern. Would her life be hers to live as she saw fit? That and the tepid explanation of the "transformation" she would undergo made her a little nervous. When she came back to the human world, where would she be, exactly? She couldn't bring herself to say the H word, like it was bad luck.

"Hello my lovely." Josh slipped into the seat across the table from her without a sound. "Sorry I'm late, I guess."

"No, I was early."

"Ah, and you are eager with questions, no doubt."

"Yes." Audray looked at her cappuccino like reading tea leaves. *Another stupid custom.* "Tell me blow by blow exactly what happens to me."

"Of course. You mean after you are dead."

Audray gave a visible shiver, shaking herself as the reality of her decision cooled her spine. "You're not making this any easier for me."

"No, I guess I'm not. It's just that I have become very comfortable with death. In time, love, you will too. Until then, the most important death is your own, so I understand how it feels."

"It feels positively creepy."

"I can see that. A transitory feeling, I assure you."

"Maybe if I knew where I was going, how I was going to change, you said, into a dark angel. Could you please give me the details I neglected to ask before?"

"Of course. Really very simple. You become dead. No explanation needed there, right?" He looked at Audray and found no protest, so continued. "You transition to a holding area where you are evaluated. You will be awake, and I will be with you the whole way. They have to identify the 'Source.'"

"Source?"

"Who has taken responsibility for the"—he paused, then sucked in a breath before continuing—"the death."

"See, even you have a problem with it."

"No, to the contrary, I have a problem finding words that you can understand. I have been doing this for centuries, three of them to be exact. I get a little jaded with my lingo—"

"Would you fucking stop it and give me a simple answer? Goddamn it, Josh. You want me to say no?"

"No. I want you to say yes, with all my heart."

"If you had one, that is."

"Oh yes, I have one. A soul as well."

"A black one."

"I'm afraid so. Audray, I came to this lifestyle the same way you will. I was guided. I was advised. I have not regretted my decision for a second. You, however, will have someone who cares more about you than my Source did. I was part of a numbers game to him. I don't consider him my friend, even though he did me a favor by turning me."

"You know, Josh, maybe I need more time."

"No, this is all my fault. I can do things quite well when I concentrate. I can see now I've been playing too much. Inappropriate. I apologize."

"Tell me. Or I am so out of here."

He inclined his head in acquiescence. "You will first wake up in a room—well, like a hospital room. Depending on the method you used, there's an entry team there that cleans you up a bit. Makes you more presentable to yourself and the Readers."

"Readers?"

"They look over your last thoughts, to make sure you really killed yourself—had no help. Not a murder. You cannot be a dark angel without this determination. There are never any exceptions to this."

"Who are these people?"

"People just like you. Volunteers, all of them. Some would rather do this than return to the human world. My dear, you are judged by your peers."

"And this is supposed to ease my nerves exactly why?"

"Everyone gets to do the job they want. You don't have someone laboring over things they hate. This is a great misconception about our world. These Readers are good at watching someone's last minutes of lifetime, verifying their admittance. I am there too, love." He added, "Our goal is to get you back to the human world as soon as possible."

"Okay. Then what?"

"There is some paperwork and such. I will try to streamline it for you. If there is a weakness in this whole system, it's in the paperwork, sorry to say. We are a little disorganized. And that's really the worst of it, honest."

Audray could not find the energy to hide her disbelief. This was making little sense. She had intended on saying yes, but now was reconsidering her choice.

"So, what am I doing while you are getting the paperwork together?"

"I suggest you give me some of your favorite reading material to bring to the other side for you. That way you'll have what you like, while you are waiting."

"You must be joking."

"You don't read?"

Audray sighed. "I find it odd I would be reading a book while I'm waiting to be admitted to, to…"

"The Underworld."

"Yes, exactly."

"I wouldn't worry about it. I have a plan that will avoid unnecessary delays. But bring a book, just in case. Things have gotten a little busier in the three hundred years since I was admitted. But I still had to wait, and I did worry. I'm trying to save you any unnecessary pain." Josh grinned.

"You don't use the H word."

"No, we don't use that word."

"So I will be assigned a permanent guide, like you?"

"Yes, well I will request that I be your guide. You will become a dark angel and sent back with me to the human world. It will probably take a couple of days, a week tops."

"What kind of a form will I be in?"

"You'll look and feel just as you do now. I'll make sure you have all the things you like. Anything I don't have, just request and it is yours. You just can't go exploring around the place until everything is finalized. After the turning is complete, you will feel absolutely marvelous, perfect. All your senses will be heightened. You will be able to feel emotions in others. You will feel absolutely powerful, and alive like you've never felt before."

"So what do I do once I am in the human world? What happens to my body?"

"Every case is different. In your case, you will just disappear, so you can come back later. Some get buried after their deaths. Those are ones that don't come back."

"What?"

"Well, it isn't a perfect science. I mean, people get carried away. You think they are going to do it one day, and then, bang!" Josh had put his fingers to his head, and with a silly grin, continued, saying, "Love, let's face it. If they are too much of a mess, regardless of what they've been promised, they can't be used. They simply can't be used anymore." Josh wrinkled up his nose.

Audray's eyes went wide.

"Look, my lovely, we want to preserve your beautiful body. I'm going to personally oversee the process. I'll devote a whole day to it. You have nothing to fear. I have a perfect track record."

"Oh, Josh. I'm getting a very bad feeling about this. Isn't there any other way?"

"No."

"Where does my body go? How does it get to where it's supposed to be?"

"It's a very complicated system. Hard to explain all of it right now. The Readers determine your manner of death and your state of mind at the very end."

"And then? After the Readers decide I am legit, what happens next?"

"You will be released to my care. Our work begins."

"And what work is that?"

"We promote the strength of the Underworld by claiming souls."

"You mean getting people to kill themselves?"

"No, we get people to agree to give up their chance at life in the human world. Not everyone becomes a dark angel. They just have to want to give up, stop the pain. We help, or suggest to them a way to get out of their misery. Ever heard of Dr. Death? They even called him a dark angel."

"He was one of you?"

"We have people in very high places, for obvious reasons. There is attrition, natural attrition."

"How so?"

"Some people are not cut out for it. They end themselves. It happens, what can I say?"

Audray had to chuckle at this. "I can't imagine the loser who kills himself and then can't make it as a dark angel and kills himself again. That's just like science fiction movie stuff. That could give you guys a bad name."

"We don't want that much publicity, trust me. Even Dr. Death was an experiment. Audray, most of what you will do is just experience the human world, but from a different perspective. You get to enjoy all the finer benefits without many of the side effects, that's all. You'll come to see our work as important, removing people from their pain. It isn't as hard as it seems to cull the human population of its weak links."

"Is there a quota?"

"It's kept track of, but we don't compare ourselves with others. That's considered unhealthy competition. There is no announced winner." He hesitated before going further. "But I have it on good authority, if there was a winner, it would be me."

"I would expect nothing less. So, what happens if you don't keep turning people?"

"You get disappeared."

"What is that?"

"No one has come back to tell us. I think it is safe to say you best avoid it. Love, if you only turn one person a year, that is enough. It isn't that hard to find someone who wants to be separated from their human form. You will see. They almost throw themselves at you."

"And my 'afterlife'…"

"Oh, that's a good word for it."

"Okay, my afterlife is totally my own, as long as I keep turning souls, right? No one to tell me I have to go after this person or that, how long to take, where to live, travel, whom to chose as a lover, any of that dictated to me then?"

"No one. I just want you to keep in touch with me. And that is only because I care about you."

"Please."

"I sincerely do. You don't believe me?"

She suspected there was a heart in the blackness somewhere. It probably made him more effective that way, she thought.

The rest of the conversation went on the same vein. In the end, Audray begged for another day or two to think it over, and Josh told her no.

"Here it is, the moment of truth. Will you do it?"

With a sigh, she shrugged. "Yes?" It came out a question. Immediately she felt sick to her stomach. Josh promised she would not feel that way when she awakened in the Underworld. He encouraged her not to think about it too much and act right away.

She went to bed that night, taking the entire bottle of prescription sleeping pills, along with a chaser of wine. Neal was out of town, so the timing was perfect. She left him a note telling him she was off to Tahiti with a new flame, a rediscovered friend. She had been bugging him to take her there, so he would believe it.

As she was drifting off to sleep she wondered whether or not her artificial breasts would have to be removed by the entry team before gaining admittance. She sincerely hoped they would not. She had paid a heavy price for them in more ways than one.

And then her last remaining thought as a human came to her in a delicious wave of expectation. She would finally get to deal with that bastard, Burt.

On her terms.

CHAPTER 30

A line of ragged men stood outside the hall Josh had rented under the excuse of holding an AA meeting. Well, something like that, he thought. They could have all willed themselves inside, but they waited for Josh, who made a point to hold the keys high above his head, in case there were any non-angel onlookers in the neighborhood.

The men shuffled in, the sounds of their mumbling and creaking of folding metal chairs deafened the heavy footsteps. Josh knew not everyone here wanted to be. Some of them didn't even want to be dark angels. He knew he had to make some examples to save the rest. Get rid of the "bad apples," although in this case, that meant the ones that were too good to be bad. He needed to exert control. Discipline had been lacking and their numbers were down.

He stood at the podium in front of his audience of thirty or so men of various ages and sizes. The room was the fellowship hall for a small country church, in need of paint, and although swept clean, the vinyl tiled floor was scraped from years of shoe marks. A four-foot high stage with a fraying beige curtain took up one end of the room. A tiny kitchen was carved out of the corner at the other end where the entrance was. Twelve step posters and religious sayings were scattered around the walls with masking tape and pushpins.

Most of the men wore black, but a few had some promise as real dressers. One showed up in full biker gear, an older angel looking for a refresher course. Josh liked that boldness. The biker was different. Nice touch. He gave him a special nod and began his prepared speech.

"Most of you know I abhor meetings. Same for lectures. But I have a unique opportunity here. We're going to do a kind of student teaching assignment. I have prepared a scenario, and I want all of you to take a look at it and come up with a solution. The most creative solution will win a prize."

There was not a single reaction on the part of the audience. Josh thought perhaps his eyes were deceiving him. What a lackluster bunch of duds these are. Only a few were his own converts.

This wasn't going well. A couple of men who Josh didn't recognize arrived late. Since they weren't part of his quota, he vaporized them on the spot just inside the doorway. That did get everyone's attention. One pair of boots remained lodged in the doorway, still standing to attention, but smoking.

"And when I call a meeting, like the first one I have called in over two weeks, I expect you will show up and be on time! Got it?"

There was a profuse nodding of heads, with more animated grumbling. Josh knew the paperwork in the Underworld as new recruits could halfway kill a new one. Otherwise, he noticed several of them might in time become fine dark angels.

"Now for the bad news." Josh smiled. How he loved the bad news. He rapped his fingers on top of the lectern, scanning the faces before him. Power surged through his veins.

"Only two-thirds of you, that means about twenty or so, will pass this next test. The rest of you, well"—he pointed to the bits of smoldering black boot—"the rest of you will join your two buddies here." He paced back and forth once in front of his class, then turned quickly. "Anyone want to just volunteer this morning, save me the trouble of the evaluation? Anyone know right now they are going to fail and just want to get it over with?" His eyes searched the crowd. Only the biker guy made eye contact. He heard someone whimper.

"Who was that?" Josh brought his brows together and squinted his eyes. A couple of hands pointed to a younger dark angel, who apparently had peed in his pants.

Instantly the two who had pointed were vaporized as well, causing the young dark to wail, sheer terror in his pathetic voice.

"That was for telling on your own kind. We stick together or we die together. Do I make myself clear?"

The room erupted in a series of "Yes sir's" and verbal acknowledgements, including one who called out, "Whooya."

"Okay. Let me set it up for you." Josh began his story. "There are lots of reasons to claim someone's soul, not the least of which is that there is attrition." He pointed to the still smoldering chairs on either side of the shivering young angel, who bolted for the back door. Josh sighed and looked down at his feet while the boy left the hall.

"Excuse me," Josh said as no one else moved or said a word. Through the open doorway he spotted the young angel crying and running, looking back in Josh's direction. Just then, a pickup truck came along and hit him, sending him flying, lying in a heap of legs and arms twisted in all directions.

They do look like a sack of bones.

Josh left the lectern and walked out the hall and into the street. He stared at the truck driver, his red eyes blazing. The pickup sped off in a squeal of rubber and smoke.

The young man was in pain, but of course could not be killed. Josh asked, "What's your name, son?"

"Felix."

"Felix? What kind of a fucking name is Felix? Didn't they give you a new name?"

The boy nodded.

"I'm waiting," Josh said impatiently. He was tapping his boot toe.

"Beelzebub."

Josh reacted like he'd been hit. "Fucking assholes. Who'd you piss off down there?"

The boy didn't look up.

"Who's your sponsor?"

"Peter."

"Okay, we're gonna talk after this meeting." Josh continued shaking his head. "Peter. Huh. What an asshole." He roughly lifted the boy up by his arm, righting him as the boy's limbs healed, solidifying quickly. Within seconds he was able to stand on his own. Sizing him up Josh asked, "He know you were coming up here to me?"

"He requested it."

This Josh didn't need. Not now. Not ever. This kid was either a spy or someone Peter wanted eliminated, Josh thought.

He led the boy back into the classroom. Josh heard the chairs creaking again, like he wouldn't know the dark angels had been glued to the windows to watch the boy's demise. If he was going to control the situation, he would to have to show them how random his mercy was, just so they could never count on anything from him but chaos. That way he wasn't categorized. That way they couldn't figure out anything he did or why. Josh wanted total autonomy.

"Maybe they didn't tell you before you came to us, but in order to stay on the 'winning' side of the cut, you have to continue claiming souls. Occasionally you will find someone you think will go dark, and they pull out at the last minute. Any of you turn anyone yet?" Josh scanned the room. Biker dude had the only raised hand.

"Okay. Lots of things can happen. But what really pisses me off is when a Guardian gets them in time and changes their mind. You're going to have to learn how to get the Guardian taken care of. Anyone want to guess what we do?"

The biker dude stood up, rocked his crotch back and forth, holding onto imaginary hips. Snickers and chuckles erupted in the room. Even Josh liked his style. Man of little words, all action. *I like that.* He made a note for later. This guy he could use.

"Couldn't have said it better myself. So, what does the Guardian want more than anything else?" The room was mum. The boy piped up.

"To save someone's life?"

"Exactly," Josh responded. "Good job, son. Maybe you're going to work out after all. In most cases, I would say to just give up when you get one of these around. Not really worth all the trouble they cause you. But sometimes the angel is a great target. Sometimes she's more vulnerable than she thinks. I got one of those for your first assignment, gents."

He gave out Daniel's address.

"As was so nicely pointed out, we want to seduce this little angel. I want you to be gentle with her at first. Then we'll take the gloves off, okay? Now remember, we can't force her—rape does not count. That will earn you vaporization. Any questions?"

There were none, of course.

"You boys are probably a bit out of practice. Hell, some of you probably never did treat women right. About time you learned." He stopped and smiled from experience. "Nothing better than turning an angel. You do it once, you'll be hooked."

He gave them a quick lesson in manners. With little else in the way of instruction, he adjourned the meeting.

For the next few days, Claire had ardent suitors wherever she went. She had flowers delivered to her, was serenaded with singing telegrams, received special chocolates, fancy lingerie, and teddy bears. One creative guy shifted into a Fabio body and showed up at the door dressed as a Spartan. Josh knew none of these things would work. He was getting Daniel primed for one last push. None of these dark angels had the powers Josh had. They were strictly amateurs.

Josh himself delivered yellow roses in person to Daniel's door. "I hear she likes the flowers. Are my guys treating her nice?"

"You're wasting your time, Josh. Leave us alone."

"You can't be serious. She doesn't find any of my boys attractive?"

"Of course not. And the flowers are giving her a headache."

"So, Daniel, still think I will give up? Can I come in and discuss it with you? You still haven't given me a chance to tell you my side of the story. Why not hear me out?"

"I think you will move on to better things. This has to be taking up an awful lot of your precious time."

"How much time do *you* have, my friend?" Josh got the door slammed in his face. He liked that he had hit a nerve. One of these times, he'd get the home run he was looking for.

CHAPTER 31

Angela looked up from her book, distracted by a sheet of rain hitting the bookstore's picture window. The impact had such force the glass bowed, and for a second she thought it would. Her gaze focused on the people outside, and she noticed a man across the street battling his umbrella, which had turned inside out by the sudden gust. Next to him, a tall man in black leaned against the green metal signal standard, one bent knee crossed in front the other. His back was turned to her. He wore knee high black boots. His head dripped wet in the rain, his hair appearing darker than the light brown she knew it was. She would recognize him anywhere—James. The human man she loved wasn't human anymore; he was a dark angel.

Her pulse quickened. Though she was in a crowded bookstore, she felt utterly alone and vulnerable.

There was a store exit around the corner and she chose to take it. Once out on the street, she turned in the opposite direction she'd spotted James, without looking for him. To summon transport all she had to do was mentally request it. That would have been safe. That would have been wise. Yet she kept walking in the rain.

The back of her neck prickled with a current that slithered down her spine. Every day for the past two weeks she'd felt watched. Now that she saw him, she knew she'd been right.

She'd recognized him by the position of his bent knee alone because she had seen him stand in that position on many occasions. How familiar she was with his long legs. And with the flat abdomen and its trail of dark brown hair leading deliciously below. She knew the sound of his heartbeat, as she'd she laid her head against his smooth warm chest and felt his arms around her for protection so many times. She had kissed the muscles that rippled under the surface of his bronzed skin while he was sleeping. Later, as their relationship progressed, she had done so while he was awake and could watch her. Her fingers had traced the dark nipples that became tighter with the delicate touch of her fingertips and tongue.

Everything along the street and sidewalk was unusually vivid. The coolness of walking in the fresh, rainy air on this grey day felt good. She loved the sounds of the cars whooshing past, spraying water to the curbside. The cold rain on her face made her skin bloom like a flower. And somewhere, behind her, he followed.

She had worshiped his body. She had worshiped this man and bore a scar on her heart—his mark on her forever—like a scarlet letter. Surprisingly, each time she looked at her naked body in the mirror, the scar didn't show through her angel skin. It had burned, growing in intensity since their parting. Today, it throbbed in her chest, causing her pain. Yet, she wanted to feel it.

The warmth of his gaze on her as she walked down the rainy sidewalk was gentle, and persistent. She welcomed the feeling. It moved from her exposed ankles, all the way up the backs of her calves, behind her knees, and under her skirt as she walked. It traced over her cheeks and found the base of her spine where it inched up one vertebra at a time. Then it fanned out and fluttered up the base of her neck into her scalp.

She rolled her head, easing and stretching the muscles. At her temples she felt tiny circles of heat. Warmth washed over her nipples. Fingertip tingles slid down her stomach into her panties. When she felt the gentle pressure on her mound she had to stop walking. She was undone. Every part of her ached for him.

He has come back to claim me.

He was clever coming to her this day—the day before she was to return home. He wouldn't interfere with her last guardianship. He probably had been watching her breathe life into the therapist. Her charge's encounter with the beautiful redhead at the symphony would keep him satisfied for two lifetimes. Angela had matched and intertwined them. The woman was creative and experimental. The therapist desired to be the student again, not the teacher. They blended together, complemented and contrasted one another perfectly. He had found true love at last. She found someone to share her healthy sexual appetites and need for dominance. It was a beautiful thing, and it would last. Her work was done.

Her bag was packed. Doris was to pick her up tomorrow morning at ten. She would meet Claire for hot chocolate first. Then Doris would take her home to Heaven, less than twenty-four hours from now.

But that was before she'd seen him.

What will they say? She hoped Claire would make a different choice than she had. She really did.

The spicy, ancient scent wafted up from behind her. He held a large black umbrella over her head, but stood just behind, out of her line of sight. She heard his breathing, as his warm finger traced the arch of her right ear, touching her for the first time. She closed her eyes and heard his husky voice.

"Angela. Angela."

She had dreamed of hearing him say her name, claiming her for himself, every day since they parted.

"My beautiful, sad Angela with the broken heart."

She started to turn, but he held her shoulders.

She felt the warm breath and the gentle brush of his lips against her skin as he whispered in her ear, "No. Not yet, my love. Soon." He leaned into her, pressing his body against her back, bringing his arm around her waist and up under the front of her sweater. "Ah, yes. I've missed this. I've missed you."

Angela inhaled sharply, straightening her spine. She couldn't concentrate on anything except what was going on under her pink fuzzy sweater.

They were still on the sidewalk a block away from the bookstore. How many cars had driven past? With a warm touch to her backside that lingered hot like she'd been burned, he urged her forward, walking slightly behind her. She stayed under the umbrella. Then she stopped.

"Are we going to my place?" she asked.

"Is that where you want to go?"

"I'm not sure. But I need to leave word."

At these words he gripped her arm and squeezed. She could tell it thrilled him. She wanted to turn to face him, but he stopped her again.

"We have rules. You know the rules."

"Yes," she said calmly.

They continued walking toward her apartment. He closed the umbrella when they entered the lobby. She heard him shake it. They headed for the stairs and he was right behind her, sometimes grazing her thigh with his own. They mounted the steps together. To an outsider it would look like she was leading him. Maybe I am, she thought. They walked down the thick carpeted hallway without a sound. Alone.

"Are you changed?"

"I'd like to think you would find it an improvement."

He put his hand up to the back of her neck and massaged it, digging strong fingers into her flesh. It was where she always carried the weight of her mission. *He remembered. He wants me relaxed. Yes. So natural under his touch.* His actions were gentle and small, but his intention screamed loudly.

At her apartment, they stopped. She put her key into the lock, but before opening it, pressed her forehead against the old wooden door and sighed. "I'm terrified. You need to know that."

"Of course. Let me take care of all that. I will be gentle with you. I want this experience to be completely pleasurable. For you, especially. There is no pain. But you will feel sad we have not joined before. You will pine for the days we didn't have. But we will have forever now."

"Forever in the Underworld, you mean?"

"Forever mine. Exclusive unto each other. Forever."

She sighed again, loving the velvet words, and opened the door. After stepping in, the door clicked shut behind them. They were completely alone together for the first time. She stood in the middle of the living room, removed her jacket, and waited for him to touch her again.

He handed her a pen and notebook from behind. "No more distractions. Just write your note and we'll finish this."

Angela bowed her head as she took the notebook and pen. She squeezed his hand as he released them. His fingers brushed her cheek. Tears streamed down her face. She tasted salt on her lips as he wiped them free with his forefinger. He pressed his face into the back of her hair, rubbing her neck and shoulders.

"Now, now. No more painful tears. You're going to love this."

She rolled her head and moaned. His attentiveness made her melt.

"How many have you turned?" She asked, barely able to speak.

"You are my first," he said as his tongue tickled her ear. "Come, let's write the note and be on to…better things."

She nodded, sat at her desk, and wrote:

Dear Doris,

He came for me.

I couldn't say no.

I will always love all my Guardian friends, forever.

Tell Father and Mother my need was too great.

I cannot fault any of their teachings, it's just

that I needed to be by his side.

Forever. Whatever the consequence, it will be worth it.

Pray for me,

Angela

She attached it with a safety pin to the handle of her yellow transport bag. She would bring it to the meeting with Claire, for her final farewell. Angela was struck with how simple it was to wrap everything up.

A lifetime as an angel reduced to a few short words. She would sacrifice her angel life tonight like shedding her clothes.

Angela looked at her apartment, mentally saying goodbye, and then dropped her gaze to her feet, following him as he led her by the hand into the bedroom. She wasn't sad, or even afraid. Curiously, she felt more alive than she ever had been.

First he removed her sweater. As he kissed her neck, she leaned back into him, reaching up with her hand to feel the side of his face as he pressed against her cheek. He undid her bra and delicately felt the flesh of her breasts release to him with her sigh. He squeezed her nipples and cupped her softly, then massaged them as his hands and probing fingers worked lower.

Her skirt was unbuttoned at the back, and he carefully unzipped her. He inhaled as the palms of his hands slid down her rear. Every place he touched burned. She could feel the heat of his huge chest against her small back. Was he murmuring something? She felt a vibration coming from him, creating a buzz all throughout her body. Her skirt dropped to the ground along with the bra. He rubbed his hardness against her. His fingers slid down between her legs and then breached the lace remaining at her upper thigh as he moved to the center of her, massaging over and under the delicate material.

"Mine," he whispered.

He pulled her panties down and she stepped through them, bending one knee and then the other. He used the opportunity to caress her buttocks and the back of her thighs. His hands moved forward again, with thumb and finger he rubbed and lightly pinched her folds, up and down, and circled her clitoris. She moaned and started to turn.

"Not yet. Almost," he said. "I like you impatient, though."

"I can wait. I will do anything you ask," she gasped.

"Oh, you will."

Angela's breathing was deep but ragged. Time was suspended. Everything she ever wanted was about to come to her and she would be slave to it.

She heard the rustling of clothes, aware that he was removing his. At last she felt his hardness pressed against her buttocks, the velvet smoothness of him so hot for her.

"Ah, my sweet Angela. I have dreamed about this almost non-stop."

"Yes, me too."

"Are you ready?"

She slowly turned to face him as her answer. She looked down as she reached and squeezed his member with both hands. It was larger than before.

He uttered a guttural, "Yes."

Then slowly, she looked from his groin, up his flat stomach and chest. The surface of his skin looked more golden than she remembered, like it glowed from a light within. She smiled at the surprise that a dark angel could glow.

"What is it, love?" he said to the top of her head.

"Your skin. You are so…beautiful."

"Oh, yes. You will enjoy all of it, too."

She leaned in and kissed his nipples, then traced a line with her tongue up his neck. Her lips and tongue were singed with the lingering taste of his skin. Her mouth watered for more.

"You have no idea how that feels," he gasped.

She had the hunger to see his face. Only then would she know if she was condemned for a decision she could not help making. She raised her head.

She was prepared to see something frightening. True, his clear blue eyes were gone. These deep black eyes were older, stronger. They created an instant erotic attraction.

Now she realized the unknown was more frightening than the real thing. His lips curved up at the corners in that familiar smile of his, the creases at the side of his mouth were still there, as were the long delicate nose and prominent jaw line that smelled of spice and faraway places. He had the same beautiful body. It was him, after all, but a more physically stunning version of him, as if tiny imperfections had disappeared, leaving his wonderful essence, but enhanced. His eyes sparkled more, his lips were redder, and the flesh of his chest and arms felt like warm marble under her exploring fingertips.

She opened her mouth a little, begging him to lower his face to her, then applied her lips to his. She needed this first kiss to calm her shaking body and to close the gap between them, to demonstrate her acceptance of his new form. She inhaled his scent like a drug.

"Yes, yes. Take it all in. It's easier the more you take inside you."

She felt smoothness in her pulse as she allowed his scent to permeate her flesh. He lightly blew on her face, and she closed her eyes, a little dizzy, but left with a warmth that washed all the way down her spine, finishing between her legs. She parted them slightly, allowing him to insert first one then another finger inside her.

"This," he said as he moved his fingers inside back and forth with careful strokes, "will become the seat of your power. This"—she closed her eyes and moaned, arching her back as he pressed further inside her—"becomes your center and will become more…important. It grows stronger when you have surrendered your soul to me." Then he added, "Mine."

"I am yours," she gasped, wrapping her arms around him, pressing her breasts into his chest, rubbing her hungry sex against his thigh.

He held her face in his powerful hands and blew in it again. "Yes, you belong to me now. You will be mine forever." He covered her mouth with his and claimed a deep kiss.

Angela felt like she was going to explode. Her fear for the crossing over only enhanced the sexual tension between them. She would be taken. She would be his.

Forever.

CHAPTER 32

Angela woke up, suddenly aware Guardians did not sleep. The events of the night before came to her and she panicked, shooting straight up in bed. She was naked. Her muscles ached. His scent was all over her.

James was sitting in a leather chair in the corner, watching her, his face in shadows. Angie's room had been furnished simply with just a dresser, and large gold mirror over it. In the corner was the chair James now sat in. Most the room was taken up with the king-sized bed. James's elbow was propped on the sidearm, chin leading into his hand with his long forefinger snaking up against his temple. It moved and then slowly crossed his red lips, back and forth. He leaned forward into the morning light, and smiled, drinking in her confusion and fear.

Oh yes, there were those black eyes again. It was still a bit of a shock, but she would get used to it, eventually. She had lots of time.

"How do you feel?"

"I wasn't sure where I was at first." She looked over her body, examining her legs and arms.

"In time your skin will change. It takes about a month."

"I feel…wonderful."

"Yes, you do."

She felt hot and red. She placed a palm to her cheek and looked at James. Beautiful James, sitting with his legs crossed, fully dressed, watching her in her nakedness.

"Your blush will remain until the change is complete. Until then, I will just have to enjoy it."

"Why does it go away—why would it?"

"It's virginal. Angelic." He came over to the bed and sat down, lifting the sheet to view his prize. His hands smoothed over her legs and up her thighs. He inhaled and untwined her arms from in front of her breasts. At the sight of her still pink skin he caught his breath. He bent his head and kissed one breast, and then the other, rolling his tongue over her erect nipples.

She arched back and moaned, the pleasure of his touch making her undone again. Her spent and satiated body began to come alive.

He moved to her ear and whispered in a husky voice, "Until then, my dear Angela, I shall experience the claiming of you again and again and again. You need to know how urgent I am for you."

She reached for his face and pulled him to her mouth so hard he fell into her. His black eyes looked over her while her breasts heaved and her cheeks burned hot. The mound between her legs was giving her tiny spasms already, faded versions of the huge uncontrollable spasms she felt all night last night. Never had she been so ravenous. Never had it felt so good.

"Kiss me."

Their tongues became reacquainted with the play. She needed his hot mouth on hers as they kissed and consumed each other. They came up for air.

He chuckled. She pulled at him again.

"More," she sighed.

"I was told how wonderful it is when this first happens. I love watching you explore yourself and all the wonderful changes going on. I didn't entirely believe it."

"Who told you?"

"It doesn't matter. A friend." He raised himself up on all fours and looked down at her, a curl of his long brown hair falling into his forehead. She could see down his shirt the trail of dark hair sparsely covering his flat abdomen. The warm scent from his chest blasted her face with emotion and she was suddenly hungry for him—for his skin, his kiss, his tongue, his touch, and for the enormous member she wanted to feel inside her. Her spasms increased in intensity at the thought of his throbbing hardness and how deep he had penetrated her, how deep she wanted him now.

She rose to a seated position, legs folded underneath her bottom. He rose with her and helped her remove his jacket and black shirt. They went up to their knees as their hands caressed each other's bodies. She threw his shirt on the floor and got to work immediately on his belt buckle. He watched her with the calm black eyes. She made fast work of it, forcing her hands into his pants; palms skin side against his lower belly until she found him. She squeezed with one hand his hard member and her other hand cupped him, just enough to make him shudder.

He stood, removing his pants, standing naked in front of her, like a Roman sentinel. She was going to take him into her mouth, but he leaned forward and deftly flipped her over on her belly, then raised her hips up. His fingers rubbed her wet sex. She rubbed herself against his hand, willing herself to come for him. She bent her head around to look at him watching her ass. He was trans-fixed, staring at her sex quivering in the palm of his hand.

"Taste me," she whispered, seeking his eyes.

He leaned in, extending his tongue so she could see, eyes on hers until he laved her, rolling his tongue and stroking her in and out. He buried his face tightly as close to her opening, biting the little folds that failed to protect her from the wonderful assault. He sucked her juices and she arched up and came. Again.

He did not wait until she had finished. He entered her from behind and was deep inside her as her spasms sent her into orbit. He pumped and stroked, pulling on her hips to slam into his groin. He leaned back on his haunches, pulling her back, still deep inside, keeping her on top of him, spreading her bent knees to the outsides of his. He pressed his chest to her back as his fists squeezed her breasts from behind. She was straddled, split with the deepness of him and the need to be used, filled, and completely claimed.

His hands pressed her little button as she rocked, feeling the full shaft of him, pushing her down on his groin. With each stroke they were deeper and more lost in each other.

His fingers moved up to her neck as one hand went around to the back of her head. He grabbed her hair and pulled her head back. He kissed the side of her face and neck as she pulsed out of control, the back of her head resting on his shoulder, her eyes closed.

"Hmm. Now you are mine." His voice was soft and gentle. "Open your eyes. Look in the mirror."

Her eyes flew open to see them reflected in the mirror, her body in an arc with breasts out, her hair falling from his shoulder down his back. His large hands encircled her delicate neck, one hand raising the back of her head so she could see how they looked together in the mirror as he pushed deeply inside her. He held her still as he filled her to the core, one hand on her throat, the other tangled in the hair at the back of her head.

She shuddered.

"Yes my dear. Now we are one." His face was next to hers as she saw them in the large mirror mounted on the wall over the dresser.

Her eyes were black.

Claire was impatiently sitting at the bookstore, by the big window where she always found Angie reading. But Angie was a full twenty minutes late. This was not like her. Doris would be upset with Angie's tardiness as well.

Angie brushed in then. "So sorry," she whispered. She wore oversized sunglasses and had her duffel with her, a note pinned to the strap like she didn't want to forget something. Dropping the bag behind her on the ground, she sank into the easy chair, delicately resting her hands and forearms on the deep armrests. Claire thought she picked up some musky smell, something earthy and dark, unlike Angie's usual warm and sunny scent.

"Sunglasses inside. Are you injured?" Claire asked.

"No." Angela smiled. It wasn't the full toothy smile. "My eyes are a little sensitive to the light today."

Claire shrugged. Something in the air didn't seem right. Something about the sight of Angie made Claire feel cold.

"So, I guess you're going back. To Heaven."

"I decided to stay awhile." Angie sounded casual.

"You got permission?"

"Well, sort of."

Sort of? Claire sat back, clutching her hot chocolate, but it didn't help. She was still shivering with a coldness that went all the way up her spine. Looking over at Angela, she noticed the angel didn't bring her usual warm, steaming mug. Instead, her hands were folded and she sat in repose, legs crossed. She wore a long pair of toeless leggings. Black.

"You had your toes done, Angie."

Angela raised her foot encased in black stiletto open-toed heels, slightly pointed at the end. Her well-developed calf muscles flexed as she pointed her toes, the nails painted a vivid red. Then she lowered her leg, crossing one over her other. "Never had it done before, so thought I would give it a shot."

"It's a strong look." Something told Claire to be cautious. "Something's changed. What is it?"

Angela looked outside the large window at the wet street. Claire thought she was searching for something to say.

Or how to say it.

Angela's reluctance to answer made her nervous. "I don't mean to pry, Angie, but you can tell me...anything." Claire hoped the encouragement would open her up. The other angel continued looking outside the window, nodding a regular rhythm, like she was tapping time to music somewhere. Her big toe did most the movement.

Claire's fear rose up, fanning her words as she spoke. "Angela, take off your glasses. I want to see your eyes."

The ends of Angela's lips curled up in a smirk. She took a deep breath, ran her fingers through her hair, and, as she exhaled, said, "Okay." She removed her glasses and stared at Claire with obsidian eyes.

Claire's palms sweated. She dug her fingernails into her skin. It would have drawn blood if she were human. She held back the urge to run as she looked at the blackness of Angela's soul, now lost to her forever. She had not seen a dark angel, other than Josh, in the flesh. It was the first time she had seen someone she knew, and liked, turned into this state.

"Claire," Angela leaned forward, seeking to clasp her friend's hands.

"Don't touch me." Claire pulled back, twisting her torso to the side, protecting her heart with arms crossed over her chest.

Angela sat back. The smile had not left her face. It seemed to intensify, had more of a seductive cast to it. "It isn't so bad, Claire. Honest. I wanted to tell you because I...care for you." She inclined her head slightly, as if wincing. "Didn't want you to hear it from someone else."

"So what do we put on your marker?" Claire's fear was turning to anger. "Shall we put a book? A cup of steaming chocolate? No, I see you've lost the need for chocolate. You've no doubt replaced it with something else entirely."

Bitterness and pain held hands in her chest. Claire couldn't afford to consider how precarious her own situation was now. But then the fear came up again.

Angie. Gone. Turned. I have no one. No one but Daniel.

She mustered up the courage to ask what she'd been dying to know. "Who did it?"

"My James."

Emphasis on MY. They don't turn, they claim each other. Always so possessive, these dark ones.

"Well, at least it wasn't Josh."

What am I saying? What difference does it make? She's gone. Angie's gone forever!

"No, James couldn't let that happen."

"Like he had some kind of a choice, you mean?"

Angela shook her head from side to side. "You don't know how it works, Claire."

"No, Angie. Only way to explain it is that James cut a deal. He cut a deal with Josh. Probably the only way he could get him to go dark. He protected you—protected you from having to sleep with that putrid sack of flesh and paid for it with his soul."

Claire was secretly happy Josh hadn't gotten Angie as a conquest, but had to go through James. But then, Angie was a blonde, not a redhead.

"Are you even sure it was James you slept with? They can shift, look like someone else. Maybe you slept with Josh after all."

"I think I would know. I am in love with him."Angela's eyes scanned her guardian friend. "Claire, it really isn't a bad thing. In fact, I am rather enjoying it. I wish I had done it before."

She did look beautiful, Claire had to admit. Her skin was whiter, more translucent. Her lips were redder and fuller. Her scent had changed to a rich vanilla and spice fragrance, rather than the flowery one her dust used to have. She could even be called sultry. Gone were her black angel slippers with the pearl button strap. Gone was her white gown with the eyelet lace. She wore her hair down now, not in the ponytail with the white scrunchie like before. She drew Claire in with her smile, the dancing flashes of red light in her dark eyes pulling her forward.

Angie is dangerous.

"I'm shocked. Disappointed." *Oh, this is not the half of it.*

"Remember when I told you about how it felt when James was my charge? Remember I told you I was the happiest angel in the universe? That was a lie, compared to how I feel now. And we have forever together, forever!"

It was a good argument.

Angela said, "Claire, take my duffel. Everything is in there: my gown, some things I brought from my room. Take it back for me, okay?"

Claire had her arms crossed in front of her, shaking her head.

"Please, Claire. I am the same person I was before. If you ever loved me before, please take this back for me. I want these things to go home with you. Please."

When Claire looked up at Angie, there were tears in her eyes.

"I'm happy, really happy, Claire. I chose this all my myself. Don't worry about me. Tell Doris, okay? Look, I've written a note to you here." Standing now, Angie dumped the bag at Claire's feet, the note attached to the strap curling up at the sides, attached with a safety pin.

"This was the only option for me. Just think about it Claire."

CHAPTER 33

Claire sat at the open-air café, collecting her thoughts. The meeting with Angie had been disturbing, but Angie had warned her about how vulnerable she'd been to James's advances. Now Claire wished she had mentioned how Angie's memory hadn't been affected by the Wash to Father when they'd met. Perhaps he could have done something. Not every human could be saved.

Apparently not every angel either. She shivered at the thought of Angie's white stone.

Her hot chocolate was cooling in front of her. Storm clouds of worry lurked in the outer regions of her mind. Claire felt ill prepared for these circumstances. She wanted a life with Daniel even though her mind failed to find a precedent allowing an angel to stay in the human world forever. Glad she'd been able to rebuff Angie's attempt to seduce her to the dark side, her nerves were eased just a bit.

Angie and James had never been physical before when he was human and she was an angel. Perhaps if they had—if they had experienced the flesh on flesh relationship she and Daniel had, there wouldn't have been the tension that ensnared Angie. Claire believed that Angie had been so overcome to love James physically that the passion had clouded her friend's judgment.

Claire had delivered Angie's bad news to Doris earlier in the day, after reading the note. She knew it would break Mother's heart, but suspected Father already knew.

A chill ran down her spine. She looked up to see Josh walk in front of her table on the outside of the café, bowing to her as he passed. Once inside the restaurant, he made a direct path to Claire's table.

"Ah, love, nice to see you again. You look good enough to eat."

"I'm not feeling it, Josh. Leave me alone. There is nothing here for you."

"Oh, but you're wrong. I am here to make you a proposition."

"I know all about your deals. I'm not interested."

"Claire, love, how long do you expect to be able to stay? Father's not going to turn a blind eye forever and you know it. How long are you going to indulge in the fantasy? It could be dangerous, you know."

Claire shrugged. She really didn't have an answer to that.

"I can give it all to you, Claire. I can give you Daniel. A love that lasts forever." Josh was watching her eyes. "And physical love, like you have now." As Claire bored her gaze into him he added, "Oh yes, I know everything." He grinned.

Her imagination focused on a life that she wanted, that felt so real in her mind. She and Daniel were sitting on a small loveseat, holding hands, watching their children open Christmas packages. She saw their daughter smile at him. The child was dark like Daniel, with red lips and strikingly white teeth. Claire was holding a baby. They all dropped to wrestle on the floor. A toddler tackled her from behind. The five of them nuzzled there in their living room. On Christmas.

But this dream could never be. The world Josh was offering did not contain children. In his version she saw a much older Daniel, sitting on the loveseat with a young blond girl, just as Claire looked now. The room was empty and there was no laughter. She would trace the lines around his eyes. They would be filled with sadness and regret for a life not lived fully. She would finger his lips, still red and luscious, but their passion would not bring forth a seed growing in her womb. No amount of lovemaking would bring to him the laughter of children or silence the deafening sounds of nothing but their own voices.

His smiles would be from remembering days when he was young, getting sunburned, lying in the fields between the vines eating cheese and drinking red wine from the bottle. The sky was so big on those days. Everything was possible and the future lay before them with brightness. But there would be no children. She would be his eternally young companion, a constant reminder of the passage of time and what they could not share. He would not have the life he really wanted. Neither would she.

"You know, Josh, what you're offering, it isn't as attractive as you would think."

Josh frowned, tilted his head. "How so, my sweet?"

"Can't you see this old man walking down the street with the young girl? Can you see the looks he would get?"

"So, you turn him too. Then you both stay young forever. Not a problem!"

"Childless. Young and childless."

"Ah, love, you ask too much. You could turn a whole family and adopt them."

"No."

"To get what you want sometimes you have to pay a price, a stiff price. But you will have him forever."

"I have forever now in Heaven."

"And it must be a fabulous place." He covered his lips with an index finger, before adding, "Curious, my pet, how there just aren't nearly as many people trying to fall into Heaven. Ever thought about that, love?" His black eyes twinkled, searching her face. He looked excited. "They all seem to be coming mostly the other way."

"It takes a certain person to want the forever Heaven offers. It clearly isn't for everyone. Certainly you would be miserable there." She looked at Josh. "I know I'm not telling you something you haven't heard before."

"Oh, but you do it so much better." He leaned on his fingers, elbows on the table, like that first day they met. He reached over and stroked the tender white flesh of her arm with his forefinger. "Ever thought about us…together?"

Claire withdrew her arms from the table, revolted. "Never. Not for an instant."

"You say such nasty things so nicely. Does Daniel ask you to say dirty things too? I'd say you have a special talent for it. I would let you say all the nasty things you wanted."

"Go to Hell."

Josh sat up straight and laughed. "Fabulous!"

"You aren't attractive to me." Claire said.

"And I generally go for redheads. I'm hoping we could get used to each other, in time. We would broaden our horizons, so to speak."

"Your offer holds no attraction, not an ounce of it. It is the last thing I would do. I would never do it. I understand rape is only a human thing."

"Sadly, yes." Josh turned down his lower lip. "Tell you what I will do. I will get Daniel turned. If I could do it without a lot of pain, blood and the kind of scene he was trying last time, would that interest you?"

"No. Besides, he won't do it. You know this."

"Wouldn't he do it for you? If you asked him?"

She shuddered, not wanting to think about it further. She saw Daniel sitting in the forest painting, in a garden of flowers among the bees and creatures that zipped through the air. She heard the sharp inhale of his breath when she touched him, when she asked for his warm mouth on hers. His life force full of passion and joy was strong. He was connected to the universe. He not only described it in his paintings, he felt it. He would never give up the universe for one little angel. Even if that angel were her.

"He's stronger than I am now, Josh. And if you took me, he would make it his mission to defeat you. That would earn him a spot in Heaven. He could become a Guardian, picking up the pieces of flesh you so easily underestimate and discard."

They both looked at their hands. Claire picked up the mug of cooled chocolate. The whipped cream had melted into it, leaving a layer of white glaze on top. She raised it to her lips, and with her eyes closed, took a sip. Josh didn't say a word, merely watched.

"I could help you with that experience."

Claire opened her eyes and smiled. "I can eat. I just prefer to taste. It was perfect without you. It was made perfect. But, I thank you for not interfering. Are you beginning to develop manners, a conscience?"

"Hardly," he scoffed a little too loudly. Claire saw she hit a nerve.

"Joshua, have you ever thought about how boring it is to cause pain all day long?"

"I like to think I bring joy now and then. I know I bring ecstasy quite often, or so the ladies tell me." He leaned over the table to get as close to Claire's face as possible. "You and I would be beautiful together."

"Beautiful? You? You want something beautiful?" She laughed. She could see it stung his ego. His eyes flashed red in return.

"I am the greatest lover in the universe. I make women want to eat themselves to get a piece of me."

"Has anyone given up life itself just to be with you?"

Josh's face was unreadable.

"Ever had someone run to you for protection from evil, when you did not take their soul? Ever love someone so much you couldn't hurt her? Have you ever been willing to give up forever for just a few decades as a human for her?" She looked at his red eyes. "Have you ever had that kind of a love, Joshua?"

"I'm not so sure that's very smart. I don't think that's love, do you?"

Claire smiled. "How on earth would you understand that kind of sacrifice? You don't know one whit about love. Now I see why. You can't love anyone but yourself."

CHAPTER 34

Claire was reading <u>Marked by Passion</u> as she lay on Daniel's bed. She glanced at the bedside clock. Sunlight no longer came through the bedroom window—it was late. She needed to tell Daniel about Angela's turning, but he hadn't yet arrived home. It was not like him to come home so much later than he'd promised. Claire hoped it meant his meeting with the new gallery owner in Sausalito today went well.

Claire slipped off her white eyelet gown and entered the shower. The feeling of warm water on her skin was heightened due to her human form, which she took almost all the time now. It felt natural to her, and she loved living as if she was human.

Daniel's strong hand suddenly pulled back the shower curtain, which startled her at first. Lust flared in his eyes, and her nerves settled. She smiled. He didn't say anything, just stared at her body, like he'd never seen it before, his boldness making her blush.

"You want some help with the soap?" he asked, grinning.

"Please." She turned her back to him and flashed a smile over her shoulder. "Or, you could join me."

She didn't have to ask him again. He left his clothes on the floor, then stepped in behind her, placing his hands on her shoulders. Tonight he gave her a delicate touch, almost tentative, though she could feel the passion underneath. She shivered.

Every time she was alone with Daniel in the flesh it felt like the first time all over again. He kissed the back of her neck and then continued down her spine. She could not imagine getting completely used to the sensuality of his touch.

"Your skin is so soft," Daniel whispered to her through the steam.

Claire felt the little bud between her legs swell, awakening the rest of her body. Daniel feathered his fingers over her back with strokes that preceded his lips and tongue. He moved closer, his body fully against hers, his erection rubbing in the groove between her buttocks. He massaged water down her flesh and touched her sex from behind, which caused her to gasp. She had missed him even though they'd been apart only a few hours.

He pulled her to him roughly, hands on her breasts, caressing them with a new urgency. The water coursed down their bodies in ribbons as he pressed one large hand on her lower belly.

"Tell me you love me. You will be mine forever." He pleaded, his voice husky.

"Yes, I do love you. And I will love you forever." She enjoyed the urgency of his demeanor.

"Tell me you belong to me and no other. Tell me you worship my body. You want my hands on your body."

"Daniel?" Claire turned and faced him, searching his dark eyes so filled with need. "You've had quite a day, haven't you?" She chuckled, smiling wide.

She didn't like that he did not smile in return.

"What's wrong?" she asked.

"I'm overcome with your beauty. I could think of nothing else today. I've wanted to feel your body all day. I need to be inside you more than I ever have."

Claire studied him carefully. His expression was filled with pain, though she could still see the lust in his eyes. She put her palms on either side of his face. "I am here, love; you don't need to trouble yourself. I am here." She leaned forward and softly kissed his lips. She coaxed his mouth open and he moaned as her tongue entered and sought its mate. Their lips and tongues entwined, then she pulled back to gaze at him again. "You don't have to take what I freely give, Daniel," she whispered.

"Tell me again. Let me hear you say it again."

"I love you, Daniel. I love you above any other. You are my angel. My Guardian lover."

He flinched at this.

"Daniel? What's wrong? Please tell me."

Claire could see he was aroused, but he was hesitant, not as familiar. She didn't feel as connected to him.

"Sorry. There's a lot on my mind. Please forgive me, Claire." He searched her face, hands gripping her, causing pain to the small of her back as she arched up to look at him. "Come, let's forget about all the worries of the world. Let's lose ourselves in each other's flesh."

Now it was Claire's turn to flinch. She stepped out of the shower and wrapped herself in a towel. Daniel opened the curtain and stood with the water at his back, watching her. His erection wilted.

"You're hiding something from me, Daniel. I want you to tell me right now. Have you been drinking? You're different, somehow."

He turned off the water and stepped out. "Different? Look at me, do I look different? I am your Daniel."

She caught a sudden red glint in his eyes and gasped. And that's when it hit her.

This beautiful man before her was not Daniel.

"Joshua!"

Daniel walked down the concrete floor of the new gallery space. The front door was open when he arrived. The light would be perfect. The building was an old warehouse, made of brick, restored and reinforced. It was located just at the end of the trendy row of other galleries and gift shops with stunning views of the bay and San Francisco's skyline. The outside of the building was covered with vines in various shades of green and hints of magenta, which softened the straight angles of the brick box. *It is beyond ideal.*

He could imagine his large jungle scenes hanging against the red brick background. Old metal-veined skylights would let in natural light. Some track fixtures would have to be installed, which would draw attention to his individual paintings. It felt like hallowed space.

The new owner said he would use Daniel's paintings as the featured artist for the gallery's grand opening celebration. He said the celebration would draw art lovers he knew from New York. Daniel could picture the crowd and took pleasure at the image in his mind. Months had passed since he'd last indulged in such a pleasant daydream. Finally he would get the respect and recognition he always wanted. He now realized how much he needed the acknowledgement of his talent.

The front door creaked open and Daniel turned. There stood Audray.

"Hello, Daniel."

"You!" He took a step back as his hands balled into fists. His fingernails dug into his palms.

"Oh, come on, sweetheart. Let's bury the hatchet, shall we?" Her smile was sickening and syrupy sweet.

"Only place I'd bury the hatchet is in your chest."

"Ah, but you see now, that won't do any good." She walked closer to Daniel, her arms outstretched. His natural instinct was to get away from her, and he took three steps back. She moved under an overhead shop light and he saw her eyes. At first he thought it was a trick of the light, but then he saw her eyes looked black, no longer emerald green.

"You've turned dark. Stay away from me."

"Love." She frowned in mock disappointment, "You needn't fear me. You know I would never do anything to hurt you. Remember how it was that first time?" She walked toward him. "Remember how afraid you were? But no, we enjoyed each other that night." She looked at his face, searching his eyes.

Her scent was exotic and intoxicating. He was getting aroused, despite his loathing for her.

"Daniel." She traced her forefinger across his lower lip. "You do remember that night? How many times did you come? What, three? four?" She blew gently into his face and Daniel felt his eyelids flutter. He fought the urge to fall into the veil of sensuality she'd thrown over him.

She walked around behind him. Daniel inhaled as she touched his ass and squeezed him with one hand. He jumped to the side but felt unable to run. She raised herself up to his ear and whispered from behind, "I have not had such a lover since. It was difficult to leave your bed, Daniel. Was it as painful for you?"

"No." He tried not to have emotion in his voice, but the words wobbled in his chest, sounding uncertain. "It was never love. You have no power over me now." As his strength regained, he turned and pushed her away. Daniel began to walk out of the space, backward.

Audray followed, stalking, smiling.

"Stay away. I am done with this."He raised his palms towards her, increasing the volume of his voice.

She stopped, shaking her head from side to side. He saw something in her eyes that looked like pity as she whispered, "No, Daniel. We are only beginning with you. With you both."

"You keep your hands off Claire."

"I've no interest in Claire. But I believe even now, while we speak, she becomes the plaything of someone else. Claire has a destiny to become an even greater angel than she is right now. And, Daniel, you could be her willing slave. Never, ever to be separated from her again. Just imagine, an eternity together!"

Daniel was horrified. *I've left Claire alone! How could I have been so careless?* He would never forgive himself if she was harmed, or worse still, if Josh turned her, like he had clearly done to Audray.

Oh my God, Claire. I've let you down. He was afraid to even think of it. The full danger and folly of their situation fell upon him like the brick walls of the gallery.

What was I thinking?

He raced through the front door, hopped in his car, and tore down the rain-soaked street. He sped up the freeway, cursing his decision for such a late meeting so far away. It would take him over forty minutes to get home. *Oh God, I will never be able to forgive myself? What have I done? How could I have been so selfish?* Would she be dark when he got there? Would she have lost her place in Heaven, her angel essence?

All the way home he clutched the smooth wooden steering wheel. His stomach was knotted and he felt nauseated as he pulled into his driveway. Josh's Hummer was parked there.

Damn. I'm too late.

He ran to the front door and stopped just inside, staring at the sight of the two of them sitting by the fireplace. He suddenly felt he was going to be sick.

Claire knew the sound of Daniel's car. Wiping the tears from her cheeks, she was ashamed she had almost risked all because of her desire for Daniel. She wished he would never know about the close call with Joshua. Resigned, she knew the dark angel and his accomplice would never allow that opportunity to slip by unreported.

It was with a heavy heart Claire stood and turned to face the one man in the entire universe she wanted to love. That very love was now putting them both in peril. She shuddered to think she had almost allowed Josh to have her. She cast a quick glance to Josh, who smiled that dark and evil smile, a witness to their torment, like a sentry at the castle gates.

She ran to Daniel and buried her head in his chest.

"Claire, are you all right? Is everything all right?" he asked, nestling his lips against the top of her head.

She tilted her face and looked up at him. He grabbed her waist, squeezing her so tight she felt she might faint. "Oh, thank God, your eyes are still blue," he whispered. She melted in his arms. How she wished she could spend the rest of eternity there.

Daniel glared at Josh, who got up and casually walked over to the two lovers, who flinched when he put one hand on each of their shoulders.

"Give me just five minutes of your time. Hear me out before you judge me too harshly. Please." Josh sighed and blew his breath over both of them. Claire felt the familiar erotic trance beginning to course through her veins as Daniel's grip on her lightened. She squeezed his hand with all the strength she could muster, bringing him back to attention.

Josh motioned to the two chairs by the fireplace and sighed again, but they turned their heads to avoid his power.

Daniel took Claire's hand, sat on one of the chairs and pulled Claire down to his lap so she rested on his thigh. He encircled her waist with one arm.

Josh made a production out of walking over to lean into the fireplace mantle, then crossed his black boots at the ankles and cocked his head to the side. He wore a white silk shirt buttoned two buttons too low. Claire noticed a gold medallion, like the one Angie wore, hanging from his neck. No doubt he brought it to put over her neck at the point he took her body. That thought left her cold, as she leaned into Daniel's immoveable chest.

"I'm going to make you both an offer, and then I will let you think about it for a day or two."

"Forget it, Josh. The answer is no." Daniel's voice was so strong it made Claire start.

"But you don't even know what I'm proposing," Josh insisted, his arms outstretched.

"We don't need to hear it. You can leave now, with our answer—it's no." Daniel looked at Claire, who nodded in agreement. She knew what the offer was. She knew what the answer was. What the answer would always be.

"It doesn't have to be this way. I can give you all your dreams. You can be together forever." Josh looked between the both of them.

Claire stood up, released herself from Daniel, walked over to Josh and slapped him across the face. "How dare you. Get out of this house right now. Leave us alone."

Josh rubbed his cheek, but Claire got the feeling he didn't mind the pain. She raised her arm to slap him again in response to the sickly sweet smile he presented her. He grabbed her by the wrist before she could strike again.

"This is unwise, Claire," Josh said coolly. You have no idea who you are messing with."

Claire jerked her arm free. "And you have no idea who you're dealing with, Josh."

"Daniel." Josh leaned around Claire, pleading with his former friend. "You need to reel in your woman. She is making this more dangerous than it needs to be." Josh's face crimped with anger and all his handsomeness disappeared. "I'm not known for being patient."

Daniel's arms pulled her back as he encircled her tiny frame from behind. She wanted to cry, but desperately held her emotions in check. She did not want to give Josh the satisfaction of feeling her fear. But, the emotions of the evening were catching up to her.

"Daniel, I appeal to you. Think about this carefully. You two believe you can win? Beat me? I have been at this for centuries. Centuries. You need to face reality."

Daniel's answer was to release Claire, grab Josh by the shirt collar and pull him to the front door. "I want you out of this house. Go find someone else to terrorize. Leave us alone."

Josh shrugged himself from Daniel's strong grip long enough to square himself and deliver a sneer. Just before going through the door, he looked at the two standing behind him. "You really think you are better at this game? You are fools, both of you. I'll never give up. How long do you really think you can last?" He directed his comment to Claire. "How long do you think He'll let you run around sleeping with your charge, Claire? Didn't they tell you what happens to angels who break the rules?"

Claire had only her active imagination to tell her what the consequences would be. Truthfully, no one had ever told her what would happen, although she was certain it would include a gravesite in Mother's locked garden.

"All it takes is once, Daniel. One time. Then she belongs to me. Wouldn't you rather keep her for yourself? I can make that happen for you. Think, man. Think!" Josh shook his head, muttering something under his breath and let himself out, through the door.

That night, in the quiet solitude of Daniel's bedroom, they lit one white candle. The moon was full. No words were exchanged. Everything was said with the urgency of their kisses, their touch, and, as Claire rose in heated climax, she was sure this would be one of the last times in her eternal life she would be able to have this mortal man while she was a Guardian.

CHAPTER 35

Daniel awoke to the feel of Claire's fingers tracing up and down his spine, inching lower and lower. She was breathing harder too. His cheek rose and fell as he lay with his head on her breast where he had fallen asleep. Her soft white flesh had become his pillow, her smell the last thing he'd experienced at night and the first in the morning. This routine had not changed since the first time they made love, not even a week ago now. He knew he was trying to hang on to her. He also knew soon he would have to let her go. But not at this moment.

"Ah, my angel. You have an appetite this morning again? You are making me old."

"I don't sleep, I don't drink other than hot chocolate, and I don't eat. That leaves only a few things I can do in my human form." Her hand found its way between their bodies to his growing erection. "Do you think it is possible to need you too much?"

Looking down at her angelic face framed in glistening blond wisps, he smiled and shook his head. "Not possible. The more you love me, the more of you I love in return." He kissed her lips, trailing down to her neck and collarbone, mesmerized in the scent of her angel flesh.

"What part of me do you love the most?" She smiled up at him, earning another deep kiss.

"These lips are wonderful. But then, so is your neck," he said as he buried his head under her ear. She giggled and raised a knee to press her sex onto his groin. Daniel's fingers found her opening and he rubbed her clit between his thumb and forefinger. "And these lips," he said as he descended on her mound, whispering to her as he licked the warm honey of her delicate pink skin quivering under his touch. "These lips belong to me. They are not yours; they are mine now."

"Yes," Claire responded as she arched up, giving herself to him.

Claire needed him more each time they made love. As soon as Daniel began pleasuring her folds, she was lost. She craved the warmth of his mouth as it laved her sex, whispering to her there, like telling secrets, as if he could turn her human, make her real. His stiff red cock plunged into her swollen peach with gentleness at first, but then thrust in and out fiercely. A long slow orgasm began to roll through her body and heat her bones like a warm bath. She felt she was made to fit over his shaft.

Her arms were pinned above her head as he held her at the wrists with one powerful hand, squeezing them down into the pillow but rubbing the whiteness of her forearms with his thumb, just to let her know his forcefulness came from his passion and desire for her. Her breasts pushed against his chest. She gasped at the pleasure she felt when he spent himself inside her, but she did not climax. Something lurked at the back of her mind.

They lay silently, breathing heavy. Claire knew this was the quiet before the storm.

A few minutes later, she looked at the almost black curls that hung down the sides of his face as he raised himself up. She watched his eyes as he slipped on his drawstring silk bottoms. With a satisfied smile and quick glance to her naked body, he left the room, but he didn't fool her. She knew he was covering up something. A sense of dread overcame her as she turned her head to the side and wept, her tears soaking into her pillow.

The sound of Daniel grinding coffee drifted up the stairs. With sadness, she noted his routine that told her he wanted his wits about him for the discussion they would soon have.

Claire was purposely lazy, avoiding what was to come. She pretended to sleep, even though Daniel knew she didn't need to, and lay back, looking at the splashes of sunlight on the ceiling. She listened for the sounds of an ordinary day beginning.

Ordinary, as if I belonged here—as if I was human.

Claire took a shower, halfway expecting Daniel to join her. Not this morning. She opened the medicine cabinet, using some of his aftershave behind her ears, and fingered one drop between her breasts, wanting to smell as much like him for as long as she could.

After donning her white gown, Claire brushed the water out of her hair and carefully applied her pink lipstick.

She stood at the top of the stairs, and when she saw Daniel sitting below on the high-backed chair by the fireplace, one leg over the arm, balancing a red coffee cup, staring out the window at the rain, her heart warmed. He was a different man than the one she met that day when he'd attempted to throw away his life. That first day she'd arrived in his life. Even then she'd known he was the only man she would love forever.

She inhaled, steeling herself against the realization of their future. Maybe somehow it would be better than she thought.

Daniel heard Claire begin the descent down the stairs and looked up to see his angel, fresh and new as the first day he saw her. Her beauty made it all the more difficult to speak with her this morning. But they had to talk. *No way around it.*

He stood up out of respect for the woman she was. His heart felt heavy, aching with need, weighted by love—maybe too much love. She ran to him and crashed into his chest so hard he spilled his coffee. She was wrapped around his body tighter today.

She knows.

Damn, this will make it harder.

"Claire, we have to talk," he said as he set his cup down.

He led her to the other chair and when she sat, he knelt before her, hands clasping hers, resting atop her knees. He kissed her fingers, pulling up the courage to say the words he was going to have to say, words she would not want to hear.

"Last night, when Josh came to you—"

"That won't happen again, Daniel. We need to have a password so we can be safe."

"And how long do you think that will last?"

245

She didn't have an answer for him.

"Last night Audray came to the gallery. They had it all arranged." At the mention of Audray's name, Daniel noted how Claire suddenly held her breath.

"Tell me she is no threat to you."

"No, love, she holds no power over me anymore. But Josh is another story. Audray more or less told me he would not stop until he claimed you. *Claimed* you, Claire." He searched her face for recognition of the danger she was in, and it pained him to see there wasn't enough. Not nearly enough. Ever so confident, she would be blind to Josh's evil plans.

"I am not worried," she whispered. She was begging him with her eyes.

"You should be! He's going to keep trying until he wins. You told me yourself there is a limit to what Father will allow. How long will He let you play out this game—a few weeks? A month? What then? Do you honestly think He will turn his back on all of this, what we have started? Turn his back on you?"

"Give me just a few days. Maybe I could go home and reason with Father. Maybe he would make an exception. Maybe he would help us."

"No, no, Claire, you're not thinking." Daniel got up and strode to the window then leaned against the frame, head resting on his forearm. Claire came up behind him and pressed her cheek against his bare back, wrapping her arms around him.

"We can do it, Daniel. I wanted to tell you last night I am not afraid. I think we can beat them."

"This is folly. Josh is right." He continued to stare outside.

"Listen, Daniel. I saw Angie. She's been turned as well. Her charge came back and claimed her." Claire moved around to Daniel's front, placing her palms at the sides of his face. "I wasn't tempted to do the same, even when she told me how wonderful it was. I wouldn't let her touch me. She knows I will never turn. I think eventually, maybe soon, they will leave us alone."

He drew her to his chest and kissed her forehead, whispering, "Sweetheart, you are more important to me than life itself. You must return home. You must go home to Heaven. I wish it wasn't so, but that is the only place you are safe."

"No!" Claire stepped away from him. "Don't say that." But Daniel could see the recognition in her eyes he wished wasn't there. There really was only one solution: they could both turn dark.

Daniel shook his head as she spoke. "Please, just give me a little more time, Daniel. I need time to figure this out. I know I can."

Daniel frowned. He looked at his angel squarely in the eyes.

"If you go dark, I will follow right behind you, Claire. You know this. So does Josh. So does Father. I doomed us the night I came to you at the planetarium and asked you to stay in human form. It's all my fault."

He could see Claire wanted to be angry. Her chest heaved as she took in a deep breath and clenched her fists. Her eyes scoped the room, as if looking for something to hit or throw. He loved her even more for it, wanting to fight a battle that could never be won.

He pulled her to him again and kissed her hard. She struggled to get away, but he wouldn't let her go. She clutched, pushed at his chest, tried to unpeel his fingers from her back and waist, and then simply went into disappear in order to escape. She turned back into human form on the other side of the room, breathing heavily.

Daniel sat down and put his chin in his hands, looking at the floor, waiting for her to come to grips with the only reality that made sense.

"When?" She looked at him with tears in her eyes. Her miserable face was still beautiful to him. It broke his heart.

"Tomorrow morning."

CHAPTER 36

The larger-than-life golden angel mannequins looked back down on them through the storefront window as Daniel and Claire strolled down the moist sidewalk. These angels appeared to weep in silence. Their heads were bent, smiles on their faces in eternal repose, hands up and fingers spread out in an expression of wonder—or was it panic? Behind them they bore white wings that looked heavy but sparkled in the display light. Claire never experienced having wings, but it was said some angels used to, a long time ago.

"They don't begin to do you justice. You are more beautiful," Daniel said to the back of her head. As he tried to lead her down the street, Claire was mesmerized by the angel mannequin's expression. She wondered if she had ever looked that way.

They sat at the open-air café under a gas heater. The morning had turned sunny, and they basked in it between light rain sprinkles. Claire ate whipped cream off the top of her hot chocolate and dipped her tongue into the warm sweet mixture. Daniel sat next to her, touching as much of her body as possible. They watched people walk by on the wet washed sidewalk.

It was all arranged. The message from Doris had came back in a matter of minutes. Father would have to bring her across the threshold himself, so great her transgression with Daniel had been. She'd been barred from the automatic return she'd enjoyed for years. Daniel told her he was relieved Father accepted her at all, even if she would pay a price for their great sin. At least she would still be alive in her angel form. He wanted her to live forever, he said.

She had packed all her earthly clothes from the attic, especially the extra pairs of blue jeans she would not likely be able to replace and now had to last for eternity. She left the yellow clogs under the dresser. On the bureau top she left the can of sparkle spray, next to her pink lipstick. No one in Heaven would believe her stories of how humans invented dust without emotion.

What would someone think if they saw these things? Would they know an angel had lived here, an angel who had fallen in love? Would they know that she had saved his soul, done her job and kept her perfect record? Would they care that she was the only Guardian in the whole universe to be able to lay claim to this distinction? And how would they feel if they knew she could save Daniel but could not save herself?

She wasn't going to tell Daniel she'd left the items there, as if, by leaving something behind, it would mean that she'd been a real woman, if only for a few days.

Claire had to admit that it had been worth it.

Daniel wasn't going to be sad until she was gone, he'd decided. He was spending the rest of the day doing things she wanted to do. He took her through the perfume counter at Macy's. He watched as she admired the twinkling lights and the brightly wrapped cellophane packages that made so much noise as she picked them up. She sampled scents, even managed to spray some on him too. He bought a white candle and a bottle of Chanel No. 5, her favorite.

"I'll wear it every day in Heaven and think of you." Then she'd sobbed again. Unable to stop her from crying, he gave up and just let her unload. It was taking a toll on her usually sparkling blue eyes, which were now red and sore-looking.

They decided not to spend their last night at the house, in case Josh had designs to spoil their plans. He rented a room with a large fireplace overlooking the ocean. It was close to the prearranged spot on the beach at Bodega Bay where Claire would ascend. Before they checked in, they took one last walk on the beach.

The beach appeared to be on fire as they watched the sun forfeit to the dark sea at the horizon. *The end of a sunny winter day, the end of the earthly life of an angel and her lover.*

This will be the last sunset I see with him.

The ground was slightly warm, even though the air had turned chilly. Claire lay back on the quilt he brought, her hands above her head in the sand, feeling the warmth on her back come through the fabric as she sifted soft sand through her fingers. She aimlessly played with little pieces of shell and stones as she looked up to a sky that would be covered in a blanket of stars soon. Daniel was at her side, stretched out on one arm, looking out at the last of the sunset, the orange glow fading on his face.

"I have a confession, Claire." He smiled and turned his gaze on her.

"Do I want to hear this? I know everything important about you, except what you will do with the rest of your life here." She rubbed his arm and he bent to give her a kiss.

"This may seem strange to you, but I grew up near the beach and..." He traced over her lips, delicately lacing his fingers under her chin. "I have never made love on the beach. Never."

She sighed deeply, watching the flickering of his shiny dark eyes and said, "Neither have I."

They both laughed.

Then his mouth slanted to cover hers and she parted her lips to allow his tongue entry. She tasted the whispered words from deep in his chest.

He removed all her clothes with care, lingering on every button, every touch of her skin as he raised her shirt over her head and slid her pants down over her hips and bare feet. She laid completely naked, nipples tightened from the chill, fully exposed to the early evening air, to the stars that were beginning to peek timidly through the deep blue of the heavens. There was not a cloud to be found in the deepening blue sky. A bright white moon was just beginning to ascend over the horizon.

He removed his clothes, laying them on top of hers neatly in the sand like a ritual they would carry out for a hundred years. Daniel lay down next to her, and as she looked at the stars, he watched her face. A few minutes later, she climbed on top of his bare, bronzed body, laying her head on his heart to hear him one more time, her knees hugging his slim hips.

"Tonight, I want you to know what it feels like to be worshiped," she said as she kissed him first on the lips, then under his jaw and down his neck. She inhaled the musty male scent of him, the wonderful smell of a man in love with her. Her body rocked over his hardness. She inched slowly down his thighs, resting on his lower legs, kissing a trail down his chest and abdomen and then put his penis between her lips. He groaned as she curled her tongue over him. His chest rose and fell in the young moonlight as he gasped.

The sight of his pleasure heightened her own inner bonfires. His urgent eyes called to her.

I will remember those moonlit eyes in forever.

He finally pulled her up onto him. His hands firmly held the sides of her face as she found him and guided him to her sex. She lowered herself as slowly as she could onto his full shaft, the lips of her peach swollen with the fullness of him. In the presence of all the stars in the sky, she rode him gently by moonlight, stopping to kiss his warm red lips.

The sounds of the surf drowned out the rest of the world as it slapped and coaxed the shore. Claire raised her arms above her head, and with her thumb rubbing between her first two fingers, produced a tiny amount of dust that sparkled in the moonlight as it fell from her fingertips, down over her breasts and belly and onto his chest. His steady breathing accepted her offering as he closed his eyes. She saw it was just enough to cause arousal but not too much to cause sleep. He opened his eyes and smiled as she felt the delicious climax overcome her body.

His hands cupped her breasts and then became claws digging into her buttocks as he arched, rocked, and spent himself deep inside her.

She loved the warmth of their two spent bodies, and rested on his chest again, listening to his heart beating, starting to slow. His fingertips lightly laced over her back in aimless meanderings. They were breathing in unison. She pulled the quilt over them both and watched him rest in the cocoon of their love.

After a time, they dressed and walked slowly arm in arm, back to the car, Daniel holding the thick quilt. Her eyes ached from all the crying she'd done this day. Of course, the pain didn't compare with the ache in her heart.

Except for the brilliant white moon and a profusion of bright stars, the sky was completely dark and night was in full force when they checked into the motel room nearby.

"Father's made an interesting choice of time and place. Crack of dawn, on a deserted beach," Daniel said as he opened the sliding glass doors to the ocean. He leaned on the railing. She soaked in the vision of his silhouette in the moonlight and knew she would never forget what he looked like there, the breeze playing with the tendrils of his dark hair. She looked over the space of their room, the place where they would spend their last night together.

"I think Father wanted to give us some privacy. I don't think He wanted an audience. Doris said not to tell anyone about the plan."

"Obviously." Daniel was looking at his toes, still peppered with a few stubborn grains of sand. "Why didn't He just send you home with Doris?"

Claire thought about that while she scanned the room. Even the large king-sized bed was dwarfed by the chipped slate fireplace that was fully ablaze. The room was furnished in simple but elegant antiques, including the four-poster bed in dark mahogany with a deep green and blue polished satin coverlet. The flooring was of wood planking that squeaked when they walked across it barefoot."He's coming himself," Claire finally said. "He has to be the one who admits me." She suddenly ran to him and buried her head just under Daniel's chin.

"Maybe He has something planned for me? Maybe He has words…" Daniel sounded apprehensive.

"I don't think you have reason to fear Him. I have to climb the stairs; I can't just will myself home any longer, not until I've been admitted back. Be prepared for a bit of a show. He is my Father, after all. And I'm coming home."

True enough, Daniel thought. *The prodigal daughter comes home to a Father who misses her.* Daniel hoped that Claire held a special place in Father's heart. Though the decision was the hardest one he'd had to make, it was the right one. Claire would be protected, and live forever. And Daniel would be loved forever, long beyond his own human lifespan. They would have a love that *would* last forever, after all.

It was worth it. Every ounce of pain would be worth it.

CHAPTER 37

Josh was seething. A human and a Guardian were making a fool of him. When word of this leaked out, it would tarnish his perfect reputation. After all, he was looked up to by all the younger darks. He was the standard. He had more angel conquests than the rest of them combined.

He was so sure Daniel and Claire would want to spend eternity together, he hadn't really think about a Plan B. The power of the dark side was way more tantalizing than the power of love, but these two were completely, utterly, unbelievably stupid.

Well, it isn't over until it's over. They were going to find out what kind of a devil they'd decided to tangle with.

It's not how you play the game, but that you never, ever lose. He drummed this into his recruits during their training.

He searched Daniel's home for some sign, some clue as to where they were going. He found nothing.

Then he tracked down Angela and found her in bed with James.

"Look at how you two squander your powerful, immortal dark lives. Pretending you're human? This you can do for all eternity. There's urgent work to be done." He crossed the bedroom, looking out the window to the night sky, at time slipping away.

"We're in love, Josh." James looked back at his sponsor across their entangled bodies on the deep maroon sheets.

Josh flared back at him in red, lunging toward them.

"How can I get hold of Doris?" Josh gripped Angela's arm, yanking her naked body out of bed so quickly she howled. James instantly shot up between them.

"Excuse me?" James' voice was confrontational. He immediately wrapped his arms around the naked and shivering Angela, who folded her head away in James's bare chest.

The smell emanating from these two lovers before him was turning Josh's stomach. Sex and sweat, a combination he liked sometimes when he needed to be serviced, but now, in the middle of a crisis, when he was about to lose his perfect record, it was a disgusting smell. The smell of too much bliss wasn't healthy for a dark angel. *It makes them soft, ineffective. Like drugs or alcohol to humans.*

"Oh, give it up, James. This isn't the time to make a stand. I've got to find them, damn it." Josh was about to toss James aside like a bag of dirty laundry, when Angela spoke up, in his defense.

"Trace all the places she took him in his dreams. You'll find them at one of their favorites." She glared at Josh.

"Fuck! I don't know where the hell she took him, Angela." Josh stepped back to brace himself, but his voice was booming, sending them both shuddering. "Daniel and I never talked about it."

Angela suggested he go look at Daniel's paintings for clues. Well, there certainly were no jungles in Northern California that he knew of, and as a human, Daniel wouldn't be able to transport, like the angel, to some exotic tropical climate. Josh didn't think looking at the jungle scenes would give him any ideas, besides, he hated looking at those awful things. *Ridiculous pink leopards and penguins.* Maybe it was good that Daniel couldn't be turned. *He'd have been another one, like James. All love, no bite.*

"Think. Think, damn it," Josh spat out, smacking his forehead with his palm. Angela jumped, but James looked like he wanted to rip Josh's head off.

All Josh's recent converts were turning out to be morons. He already regretted his decision to admit this pair to his brotherhood. *These two would rather make love than claim souls. They're too soft for this work.*

Josh was so angry he considered doing away with them, but he was concerned he might need Angela to lure the Guardian to him. And having new recruits made Joshua more powerful.

He could tell Angela was rethinking the wisdom of her decision to turn dark. Josh knew it would only get worse as she learned the nature of her new dark friends. Probably thinking about finding a way out already.

Well, big deal. Nothing was turning out the way it was supposed to anyway.

Josh had to get away from them. Their love scent was overpowering, blurring his vision, making his ears buzz and his nose itch. It annoyed him more than he thought it would have. *All these people who can't live without each other. Damned idiots!* He'd have to make an example out of Angie and James in the very near future, otherwise he would never be able to exert control over his new recruits.

But first, he had to find the angel and her painter. Maybe he'd vaporize Daniel just for spite. No angel had ever humiliated him so much. He'd make her pay. Hatred boiled over inside him like a thick black sludge.

What was going on? Why were they not at the house? Where could Doris have transported them? Or did they go on their own? He knew they weren't leaving the area completely; Daniel had left behind all his things, including his paints and his work.

Josh searched downtown haunts. He went to a Latin disco. He went to all the twenty-four-hour Laundromats he could find, scaring half the homeless population in the downtown area who were trying to find a little shelter from the rain. He searched the paintings at Daniel's house, looking for evidence. One of his new paintings depicted pieces of colored glass discarded on a smooth white beach, glistening in the sun.

Where are they?

CHAPTER 38

Daniel put the little star pendant around Claire's neck and kissed it where it lay in the hollow below her collarbone. "I hope he will let you have this, and I hope you remember our time together whenever you see it." Daniel leaned down to kiss her, whispering, "Know that I love you." The star twinkled, like the droplets of tears in the corners of her eyes.

He was aching with the hole in his heart, too.

"Don't. Don't cry, Claire. It's going to be all right. You'll see. This is for the best." He stood naked in front of her and then pulled her to him. Their arms entwined. He claimed her mouth, hungry and waiting.

He wondered if he could stay up all night. He didn't want to waste a minute of their time together. He led her to the bed where he sat, reaching out to her.

"Come to me, Angel."

Claire was in his arms and showering him with kisses. She straddled him as he lay back on the bed, her breasts pressing to his chest. She drew her fingers through his shiny hair and kissed his forehead.

He lowered her down and to the side, turning her body so his chest encased her back. She felt his kisses to her neck as his arms pulled her into his groin, his hand playing with the folds of her sex. When he entered her from behind, she was panting into the pillow. As he thrust inside her, she was grateful he could not see the trail of tears covering her cheeks. She felt the ripple of pleasure course through her body, but it increased the dull ache in her heart.

Even the pain of this last pairing I do not want to be without. The more he gives me the more I am mortally wounded. Wounded forever. This is a pain I will bear forever, gratefully. At last, he moaned her name at the back of her neck, pulling her into him.

Later, they sat on the balcony overlooking the roar of the ocean, wrapped in the bedspread. The wind was cold on her skin, but she was on fire with need for him, a need that would live for centuries.

For the rest of the night Claire tried to keep Daniel awake, but she was having a hard time doing so. He dozed in and out of a sleep. She knew his brain was willing, but his body had given up after the second time they made love.

She watched as the skies turned from dark to light grey and then blue, with a blush of pink coming from a sunrise on the other side of the motel. *Another ordinary day starting. I'll let him sleep five minutes longer.* She heard the gulls calling to each other over the regular pulse of the waves tumbling to shore.

At six they got a call on the room phone, the ringing waking Daniel. Daniel looked startled as he shot a quick glance at Claire. He put the call on speakerphone and they listened to a nervous clerk inform them he'd been persuaded to give their room number to a man. A man who was on his way to their room at that moment.

Daniel gaped at Claire, then they rushed to get dressed. They were racing down the hallway before the clerk even knew that no one was listening to her any longer.

CHAPTER 39

They left the passenger door on the Mercedes ajar and ran to the beach for Claire's transport back to Heaven. Daniel pulled her forward, hiking her duffel up onto his shoulder. Glancing over her shoulder, she gasped when she saw Josh's black Hummer roaring down the rise of the highway about a quarter mile away.

The two of them flew over the sand dunes and the uneven ice plant that bloomed bright pink. Mounds of brittle brown seaweed littered the beach, scorched crisp after days in the sun. Salty sea excrement assailed her nostrils. Out to sea, a thick fog had been pushed back, waiting for a chance to pounce.

The muted sea sounds and the icy cool early morning air chilled Claire to the bone. The stiff breeze tugged at her tears. Her heart was racing and her mouth was parched. She was coming up to the threshold she had dreaded for so long. This was like Daniel's act of jumping out of the airplane to an unknown future, she thought. She was not entirely sure there was one, but she rushed toward it anyway, terrified not to make it in time. Terrified to leave. Terrified to leave Daniel forever.

Forever!

The sun was low, just peeking behind the mountains at their back. Large white clouds writhed in an otherwise clear morning sky, then spread out and began to grow in ominous proportion.

Daniel and Claire continued running for the water's edge. They stopped when small foamy waves lapped at their feet. As the water pulled away, the slick beach was littered with black holes and bubbles that hissed and then went silent.

Creatures heading for cover. Back to their homes in the sand from a trip to the big ocean.

Daniel turned to her, cupping her face in his hands. She heard the screech of tires as Josh's car turned off the highway and onto the frontage road.

Daniel gazed at her tears, wiping them with his thumbs. His face reflected her own pain but somehow his eyes still smiled, as they always did for Claire. Love etched his features. She would always remember him this way. Strong. Handsome. His face full of love and his heart full of passion.

Would he still have those same eyes as the days and months passed without me? Would they shine for someone else when he found his true mate, the woman meant to share his human life? Will I fade into distant memory with the passage of time?

His eyes went to her mouth and he covered it urgently with his own. She had heard the expression before, "gallows kiss" and this was one. Their love would live forever in her heart. She would count every year of his life and then go on alone.

So unfair. I would trade places...

She didn't want to miss the warmth of his lips. She could stay forever, but he pulled away. Behind him a large amber stairway was forming in the clouds. The massive marbled yellow and golden structure reached halfway to the beach. A small figure in white stood at the top of the stairs.

Father has come.

Daniel took in the sight before him, his face filled with wonder, then she watched the worry lines appear at his forehead and bridge of his nose. She read regret and sadness as he turned to her.

"It has to be done." Daniel said, reaching out to her, engulfing her in his long arms. For a second, she thought perhaps he wouldn't let her go. His breath was warm and raspy as he whispered into her ear, "You have taught me to have faith. I know somehow we will see each other again. If it takes a century, or another lifetime, I will find you. Somehow."

"If you tell me to stay, I will," Claire pleaded.

"Yes, I know, my love. But I am asking you to go. Do it for me. Can you live for me, Claire?"

"For you, but without you."

"Yes. It has to be this way."

She nodded, unable to speak.

"You will still be with me, here." He said as he placed her palm at his heart over his strong muscled chest—that place that had been her sanctuary. "Forever, Claire. You have to believe that." He grabbed her again. "Please believe for me. Live for me, Claire."

"I will love you forever, Daniel."

"And I will love you forever, my angel. My Claire."

The stairway touched down to the sandy beach with a deep rumble that shook the ground and then was silent.

Josh appeared at the top of the dunes and hesitated. Claire saw a red bolt of light flash just short of where she and Daniel stood. He wouldn't miss the next time.

"You must hurry," Daniel urged. She knew she had to go of her own volition, as he was not going to push. Her legs betrayed her and she wobbled for the bottom step, and then turned to look at him.

The first stair made her safe from anything Josh could do. She saw the red laser light sent from Josh's eyes was truncated at the golden aura surrounding the stairwell, engulfing her in Father's protection. Daniel breathed a sigh of relief.

He wants me to go. He actually wants me to go!

Each step got remarkably easier. As she ascended, her sandy slippers made scratching sounds on the massive steps. Daniel became smaller and smaller. Finally, he was just a toy figure on the beach with another speck of a figure beside him.

Josh had joined him. She took one long look, then turned and approached Father, who stood tall at the top of the stairs, light dancing with a swirl of golden clouds at his back. His face was stoic, but Claire thought she saw a tear glistening in the corner of one eye.

Claire's own cheeks were shiny with tears. She wanted to walk past Father into the clouds. He stopped her, turned her around to see Daniel one last time. Father bent down and put his face next to Claire's, watching with her, his cheek pressing against her angel flesh. With hands on her shoulders, he held her up and steady.

"He will be safe now, Claire," Father whispered.

Claire wasn't so sure. Father knew the concern in her heart.

"If we have to, we can send someone down to watch over him. But I think Josh will give up now that you're gone, and Daniel knows the rules. As much as I hate to admit it, you have armed him with the rules, and that will help."

They continued watching the two specks on the sand as the stairway started to retreat.

"Do you want a new Guardian for Daniel?"

"No." Claire didn't have to think twice about it. She felt oddly reassured. Daniel was still there, standing, unharmed. And she was safe. Safe forever.

This is just not worth it. But Father said you will be safe, my love.

The stairway removed itself, as it had appeared, one step at a time, until at last the top step with the two small figures was lost in the white cloud. Then the cloud imploded back on itself, the last bit of white swirling mist evaporating into thin air, leaving a blue clear sky. Daniel sighed. Josh shot a quick look at him. The man had been holding his breath.

"You didn't have to do this," Josh said. "There was another way. You two never gave me the opportunity to explain how differently this all could have ended."

"And I should believe you why?"

Josh shrugged.

"What, no witty repartee? No dark understatements? No jokes from the man responsible for taking..." Daniel did not finish. He turned his back on Josh and made a bead for the car.

"Look, okay, I misjudged everything. It wasn't going to work, anyway. This whole scene was inevitable. You two were just the last to get it. Everyone else knew." Josh was still talking to Daniel's back. His words bounced off Daniel like a gentle breeze. Daniel did not slow or veer off course. His determined gait carried him toward the parking lot, concentrating on one step in front of the other. "You want to be angry at someone? What about Him?" Josh pointed to the Heavens. "He knew this was going to happen. He chose her to come to you. He did it," Josh said to Daniel's back.

Daniel stopped, slowly turned. He marched back towards the dark angel until he stood a foot from him. Daniel leaned in further as he spoke.

"You lost." Daniel tapped Josh's chest with a stubborn forefinger right over the angel's heart. "The big bad dark angel lost the battle. Face it, freak. No one in the universe cares anything about you. You don't have what I have. You've never *owned* what I've *lost*." He started to step away, backwards, anger increasing the volume in his chest, waving his hands through the air as he continued.

"You're insignificant. Irrelevant. Unnecessary. How does it feel to be measured by what you take away and not what you give?"

Josh stood motionless as Daniel rounded the top of the dunes and disappeared. He heard a car door open and close. An engine revved, tires screeched and then all was strangely calm. Josh felt alone in every sense of the word. He shrugged his shoulders, rolled his head from side to side, and sighed.

His anger had evaporated into fear at the sight of the golden stairway and the man at the top. He was glad none of his recruits saw how he lost the angel, and how small and afraid he'd felt staring into the face of Father himself.

CHAPTER 40

Claire walked with Father down the path from the reception hall. He kept his arm around her but was silent except for the methodical crunching of his feet on the diamond dust pathway. She clung to the side of him, hiding as much of herself as she could, leaning into him for support. Several angels stopped what they were doing, but did not venture to come close or look into her eyes. This was not the usual type of homecoming. Claire knew the word had spread, the way it always did. The profusion of flower petals, cherub choirs and hugs after a successful venture—the closest thing to a ticker-tape parade in Heaven—would not be today's welcome. With her face still streaked with tears, her dress disheveled, she honestly didn't know when she'd be able to stand straight, stop crying, and look back at them.

Someday.

Claire had forever to perfect closing down her emotions, but her heart wasn't into making the adjustment any time soon. Maybe now the other angels would leave her alone.

Father didn't let go of her as they passed by her dorm. Dark green ivy clung fiercely to the stone walls. A group of young angels were reading on a bright green lawn and a couple of them tittered, which caused Father to stop and frown at them until they bowed and scurried into the dorm like a flock of birds. They passed a group of three angels gardening, their white gowns tied between their legs, making them look like they wore huge diapers. As they stood up to stare back, leaning on a hoe or shovel, their faces, hands and cotton smocks were smeared with the dark reddish-brown soil, the lifeblood of the flowering plants and trees that grew there.

The pair walked past the Playhouse with its spires looking suddenly more golden, as if recently polished. Long banners snaked through a gentle breeze, flapping like the wings of a firebird blazoned with an overwhelming palate of color. An older Guardian wheeled a clothes rack of colorful costumes towards one of the side entrances. The rack's wheels on the crushed diamond path were giving the angel some difficulty, and she muttered under her breath, unaware of Father's scowl. The enormous Playhouse looked like it was growing up from a bright cloud of white and yellow rose bushes. The intensity of Heaven's light was brighter than Claire remembered, and she squinted.

There was activity all around them as they silently walked up the glistening path lined with blooming flowers bursting with heady aroma. It was the way to Father's office complex, one she knew well in happier times. Although it was winter in Daniel's world, Heaven's blossoms of narcissus, snapdragons, stock, and bushes of lilac stood tall, invigorated by the mist that covered them several times a day. If only Claire could enjoy these sights, these scents.

Father opened the tall, etched glass-and-metal door for her. Claire dropped her duffel into the chair just inside the entrance, suddenly exhausted. She covered her face and sobbed.

Most humans want to go to Heaven. *Without Daniel, this is Hell itself.*

"Come, Claire, we have to talk." Father held out his hand, and escorted her down the hallway into his private office. The long hall that led to Father's office echoed like a lonely mausoleum.

Once a warm room where a young angel would tell stories of the human world to the rapt attention of the old man she felt closer to than anyone else in the universe, now the space chilled her to the bone. Claire's happy memories collided with the gaping hole she felt in her chest.

Of course they had to talk. She'd been so wrapped up with how miserable she felt, she'd temporarily forgotten about the consequences of her indiscretions with Daniel. She shivered, her teeth chattering.

"Sit here, child." He pointed to the leather chair, warmed by the fireplace nearby. It was the chair she used to sit in during their long afternoon chats, like the day she created her first dust mixture or the morning she returned from her first successful mission. He made a point to be available to her, avidly listening to her theories on humans and why they behaved as they did. Claire found it curious how fascinated he was with all his creations.

Father's tall statuesque form was motionless as he looked out the rosette window, his face awash in color and light, overseeing the Guardianship and the activity of the day spread out in front of him. He sighed.

Here it comes.

"I am gravely disappointed in you, Claire. I thought you were better prepared for this sort of mission." He turned around to look at her.

Claire tried to stuff the emotions raging in her chest, but at last gave up. Overwhelmed, she dropped to his feet. "I am so sorry. Your trust and faith in me was all I ever had. But for just a few days, Father, I felt as if...as if...I were..." She looked up at him.

"Human," he finished for her. "You actually thought you could live like a human? You're an angel, Claire. Your human life was over years ago. You know this." His voice was resolute, unwavering.

Claire knew it was absolutely the terrible truth. She nodded, wiping the tears from her cheeks with the back of her hands. She remained at his feet, while Father continued to stand gazing through the window. He touched the top of her head, then pulled his hand away and did not utter a word.

There was a light rap at the side door.

"Come in," Father's deep melodic voice consumed the whole room, rattling the windows just enough to make Claire flinch.

"Sorry, sir, this is for Claire."

When she spotted Father's personal assistant, a steaming mug in his hand, her mood lightened. He handed her a hot chocolate, filled to overflowing with whipped cream. Claire had enjoyed this ritual bestowed upon her many times before in Father's office. Cedric was eternally kind to her, and appeared to be much older than most of the other angels in the Guardianship. His silver hair glistened in the sunlight as his bent frame stooped lower in a bow. He rose and extended the warm mug to Claire and gave her a private wink.

"Welcome back, Claire. So glad you have returned to us at last."

"Oh, thank you, Cedric." She immediately stood, taking the mug with a smile. Her hands were cold and the heat felt good. She inhaled the sweet warm mixture with eyes closed, just like she always did. Melted whipped cream spilled onto the white marble floor and on Claire's dress.

"Oh, I'm sorry," Cedric began. "I just wanted to help…"

Claire shook her head. "No, I'm grateful. Don't worry about it."

Instantly on his knees, Cedric produced a damp rag and wiped clean the white marble floor and then looked at Claire's dress, streaked with two long brown lines.

"Cedric, I need a private word or two with Claire. We aren't finished," Father said with irritation. The bony assistant nodded and bowed, heading backwards toward the exit. Claire caught a conspiring smile and wink just before he disappeared behind the doorway. Father didn't notice.

She mused at this small kindness, which warmed her heart as well as her hands, and felt a swelling of courage in her chest. Recalling the day she met Josh at the café when he made her spill her hot chocolate, she remembered how she found the courage then to stand up to the dark angel. She suddenly felt hopeful, although she had to admit, she missed the battle between the dark and light forces already. Giving up and retreating to safety was never her plan. Claire thought they could win the war. Now she was beginning to doubt whether or not she made the right decision to return.

Did I give up too soon? I should have died fighting.

"Please." Father motioned her to sit again, then sat across from her in the other leather chair. He watched the fire and sighed. Behind him, ancient symbols carved in the dark grain of his old desk were highlighted with sunlight. They almost seemed to dance.

Claire made a big show of loudly slurping the white topping as Father's eyebrows arched up. She didn't care how much of it spilled onto her dress now. They'd just wash and send it back tomorrow, perfectly white, or get her a new one. But then of course she wouldn't want a new one. It wouldn't smell like Daniel anymore. It wouldn't be the dress he pressed close to his chest when he said goodbye this morning. No, this dress would never be laundered. It would stay in her closet in her room, stains and all, marked forever with her tears.

She sat before Father and tried to compose herself. How nice it would be to just take a long nap, to wake up and find this all had been a bad dream. That she was in fact a real woman, sleeping safely in Daniel's strong arms, suffering a nightmare that she had turned into an angel and had to return home to Heaven.

Father was studying her.

"Your days of being a Guardian are over, Claire. I need you to accept that as soon as you can." He added softly, "I'm sorry it worked out this way for you. In time, you will mend."

She nodded. She was going to try very hard to feel cold inside to quell the pain. Then later, she might start to feel alive again.

"We have to find something useful for you here. Mother has some good ideas. Perhaps a teaching position, or work in the Playhouse? Maybe the library?" He didn't make eye contact so did not see the stare Claire drilled into him.

At last, Claire worked up the nerve to speak. "I have a question."

Father looked slightly irritated with the request. "Yes, what is it?"

"You haven't once said anything about all the rules I broke. I understood that perhaps I would be retired, banished, or buried in your cemetery out behind the greenhouses."

"No, those angels didn't come back. They have gone dark."

"What do you mean, they didn't come back? They are buried there, aren't they?"

"No, they're not. The white stones are reminders. For me."

Claire looked up at his face, puzzled.

"I couldn't just let them leave, be gone. I wanted to remember them, all of them. Over the space of time, there have been only a few."

"Like Angela," Claire whispered as she began to understand.

"Exactly."

"I saw her, you know. She came back to say goodbye to me. She gave me her bag."

"Yes. I knew."

"So those angels are still alive?"

"Alive? No, but you're not alive either, Claire. Do they exist, is that what you mean?"

She nodded.

"Yes. Somewhere, but out of my reach right now." He winced as he continued. "They choose not to be found right now."

"So they can come back?"

He smiled. "All things are possible. You know this, my dear."

She saw the ancient face of a truly supreme being, secure, satisfied, and confident in his work. When his eyes fell upon her she felt ignited, almost human. He always had that affect on her.

Then she remembered herself—the reason for this meeting—and grew sad. "Except for a life with Daniel," she whispered.

"Only as a dark angel. Do you want that? Really want that?" He was furrowing the large brow on his smooth ageless face.

Claire knew in her bones he could make it happen. He could just snap his fingers and she would be right back in the human world, but as a dark angel.

It took every ounce of her spirit to give him an answer.

"No."

"The human world is intoxicating. I should know. I made it that way." His steel blue eyes bored into Claire, and she saw in them ancient battles, heard cries of pain and joy. The rhythm of life was all around him. And he let her see it.

"I give humans choice, free will. I give angels the same, but each of you are two different sides of the same coin. Each of you has different choices available." He got up, came to the end of the desk and sat on the edge in front of Claire. One knee was bent, the other straight, supporting his frame. Claire bowed her head and focused on her chocolate.

"You were supposed to go down to the human world and save this man, which you did. He probably won't ever be in danger of doing himself harm again. But he knows about us now. It's supposed to be his faith that saves him, that makes him strive to be a better man. He's put his faith in an angel. I wanted him to believe, not know. Do you see the difference? In a way, Claire, you've robbed him of that. You've robbed him of his faith."

Claire felt punched. "We fell in love!"

He stood up quickly, walked over in front of Claire, his scowling face leaning into her. "How dare you! How dare you place your own selfish needs above what we do here in the Guardianship. I chose you to become a Guardian because I saw in you a special quality all the angels have here, the capacity to serve, to help humans understand the power and beauty of life. Guardians serve unselfishly, wishing nothing for themselves. What you've brought this man is a relationship of the flesh, Claire. You gave him your body. He gets his inspiration from loving you, an angel. That's not how it's supposed to be."

Claire saw something in Father's logic. A flaw. A fatal flaw.

"Excuse me, sir. I need to understand something. You created the choices; you created the attractions. You created my body and then took that life away from me. You took me from my parents. I know they must have grieved. But I don't know anything else about them—you wiped clean every ounce of my memories; you did this because you chose me to serve." She stood up.

"And I have served you, Father. I have saved more humans than any of the angels here, without one single failure. I have inspired others at the Guardianship to be better angels. I have lived with their gossip and their criticism of my ways and of me. I have had my room searched and my personal things borrowed without permission. And I have never complained about any of it."

The look on Father's face was a mixture of anger and shock. His eyes clouded over, began to water.

"And I have given up the love of a man. You created that in me. You made that possible, gave me the choice. Now you want to take that away from me as well?" Claire looked at her feet, then back up to Father's face.

"Is it necessary that you sacrifice me for your Guardianship? Because it isn't my Guardianship. It's yours. Who is the selfish one now?" She stepped closer and said to him softly, "It's time to let me go."

"No," He whispered. "Your work is here."

"No, Father, my work here is done. The battle isn't in Heaven. The battle is down in the human world, where I belong." Claire stepped back away from Father's imposing figure, suddenly with more courage than she'd ever known. "I have done something you have not. For a few days I lived and loved as a human. I found my soul mate. That's where I belong."

Father went over to the window again, his back to her, and sighed.

Claire carefully continued, "You know my thoughts, you know the choice I'd make if I could, truly could. If we really do have free will here, I'm asking you to prove it."

He turned to face her and quietly gave the edict that would ring in her ears for the next several hours. "But you are back here. You made your choice. You are a Guardian Angel. Your choices are to have your memories washed or bear the burden of your actions every day as you seek to find a way to contribute. But here you will remain for all eternity. It isn't useful to think otherwise, Claire."

THE LETTER

The four steps up to the lobby entrance at her dormitory seemed higher than Claire remembered. She used to take them two or three at a time, once doing all four in one leap. Not today, though. She took each step with deliberate, careful movements, as if in pain, her yellow duffel bag slung over her right shoulder. Though nearly empty, it still felt heavy.

The lobby was full of angels. They lounged in all positions, reading or whispering to each other in small groups, relaxing on white couches in front of the stone fireplace mantle. Many of them looked up. Several pairs of eyes followed Claire through the lobby and up the grand curved staircase. Claire felt their stares on her back with each painful step.

Upstairs, the floor was deserted and eerily quiet, like the evening Claire left. Most angels were in classes. She gripped the doorknob, which was never locked, and burst into her old room, unsure whether it felt like a sanctuary or prison. Sunlight poured in from a small window over the settee filled with colorful pillows, her favorite reading place, as well as through the clouds overhead. Dropping her yellow bag with a thud, she sighed as she noted the first of Daniel's large paintings hanging from a skyhook next to the window. It was the one she touched at the gallery. The pink lioness and brightly colored birds perched on multi-shades of thick green leaves. She turned around, soaking up the vision—her walls dripping with the splash of colorful paintings, the outpouring of Daniel's soul. She felt the lack of him there beside her and started to cry. She loved his artwork, but missed the man.

It seemed like long ago her fingertips had touched his red lips and traced the little laugh line at the right side of his mouth. She bent and kissed the painting. The acrylic surface gave back its sharp scent in rebuke. Daniel's talent was there before her, but the scent of his body was relegated to her memory.

Next she walked into the white marble bathroom and turned on the hot water of the pedestal tub. From her yellow bag she brought out lavender gel and poured a healthy dose into the steaming bath, like creating a witches' cauldron. She lit the Chanel white pillar candle Daniel had bought her. It sputtered on the white marble vanity. Carefully removing her dress, she hung it up in the closet, inside out. She slipped off her angel-issue black slippers with the pearl button.

She eased her naked body into the warm, sudsy water and leaned back against the tub wall. She sighed, lost in the sensuality of the steaming liquid and the soothing lavender scent. Turning her head slightly to view the burning candle, she remembered the white candle altar in Daniel's bedroom that first night they slept together as man and woman. She decided that she would burn a white pillar every night, for however long she had in the Guardianship, and would sit in the dark, in the warm bath, creating a new ritual that might last for centuries. Then she could pretend she was human again. She could star in her own dream fantasy. The candle made fluttering sounds like the wings of a small bird.

There was a rap on the door.

"I'm in the tub." She thought they would leave her alone, at least tonight.

"Claire, it's Ava. Can I come in?" The young angel's voice floated through the door.

"Oh, Ava, yes, please." Claire suddenly remembered her friend.

A young blonde angel with a long French braid walked through the open bathroom door and gave Claire a kiss on the forehead. Ava smiled. Her eyelet lace top had been embroidered with yellow daisies and sunflowers.

"What's so funny?" Claire asked. Then, as she looked down, she saw bubbles everywhere, overflowing onto the floor. She grinned at the mess. "Oh, I see. I don't care anymore." She leaned back again and closed her eyes, letting out a long sigh.

Ava giggled. "So how was Father?"

Claire scrunched up her face but kept her eyes closed. "Not one of our most pleasant conversations. I probably went a little too far." She moved her legs back and forth under water. "Truth is, I got pretty angry with him."

"Oh. Um, is everything all right, then?"

"No. And I don't think it could be all right. I'm still here, but I have no idea what he's going to do with me."

"Can't believe you got angry with Father. Don't think I've ever heard of that happening before."

"Well, I broke most of the big rules. Might as well break them all, I guess." She slowly opened her eyes to take in her rosy-cheeked friend.

"So, can I ask you what happened, down there?" Ava pointed to the floor.

"I don't think they want me to tell you. The gist of it is I fell in love with him. I fell in love with Daniel." Claire's voice trailed off to a whisper. Her eyes filled with tears.

"I'm so sorry, Claire. What happened to him?"

"He's fine. He's got the rest of his life ahead of him. He'll probably get married, have kids. He's going to be fine." Claire looked at her pink fingers holding onto the sides of the tub. In a whisper, she said, "He'll be fine without me."

Ava paused before speaking. "So he didn't go dark?"

"No. Did someone say that?" Claire sat up swiftly, eyes wide, oblivious to her lack of modesty.

"I just thought maybe that's why you came back."

Claire sighed and eased back down into the warm bubbles. "No, I came back because he asked me to. Daniel's stronger than I am, Ava. I was the one in danger of turning dark, not him. He convinced me to come home. He saved my life."

"And now what?"

"And now I'm completely miserable."

The water had turned cold, so Claire got out of the tub, dried off, and put on another gown. She started to unpack her duffel when she found a letter in the bottom of the bag, sealed, with her name on it, written in Daniel's distinctive scrawl. Her fingers touched the paper where his pen had been. She smelled the cream vellum of the envelope and closed her eyes. Yes, his lemon aftershave scent was there. She wondered how long it would last.

"What is it, Claire?" Ava asked.

"It's from Daniel," she said as she made her way over to the settee and bur-rowed herself among the pillows, under the watchful eye of the pink lioness.

"I'll come back later." Ava turned to go.

"No, stay. Sit here next to me and help me read it, please."

Ava sat at the corner of the daybed, at an angle to Claire as she opened the letter and took a deep breath in, beginning to read silently.

My Love,

I thank you for the love you brought into my life, and I promise to use every day enjoying it, using this gift, even though you will not be by my side. I don't want you to worry about me. You have brought my world back, and if I can't have you, well, then this will have to be enough. It is more than most people get, anyway.

I've made the decision to never marry. There will never be another woman in my life but you. You have not asked for this, but I give it freely. The few days we had together are more than most men get in a lifetime. Perhaps someday we will be together again, in Heaven. Maybe I could teach painting? Would you still love me if I were white haired and wrinkled? Would you let this old man touch your body and hold you close? Would Father let us have each other someday again? Put in a good word for me. I promise to live a life so that I would make an excellent addition to the Guardianship staff. All in due time. Who knows when that will be? I'm just going to focus on that every day, and keep painting.

We really scared Josh. I could see it in his face. I think we were his first defeat. We were pretty powerful, you and I together. Look at what we did!

I hope they treat you like the precious jewel you are. I hope they understand how wonderful you have made me feel, Claire. I pray they make your life easy, that they shower you with love and affection, as I cannot. I hope that in time you come to accept our separation and you find meaning in your work there. I can't believe Father would do you harm. Perhaps I'm naïve, but I just don't see it.

But I miss you already, even as I'm writing this, listening to you in the next room packing...

Claire leaned back into the pillows and put the letter to her chest, sobbing. Ava moved closer and embraced her.

"Shhh. Shhh. It's all right. It's going to be all right, Claire. I'm so sorry." Ava's tone was warm and soothing, her strong little arms held onto Claire tightly.

At last, Claire broke away and continued to read the letter. Ava sat back to give her privacy.

If possible, send me word. Maybe Doris would help out. But don't worry, I won't expect it. You gave me everything you could. And for that I will be grateful for the rest of my life.

Take care, my love. Read your books and poems, and dream of me, dream of us, holding each other and of the love that still burns inside my heart. For I will have something most men cannot have. An angel will love me forever, long after my earthly life is over. That's the greatest gift of all.

Love, Daniel

Claire's breath was ragged, her cheeks streaked with tears again. She folded the letter up carefully and placed it back in the envelope. She tucked the letter under one of the pillows. It was her match to Daniel's box of treasures under his pillow as a boy, hoping for a bright future.

ALONE

Daniel awoke, the rose glow of sunrise warming his face and chest. His eyes burned in the light. He pulled himself up off the bed; he was alone. *Of course I'm alone.* He looked at the pillow where she used to wait for him to wake up. A few golden pieces of dust remained—the only physical part of their love that was left, except for the dull ache in his heart. And who knew how long that would take to fade? Maybe never.

He sighed and clambered out of bed, resting his forehead against the upper trim of the window frame. Staring out to the distant sunrise, he could hardly believe the hole in his heart, now that she was gone. And he wondered about a God who could do this to him, who would give him something so precious and then take it away, just like that. He'd thought somehow they would figure out a way to be together. But in the end, it was not to be.

He was pretty sure he couldn't spend a lifetime without Claire, but he had promised and he intended to keep that promise. He just wasn't too sure how he would get through today without her, as he could taste her still, feel her young body giving herself up to him so freely. He could still smell the lavender and citrus of her breath, of her hair, and the salty tears he fed on over the course of their last night together. When he closed his eyes, he felt like she was still there next to him, naked, her heart beating like a kettledrum in her small body.

Perhaps this would be enough for today. How he wished this sunrise could be the start of their life together and not the back cover of a good book. He knew Claire didn't make sunrises and sunsets—this was Father's cruel shell game. *He takes Claire; he gives me this sunrise in return.* This was not a fair trade, but the only one offered.

His memories were his, totally his, as long as his brain held up. Daniel looked around him at the white candles he used to light the room so he could see the wonder of her body, and the pleasure of their lovemaking forever etched on that face he would never forget. He wanted to be able to remember every detail and hoped the image of her face would the last thing he saw before he died.

HOME

Claire had a tearful reunion with Mother the next morning. They'd had no word yet on what she was to do, so Mother suggested she write something, instead of reading one of her novels.

"Write what you learned. Tell us the story of your experience there. How would you counsel a young angel about to take her first charge?"

The request felt reasonable, except Claire's heart wasn't into anything. She wasn't sure what advice she would give. And it was difficult to think about it, not knowing what the future held for her.

"Why do you think your human memories don't last when you pass through as a Guardian?" Mother had asked her.

"So we won't spend immortality searching for them again," Claire answered.

"Yes," Mother answered as she closed her eyes. "It's Father's blessing, removing all hurt, all regret, all knowledge of the pain in the dying."

"But there's something I have never shared with you. I remember some things. I'm sure they are about my life as a human."

Mother's stern eyes fastened on Claire's. "That's just not possible, Claire."

"But it's true. I never told you, but I remember—my—death."

Mother looked at her bony hands folded in front of her. "Father has talked to me about what we are to do with you. He's pained, seeing you so miserable."

Claire nodded. *I'm the one feeling the pain.*

"You have to move your human memories to the back of the screen." At Claire's wide-eyed expression, she added, "You don't have to send them away, Claire, even if you could. Today I think you can't." Mother replaced her look of concern with the placid smile she was known for. "Just move them to the back."

Claire stared at the embroidery at her hemline.

"And if you can't do that, the only other option is to volunteer for the Wash."

At the mere mention of the Wash, Claire was jolted to action. They could erase all her memory of Daniel forever in that room. She'd seen an angel or two led there in tears, and now she knew why. Could they make her do it?

She darted from Mother's office and down the stairs out into the pathway. She ran around the front of the classrooms, past the teaching garden, around the back of the greenhouses, and rammed into the metal gate at the cemetery. She pressed her face through the bars until it hurt, but could not see them—see the stones. How she wished her powers of disappear and transport worked in Heaven. She was grounded behind the gate, as any human woman would be. She fell to her knees. *Am I going to be able to do this? Am I seeking death?* She wondered, just wondered, what a white stone would look like with her name on it. She reached through the bars of the gate, as if she could touch the cold granite of those markers. *What would my symbol be? Not a harp, not a rose or music notes...*

"It was going to be a shooting star."

Claire whirled around to find Father standing behind her. His eyes were filled with pain and compassion. He seemed to drain all the hurt from her soul. She stood and ran into his arms.

"I won't do the Wash. I can't do that." Claire said into his large chest.

"Nor will I make you, my precious little star." He held her tightly and let her cry. He stroked the top of her head, murmuring things to her to soothe her anguish. Claire felt the calming effect he had on her and was grateful.

He parted them, holding her face between his two large hands, hands that were warm. He stared at her, hesitant to speak. "My precious little one, born of light and made to love," he said tenderly. He drew her into his chest again and held her tight. "You are a wonder, even to me."

Claire broke away and looked up at him. "Father, don't make me wash it all away. Even if it's the pain, I will live with it for eternity. Don't make me give up these memories."

"Child, my little angel child."

"What's going to happen to me? Please tell me." She looked at the turquoise pools of love she used to lose herself in.

He sighed and dropped his arms to the sides.

"If it's real you want, it's real you'll have, my dear."

She couldn't believe what she heard. He nodded as he smiled. Recognition of his gift overtook Claire like a warm wave.

"Remember, Claire. I can only make you human. Only Daniel can make you real."

"I can go back?"

"If that is truly what your heart desires."

"Oh, thank you. Thank you."

She hugged him, suddenly feeling a change coming over her body as she looked at her hands and felt her legs tingle. She felt little capillaries all over her skin, blood pumping so loud it hurt her ears.

"Hurry, pack your things. I'll have Doris deliver you to him. Go, save each other, Claire."

She started to run, then turned back on the path, seeing the bright whiteness of Father's form move toward the gate.

"Father, one more thing."

He turned quickly, eyes wide. She could see he was surprised.

"Actually, I have two things."

Father looked down, with his hands on his hips and shook his head.

Her chest heaving, she blurted out, "Can you give Ava my room? Can she take care of Daniel's paintings?"

"Done. What else?"

"Will I ever see you again?"

"Does it really matter, Claire?"

She walked back to him and stood facing the fullness of his eternal body. "Yes, Father. It matters. What you do here matters. It always has and it always will."

She turned and began to leave, leaving a wafting of angel dust in her wake. She looked back to catch one more glimpse of Father, who leaned his head back, and with outstretched arms, let the golden particles of dust fall on his face as he laughed in the sunlight.

Doris had driven frantically across town several times. Claire had her nose pressed against the steamy windows of the transport, looking for some glimpse of the dark haired man who had stolen her heart. He hadn't been at the planetarium; he wasn't at his house or in the garden behind. He wasn't in the bookstore or at the gallery. He wasn't at the Laundromat, nor at the deserted Farmer's Market, not at the coffee house on 4th Street, or the little Latin disco filling up with people.

"Where should he be? We've checked everywhere." Claire's fingers and white knuckles gripped the back of the transport front seat.

"Any place you went with him we didn't see today? How about a winery?"

"No, I don't think so, Doris. It's too late. He wouldn't go there alone. I hope Josh didn't get to him. What if I'm too late? After all this—oh my God—I'm too late!"

"Claire, think about it. Where did you spend your last night together?" Doris' red hair was even redder today. Her eyes sparkled. She was into the hunt.

"The beach. Oh my God. He's at the beach!"

Doris laid her foot into the pedal of the transport like her life depended on it. The vehicle leaped forward, emitting a cloud of light grey smoke. For the first time, there was a human woman occupying the transport's back seat.

At last they came to the beach where Claire had ascended the stairway to Heaven. Golden yellow and peach clouds were rapidly turning deep rose and purple. Sunlight was making a hasty retreat. That's when she saw him.

"There he is, Doris!" Claire leapt from the transport before it stopped. She almost stumbled, then righted herself and made it up the crest of the sand dune covered in ice plants and seaweed.

"Hey, kid!" Doris quickly stood up and out of the cab, yelling to Claire over the top of the roof.

Claire stopped for a moment to listen to her farewell, grinning from ear to ear.

"Have a great life, OK? You're doing the right thing. Who knows, maybe someday I'll join you!" Doris smiled and waved to Claire, who immediately turned and resumed her run to the beach.

Claire ran with new legs. Her jellies hurt. Little pieces of sea grass and sticks of driftwood got stuck inside. The pinching pain was delicious. The duffel was getting heavy too. She was out of breath as she scampered through the ice plant, trying not to fall. The last vestiges of sunlight shone on the waves, buckets of the deep yellow gold and copper spilling onto the beach.

She could see Daniel watching the sun set, sitting with his legs spread, playing with a pattern in the sand with a stick. He wouldn't be able to hear her running on human legs. He couldn't hear her breathe as her chest gasped for air, almost making her cough, or hear her drop the duffel from exhaustion. She tripped and fell to her knees, scraping her knees on the sand, then laughed at the sensation. *So this is pain. It isn't so bad. Oh, I love how it feels!*

She clambered to her feet, and the wind whipped at her flowered dress as she laughed at the bronze clouds, the water, the way Daniel's hair blew in the wind, and the jacket that billowed out behind him like a sail. She was a child of the earth, after all. All these visions belonged to her now. This was all now part of her life, the miracle of her wonderful human life.

She stopped a few feet behind him and sobered, walking with caution. *How do I surprise him? What do I say?* She gave up. No plans. Just live.

She bent down, placing her hands over his eyes. How many days and nights had she daydreamed about this, flesh on flesh? She inhaled, feeling his warm face under her fingertips, feeling him jump in recognition. Her thighs hugged the outsides of his thighs, her mound pressing into the small of his back. All her angelic self-consciousness was gone. She inhaled the wonderful scent of her man like it was the first breath of life. The chemistry between them was stronger than all the angel dust she could generate in Heaven.

He grabbed her wrists. In an instant he was on his knees and they faced each other.

"Claire! You came back. But—"

She was kissing him, unwilling to answer yet. He grabbed her arms again and pulled her back to face him, then looked straight into her eyes. She drank in his beautiful gaze. His beautiful, beautiful *brown* eyes. Not black.

"How much time do we have?" His palms went to the sides of her face. His eyebrows arched, two little worry lines between them. He kissed her with tenderness as she inhaled his lime aftershave and the taste of his tongue on her lips.

"We have all the time in this lifetime, Daniel. I am real at last. I'm human." Her tears flowed freely. He was kissing them away, saying things she couldn't understand, but she was nodding, agreeing to everything he said, comprehending without knowing a word of it. "Anything, Daniel. Yes, Daniel, my love."

On the way back to the car, they would take two or three steps, and then stop and kiss, hug each other, and laugh until their insides hurt. Her duffel was slung over his shoulder. With locked arms and legs, touching as much as possible, tripping over each other they made it to the car. The blustery early night air was refreshing. It was a perfect backdrop to a day that had made all things possible again.

He leaned her against the side of his car, pressing himself the full length of her body. She could tell he was overcome with emotion as she heard what sounded like a sob when he wrapped his arms around her and squeezed so tight she could hardly breathe.

"Where do you want to go?" He continued to press into her with urgency. She could see in his eyes he would take her to Paris if she asked. But she didn't need to go that far.

"Home, Daniel. I want to go to our home."

As they drove, they held hands, interlocking fingers and kissing each other with tenderness. Several times he had to stop at the side of the road to finish a kiss that threatened to run them into traffic. When they arrived at the house, they stayed in the car where he leaned over the center console to plant kisses down her neck. Her dress had migrated way above her knees. He filled her panties with searching fingers. His thumb focused on the little hardened knob at the top of her sex. She arched, throwing her head back between the seats. He spread her knees, and she gave no resistance.

She thought for a second that her first lovemaking as a human might be in the front seat of his car, but the tight quarters became laughable. He got out, extending a hand to peel her out of the front seat and then splayed her against the car door, pressing himself against her again.

She felt his growing hardness as her hands explored him, lingering to smooth the length of him and then squeeze. They stood together, breathing heavily. He reached around her waist and drew her to him tight, ravishing her with hot kisses. Their hands wandered, seeking each other's flesh like they had been separated for centuries.

"Come. Let's go inside," he urged. He fumbled with his keys at the front door and dropped them, cursing. She saw this as an opportunity and leaned forward, pressing her breasts against his back, and as he straightened, she slid her hands into the front of his pants. He jumped. She bit his neck and squeezed him. She raised his shirt from behind and kissed all the way up his spine as she attempted to undo his belt buckle. This made him chuckle.

He finally got the door open and he turned to her, pulling her hard against him just inside the door. They locked themselves in an urgent embrace, whispering to each other between kisses. He kicked the door closed behind him, dropped the bag and then traversed the room in three long gaits as he pulled her along behind him. He walked up the stairs backward, holding both her hands in his, kissing her fingers, smiling.

At the bedroom entryway he led her toward the bed. She redirected him to the bathroom where she quickly removed her gown, slipped off her shoes, and stood in front of him naked. He removed his clothes and stood before her with a full erection. Their bodies just barely touched. He stepped into her and they melted, flesh against flesh. She gasped. His kiss was hot, needy.

He pulled her into the shower. Steam began rising around them as he picked up the lavender shower gel and began to massage her chest. He lathered over her breasts, down her hips to her smooth ass, fingers touching her gently between the crack. She leaned into him, sheltered by his warm chest, feeling the muscles of his arms and torso working to support his hands rubbing all over her. She kissed his neck, her hands finding his member and covering it with the lavender soap bubbles. She rubbed his chest with the lather from her breasts and he groaned, bending to kiss her again.

He held her with a strong hand at the small of her back and pushed his other palm up from her lower belly over breasts and up to her neck, making her arch backward. She raised a knee to rub her sex into his upper thigh. His soapy fingers found her spot.

Standing her upright, he spread her knees as he bent to his. She rubbed the lavender bubbles in his hair. His nose and forehead were covered with white soapy foam as he kissed her lower belly. His tongue found its way through the wet soapy hair of her cave and flicked into its opening. Claire directed the warm water from the shower to cover the top of his head and sluice down over her lower torso.

As water rinsed all the bubbled gel from them, he pleasured her with long strokes of his sandpaper tongue. He held her thigh up behind the knee. He kissed the red abrasions from her fall at the beach. He blew on the injury, taking care to concentrate on every tiny red line, like he was willing her skin to heal.

Claire couldn't believe how enraptured she felt at this small gesture. He followed with gentle kisses, extending them up her thigh to the spot between her legs. He sucked on her sweetness, feeling and tasting her folds, while his other hand brought her mound into his face. Then one finger began to pleasure her, then two fingers as she jerked and arched back. Claire was actually shouting, screaming out. He started to laugh, stood to cover her mouth with his fingers, which she drew inside with her hungry lips, tasting herself for the first time.

"Sh, Claire. They will think I'm ravishing you." He was softly saying to her, the deep timbre of his voice vibrating against her neck, driving her crazy.

"Who?" she asked.

He pointed to the ceiling. "Don't they watch?"

"Oh, I hope so. I want to make love to you in front of the whole universe. I don't care who sees. Take me, Daniel."

She reached for his cock, stroking it back and forth. She dropped to a kneeling position and sucked him as hard as she could. She fondled him at the base where her lips were buried in dark curly hair. She tasted his salty drops of readiness. He was lurching now with every lick from her curled tongue, every suck elongating him, pulling him toward her.

He knelt, laying her back against the soapy bubbles at the back of the tub, positioning her scraped knees carefully up and over his shoulders. Under the rain of warm water sluicing over them he entered her, his rigid member splitting her all the way to her soul. He moved back and forth inside her with fury, each thrust becoming deeper. Claire pushed herself down to completely encapsulate him deep inside her.

Real. This is real.

She was grateful for the art of his love making experience; oddly thankful he had pleasured dozens of women first. She would be the last. She would be his insatiable and most willing partner.

She gave her body up to the spasms that overtook her, muscles deep inside clamping down upon his hardness and finally forcing him to explode inside. They shuddered together, spent.

The morning sun was just pushing its way from the widow. The room was fading from a pink glow. Daniel awoke to the sound of snoring. He was lying naked on his back. He almost expected to see Claire sitting next to him, smiling, as occurred so many mornings, that is, when she was patient and let him awaken to the day naturally. Before being sent back to Heaven, her appetites were such that she hadn't let him sleep. He smiled at the memory of waking up to her lips covering and milking his cock.

This morning, however, she lay at his side, curled in fetal position under his arm, resting close to his chest, her knees holding one of his thighs between them. She snored again and he had to laugh at her lack of grace and control. *She snores like a soccer player after too much sex and tequila.* She would think this funny.

With care, he slid down the bed so he could see her face, partially obscured by her curled hands that lay together in front. Her head was buried in his soft pillow, mouth open. He had never seen her unconscious. As with most things, she did that too with abandon. *She will awaken to good old morning breath*, he thought with amusement. But today he found even that sexy.

He wanted to see the look in her eyes when she first saw him. He wanted to be the first thing she saw every day when she awoke, like she had been for him. As he watched her sleep, he wondered what dreams she had. Would she remember them? *Am I in your dreams, Angel?* His heart danced. He was a young child at the beach again, picking up pieces of sea glass and sketching the pretty girls that walked past with charcoal from the campfires. He looked back at her sleeping next to him. *My angel sleeping in my bed.*

He traced a line with his forefinger from the center of her palm, down the length of her curled middle finger. Her reflex action was to squeeze her hand into a loose fist. Then she opened it, then the other hand as she inhaled, a smile on her lips. He needed to kiss those lips again. He wanted to make them hurt. She opened her eyes and looked at him. His errant finger began a journey lower on her belly.

"Hi." He sighed.

"Hi." Her warm pink hand reached for his face and stroked his cheek with the back of her fingers.

"What would you like to do today?"

"Hmmm…" she stretched, arching her back, raising her breasts, which brought his hand over them immediately. She smiled, then rolled over close to him, her body searing hot like a torch. "I think I'd like to take a shower, after a bit." She kissed him. Her fingertips played with the muscles on his chest, and worked their way up his neck to trace his lips. His fingers had worked their way south as she let his hand part her knees. She was ready and wet. She sighed and squeezed her thighs together against his forearm.

"Then I would like some strawberry pancakes with real maple syrup, maybe a hot chocolate with lots of whipped cream that sticks to my upper lip."

"And then?" His fingers called to her, tickling and tracing up and down her folds. He rested at her opening, waiting.

"There is a tradition I read about. The famous music couple who wanted to stay in bed in New York until they got pregnant. Daniel, can we do that?"

"The staying in bed or the getting pregnant?"

"Both."

"Does it have to be in New York? In a hotel?"

"I was thinking right here would be fine."

He lay back and laughed harder than he had in months, perhaps years.

"Yes, Angel, I think we can."

THE END

OTHER BOOKS IN THE
SEAL BROTHERHOOD SERIES:

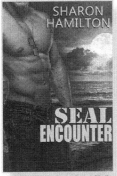

SEAL ENCOUNTER

PREQUEL TO BOOK 1

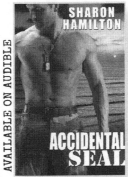

AVAILABLE ON AUDIBLE

ACCIDENTAL SEAL

BOOK 1

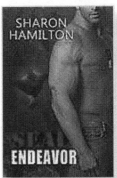

SEAL ENDEAVOR

PREQUEL TO BOOK 2

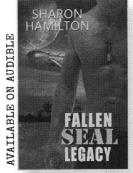

AVAILABLE ON AUDIBLE

FALLEN SEAL LEGACY

BOOK 2

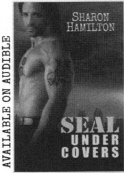

AVAILABLE ON AUDIBLE

SEAL UNDER COVERS

BOOK 3

AVAILABLE ON AUDIBLE

SEAL THE DEAL

BOOK 4

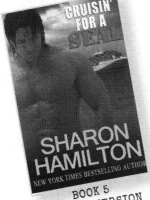

CRUISIN' FOR A SEAL

BOOK 5
AUDIBLE VERSION
COMING SOON!

Connect with Author Sharon Hamilton!

sharonhamiltonauthor.blogspot.com

sharonhamiltonauthor.com

facebook.com/AuthorSharonHamilton

@sharonlhamilton

http://sharonhamiltonauthor.com/contact.html#newsletter

OTHER BOOKS BY SHARON HAMILTON:

The Guardians Series

(Guardian Angels, Dark Angels)

PURCHASE ON
amazon.com

BOOK 1

BOOK 2

The Golden Vampires of Tuscany Series:

PURCHASE ON
amazon.com

AVAILABLE ON AUDIBLE

BOOK 1

BOOK 2

Made in the USA
Charleston, SC
19 April 2015